ANGEL IN THE
FULL MOON

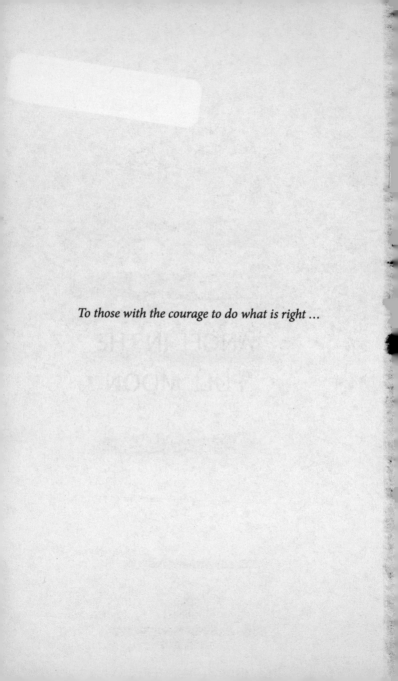

To those with the courage to do what is right …

ANGEL IN THE FULL MOON

A Jack Taggart Mystery

Don Easton

A Castle Street Mystery

THE DUNDURN GROUP
TORONTO

Editor: Barry Jowett   Design: April Duffy
Copy-editor: Shannon Whibbs   Printer: Webcom

Library and Archives Canada Cataloguing in Publication

Easton, Don
    Angel in the full moon / Don Easton.

(A Jack Taggart mystery)
ISBN 978-1-55002-813-3

    I. Title. II. Series: Easton, Don. Jack Taggart mystery.
PS8609.A78A66 2008   C813'.6   C2008-900678-X

1   2   3   4   5   11   10   09   08   07

We acknowledge the support of The Canada Council for the Arts and the Ontario Arts Council for our publishing program. We also acknowledge the financial support of the Government of Canada through the Book Publishing Industry Development Program and The Association for the Export of Canadian Books, and the Government of Ontario through the Ontario Book Publishers Tax Credit program, and the Ontario Media Development Corporation.

Printed and bound in Canada

www.dundurn.com

Dundurn Press	Gazelle Book Services Limited	Dundurn Press
3 Church Street, Suite 500	White Cross Mills	2250 Military Road
Toronto, Ontario, Canada	High Town, Lancaster, England	Tonawanda, NY
M5E 1M2	LA1 4XS	U.S.A. 14150

Nguyễn thị bích Thủy

Thank you, Thủy, for the help you have given me in completing this novel.

chapter one

It was ten o'clock at night in Hanoi as Biển stood at the back of the cargo van with his twelve-year-old daughter. The incessant January rain, coupled with a light breeze, made the fifteen-degree Celsius temperature seem colder. Biển had no idea that his dream for the future was about to become a permanent nightmare — or that the rear doors on the van opening in front of him were the gates to hell.

The driver turned in his seat and gave Biển an impatient nod. Biển grimaced and shoved the plastic bag containing Hằng's belongings into the van. Saying goodbye was difficult and it was more than the rain that made his cheeks wet.

Hằng was the older of Biển's two children. When Biển was given the opportunity for both his children to go to America he could hardly believe his good fortune. There was little future for them in Vietnam. He bent over to give Hằng another final hug.

A swarm of motor scooters zoomed past like angry, wet

hornets and disappeared into the night. Hanoi was like a hive when it came to scooters. Few people could afford cars.

Biển ignored the scooters and forced himself to smile at Hằng. She smiled back, but the corners of her mouth twitched, revealing her nervousness. On impulse, she checked the pocket of her new coat again. Yes, the gift was still there. Wrapped in a small piece of tissue paper and tied with a pink ribbon.

The silver necklace with the pearl from Halong Bay had cost Biển the equivalent of sixteen American dollars. *An exorbitant amount of money,* thought Biển. *But the American lady will be grateful.*

Biển's mind turned to Hằng's new coat. *She will need it. It can be very cold in the United States.* A long blast from the van's horn interrupted his thoughts and he watched as Hằng quickly climbed in to join a handful of young women who sat on the floor of the van. Biển had opted to leave his other daughter, nine-year-old Linh, back at their apartment with her grandmother. It wasn't simply that he didn't own a car. He often pedalled with both children on his bicycle. The real reason was he was afraid he might cry. He didn't want Linh to see him cry. Especially when she was scheduled to leave next.

The children's mother died of cancer when Linh was six months old. Biển's own mother lived with them, but time had been hard on both her body and her mind. Hằng, despite being only three years older than Linh, had taken on more of a role of a parent than that of a sister.

Biển started to close the doors but Hằng looked at him and quickly blurted, *"Con thương cha thật nhiều."*

Biển replied, "English now, Hằng. You speak English." He paused and said, "And I love you a lot as well … but now it is time for you to be strong."

"I am strong," she replied, trying to make her face look stern.

Biển hid his smile and said, "I know you are. I will be anxious to talk with you."

"I telephone in United States," said Hằng. "Six months."

Biển shook his head and replied, "No. The word is weeks. Say weeks."

"Yes. Weeeks," replied Hằng. She frowned at her mistake.

"Good. That is good. You call. Linh and I will be waiting. You be sure it is good before I send Linh."

"Con có thể hy sinh tất cả vì chả."

"English … please."

Hằng sighed and said, "I will do …" she hesitated, searching for the word she was looking for, *"whatever … you ask."*

Biển smiled and said, "Good. Very good. I know you will do *whatever* I ask. I ask that you do *whatever* for Linh, too."

Hằng nodded seriously as Biển closed the doors.

Minutes later, Biển held his bicycle and stood silently in the rain staring at the empty street. His heart and stomach felt like they were being wrenched from his body. The image of Hằng waving at him through the back window of the van would forever be etched in his memory.

Biển climbed on his bicycle and pedalled toward his apartment. He brooded about his last-minute decision not to send Linh to America on the same boat as Hằng. People were angry with him, but eventually he was told that the American family understood.

The American family had lost two daughters in an unfortunate accident. The Americans wanted to fill the emptiness they felt and were willing to take his daughters into their home. They would pay for them to go to school in America.

Perhaps, some day, Biển would be allowed to go to America, too. For now, they agreed that Hằng would travel first. Another boat was scheduled to leave when it was known that the first boat arrived safely.

Not that there was any real danger, Biển had been told. The passengers would be smuggled into the United States from Canada. Even if the authorities caught them, the worse that would happen is that they would be returned to Vietnam.

If that happened, Biển knew, he would face some criticism from his own government. The opportunity for a prosperous and happy future for his children was well worth that risk. He was told that if all went well, eventually the right people in America would be paid and both his daughters would become American citizens.

Biển heard that there were many other passengers being smuggled. All young women who were being given jobs in the hotel industry. They would have to work to pay for the cost of being brought to America. That would not take long. There was a tremendous amount of money to be made. They would have no problem paying off their debt, even while sending money home to their families.

Biển knew that for many of the young women, their fate would no be so. He had heard rumours that some of the young women lacked morals and became greedy, opting instead to make more money by selling their bodies. Some sent money home to Vietnam for their parents, who became rich, but when asked about their daughters, the shame was evident. They said their daughters worked in hotels or restaurants, but few believed it. Maids in hotels were not paid that much.

Biển had talked at length about this to both his daughters. He had also spoken to the smugglers. If there was even a suggestion that they engage in any impropriety, he would go to the authorities. He was assured otherwise. This family was decent, heartbroken over the loss of their own daughters. He was told that he was foolish to worry. Still, these were his daughters. What father would not worry?

Biển's daughters were fortunate. They would not have to work at all to pay for their voyage. His was a special situation. Biển's contact had taken a picture of Hằng and Linh standing in front of the *One Pillar Pagoda* close to where Biển worked. The picture was sent to America and Biển heard that the family instantly loved his daughters. He was told that if his daughters were truly unhappy, then the American family would pay to return them to Vietnam.

Biển thought about the Westerners' use of the word *love*. He decided that it was a word they used as if they were saying hello. From Westerners, it sounded about as genuine as the fake Rolexes sold at the market. The Vietnamese expressed love more often through action, by doing something nice for the person. It had more meaning.

It was the same with Western names, Biển mused. They never stood for anything. His own name, Biển, meant *ocean*. Western names did not usually have meaning. Biển was told the name of the American family was Pops and it meant *friendly father*. Believing the name to be real, he felt reassured. Had he known it was a nickname with a secretive, twisted, and perverse meaning, he would have been aghast.

Biển reflected upon the picture of his two daughters. His contact had graciously provided him with a black and white photocopy. In the picture, Hằng held Linh's hand. *Not that she was afraid Linh would run out into traffic. She knew better. She held Linh's hand because she loved her. Their spirits entwined like one. Anyone looking at the picture could see their true beauty. Perhaps the American family were sincere when they said they loved my children? It would be impossible not to ....*

Biển had not always lived in Hanoi. As a child, he was raised in the South. Saigon. Biển still preferred the city by its old name, but while working in Hanoi, he was careful to refer to it as Hồ Chi Minh City.

Biển's father had served with the South Vietnamese army and fought alongside the Americans until the Communists achieved victory in 1975. His father had learned English and taught it to Biển, who in turn, taught it to both his daughters. After the war, Biển's father was placed in a re-education camp, where he died thirteen years later. Biển scoffed at the term *re-education*. It was a camp of forced labour and brutality.

Biển's wife, formerly from Dong Ha, had been exposed to heavy concentrations of Agent Orange during the war. Their daughter, Hằng, like many second generation children, was born with an abnormality. She had an extra thumb protruding off the thumb of one hand. This was only a minor imperfection, Biển decided, when so many other families had children who were born without feet or arms.

Hằng's extra thumb was not something that had been hidden from the American family. Biển was told that Pops would have an American doctor fix it, but only if Hằng wished. Biển knew that Hằng would wish it to be so. She wanted to be perfect. *She does not understand that she already is.*

Linh was born without any abnormalities. Something that was cause for extreme joy. A sign that the future would improve, thought Biển. He had received a teaching degree just days after Linh was born. He felt like their lives were complete and that their future would be good. But it was not good.

Biển's wife died six months later of organ failure brought on by the dioxin in her body. The closest Biển ever came to being a teacher was doing janitorial work at a school. The Communist party was only too aware of his family's sympathy to the South during the war. He would not be allowed to teach.

It was not until recently that the government recognized the benefit of tourism and knew that Biển's ability to speak

English could be an asset. He was sent to Hanoi to act as a tour guide at Uncle Hổ's Mausoleum.

Biển lived in a one-room apartment facing an alley that he shared with his daughters and his own mother. His kitchen, like others in his neighbourhood, was a small plastic table and chairs set out on the sidewalk at the front of the building. The rest of his kitchen consisted of a hot plate set up on wooden boxes in the alley. The boxes were on their sides and a piece of cloth wired to the boxes acted as a curtain to keep the dust off the dishes. All this was enclosed with a wrought-iron grate bolted to the alley wall, which protruded just over an arm's length away from the boxes. Entry was through a padlocked door.

For the first few months, he was paid barely enough to buy rice and noodles. Later, he learned to become a little shrewder about accepting tips from the tourists. Soon he would be able to afford a bigger apartment. One that would give his mother her own room to snore in.

It was midnight when Biển pedalled back through the Ba Dinh district of Hanoi and quietly carried his bicycle into his apartment. Tomorrow he would face questions. He did not like the fact that he had to deal with smugglers. Lying to friends about where his daughter went made him feel guilty — but he understood the need for secrecy.

Hằng sat quietly on the floor as the van continued through the streets of Hanoi, occasionally stopping to pick up more women. Hằng figured they were all about six or seven years older than her. She caught the friendly smile of a younger woman who had been in the van when Hằng got in. Hằng forced a quick smile back before turning away — directing her attention to the floor of the van. She remembered her vow to stay strong and did not want anyone to see the tears on her face.

"*Em tên là gì?*" the young woman asked her.

"Hằng," she answered, continuing to stare at the floor.

"You … talk … English," she noted, slowly enunciating the words of this foreign language.

"A little," replied Hằng.

She smiled again. "Yes, me talk a … small … English," she said, holding her thumb and finger close together to emphasize her point. "My name Ngọc Bích. You, me, we teach English each other, okay?"

"Okay," replied Hằng, looking down at the van floor.

"You cold?" asked Ngọc Bích.

Hằng shook her head.

"Very cold in America. I think you cold now," said Ngọc Bích, while changing positions and sitting beside Hằng. "You be okay," said Ngọc Bích. "Okay to be afraid," she added, while putting her arm around Hằng's shoulders.

"I'm not afraid," said Hằng, glancing up defiantly at the other women in the van.

Ngọc Bích caught Hằng's expression and said, "That okay. They no speak English. They no understand what me say with you. I see you cry. I am sorry with you."

Hằng paused for a moment, and said, "I'm not afraid. I only miss my family."

"My family live in Nha Trang," said Ngọc Bích, pulling Hằng closer. "My father dies two years before. I cries. The day last, my mother say goodbye to me in Nha Trang. I am oldest five kids. Two brothers. Two sisters," she said, holding up two fingers on each hand. "It is good I send money from America — but yesterday I cry the same as you. You father and mother many kids?"

"One sister. No mother," replied Hằng.

Ngọc Bích paused briefly and said, "It okay to cry."

Hằng solemnly studied Ngọc Bích's face but did not respond.

"I cry for my brothers and sisters today. You want, you … me … be sister now," added Ngọc Bích.

Hằng reflected upon this briefly, before nodding. They each smiled and hugged each other.

Eventually the van came to a stop and everyone got out. The driver warned them to be quiet and to follow him. Hằng slung her bag of belongings over her shoulder and, along with everyone else, obediently followed. They entered an apartment building, trudged up four flights of stairs, were led to a room halfway down the hall, and ushered inside.

Hằng and Ngọc Bích quietly sat on the apartment floor with a dozen others. The driver left but two other Vietnamese men remained in the room. The men told everyone to sit quietly and not to speak.

Later, there were more soft knocks on the apartment door as several more groups of young women arrived. Hằng counted thirty-five women but lost count when the room became too crowded.

An hour passed, and the silence in the room made Hằng more conscious of the humidity and the sticky feeling from the heat generated by their cramped quarters. Eventually there was another knock at the door.

Another Vietnamese man entered the room, followed by two other men who were both foreigners and appeared to be about fifty years old. One foreigner was lean and tall, with a thin, grey moustache that matched the colour of his brush cut. His face was pointed with sharp cheek bones and large dark eyes peered out from a nose that reminded Hằng of a beak on a bird. *Like a long-billed vulture* … She heard the Vietnamese man call him *Petya*.

The other foreigner took off his jacket and Hằng saw that

he was wearing a golf shirt and slacks. His head was shaved bald and he had a large pot belly ... but it was his arms that caught Hằng's attention. She had never seen arms covered in so much thick, black hair. More black hair unleashed itself from the open neck on his golf shirt. It made Hằng think of a bald ape and she quickly looked away so as not to be seen as being rude.

The two foreigners spoke to each other in a language that Hằng did not understand. After, the bald ape turned to the Vietnamese man.

"Tell them all to stand," said the bald ape, speaking English.

"Yes, *Styopa*," replied the Vietnamese man. He then gave the command in Vietnamese and everyone got to their feet.

For Hằng, the names *Petya* and *Styopa* were too foreign to pronounce. She would just think of them as the vulture and the bald ape.

The vulture and the bald ape approached each woman and pointed for them to stand on one side of the room or the other. As this happened, the Vietnamese man wrote everyone's names down on two lists.

It is the Vietnamese custom not to look into a person's face. To do so could imply a lack of respect. In this case, Hằng sensed it was an uncomfortable shame the women felt as they stared down at the floor, wondering what the selection was all about. When the men reached Hằng, the bald ape lifted her chin to face him, but she continued to avert her eyes.

"You are the young one," he said. "You speak English?" he asked.

Hằng nodded, but the man still gripped her chin, making nodding difficult.

"Let me hear you talk," he commanded.

Hằng swallowed and said, "Yes, I speak English. My

father taught me."

"Good. And you are going to the States to live with an American family, correct?"

"Yes, to live in the house of Mister Pops."

"*Mister* Pops!" The bald ape glanced at the vulture and they both chuckled before turning back to Hằng. "Your English is good," he said, releasing her chin. "Your sister was supposed to come. Why didn't she?"

"My father wanted me to go first. To make sure it would be good for my sister."

"That is very prudent," said the vulture. "Your father is a wise man, but you will see that you are very happy there."

The bald ape grabbed Hằng's hand and held it up to show the vulture her extra thumb. Hằng felt her face flush with embarrassment. The vulture spoke harshly to the bald ape in his own language and the ape dropped her hand. Hằng felt his eyes upon her for a moment before they moved on.

When the men finished dividing the women into two groups, the bald ape walked back to one young woman and poked her in the ribs with his finger and turned to his Vietnamese colleague and said, "This one is too fat. Nobody will want her."

The Vietnamese colleague said, "She is fat now, but she will be much thinner in six weeks when she arrives."

The bald ape blurted out a laugh.

Hằng had been warned that the voyage on the ship would be cramped, with little time on deck. It would be a tough journey, but one they were told they would forget completely once they arrived in America. *Still, his cruel laugh — he is like the rats who live in the sewer. The sewer I must cross to America.*

She risked glancing at the vulture. His face was cold, without expression. A slit under his beak cracked open and he said, "They are all okay. Get them to the ship."

Moments later, Hằng found herself crammed into the back of a large cube van. There was standing room only and she was glad that Ngọc Bích had remained by her side.

It was three hours later when they hurried up a wooden gangplank in the dark to the deck of a ship. The women were told to remain in the two groups they had been divided in. Each group was directed to a separate cargo hold.

They were told to climb down a ladder leading below deck and a man stood at the top of each ladder to help. Hằng stooped to get on the ladder and felt the man grab the cheek of her buttock and squeeze tight while emitting a laugh.

Hằng gasped but before she could respond, Ngọc Bích slapped the man hard across his face. He released his grip immediately and pulled back a fist to punch Ngọc Bích in the face. At the same time, another man's voice uttered a command from the darkness for them to be quiet.

The man who had grabbed Hằng scowled and lowered his fist. He grabbed Hằng by the arm and made her go with the second group of women. She quickly made her way down the ladder into the cargo hold and, along with the others, stood waiting for further instructions.

An hour passed and, following the shouts and commands from above, the diesel engines coughed and rumbled to life, causing the ship to shake before it slipped away from its moorage.

A crew member eventually came down the ladder and told them the cargo space they were in was their home for the next six weeks. He pointed to a plastic pail that they could use for a toilet and pieces of cardboard on the floor for them to lie on. Nobody would be allowed up on deck for two weeks, after which they may be allowed up on deck at night only. The passengers looked at each other in shock as the crew member climbed back up the ladder and closed the cargo doors behind him.

Three of the young women started crying. Hằng stared at them blankly for a moment before picking up a piece of cardboard and selecting a spot near the hull of the ship to lay it down. She was cold, even with her new coat, and brought her knees up close to her chest. She lay with her back to the hull, but felt the vibration of the ship's engines and readjusted the cardboard.

When she was settled once more, she stared at a black cord with a yellow light bulb that hung from above, swinging with the movement of the ship. The dim light did not hide the fear she saw in some of the faces around her. She wished Ngọc Bích had not slapped the crew member. She felt exhausted. Maybe later they would be allowed to be together …

Hằng suddenly awakened to the sound of someone vomiting beside her. She felt nauseous, too, and moaned, grabbing her head as a piercing pain reduced her vision to flashes of light. The smell of diesel was overwhelming and water had leaked in, turning much of the cardboard mattresses into soggy masses.

The woman who vomited faced a string of obscenities from another neighbour, which only brought more angry voices and commotion from others. Another woman climbed to the top of the ladder and yelled and pounded on the cargo door. From somewhere in the ship, Hằng heard Ngọc Bích yelling and the pounding clang of metal being struck with a pipe.

The cargo doors were opened and the women rushed to stand beneath as fresh air and rain came in from above. The crew member took only the first few steps down the ladder before cursing and going back up. He returned a few minutes later and tossed down a mop while ordering another woman to bring up the plastic pail so that it could be dumped overboard.

Three weeks passed and, despite the promise to be allowed on deck at night, had that luxury rescinded because of severe storms. The ship rocked and creaked as it was blasted by the wind and heavy waves. During this time, the cargo doors were closed again to prevent flooding. It was also the time when most people were sick.

On this night, the storm was worse than usual and Hằng was one of the few who had managed to keep her food down. She waited until most of the others were asleep before deciding to take the opportunity to squat over the plastic pail.

She balanced her steps on the rollicking floor of the ship as she headed for the pail, only to see that it was overflowing. She wondered what to do just as the ship gave another violent heave, sending the pail sliding across the floor and tipping over. She decided to wait.

On the following night, the storms abated. It was January 29th, this year's official beginning of the celebration of Tết Nguyên Đán, or "TET," as it is commonly called, marking the lunar New Year. This year was the Year of the Dog. Today, their daily rations of rice, noodles, and fish soup was replaced with ample quantities of chicken, pork, and vegetables.

As soon as darkness came, everyone was allowed on deck. It didn't take Hằng and Ngọc Bích long to find each other. They decided to speak Vietnamese to each other. Tonight would be a night to relax. Even if they couldn't be together on the ship, they promised each other they would remain friends when they got off. Then there would be plenty of time to practise English.

They watched as a couple of the crew members waved bottles of wine and invited some of the women back to their rooms with them. Some of the women went and Hằng caught the look of disapproval from Ngọc Bích as she stared after them.

"The crew ... their rooms will be warm," said Hằng. "Is it wrong to drink wine?"

Ngọc Bích turned to Hằng and smiled and said, "You are a child, my new sister. It is not just wine that these men want to put in the women."

Hằng felt embarrassed but said, "The women, maybe they will just enjoy the warmth and then say no, and leave."

Ngọc Bích shook her head and said, "That is why the men will share the wine. These young women will be too drunk to say no ... and if they do, the men may not listen. Never dishonour your family by such behaviour."

Hằng was appalled that Ngọc Bích would even feel the need to convey that to her. "I never would. Yuk! Never!"

"Good. No man would ever want you for his wife then," said Ngọc Bích seriously.

"I will never dishonour my family," replied Hằng solemnly. "My father has told me about such women. Greedy women, who give their bodies to men."

Ngọc Bích nodded. "Always respect what you do and respect yourself. In America I am going to be trained to give massages and work at a hotel where the very rich go," said Ngọc Bích. "I will make lots of money and then," Ngọc Bích paused as her eyes twinkled, "when a man with a bottle of wine invites me to his room ... I will go."

"You will go?" exclaimed Hằng.

"Yes. Because that man will be my husband."

Hằng laughed and Ngọc Bích joined in. Hằng could not remember the last time she had laughed. Ngọc Bích's comments made her realize how lucky she was ... or would be in three weeks when they arrived. She was told that the home of Mister Pops was so large that she would have her own bedroom. He was even so rich that when Linh came, she would also have her own bedroom.

Pops turned the radio on to maximum volume before flushing the toilet and crouching down to hurry through the short passageway that led to the television room in his basement. Once free of the passageway, he pushed the square doorway shut behind him.

He stood panting for a moment. Not that he was out of shape. He was a big man with a narcissistic drive that compelled him to maintain a daily routine of bodybuilding. His panting was not from physical exertion. It was from excitement.

Pops's house was a four-level split built over the side of a hill. In the basement of the home, he had discovered a small trap door leading to a dead space in the earth behind his foundation. The trap door was intended to gain access to some plumbing pipes that led from the upper levels down to the run-off pipes in the earth below.

When Pops first stuck his head in the hole and shone a flashlight around, he saw a space that ran the width of his house and was several metres wide. It was partially back-filled with dirt and debris from when his house was built. The area was completely sealed off by cement foundations that supported the upper levels of his house farther back on the hill.

For many months, Pops lay awake and fantasized about what special use he could make of this newfound space. His fantasies were about to become real.

Now Pops stood and held his breath and listened. *Not a sound!* He placed his ear to the wall and could hear a slight sound from the radio, but if he had not known better, he might have deduced it came from some other home in his neighbourhood.

"Yes!" he shouted with elation, while punching his fist into the palm of his other hand. The heavy thickness of soundproofing worked! He opened the passageway door and ducked back inside to retrieve the radio.

The room he had built was basically a smaller room within the space. It was like a huge rectangular plywood box with an igloo-style passageway that led into it. There was a drain on the floor, along with a foam mattress, a toilet, and a set of shackles and chains fastened to the floor at each end of the room.

chapter two

Corporal Jack Taggart glanced at Constable Laura Secord as she patiently sat at her desk while flipping through the Royal Canadian Mounted Police *Gazette*. Her desk butted up to his and space was at a premium.

The Intelligence Unit targeted organized crime, which meant gathering information on secretive societies. Investigations often fanned out like inverted pyramids. One criminal would lead to others and these others would lead to others and so on, as investigators tried to determine who were involved in criminal enterprises and who were just associates.

Jack and Laura's office slowly collected more and more file cabinets that in themselves became like Pandora's boxes for those who would look inside to try to grasp the nature of the beast.

It was late Friday afternoon and their shift should be just about over. Should be, but wouldn't, grimaced Jack, while waiting to receive a text message on his BlackBerry.

He knew Laura wouldn't complain. Personal life often took a back seat as they adjusted their hours to match the hours of people who worked without schedules. At least it did if you were to be effective. Effective in your work. Not effective in your personal life.

His thoughts went back to the person he was waiting to hear from. *Why? Why would Damien make such an obvious faux pas? The National President of Satans Wrath .... You didn't end up in charge of the top organized crime family in Canada by being stupid. So why?*

Satans Wrath had chapters in dozens of countries. They operated like an international corporation with paramilitary discipline. In many countries, including Canada, they were at the top of the list when it came to organized crime. Each chapter had its own president and each country had one national president. In Canada, that was Damien.

Jack felt a vibration on his belt. *Finally ...*

Laura saw Jack grab for his BlackBerry. She studied his face as he read the text message. Jack was more than her boss. Next to her husband, Jack was her closest friend.

He glanced up and said, "It's him. Montrose Park in forty-five minutes."

"I don't know it," replied Laura.

"Near Second Narrow Bridge."

"I'll call Elvis," said Laura. "You mind dropping me off at home later? We rode in together this morning."

"Hopefully he's not already waiting outside to follow us," said Jack.

Laura pursed her lips to hide her grin. Her husband worked on the Anti-Corruption Unit, which handled the more serious investigations directed to Internal Affairs. Jack's name was familiar to everyone in her husband's unit. He had been the subject of more than one investigation.

Not that it did them any good, mused Laura. *Jack does operate under his own set of rules and his methods are unorthodox — okay, illegal — but never corrupt.*

It sometimes left Laura in an awkward position with Elvis, but he trusted her own moral judgement … and she trusted Jack's. Her marriage was something of a balancing act, not just for her, but for Elvis, too. They had elected not to discuss work at home.

Since being transferred to work with Jack on the Intelligence Unit last year, Laura really appreciated just how necessary it was to have an Anti-Corruption Unit. Organized crime specialized in turning what were once good cops into dirty cops. Elvis did not have an easy job. Something that made her love him all the more.

"Sure I'll drop you off," said Jack, continuing their conversation. "I'll give Natasha a call, too."

Laura dialled Elvis, who put her on hold. She watched as Jack called his wife. Natasha was a doctor who worked in an emergency clinic on the downtown east side. *Not an easy job, either.*

Laura heard the first few words of Jack's conversation to Natasha. "Hey honey, I'm going to be a little late. Maybe around seven. Laura and I have to go meet a friend …."

Laura's thoughts went to who they were really meeting. Meeting *a friend* meant meeting a confidential source. Real names were never used. Jack was extremely protective of any of his sources. Their *friend* in this case was Damien. Not actually an informant, but as a top criminal, Damien and the police sometimes had common enemies. Laura knew that only too well.

Last year a Colombian drug lord by the name of Carlos planned to murder Damien and had tried to kill Jack. The biker's rules stated they would never phone the police or cooperate with them. Last year was different. Damien was scared for his own family and reluctantly agreed to go along with Jack's plan to neutralize Carlos. *Can't believe my mind thought the word* neutralize — *Jack's influence no doubt I should have thought* murder.

Jack convinced the brass to let them travel to Colombia on the pretext of arranging an undercover purchase of a shipment of cocaine by using Damien as an informant. His real plan had Damien introduce them to a rival Colombian drug lord by the name of Diego Ramirez and convincing Ramirez to kill Carlos. The plan worked. Ramirez never did find out that Jack and Laura were undercover police officers.

Ramirez used a string of shoe stores and leather factories to launder his money and aid in his exportation of tonnes of cocaine. When they all met last year in Colombia, it was obvious that he was attracted to Laura.

At Christmas, Ramirez sent a box full of expensive shoes to Damien to pass on to Laura. Damien held on to them for over a month before sending them to her house. Laura thought Damien should have known better. Gifts from Damien or a Colombian drug lord would definitely attract the attention of the Anti-Corruption Unit. She was glad that Elvis was not home when they arrived and did not see her take them out to the trunk of the car.

This resulted in another secret that she kept from him. Keeping secrets from her husband bothered her immensely. Elvis always knew when she was up to something ... but was kind enough not to probe too deep when it came to the job.

When Laura finished talking to Elvis, Jack said, "Come on. We'd better tell Quaile something."

Moments later, Jack walked into Staff Sergeant Quaile's

office with Laura at his heels. Quaile was in charge of their particular Intelligence Unit, having arrived from a Commercial Crime Section in the fall.

Quaile was pegged as a high flyer. Someone who was rapidly climbing the corporate ladder. Jack knew that Quaile obviously had the backing of some high-ranking officer from somewhere in his career. His transfer to the Intelligence Unit was just another step in balancing his experience. *Which means he won't be here long.*

Jack waited until Quaile looked up and said, "Laura and I are heading out to meet a source. We'll be gone for the day."

Quaile glanced at his watch and said, "Thirty minutes before your shift ends? Is that what you are really doing — or are you just skipping out early?"

Jack felt his jaw clench, and replied, "We are meeting a source." There was a noticeable edge to his voice.

"Really? What source?" Quaile's tone now matched Jack's.

Damn it, why antagonize a snake? Jack thought. *I'll only be bitten.* Jack's voice returned to normal and he replied, "Fred Farkle. He's a dope dealer."

"Oh," replied Quaile. He stared at his own hand for a moment while drumming his fingers on his desk. Reaching a decision, he abruptly looked up and said, "Okay, but you're not claiming overtime for this. You should have rescheduled to a more appropriate time."

"We won't claim overtime."

Quaile nodded and returned to reading the policy manual.

Upon entering the parking garage Laura snickered and said, "Fred Farkle? Couldn't you come up with a better name than that?"

"If Quaile was smarter, I would have," replied Jack, opening the car trunk and passing Laura her bag of clothes.

"And this is another thing," replied Laura. "Having to

change clothes so we don't look like two J. Edgar Hoover FBI agents — doesn't he appreciate the type of work we do?"

"Apparently not. Just remember to change back when we return."

"What the hell are you up to?" said Jack, while throwing the box of shoes down on the path at Damien's feet.

"What?" replied Damien, looking first at the shoes sprawled out of the box before gazing at Laura. "Wrong size?"

"This is bullshit," said Jack. "You know better. What's going on?"

Damien glanced around the park, nodded and said, "Let's keep moving."

They left the discarded shoes on the ground and strolled down a path together. "Sorry," said Damien. "I got inebriated the other night and decided it would be funny. That's all there is to it."

"That's all there is to it?" said Jack heatedly. "Making it look like Laura could be getting a bribe — speaking of which, did you know her husband works in Internal Affairs?"

"Internal? I heard he was in the Anti-Corruption Unit," said Damien, before quickly adding, "Oh, I guess it's the same thing. Besides, he wasn't home at the time."

Laura felt her spine tingle. *Damien knows a lot about us … too much!*

As if reading her mind, Damien looked at her and said, "Don't worry. Just routine survival stuff. You know, keep your friends close, your enemies …"

"So, you're telling us you did it because you were pissed the other night?" said Jack.

Damien studied Jack's face momentarily before answering, "No, I said I was inebriated. There you go again.

Typical cop, thinking you have to lard on the tough talk."

"So inebriated," said Jack, "that you decided to advertise that you were back in the cocaine import business again?" Jack looked at Laura and added, "What am I saying? Why did I think he was ever out of it?"

Damien shook his head and said, "No, I am *not* importing cocaine from Ramirez. After what we went through with him last year? Give your head a shake!"

"New supplier?" asked Jack.

"It's not *us* you should be wasting your time on," said Damien.

"I've never found working on Satans Wrath to be a waste of time," said Jack.

Damien eyed Jack briefly and said, "Maybe in this new day and age you should set your sights higher. Start thinking outside the box. The world doesn't end at the Vancouver city limits."

"What are you saying?" asked Jack.

"I'm just saying that your time could be better spent than hassling a few of my boys who might have crossed the line once in a while."

"May have crossed the line once in a while?" said Laura, sarcastically.

Jack gave a slight shake of his head to Laura, signalling for her to be quiet. *Damien sent the shoes because he wants us to know something … but what?* Jack looked at Damien and said, "Set our sights higher? On who?"

"I don't know. I'm not a rat, but — just for example — I did hear of a couple of Russians who were asking a lot of questions about how to bypass something through the Port of Vancouver. Maybe you should be looking at them."

"And what do they intend to smuggle?" asked Jack.

Damien stared intently at Jack for a moment, and said, "I

really don't know. I'm not having anything to do with them. Neither is anyone in the club."

Jack sensed a look of fear in Damien's eyes. *What is he afraid of?*

"Russian mafia?" asked Laura.

"Probably connected," shrugged Damien.

Jack watched Damien nervously look around as he spoke.

"You talk to them personally?" asked Jack.

Damien nodded and said, "For some reason they seemed to think that we had a connection at the Port."

"You do," said Jack.

Damien flashed an irritated glance at Jack and said, "We met briefly. It was real brief. I did all the talking. I told them we would have nothing to do with them. If you guys, or whoever, were watching — I'm just telling you that we are not involved with anything they might be up to."

"And you don't know what they are up to?" asked Jack.

"That's right! I don't!"

"Who are they?" asked Jack. "What do they look like?"

"I don't remember. That's all I've got to say."

"I thought so," said Jack. "You are involved with them and are protecting them while trying to cover yourself."

"I'm not a liar!" said Damien, before clenching his jaw.

"Then quit playing games. You didn't call us here for nothing. What is it? Something is eating away at you."

Damien glared at Jack for a moment. He took a deep breath and slowly exhaled. "Okay, okay. I know I owe you for what you both did in Colombia last year," he said, lowering his voice. "So I'll tell you a little something about them. This is just between us, right?"

"You've got my word on that," replied Jack, glancing at Laura, who nodded her head.

Damien stared at Jack, nodded in return and said,

"They're both about my age."

"And you turned fifty-three last April," said Jack.

Damien frowned and Jack added, "It's like you said, know your enemies."

"Yeah," replied Damien gruffly. "Early fifties. One guy is tall, thin, short grey hair, grey moustache, and a prominent nose that sticks out like a beak. The other is short, fat, and bald with hairy arms. Looks like an orangutan. They mentioned they used to be schoolteachers in Russia."

"Schoolteachers!" exclaimed Laura.

"They're lying," said Damien. "These guys are different."

"How so?" asked Jack.

"I know authority types. The tall one for sure has government written all over him. Maybe military ... maybe police ... something. They're sure as hell not schoolteachers."

"So, what are you suggesting?" asked Jack.

"I'm suggesting that you should be working on them rather than bothering a bunch of working stiffs who occasionally like to get together and ride bikes."

Jack started to laugh but Damien interrupted and said, "No, seriously. Whatever they're up to, I'm not interested. And neither is anyone in the club. Understood?"

"I understand what you're *telling* me," said Jack.

"Damn it, Jack! I'm telling you the truth. We are not involved with them!"

"How do I find them?"

Damien glanced around and after not seeing anyone, he handed Jack a slip of paper. The names *Petya* and *Styopa* were on the paper, along with a cellphone number and an apartment address.

"There are only three guys on this planet that make me ... uncomfortable," said Damien. "You," he said, pointing a finger at Jack, "and these two."

Jack studied Damien's face as he spoke. *He is nervous …
so what the hell is going on?*

Damien gestured to the slip of paper in Jack's hand and
said, "They think the cell number is cool so it could prove
interesting to you. They also don't know I know their address.
It's a penthouse suite backing onto Stanley Park. Fairly lavish.
Two bedrooms, mini-bar, plasma television, one desk with a
laptop computer and … a bunch of textbooks."

"And they don't know you know their address?"
commented Laura, with a bemused look on her face.

Damien ignored the comment.

Textbooks? wondered Jack. *Odd comment.* "What type of
textbooks?" he asked.

"They were in Russian." Damien stared at Jack and said,
"So I don't know for sure."

Jack sensed that there was more to this than Damien was
letting on. *Or is he uncomfortable admitting that he had his
guys break into the Russians' apartment?*

"You might be interested in who visits them there,"
Damien suggested.

"And who would that be?" asked Jack.

"How the hell should I know?" Damien pointed to the
paper in Jack's hand and said, "Don't lose that. I didn't make
a copy and will have nothing further to do with these guys.
That's all I've got to say on the matter."

Damien turned away and took a step, but stopped and
added, "Oh, by the way, I almost forgot. The shoes didn't
arrive how you might think. But I guess if you had toxicology
check them for powder you probably already know that." He
handed Laura another piece of paper and walked away.

"Customs declaration," said Laura. "The shoes were
mailed to him directly. No cargo ship involved." She stared
after Damien. "So, what was that all about? Do you think he's

trying to sidetrack us into working on someone else instead of them?"

"I don't think so."

"Maybe he wants us to get rid of the competition for him."

"He has his own surveillance team and hit squad for dealing with the competition."

"Complete with locksmith," added Laura.

"Probably the one they call Sparks, from the east-side chapter. He does bugging as well."

"Figure he's bugged the Russians?"

"I don't think so. Not after telling us. He'd be afraid we'd find out. No, I think he's telling the truth when he says he doesn't want anything to do with them."

"So what do you think? That these guys are with the Russian mafia and have got him rattled?"

Jack shook his head. "Satans Wrath had a problem with the Russian mafia a few years ago. Four Russian brothers were the ringleaders. It took a year or so, but when the bullets stopped, there were three dead Russians and the fourth fled back to Moscow. This is what's so strange. Stuff like that doesn't scare him. He said that these two guys make him uncomfortable. For him to admit that — I just never would have believed it possible."

"Why doesn't he just kill them?"

"That's just it. I don't understand." Jack spoke his thoughts aloud. "There's something he isn't telling us. Some potential consequence that scares the hell out of him."

"So what should we do?"

"I think we better do as he says. Check these guys out."

It was late afternoon as Assistant Commissioner Isaac sat at his desk and gazed at the picture that stood upright on his desk next to his Bible. It was a picture of Sarah and Norah. His wife and daughter. Norah was only seventeen when an impaired driver raced through a red light, striking the side of the car that she was in. She died at the scene. Her friend, who was driving, was also seventeen and Isaac knew that she still blamed herself.

It was not her fault ... I pray that some day she realizes that. The impaired driver was convicted and lost his licence. *Little compensation for losing our daughter.*

"Staff Sergeant Quaile here to see you," announced his secretary.

Moments later, Quaile was seated in an overstuffed leather chair facing Isaac's desk while nervously wondering why he had been summoned.

For management purposes, the Royal Canadian Mounted Police was broken down into four nationwide regions: the Atlantic, Central, NorthWest, and Pacific Regions. Isaac was the Criminal Operations Officer who oversaw all the operational investigations in the Pacific Region. It made Quaile feel like he had just been invited into the inner sanctum of power.

"You've been in charge of the Intelligence Unit for three months now," observed Isaac.

"Yes, sir," replied Quaile. "Three months today, actually."

Isaac nodded. It was a date he had already noted in his Day-timer from when Quaile first arrived to the section. His piercing eyes examined Quaile closely and he said, "I wanted to wait until you had ... a feel ... for the office before having this conversation with you. A conversation that for now will remain between the two of us."

"Yes, sir?"

"I want to talk with you about Corporal Taggart."

"Sir?"

"Are you familiar with the more unusual aspects of some

of his past investigations?"

"I heard he was in a shootout with some bikers two years ago. Also that someone tried to kill him last year."

Isaac nodded knowingly and said, "He's had a rather lively career. Outstanding in some aspects. But ..." Isaac paused and glanced down at his desk before continuing, "I'm not exactly sure how I should word this. There's never been any proof," he muttered, more to himself than to Quaile.

"Proof, sir? Of what?"

"Of any wrongdoing on the part of Corporal Taggart. This is the dilemma. He could be completely innocent. Incredibly lucky, perhaps. His predictions in his reports about organized crime families have been remarkably accurate."

"That concerns you, sir?"

"No," said Isaac, brusquely. "That is *not* what concerns me. What concerns me is that key people he works on end up dead! That is what concerns me!"

"Dead?" said Quaile, sounding dumbfounded. "You mean like — I don't understand."

"I'll give you a quick history lesson. Three years ago, Corporal Taggart worked on a notorious French bank robber who was the ringleader in a gang that robbed banks across Canada. They were responsible for wounding and paralyzing a female officer in Quebec. Two months after Taggart starts to work on them, suddenly the gang believes their boss is an informant and kills him."

"Was he Taggart's informant?"

"No."

"Oh, I see," said Quaile, wondering what Isaac meant.

"That investigation followed another where a corrupt prosecutor working for Satans Wrath had ..."

"Had the bikers go after Taggart's niece and nephew. I heard about that," said Quaile.

"And did you hear that this prosecutor was later found dead in his swimming pool?"

"Yes, sir. An accidental drowning, I was told."

"*Maybe* it was — but it happened in Mexico at the same time Taggart was in Mexico."

Quaile swallowed nervously when he realized the implication.

"Perhaps that was just a coincidence," continued Isaac. "Then, last year, a Colombian drug lord tried to kill Taggart and terrorized the family of Constable Danny O'Reilly, who was Taggart's partner. A short time later, Taggart went to Colombia, allegedly to work on an unrelated investigation. Within a day of his arrival the drug lord and thirty of his men were murdered."

"Taggart did that?" asked Quaile, his eyes wide and his mouth dropping open.

"No, I'm not saying that he did. It's just that … well, quite frankly, it has crossed my mind if he wasn't somehow responsible. All this might simply be the suspicious brooding of an old man who has been on the job too long."

"I don't think you're old, sir." Quaile caught the frown that passed over Isaac's face. *Smart old fart. I'll have to be more tactful …*

"What I'm asking," continued Isaac, "is that you keep an eye on him and report anything suspicious to me. Understood?"

"Yes, sir. You may be pleased to know that I'm already on top of it. I've sensed he was a bad apple ever since I first arrived."

"You have?"

"I've found him to be contemptuous in nature and he is not someone I feel is properly groomed for the duties he is now responsible for. I'm surprised that his predecessor did not identify this."

"I've noticed that your office seems … well, more

spruced up since your arrival."

"Thank you, sir. Shoddiness, tardiness, insubordination … are all things I will not permit under my command. Unfortunately, Corporal Taggart has required discipline in all these areas. I also suspect he is a bad influence on the more junior members in the office. Now, realizing his history, perhaps Taggart is someone who should be given a less significant position?"

Isaac let out a sigh and said, "I hope you haven't misunderstood me on this matter. Taggart has done excellent work in the past. He is a particularly gifted undercover operative, exceptionally astute, and if I were a criminal, quite honestly, he is the last person I would ever want on my trail. All I'm asking you to do is to keep close tabs on him. Treat him fairly, but at the same time, I will not tolerate any deviations from policy. Is that clear?"

"Yes, sir," replied Quaile. *The first real test of my leadership! Thank you for the opportunity, Corporal Taggart!*

chapter three

Hằng's wet hands grasped the rope ladder to the fishing trawler waiting below. A mixture of rain and snow lashed at her face but she did not care. The excitement of finally arriving made everyone slightly giddy. The fact that their ship was three days ahead of schedule made it even better.

As soon as her feet touched the deck of the trawler, she anxiously pushed her way past the others to the outside edge to see if she could see any lights on shore. She saw only darkness.

Hằng felt an arm around her shoulders and smiled at Ngọc Bích. "We've made it," said Hằng, feeling breathless.

"They told me we would be on land in an hour," replied Ngọc Bích. "We haven't made it yet."

"If it is only an hour, I think I could swim that far," replied Hằng.

Ngọc Bích laughed and said, "Not here. You would become like a block of ice at the fish market."

"Quiet everyone! Lie down!" came a man's hushed voice

from the ship above.

Hằng quickly did as instructed. Soon the reason was clear as she heard the sound of a third boat. It chugged closer and closer … before continuing past.

Hằng peeked over the railing and saw that it was another fishing trawler heading out to sea. Everything was okay.

Their trawler did make land in an hour and moored alongside a wharf. Two vans took turns relaying the passengers to their next destination. Eventually it was Hằng and Ngọc Bích's turn to stumble down a wharf into a waiting van.

"My legs … they are acting strange," said Hằng.

"We are like sailors," said Ngọc Bích. "At sea many days."

They reached the van and crawled in the back with several other passengers. The driver was a Vietnamese man. He told them he was a fisherman and would take them to his home nearby.

"Just like Hanoi," commented Hằng, gesturing around the van from where she sat on the floor. "Another crowded van filled with the same people. Maybe we're still in Hanoi."

Ngọc Bích smiled. "Same, same, only different. It is colder. We are in Canada."

The fisherman's home turned out to be a house set back from the highway in a forest. Hằng had a glimpse of the heavy moss on the roof of the house and the peeling olive-coloured paint on the siding while being ushered inside to join her fellow passengers in the basement of the house.

Once in the basement, Hằng felt like she had entered paradise. The room was warm and the floor was scattered with blankets. There was a bathroom, complete with a shower for them to use, and even a television set. Few people from Hằng's neighbourhood would ever be able to afford a television set.

Hằng and Ngọc Bích looked at each other and smiled. Excited voices drew Hằng's attention to the far side of the room where several of the passengers were standing near a stove. *A real stove! Not a hot plate.* Hằng was awed. *That a simple fisherman should own such a place — is it possible?*

A large pot of boiling water was on the stove and some of the passengers who had arrived earlier were dumping Dungeness crabs into the pot. Hằng and Ngọc Bích quickly joined in.

A short time later, Hằng crawled under a blanket. Her stomach was full and it didn't take long for her to fall asleep.

It was many hours later when Hằng awoke to the sound of a woman speaking English. The voice came from the television set and she saw Ngọc Bích staring at it intently.

Hằng joined her and Ngọc Bích said, "Good to look. Learn English."

Hằng found herself watching a show called *CSI*. It was about the American police. It was a show she found engrossing. *They are the police and they are scientists. Very smart these American police …*

The fisherman came downstairs to tell them that because the ship was early, they would have to stay in the house for another three days before continuing on.

Hằng smiled. She was anxious to meet her new family, but after what she had been through in the last six weeks, this was like being told she would have to stay in a palace.

The fisherman produced the list of paper that Hằng had seen prepared by the bald ape and the vulture in Hanoi. The names were called out and everyone was divided into two groups, except for Hằng, who remained standing alone.

Then came the bad news. Only half the women were being smuggled into the United States. The other half, including Ngọc Bích, would be staying to work in hotels in Canada.

Hằng pushed through the group and grabbed her friend by the arm. "Say something! Come to America with me!"

Ngọc Bích took the fisherman aside and talked to him quietly. Hằng saw him shake his head and she felt a lump in her throat. She wished that her father had sent Linh with her. Now the loneliness crept into her body like the morning fog that swirled past the doors of Hồ Chí Minh's mausoleum.

Ngọc Bích returned and said, "It is not all bad. I must work in Canada for only a few months. Then I will be sent to America. I have been selected to work at hotels owned by three men. They are Vietnamese. The Trần brothers. I am told that one of them is taking you to your home in America. He will know where you are. We will see each other in a few months."

Hằng looked at Ngọc Bích and said, "You will not forget me?"

"You would forget your sister?" asked Ngọc Bích.

"No. I wish she was here now," grumbled Hằng.

"In Hanoi I told you I would be your sister as well. I will not forget you any more than I would forget my other brothers and sisters in Nha Trang."

Hằng looked solemnly at Ngọc Bích before hugging her.

The next couple of days went by quickly for Hằng. She spent much of her time watching back-to-back episodes of *CSI*. A cube van arrived one morning and the women who had been selected to go to the United States were called.

Hằng collected her clothes and turned to hug Ngọc Bích, but the fisherman touched her shoulder and said, "Not yet. You must stay here with these other women until more arrangements are made."

Hằng felt happy. The longer she was with Ngọc Bích, the better.

Later that night, another cube van arrived and the fisherman came downstairs with a young Vietnamese man. The fisherman pointed to Hằng and the young man immediately approached her.

"You speak English?" he asked.

"Yes," replied Hằng.

"My name is Tommy. I was born in Canada. My Vietnamese is not so good. Explain to the others that we must leave here at midnight tonight. We have to catch a ferry at quarter after five in the morning."

"Another boat?" asked Hằng.

"Not long. Only two hours. Everyone will ride in the back of the truck. Tell them to be quiet. I do not want anyone to know there are other people in the truck."

"And after this ferry ride I go to United States?" asked Hằng.

"I do not know. I work for Đức. He told me and Cường to bring everyone, so you're coming to."

"Cường?" asked Hằng.

"He is driving the truck. He works for my boss, too."

"Mister Đức is one of three brothers?" asked Hằng.

"Yes, Đức has two brothers in business with him."

"Now I understand," said Hằng. "Mine is a special situation. I will not be working in the hotel business. Your boss is going to take me to live with a family in the United States."

"Lucky for you."

Hằng gestured at the *CSI* show on the television and said, "Lucky — only if I do not get caught by the police. The American police are very smart. They are scientists."

Hằng believed her worry was justified and was startled when Tommy started laughing.

"You laugh that I may get caught? After what I have been through!" she said angrily.

"No … this is just television," Tommy said with a smile. "You need not be afraid. What you are watching … that is not all the police in the States. CSI are a special type. They only work on dead people. Believe me, if my boss is looking after you, you will not have to worry about the police."

"You are certain?"

"Yes. My boss does not take chances."

Their midnight truck ride, followed by the trip on the ferry, went without incident.

It was eight o'clock in the morning when Hằng accepted Ngọc Bích's helping hand as she climbed out of the truck. The truck had been backed up to a garage where a man ushered everyone to the rear of the garage. The overhead door was shut as the truck drove away.

The man inside the garage said his name was Giang. He said they would only have to wait a few minutes and would be on their way once more.

As they waited, Hằng saw Giang leering at the women. His eyes settled on Ngọc Bích and he stared brazenly, with a thin smile on his lips. Hằng knew Ngọc Bích was perhaps the prettiest, but to be so bold as to stare …

"I do not like that man," whispered Hằng, while clutching Ngọc Bích by the hand.

"If he were an animal," said Ngọc Bích, "he would be a pig."

Hằng smiled and said, "You think of people as animals or birds?"

"Sometimes."

"On our voyage, did you see a bald ape and a long-billed vulture?"

Ngọc Bích paused for a moment, and smiled. "Yes. The two foreigners in the apartment in Hanoi!"

They both giggled but Giang cut them short by stepping

closer. "What are you saying about me?" he snarled.

Hằng stepped back, fearfully tugging on Ngọc Bích's hand but she remained firm and looked Giang in the eye and said, "Who are you that we should talk about you? We were talking about Hanoi."

"That …" Giang's response was interrupted by a doorbell and another Vietnamese man hollered to him from inside the house. Giang immediately disappeared, only to return moments later with two more Vietnamese men.

These two men repeated the pattern that Hằng had seen in the apartment in Hanoi. The remaining women were once more divided into two groups, while she was left standing alone.

Minutes later, one of the Vietnamese men backed a van inside the garage and the first group of women were driven away.

The second Vietnamese man pointed a finger at Hằng and said, "You will wait here. My brother will be along soon." He looked at the remaining women and said, "Wait until I back my van up to the garage and then get in."

Hằng realized that Ngọc Bích would be gone within a minute. She felt Ngọc Bích's fingers on her arm and they looked at each other and tried to smile. Ngọc Bích fondly massaged Hằng's arm and said, "Only a couple of months. It will go fast."

"You are my first friend in America," said Hằng.

"No," chided Ngọc Bích. "We are sisters."

Hằng heard the harsh command telling the women to hurry as they climbed into the second van. The overhead garage door closed again and Ngọc Bích was gone.

Hằng was now in the garage alone with Giang and she fearfully glanced in his direction.

"Sit on the floor and wait," he said, and turned and went into the house.

Hằng was glad to be alone.

Half an hour passed before Giang returned. "Mister Đức is here," he said, opening the garage door. Đức drove a car into the garage and Giang closed the door behind him.

The man got out of the car and smiled at Hằng. "I am here to take you to your new family."

Hằng saw that Đức was a small man, with skinny arms and legs. *If he were an animal, he would be a spider monkey.* She nodded respectfully and asked, "Mister Đức, may I ask if the journey will be long?"

"You may ask whatever you like! No, your journey will not be long. We are in a place called Richmond. It is close to the American border. You will be in your new home in less than two hours."

"In two hours!" Hằng felt the adrenalin pump through her veins.

"I must apologize that you will have to ride in the trunk of my car. It will be uncomfortable, but I have put several pillows and a blanket in there to try and make it more comfortable. There is also some bottled water."

"Thank you, Mister Đức."

"I have a rear seat that folds down and for a little while, we will leave it down so you can talk if you wish. Once we get close to the border you will have to pull the seat closed and be very quiet as I clear U.S. Customs. Leave it closed until I tell you that it is okay."

"They will not search your trunk?" Hằng asked.

Đức smiled and said, "Some money will be passed. It is arranged, but it is still better if you are quiet."

Đức turned to Giang and said, "Be at the Orient Pleasure tonight at closing time. Bring the guys. I will be at a party and may be late. No matter if I am there or not. Start the …" Đức glanced at Hằng before continuing, "the training without me."

Hằng could not help but notice the harsh tone of Đức's voice when he spoke with Giang, who nodded obediently while staring down at his own feet.

Mister Đức may look like a spider monkey — but he is powerful!

Đức opened up the trunk to his car and gestured for Hằng to get in. She climbed in and made herself comfortable on some pillows. Đức opened up half of the rear seat and from her position, Hằng could see out the car windows at an angle looking up.

"When we get close to the U.S. border, I will tell you and you can just pull on that strap and the seat will close," said Đức.

Hằng nodded, feeling her body tremble as the final leg of her journey began.

Street lights and overhead signs passed by quickly as they drove. Hằng saw that they were on a highway marked 99.

"Up ahead, Hằng!" yelled Đức. "Look! See it?"

Hằng strained her head up to see what Đức was pointing at. *Canada–U.S. Border! This is it!* "I see it! I see it!" she said.

"Pull the seat closed! Quickly!" yelled Đức.

Hằng yanked hard on the strap and the seat closed tightly into position. She was now in complete darkness. She worried that the pounding of her heart could be heard. When she heard the blast of music as the radio was turned up she breathed easier. *Mister Đức knows what he is doing …*

Đức smiled as he turned off at the 8th Avenue exit, just prior to the U.S. border. He made a couple of more turns and slowed down as he inched his way along in a lineup of cars.

Hằng could hear little due to the loud music, but she felt the motion of the car as it would slowly pull ahead, stop, pull ahead some more. Her feet touched the plastic bag containing her clothes and it made a rustling sound. She froze, holding her breath, but the car inched forward again.

Đức picked up his coffee at the drive-through window and continued on.

Hằng breathed a sigh of relief as she felt the car pick up speed. Đức turned the radio down and yelled back to her, "Don't open the seat. We're through, but there are lots of big trucks beside me. I don't want anyone to look down and see you. Should only be about another twenty minutes."

Twenty minutes later, Hằng felt the car stop and heard the sound of a garage door. Đức pulled into the garage and she heard the garage door close. The trunk was opened.

Hằng saw a large man standing next to Đức. He was about the same age as her own father, but he was wearing sweat pants and a white T-shirt. Hằng had never seen a man with arms bulging with such big muscles.

"Hằng," said Đức, "I'd like you to meet …"

"Pops," the big man beside Đức said. "Just call me Pops." He smiled and said, "Here, let me help you out of there. I bet you're really uncomfortable."

Before Hằng could answer, he bent over and lifted her out of the trunk and gently set her down beside him. "Welcome to the States," he said. "Come, I'll show you your new home," he said, opening a door that led into the house. "You must be tired … and hungry too, I bet!"

Hằng felt dumbstruck as she was shown around the house. Đức trailed along behind and seldom spoke. To Hằng, the house was huge. There was a large kitchen and a sitting room with a fireplace.

"How many other families live here?" asked Hằng.

Pops chuckled and said, "Just us. No other families."

Hằng shook her head in amazement, and asked, "Where is Mrs. Pops? Is she here? I have something to give her."

"She is not home right now. Her mother is sick and she

had to go away for a couple of days."

"I am sorry," said Hằng, hoping her question did not cause discomfort.

"That is okay. Come, let me show you the rest of the house. For now, we have to keep the drapes and blinds shut. Nobody must know you are here until we receive the proper documentation."

Pops shoved open a door and said, "This is my bedroom."

Hằng looked inside and saw that on the opposite side of the bedroom was the bathroom. *To get to the bathroom you have to walk through Mister Pops's bedroom! Poor to build a house in such a manner.*

Hằng was led farther down the hall and Pops opened the door to another room.

"This is your bedroom," said Pops, placing Hằng's bag of clothes on the floor. "You can hang your jacket in the closet."

Hằng gazed around the room in awe. It was huge. Her eyes wandered from a big stuffed teddy bear lying on the bed to something that startled her.

"Mister Pops! There is a television in my room! Do we watch it in here?"

Pops laughed and said, "No, that is just for you."

"For me!" Hằng exclaimed, putting her hand over her mouth.

"You can watch it in here if you want to be alone. I'll show you another television that you can watch if you do not wish to be alone. It is much bigger, but first, I want to finish showing you around up here."

Hằng opened the closet door and saw that the closet had more space than the area that both she and Linh had when they slept at home.

Pops opened another door beside her bedroom. "This is your bathroom," he said. "If there is anything you are missing or anything you need, please just ask me."

"Mister Pops, this is … for me, too?"

He grinned and said, "Mister? No, no, no. Just call me Pops. Yes, this bathroom is for you until your sister comes. Then you'll have to share the bathroom with her. Of course," he said, opening the door to another bedroom, "she'll have own her room."

"I'll go now," interrupted Đức. He handed Pops a cellphone and said, "For later."

Pops had Hằng wait in the kitchen while he went to the garage with Đức. As soon as Đức was gone, Pops returned and said, "Come, follow me. I'll show you a real TV set."

Hằng was in a daze as Pops led her to the basement, where they entered a large room with wooden panelling on the walls and thick wall-to-wall carpet. There was a leather sofa, two upholstered chairs, and a coffee table in the room.

"Help yourself whenever you want," said Pops, gesturing to a bowl full of candy on the table.

Hằng gawked at the wall opposite the sofa. Hanging on the wall was the largest television set she had ever seen.

"And this room over here is just another bathroom," said Pops, gesturing to another door. "The room beside it just has my weights for working out."

Hằng started to cry. She tried to stop, but she couldn't help herself.

"What is wrong?" asked Pops.

Hằng flung her arms around him and said, "Nothing. It is so much just for me. My tears are happy tears."

Pops hugged her back and said, "Why don't you go back upstairs and freshen up? Take a hot bath or a shower. There are clean towels in the bathroom for you. It is also lunchtime. While you're doing that, I'll order some pizza."

Pops stared at Hằng for a moment and said, "If you like

pizza? Otherwise I can order something else?"

"I like pizza," said Hång, using her hands to wipe her tears. Later, while gorging herself on pizza, Hång turned to Pops and nervously said, "My father has a phone. He asked that I call him."

"I think you should. He must be worried."

"I have not talked to him for six months — no, weeks," replied Hång. "I worry about my sister and grandmother, too."

Pops checked his watch and said, "With the time difference, it is now about four in the morning there. Maybe a little early for a call. Let's wait a few hours."

Hång nodded in agreement.

Pops spied Hång's extra thumb and gently reached out and touched it. "I was told about this. Does it cause you pain?"

Hång quickly withdrew her hand from the table and placed it on her lap.

"Please, I did not mean to embarrass you," said Pops. "I just wondered if it caused you any pain."

"It does not hurt" replied Hång, matter-of-factly. "Only in my head it hurts. Not real pain."

Pops smiled knowingly and said, "If you like, in time, I will have a surgeon remove it for you. But that will be your decision. It does not bother me at all."

Hång smiled and brought her hand back into view. "I think I would like that. To be the same as other children. My sister does not have this problem. She is perfect."

"Your sister … I understand the next ship leaves in three days. Do you think she will like it here? I bet you miss her?"

"Yes, very much," she admitted.

"I hope you will be happy here," said Pops.

Hång beamed. Words were not necessary.

"Your English is very good, but in a few days we will start you on home-schooling. Right now, I bet you are exhausted."

Hằng smiled and said, "Yes. I am very tired."

"If you've had enough to eat, go to your room and take a nap. I'll wake you in a couple of hours and then you can call your dad."

Hằng went to her room and climbed into bed. She had never slept in a bed so big. Or on a mattress and pillow that was so soft. Too soft for what she had become used to. She elected instead to lie on the floor and cover herself with a blanket. She fell asleep immediately and slept soundly until she was awakened a few hours later by a gentle knock on her door.

A few minutes later, she sat at the kitchen table with Pops, who picked up a cellphone on the table.

"Do not say anything on the phone about the ship or the name of who smuggled you into the States," he cautioned. "It is risky for you to call home now, because the American police monitor calls to foreign countries. Especially a communist country like Vietnam."

"I understand," said Hằng.

"Tell your dad how excited you were to see the American border sign when you arrived. That would be good. If the police are listening, they would think you drove across the border as people are supposed to."

"Okay," said Hằng.

"Do you think your sister will be happy here? I understand the next ship leaves in three days."

"It would be an honour for her to be in your house, Mister Pops."

"I think it would be better for you if she was here. There is another girl that wants to come. It must be decided now. I can only have two girls and I think it better that you have your sister. Don't you?"

Hằng was startled to learn that there was a possibility that another girl may be selected. "Yes, I want my sister," she said quickly. "She is kind and polite. She will be no trouble for you."

"Your dad must miss you. Won't it be nice when he can come and live here, too?"

"You think he can?" asked Hằng.

"Not right away. But think about it. You are free to become anything you want in this country. You could become a lawyer if you want. Then you could draw up the papers yourself to allow your father to immigrate here."

"He really wants to come to America."

"Good. I think we can risk one call right now. In a couple of weeks, when certain papers are in order, you can use the regular phone in the house and call home whenever you like."

Hằng gave Pops the number and he dialled. "It is ringing," he said, while passing her the phone.

Hằng's call was an excited combination of tears and laughter as she spoke of her new surroundings and her dreams for the future. Pops was generous with the time she could talk and when she was finished, she had spoken at length with her father, Linh, and even her grandmother.

As soon as she hung up, she felt sorrow. She had never been completely away from her family before. Occasionally, in the past, before her father had become a tourist guide, he had to go away for a couple of weeks to work on farms. Even then, Hằng still had Linh, who helped her look after Grandmother.

"You look sad," commented Pops. "Is everything okay?"

Hằng nodded and said, "I am okay. I am only sad because I miss them."

"That is why I wish your sister had come with you. It would make it easier. Your father was told that."

Hằng's face brightened and she said, "She will come now. You do not need that other girl. She will start the voyage in three days."

"That's great," said Pops, sounding relieved. "Oh, there is one thing I forgot to show you. It is in case the police should ever come before your papers are in order. I have built a secret room in the basement for you to hide in. Come, I will show it to you."

chapter four

Jack and Laura started their shift by checking with the property managers of the apartment building that the two Russians lived in. The office was located in the main foyer, next to the front entrance of the apartment building itself.

Jack noticed the building was secure, complete with intercom and security cameras, inside and out. After producing identification, Jack and Laura learned that the actual apartment manager was a retired Vancouver city policeman by the name of Derek. A phone call was placed and Derek soon joined them in the office. He was more than willing to assist.

The lease agreement indicated the names were Petya Globenko and Styopa Ghukov. Their occupation said that they were retired schoolteachers. They had each provided Russian passport numbers for identification. The penthouse suite came with two free underground parking stalls, but the Russians indicated they did not have a car.

"Taxis," commented Laura. "Makes our job easier."

"Until you turn a corner and suddenly see three taxis in front of you and have to play the old shell game," replied Jack.

"They usually use a limo service," said Derek. "From what I've seen, they're big tippers. I presume they're dopers?"

"We're not sure," said Jack. "We were just given their names and told they were bad guys worth looking into. At this point we don't know anything about them yet."

"They speak perfect English," said Derek. "Petya goes by the name Peter. He's tall, thin, and has short grey hair and a moustache. Styopa is short, chubby, and has a shaved head. They always pay on time and with cash. Guess I don't need to tell ya, their place costs a bundle to rent. They fit the profile of dopers."

"I'll never keep their names straight," mumbled Laura, before trying to repeat them in her head.

"How about Moustache Pete and the Fat Man?" suggested Jack.

"That's easier," she replied.

"Do you know who they associate with, or if they have many visitors?" asked Jack.

"Not that I've really noticed ... but come to think of it," replied Derek, reaching for a journal on the desk and flipping through some pages. "The building has a party room," he muttered, gesturing to a room with double doors just across the foyer. "They came to me about a week ago ... yes, here it is. They booked the room for tonight. The party starts at nine o'clock."

"You free tonight?" asked Jack, looking at Laura.

"You bet," she replied.

"They're allowed to come in early to set up," said Derek, "but are required to have everyone out no later than two. The room holds fifty people easy. There is also an apartment directly above this office that you can rent for a day or two if you have company arriving. It's right beside the elevators. They booked it also and said it might be used if any of their party guests drink too much."

"We would really like to see who attends the party," said Jack.

"If you like, you could sit in here tonight and watch," suggested Derek. "Whoever comes to the front door will have a key if they're a tenant. If not, they will have to be buzzed in, either from an apartment or from the party room. If you're in here watching you'll be able to see who goes to the party and who is probably just visiting other tenants. We turn off the lights and close the blinds in here at night so nobody would know you were in here. You want a key?"

Jack smiled, held out his hand, and Derek gave him a key to the main entrance of the apartment and a separate key to the office.

"The office one, I would prefer it if you leave it on the desk tonight when you're done. As far as the key to the main doors goes, you can keep it until you're finished your investigation."

"Much appreciated," said Jack. "I notice you have security cameras. If need be, could we get a copy later to see who attends the party?"

"That could be arranged. We only hang on to them for a week."

"Long enough for us to decide if we need them. One more thing."

"What's that?" asked Derek.

"What's your favourite brand of poison?"

Derek smiled and said, "Thanks, but no. I don't drink anymore. Since I've quit the job, I haven't had to. Anything I can do to help you catch bad guys is fun enough."

Back at the office, Jack called a contact and learned that the cellphone being used by the Russians was listed to a massage parlour in Surrey called the Orient Pleasure. As the day progressed, he also obtained a list of phone numbers that had been dialled from the cellphone within the last month.

Jack made a photocopy of the list and handed it to Laura and said, "Check out who the Canadian numbers are registered to. There are a lot of area codes here I don't recognize. I'll …"

"What are you two up to?" asked Quaile, entering their office.

Jack glanced at him and said, "Laura and I are working on a pair of Russians."

"What are they involved in?"

"Not sure yet, we're just getting started."

"We're a little too busy, don't you think, to be working on people when you don't know what they're even involved in?"

"We know they've met with the higher echelon of Satans Wrath. We think they're worth looking at."

"Satans Wrath again? Still working on bums, I see. Well, keep me apprised." With that comment, he turned and sauntered back to his own office.

"What was that all about?" wondered Jack.

"Maybe he's decided to take an interest in police work," suggested Laura.

"As long as we dress like we're going to church and don't claim overtime, he's never cared before."

Jack shrugged off Quaile's intrusion and checked to see who owned the Orient Pleasure. It was listed under the name of Trần Đức, who, Jack discovered, lived in a house in Surrey. A further inquiry revealed that Đức had a lengthy criminal record for assault, armed robbery, keeping a common bawdy-house and extortion. Most of the convictions were more than six years old and there was nothing recent.

As the day progressed, Jack and Laura discovered that many of the numbers called from the Russians' cellphone were to such places as Afghanistan, Russia, Iran, Saudi Arabia, Thailand, Vietnam, and Korea. A couple of others were to Sweden.

"These guys work for the United Nations?" joked Laura.

"Afghanistan is a great country to go to if you want to buy a couple of tonnes of heroin," replied Jack. "Some of these Arab and Asian countries could be smuggling routes."

"Makes sense," said Laura, thoughtfully.

"It would, except that why would it make our friend nervous? You think he'd be glad to cut himself a piece of the action."

"Either that, or simply kill them if they're too much competition," said Laura.

"Exactly. I'm going to pass some of these numbers on to Interpol. See what pops up."

"Don't hold your breath waiting."

"Yeah, I know."

"It will be interesting to see who shows up at the party tonight," said Laura.

"If any Arab women show up, do you have a burka you could put on, so you could slide in and mingle?"

Laura glanced at him and said, "Excellent idea. And you could put on a pair of donkey ears and come along as an ass. Oh …" Laura paused and continued, "maybe you don't need the ears."

Jack brayed like a donkey and they both laughed.

Hằng followed Pops back down to the basement. Pops gestured to the walls with his hand and said, "Watch this."

Hằng saw that the upper half of the basement walls were

covered in wood panelling, while the lower half of the walls
consisted of dark brown boards that framed large, square
pieces of brown panelling.

Pops pushed on a segment of the dark brown board and
Hằng heard a metallic click. A magnetic latch behind the
panel opened to allow the panel to protrude slightly from
the wall. Pops pulled on it to release the rest of the magnetic
latch and a thick square section in the wall opened up to
reveal a passageway.

"See how it is done?" asked Pops. "There is a wooden
handle on the back of the door for you to pull shut after you
go inside. I do not think you will ever have to use this room,
but it is good to be safe." Pops demonstrated once more, by
closing and opening the door again.

"I understand," said Hằng, admiring how perfect the wall
looked when the secret door was closed.

"Follow me," said Pops, crouching down as he took a few
steps into the passageway.

Hằng followed, pausing briefly as Pops reminded her
to close the door behind her. After, she turned and accepted
Pops's hand to stand up as she entered the secret room.

Pops flicked the switch on the wall and a bright overhead
light recessed behind wire mesh in the ceiling lit up the small
room. Hundreds of shiny brass-coloured screws shone down
from where the bare plywood was screwed to the ceiling. The
walls and floor were covered in crimson enamel paint.

Hằng saw a toilet in the centre of the room, close to a
sponge mattress on the floor. On one wall was a large calendar.
How long do I have to hide if the police come? The room was
dank and musty. Hằng shivered and saw a propane bottle
attached to a portable heater sitting beside one wall. It was
not turned on.

"Nobody would ever find me in here," said Hằng.

"That's right. They won't," nodded Pops with satisfaction.

Everything made sense to Hằng except for one thing. Two piles of chains lay on the floor on each side of the room. She walked over and picked up a handful of chain and asked, "What is this for?"

Pops just smiled.

She saw that one end of the chain was bolted to a metal ring on the floor … and she spotted the shackle on the end that dangled in her hand. Fear gripped her body like a vice as she slowly turned her head to stare up at Pops.

"Put it on," he said. His voice was menacing as he loomed over her, threatening her with a fist.

Hằng shook her head, too frightened to speak. She stepped back and quickly tried to swing the chain at Pops's face, but he grabbed her around the throat with one hand, smashing her down on the floor and landing on top of her.

Hằng tried to yell and clawed frantically at the hand squeezing her throat. He grabbed at her fingers with his other hand. She heard a sound like the crunch of celery and felt the searing pain in her fingers when he snapped them backwards.

Hằng writhed and kicked out violently with her feet. Pops punched her hard in the side of her ribs. She continued to squirm and gasped at the intense pain in her side with every breath she took. His next punch buried deep into her stomach, forcing what air she had to come gurgling past the hand clamped to her throat and out through her mouth and nose.

She realized Pops was standing at the opposite end of the room with a bemused look on his face. She leapt to her feet and dashed toward the passage door. The chain went taut and she fell on her hands and knees, far short of her goal. It was then that she looked down at the shackle chained to her ankle and realized that she had been unconscious.

Hằng knew she had nothing to lose and screamed as loud

as she could, while cringing and waiting for the next attack.

Pops did not move. Instead of trying to silence her, he started to laugh. She screamed again and again …

"Go ahead!" yelled Pops. "Louder! Louder!" he shouted with glee. His laughter and Hằng's screams filled the room. "Come on, you can do it!" he shouted. "Let me hear you scream!"

Hằng's screams eventually became hoarse rasping cries of anguish. She stopped and held her face in her hands, before dropping to her knees on the floor and sobbing.

"Please, Mister Pops," she cried. "No. Why are you doing this to me? Please let me go."

"Maybe some day I will," he said. "Or maybe I won't."

Pops took a red felt marker from his pocket and with a smile at Hằng and a flourish of his arm, circled a date on the calendar that was exactly two weeks away. He made three more circles on the calendar in the week following the first circle.

"You will have two weeks for behaviour modification," he said. "These circles represent something special. There will be a different surprise for you on each red-circle day."

Pops hesitated as his hand hovered near the light switch and said, "I'll leave this on. Have a good sleep." He ducked into the passageway and Hằng heard the click and the creak of the secret door as it opened and closed behind him.

She immediately got to her feet and walked to see how far the chain would let her go. She could just reach the centre of the room where the toilet and mattress were. She carefully checked out the chain where it was attached to the floor. There was nothing she could break or undo.

She hopelessly looked around before sitting on the floor, using a loop of chain to smash at the padlock. She tore the skin on her leg and bruised her ankle before giving up.

She started to cry and sobbed uncontrollably as she

crawled over to the toilet and dipped her broken fingers in the water. The coolness of the water did little to soothe her. Eventually she quit crying and stared blankly at the calendar on the wall. *What does it mean? What surprises do the red circles hold?*

As her eyes settled on the other pile of chain on the far side of the room, her terror reached a new crescendo.

chapter five

"You there, Jack?" whispered Laura, from where she sat in the darkened room of the property manager's corner office. The blinds were open just enough to give her a glimpse of the entranceway outside, as well as a view of the main doors to the party room across the foyer.

Jack was parked out on the street and sat slouched in the passenger seat of the car. From the perspective of anyone walking by, it would appear that he was waiting for the driver to return.

He clicked the transmit button on the police radio and said, "Copy. Go ahead."

"Moustache Pete and the Fat Man are just opening up the doors to the room. They're each carrying a case of vodka. Looks like they expect a few people tonight."

"Ten-four. Over an hour to go before the party is supposed to start," observed Jack.

Minutes later, Jack watched as a taxi van pulled into the

crescent-shaped driveway in front of the apartment building and parked under the awning in front of the main doors. He reached for the binoculars.

"Got it, Jack," came Laura's voice. "Can see the plate from here. Oh, it's a taxi."

Jack watched as seven young women exited the taxi. They were all smartly dressed and wore high heels. Two of them wore coats that were trimmed with fur. The other coats appeared to be made of wool.

Despite the cool February night, their coats were open and Jack could see that they all wore skirts. They also had something else in common. They were extremely beautiful. Three of them were blondes, the others were brunettes.

Laura remained still and heard the women chatting as they buzzed the intercom.

"There's no answer," one woman said.

"Try again. These guys have used our agency before."

"You've worked here before?"

"Oh, yeah. I call them Nikolai and Doctor Zhivago. They like that. Both pigs, but if you make them happy, they're not afraid to open their wallets wide for a tip. Here, let me try the party room."

Seconds later the women were buzzed in and Laura saw the two Russians come to the entrance to the party room and wave them over.

"Escort service," Laura relayed to Jack.

"Maybe the party is starting sooner than we thought," replied Jack.

Laura watched as the two Russians carefully examined the women, before taking one on each arm and heading for the elevator. The other three escorts remained in the party room.

"Our boys aren't greedy," radioed Laura.

"How so?" asked Jack.

"They only picked two each and headed up to their room. Must be saving the other three for later."

An hour later, the entourage from upstairs returned. One woman made a motion to re-button the top of her blouse but the Fat Man playfully slapped her hand away. He laughed and shook his finger and said, "No, no, no. I like to look."

Laura noticed that both Russians had changed their clothes and were now wearing expensive-looking shoes, slacks, and silk shirts open at the neck.

The next hour went by relatively quietly and a mixture of men and women started to arrive. As this happened, Jack would walk down the sidewalk while using the voice-activated tape recorder in his inside jacket pocket to record license plates. When people entered the apartment, Laura confirmed who was of interest and who wasn't. In the end, Jack had recorded over two-dozen license plates and he estimated that, with the taxis included, approximately forty to forty-five people were at the party.

Several hours passed and Laura whispered into her radio, "Jack, just to let you know that the apartment above me is being used … about half an hour at a time."

"The seven escorts?"

"So far, five of them. Five different guys, too."

"Special guests getting their treats upstairs," radioed Jack. "Let me know when they leave. I'll try to identify them."

"Getting their treats? Is that what you call it? You must have been *very* disappointed as a kid on Halloween — stand by! Three of the guys who were *treated* upstairs are now giving Moustache Pete a hug at the door … he's kissing each one on the cheek. The three of them are heading for the entrance now. You can't miss them. They're all Asians and looking a little whiskied. Incidentally, all of them preferred blondes."

Jack had no trouble following the three men and was pleased to see that they each drove away in separate cars. He recorded three licence plates, ones he had seen earlier, as now being of particular significance.

The other two men who had been entertained upstairs eventually left separately. The first one drove away in a Jaguar while the second drove off in a Porsche. Jack didn't need to double check these plates. He had remembered them from when they first arrived.

It was three o'clock in the morning when Jack dropped Laura off at her car to drive home.

"Something was really out of place at the party tonight," said Laura.

"That being?" asked Jack.

"All the guests. With the exception of the seven hookers who arrived first, everyone else was either dressed — or acted — like lower-class hoods and gangsters."

"Hoods and gangsters … there's an old expression. You been watching *The Untouchables* again?"

"You know what I mean. Walking around with real attitude. Wearing too much gold jewellery. Doused in enough aftershave to make you gag."

"You smelled aftershave? Did you go inside?"

"Didn't have to. I could smell it coming through under the door."

"Good. Don't know how long we'll be working on these guys. I don't want them seeing our faces until absolutely necessary."

Laura nodded in agreement and continued, "I guess all I'm saying is I wonder why the Russians would hang out with these guys?"

"Maybe it's strictly business? Nothing to do with friendship."

"Maybe."

"High-class hookers. I would say it was a corporate party. Likely celebrating something. Wish we knew what."

"Two of the hookers were never used, although our Russian friends always had one latched to their arm all night."

"Big egos require a big show. We'll find out about the guests tomorrow when we run the plates," said Jack.

It was four in the morning when Jack slipped into bed beside Natasha and gently kissed her on her bare shoulder before pulling the blanket higher. She rolled over to face him and lay with her head on his chest.

Jack felt her hand slowly drift up the inside of his thigh and tilted his pelvis slightly while unconsciously opening his mouth in the expectation of pleasure. She stopped and moments later her breathing indicated that she had gone back to sleep. Jack let out a sigh and tried to relax. It took him over an hour to get to sleep.

It was nine o'clock at night in Hanoi when Biến felt Linh's skinny arms squeezing his lungs. She was clinging to his waist while he pedalled his bicycle. It made taking deep breaths difficult, but he didn't mind. They were plenty early to meet the van.

Eventually, Biến pulled up to the appointed location and carried his bicycle up onto the sidewalk while Linh carried the plastic bag containing her clothes.

"Forty minutes early," said Biến.

"I do not think the American lady will be happy to see me," sniffled Linh.

"And why not?" asked Biển, although he knew what the response would be before he asked.

"I have no gift to give her."

"We do not have the money for two gifts. The pearl necklace cost much money. It is worthy of being a gift from the both of you."

"Maybe Hằng forgot to say so."

"Do you really think she would do such a thing? Leave her little sister out?"

Linh put her head down and said, "No. I do not think that."

"There is something you have to give that is much more precious than a stone from some oyster," said Biển.

"What is that?" asked Linh with surprise.

"Your smile, little one," answered Biển sincerely. "I would not trade your smile for all the pearls in Ha Long Bay."

Linh tried to frown as she looked up at her father, but there was a twinkle in her eye and she soon smiled and giggled.

At nine years old, some might have found her mixture of baby teeth and adult teeth somewhat less than attractive, but to Biển it was a beautiful smile.

chapter six

The next day Jack identified the three Asians from the party and did background research on them while Laura looked into the backgrounds of the two men they referred to as Mister Porsche and Mister Jaguar.

Jack discovered that the three Asians were Vietnamese brothers who were the owners of two massage parlours. One massage parlour was called The Asian Touch and was one-third owned by each of the brothers. Their given names were Đức, Hữu, and Thạo. Their family name was Trần. Đức was also the sole owner of the Orient Pleasure, the establishment to which the Russians' cellphone was registered.

Hữu and Thạo did not have criminal records, but Jack learned that the Combined Forces Special Enforcement Unit had encountered one of the brothers on an investigation two years previous.

Jack told Laura the information and she groaned.

"What's wrong?" he asked.

"I'll never keep these guys straight," she said.

"I think the important one to remember is Đức," said Jack. "He owns part of what his brothers have, plus the Orient Pleasure, where the Russians' phone is registered. He's also the one with a criminal record."

"So it's Đức and his brothers."

"For now. Incidentally, if you ever read or hear their names someplace, the Vietnamese put their family name first, followed by their middle name, and then their given name. Formally, they address each other by their given name. I would be known as Taggart, Bruce Jack, and if formally addressed, would be called Mister Jack."

"Okay, Mister Jack, so neither of the two brothers have any criminal history?"

"No convictions, but Thạo was the owner of a couple of rental properties where the Vietnamese tenants had grow-ops. They were taken down two years ago by CFSEU."

"Doesn't take these guys long to learn about B.C. bud," said Laura.

"How are you making out with Mister Porsche and Mister Jaguar?" asked Jack.

"They are both well known," replied Laura. "No convictions, but I just got off the phone with Drugs. Mister Porsche beat an importation charge a few years ago when he tried to smuggle a boatload of hash into B.C. He beat the rap in court by claiming that the dope was on its way to Alaska and that a storm blew them into Canadian waters. The judge said there was no intent to commit a crime in Canada. Mister Jaguar is a major cocaine dealer but has never been caught."

"Jag and Porsche work together?"

Laura shook her head. "Not as far as any records show. They appear to be independent of each other."

"Our Russians are the common denominator," declared Jack.

"I've also checked for criminal records on the rest of the partygoers," said Laura. "Lots with criminal records, but all minor stuff. Low-level drug dealers, that type of thing."

"I think our Russians were just throwing their version of an office party," said Jack. "I doubt that any of these people are really their friends."

"So where do you want to go from here?"

"For now, concentrate our time on the Russians. If we lose them, then we'll work on Đức as a backup."

"Sounds good."

"I'm going to give VPD a call and see what they have on these guys. The Asian Touch is in their turf."

Jack's phone call to the Vancouver City Police soon found him transferred around where he ended up speaking to Detective Rocco Pasquali of the Anti-Gang Unit.

Jack had met Pasquali on past investigations and knew him as a good cop who was not afraid to work. More importantly, he didn't let inter-agency rivalry affect his work. All he wanted was for bad guys to go to jail.

"The Trần brothers are well known to us," said Pasquali. "Guess I don't need to tell you that the massage parlours are just a front for prostitution, but there's a lot more to him than that. Đức expanded his operation out to Surrey last year."

"The Orient Delight," said Jack.

"You got it. Physically, he's a small man. A good fart would probably knock him over, but he's got the power. He heads a Vietnamese gang of at least fifty. They're into just about everything. Extortion, robberies, drugs, juvenile prostitution … you name it. They're extremely violent. Not afraid to take a machete to someone just for making eye contact with them."

"I'll keep that in mind."

"Lately, the asshole has insulated himself enough as to be basically untouchable. His top lieutenant is a guy by the name of Giang. A real psychopath. I mean that. He deals coke at the pound level. He came to Canada when he was seven I really think the Vietnam War did something to him before he came over. He really is one disturbed individual."

"So Giang gets his coke from Đức?"

"No, Giang freelances that on his own. Đức uses him more as an enforcer and to keep his girls in line. The two don't hang together as friends. Giang uses a place called Lucky Lucy's Bar and Grill as his base of operations. That's downtown here in Vancouver, on Kingsway, close to The Asian Touch."

"Any other hangouts?" asked Jack.

"There is also a restaurant close to Lucky Lucy's called the Mekong Palace. The owner of the Mekong is a nice old guy. Doesn't want these guys in there but doesn't have much choice. If Giang is not at any of these places, he usually can be found hanging out with the other punks in Đức's gang at Billiard Bill's out in Surrey. That place is just a block down the street from the Orient Pleasure."

"I really appreciate this, Rocco."

"No sweat. I'll send a copy of everything we have on this group over to you. You need a hand with anything — surveillance, takedowns, you name it — give me a call. Day or night, doesn't matter."

"Sounds like you want him bad," said Jack.

"I do. Đức's gang ... half of it is composed of juveniles, for Christ's sake."

"Their conscience isn't as developed. They don't think of the real consequences of their actions. Explains the extreme violence."

"Yeah, and they're more easily influenced and brainwashed ... and usually get probation. You catch Đức and there's a bottle of tequila in it for you."

"Thanks. Actually I've switched to gin martinis."

"Catch him," said Rocco, "and I'll be buying the gin."

"No reward for Giang?" asked Jack.

Rocco chuckled and said, "What are you trying to do, bleed me dry? Giang's not real smart. He's been caught before. Unfortunately he's smart enough not to cross Đức."

"Tell you what," said Jack. "When I nail Đức, you buy the gin and I'll bring the vermouth. If I happen to nail Giang along the way, then you can bring the olives, too."

"That's a deal!"

The next week and a half went by quickly for Jack and Laura. They focused their energy by doing surveillance of the Russians while doing intermittent surveillance on Đức.

Đức had a routine of sleeping in late and then going to the Orient Pleasure for an hour over lunch. He would generally spend the rest of his day and evening at the Great Canadian Casino in Coquitlam. His skill as a gambler left much to be desired.

Surveillance of the Russians showed that they varied their sleep patterns. Sometimes they would appear early in the morning and go to a restaurant for breakfast. On these occasions, Jack surmised that they had not been to bed yet, or, at least judging by the escorts that left the building moments before they appeared, they had not been to *sleep* yet.

Other times the Russians would not appear until early afternoon, when they would go and drink espresso in different restaurants. At night, they would throw their money around at various nightclubs or go to more expensive restaurants. If they didn't pick up any women at the nightclubs, they would often call an escort service when they returned to their penthouse.

Hằng lay on her side on the foam mattress, staring at the calendar. Pops never shut the light off and she found herself switching her attention back and forth between the calendar and the chain and shackle at the opposite end of the room.

Now she felt so weak that she could barely move. Going by the large X marks that Pops penciled on the calendar each day, she had been there thirteen days. She had been given a plastic cup to drink water from out of the toilet tank. The only food she had been given was one loaf of white bread.

Her fingers had quit throbbing, but any attempt to move them brought immediate pain. The same went for her ribs and she had learned to take shallow breaths.

On the first night she was chained, Pops had returned and flung all her clothes and belongings at her. The room had a high humidity and at first when she wore her new coat she was too warm, but now she felt weak and shivered constantly.

Pops would see her for a few minutes each morning and again at night. Except for hurting her the first night, he had not actually touched her.

One night he dragged a garden hose through the passageway and said he was going to give her a shower. Despite the incredible shame she felt at undressing in front of him, her fear made her obey and she squatted obediently on the floor and tried to cover herself with her hands.

"You are a filthy, worthless little child," he said. "No wonder your father gave you away," he said as he urinated on her, before taking the hose and spraying cold water into her face.

Every time Hằng heard the familiar creak of the passage door, she automatically cringed and drew her knees up into the fetal position as she waited for Pops to enter, mark the X on the calendar, and announce how many days were left until "red-circle day."

Tonight was different. Pops shoved a large cardboard

box ahead of him through the passageway opening and set it down out of Hằng's reach. The box was big enough that it could have held an object the size of a kitchen chair.

"There are special things in here for you," said Pops. He marked another X on the calendar and said, "Things for red-circle days. As you can see, the first such day is tomorrow."

Hằng didn't respond, but just stared at him from where she lay.

"What do you think is in the box?" asked Pops.

Hằng continued to stare.

Pops tone turned to anger and he said, "Well, you've got twenty-four hours to think about it!"

Hằng closed her eyes and, a moment later, she heard the creak of the door as Pops left her alone. She immediately got to her feet and got as close to the box as her chain would permit, but she was too far away to see inside it. She went back to her mattress, sat, and stared at the box.

What does it mean? She looked at the calendar again. *Four more weeks and Linh will be here … and I told her to come!*

Hằng cried in anguish. Eventually she caught her breath between sobs and looked at the calendar. *Tomorrow is the first red-circle day. There are more circles later. What do they mean?*

chapter seven

It was eight o'clock at night when Jack and Laura saw the Russians return to one of their favourite restaurants.

Jack lowered his binoculars and said, "Table for two. Doesn't look like they expect any company. Let's knock it off and go home and introduce ourselves to our spouses."

"Looking for a treat, are you?"

Jack chuckled and said, "Something like that."

"Well, I figure we're likely wasting our time out here at the moment."

"Something is going on with these two," said Jack. "Retired schoolteachers don't have that kind of money to throw around. Not to mention they had the clout to meet with the top exec of Satans Wrath."

"I'm not saying we shouldn't work on them. I know the type. Whatever they're involved in is big enough that they aren't standing on the corner dealing ounces. Working on this type ... it's always peaks and valleys."

"And right now we're in a valley," said Jack. "What we really need is an informant. Someone on the inside."

"Who and how?"

"Don't know yet. Tomorrow I'm going to go to a bookstore. Start learning a little Russian and Vietnamese. Will help build a rapport if we do find someone to turn. Besides, it'll give me something to read when we're on surveillance."

It was midnight when Jack glanced out of the ensuite bathroom just as Natasha was getting into bed.

"How good is your Russian?" he asked. "Could you teach me some?"

"With a name like Natasha Trovinski, how good do you think it is?"

"I don't really know. I've heard you talk to your parents."

"*Lazhites' syooda,*" she replied.

"What did you say?"

"Lay down over here."

"That sounds real good to me!"

The next afternoon Jack and Laura watched as the Russians left their apartment and got into a waiting limousine-styled taxi. They followed them to a location on the west end of Vancouver where the Russians had the limo wait as they went into a store. Laura stayed in the car while Jack took a portable police radio and went on foot.

Jack returned a few minutes later just as the Russians were returning to the limo.

Jack grinned at Laura and said, "They popped into a store called West Marine. They were asking for marine charts for around Seattle. The clerk said they didn't carry any for Puget Sound. They only carried charts for places north of the forty-ninth."

"They're looking for a place to bring a boat in," said Laura.

"Definitely. Our friend wouldn't help them with the Vancouver Port so now they're checking other possibilities."

"Seattle!" said Laura. "Are they nuts? With what's going on in the world these days I wouldn't want to get caught smuggling something into that area. The Americans are liable to shoot first without ever asking any questions."

Jack's call to the DEA came up empty. He looked at Laura and said, "They've never heard of them. If something crops up, they said they'd call."

"You two!" said Quaile. "Are they not paying you enough?"

Jack looked up to see Quaile standing in the open doorway. He had his hands on his hips and was staring at the both of them.

"My salary is adequate," replied Jack.

"Then tell me why you've worn the same tie for three days in a row? Not to mention your shirt looks like you've slept in it! Laura, you're not much better. With Jack, somehow I'm not surprised, but with you, I am very disappointed."

Quaile stared briefly at Laura. If he was expecting to see a look of embarrassment he didn't. Her look was that of utter contempt.

"I can only imagine that you are being unduly influenced," he added. "From now on, and until I say otherwise, I want to see the both of you in my office at o-eight-hundred every morning. If you're not suitably attired, or look shoddy in any way, I'll send you home to change. You got that?"

"Come on, Staff," said Jack. "We've been doing a lot of surveillance. Bound to get a few wrinkles. Sorry about the tie. I'll increase my wardrobe, but …"

"But nothing! Looking sharp is critical to success."

"I was going to say," continued Jack, "that the criminals we work on don't work eight to four shifts — let alone wear suits and ties."

"That is another thing! I've seen your reports. You're working on a pair of Russians that have no criminal history and who aren't doing anything."

"They're also connected to a Vietnamese gang," said Jack, "who have a criminal history of …"

"Half of which are children! My God! It's me that has to sign off on the bottom of your reports. I'm embarrassed to be sending them forward."

"Children *are* being used," said Jack, assertively. "All the more reason to nail these guys for turning these kids in the first place."

Quaile stared blankly at him.

"You must admit," continued Jack, "you're relatively new to this section. Give us a chance. We'll get results and then you'll see the bigger picture. You'll understand how the tentacles of organized crime work."

Quaile acted like he didn't hear. "Eight o'clock tomorrow morning!"

"Staff, you're being obtuse," said Jack, louder than he had intended. "Laura and I are working our asses off here. We don't need …"

"Obtuse!" sputtered Quaile, before turning on his heel and retreating back to his office.

"Well, I think that went well, don't you?" said Laura quietly after he left.

"I'm not sure," replied Jack, taking a deep breath. "Perhaps it's that sixth sense I've developed as an operator, but I have a feeling that he wasn't entirely happy with us."

"I sort of detected that, too. Any suggestions? Box of chocolates or something?"

"I was thinking more of throwing a shovel in the trunk and looking for a cemetery."

"Shoot, shovel, and shut up," commented Laura.

Jack sighed and said, "I've seen his type before. All he wants is to climb the corporate ladder. He won't be here long. Try and humour him. With his background in Commercial Crime, it may take a while to educate him."

"I think you're giving him too much credit."

"We'll get results soon. That should open his eyes and give him perspective."

Laura made a fist and said, "I think I'd rather shut his eyes."

Hằng watched fearfully as Pops entered the room. He smiled when he saw her eyes dart from the cardboard box back to him.

"That's right," he said. "This is your first red-circle day — but every red-circle day will be different." Pops lit the propane heater for the first time. Within seconds, Hằng could feel the heat start to engulf the room.

Pops peered in the cardboard box. He glanced at Hằng and smiled. She heard the sound of metal objects as his hand moved around inside the box. He took out five candles and placed them around the room while lighting them.

Hằng stared at him when he flicked off the lights. His eyes glimmered as shadows danced across his face from the glow of the candles and the heater.

Without a word, he disappeared back out into the

passageway, only to return a few seconds later carrying a circular cardboard carton. Hằng did not need to ask what was inside it. The smell of fried chicken permeated every corner of the room and she immediately began to salivate.

Pops handed her the carton. On top were paper napkins and she tossed them aside and tore the lid off, grabbing the chicken with her hands and eating as fast as she could.

Pops sat beside her and wrapped his arm around her shoulder and said, "It is all yours. Eat as much as you like. Take your time, there are fries in there as well."

Hằng continued to eat, but soon found that she was full. Her stomach had shrunk and the food soon gave her cramps.

"Wipe your hands on the napkin."

Hằng did as instructed.

"It is too hot in here now," said Pops as he got up and shut the heater off. "Much too hot," he said, taking off his shirt to expose his bare chest as he strut back across the room.

He smiled down at Hằng while slowly flexing one bicep at a time before sitting down beside her. She felt his hand on the back of her head and tensed as he drew her toward him.

"You will kiss me now," he said. "On my stomach … just below my belly button."

Hằng nodded obediently and put her head down, grabbing a fold of skin around his navel with her hand, before sinking her teeth into it.

Pops roared, punching her on the side of the head and knocking her over as he leapt to his feet.

"You filthy little bitch!" he screamed, kicking her in the stomach. "You do not appreciate my generosity!" he yelled.

Hằng was too frightened to notice the blood dripping from her ear as she curled up in a ball on the mattress before vomiting.

Pops turned on the light and then extinguished the candles before throwing them back in the box. He left the room, only to return with a pair of pliers.

chapter eight

Early one afternoon Jack and Laura followed the Russians as they left their apartment building and walked a few blocks to a pay phone. Moustache Pete gestured to the phone and reached into his pocket and looked at his change. Fat Man did likewise and pointed at a nearby confectionary.

"This could be good," said Jack. "Pay phone call instead of using their cell. They're up to something."

"It's too deserted there to stand nearby and listen," noted Laura. "They'd make us."

"Wait here," said Jack, before darting over to the telephone.

Now what's he up to? Laura spotted the Russians coming back out of the confectionary store, but it was apparent that Jack had already seen them and was moving off farther down the street.

The Russians used the pay phone again before walking back toward their apartment building. Moments later, Jack returned.

"Let's see what we got," he said, holding up his voice-activated tape recorder.

"You just did an illegal wiretap," said Laura. Her comment was said more in surprise than it was to rebuke.

"I would never do that," replied Jack. "I was just going to use the phone and accidentally forgot my recorder when I was there. Glad I remembered it."

"Right, do you think you're talking to Quaile or Internal? Come on, let's see what's on it! Hope they spoke English."

"If they didn't, I'll call Natasha."

English was spoken, but between passing cars and the muffled-sounding voice of Moustache Pete, much of the conversation was missing. Two things were heard. It was evident that a meeting was to take place in Costa Rica within the next two weeks. Moustache Pete also said, "The shipment will be as white as snow."

"Bingo! Coke shipment," said Laura.

"For sure. Let's go back to the office. I've got the pay phone number. Let's find out who he called."

"Glad you're back," said Quaile, motioning them into his office. "Have a seat," he said, sounding friendly.

"We just got something on the Russians," said Jack. "I happened to overhear them at a pay phone. It sounds like they're planning to bring a boatload of coke up through Costa Rica."

"Oh, good," said Quaile. "Pass it on to Drug Section. I've got …"

"We haven't reached that stage yet," said Jack. "We need to …"

"Don't interrupt me," responded Quaile with a noticeable

chill to his voice. "This office is done working on degenerates. We're stepping things up around here. I just got off the phone with Inspector Penn at Commercial Crime. They have a huge stock manipulation case on the go. He said he would be glad to get the extra help."

"Stock manipulation," said Jack. "That should be left up to Commercial Crime. The organized crime we target is ..."

"Considering you work on an Intelligence Unit," said Quaile, "I'm astounded at your lack of knowledge. Perhaps you should review what organized crime is. The Canadian Intelligence Service of Canada says that it is two or more persons consorting together on a continuing basis to participate in illegal activities."

"Yes," replied Jack. "The Criminal Code, which is more suited for the RCMP, defines it as three or more persons. But that is not the point. I am personally familiar with *real* organized crime. It ..."

"Then you will appreciate that your new assignment is within our mandate! I'm sure they appreciate our offer to assist."

"They never even asked for assistance?" said Jack, angrily. "You just decided to call and butt in?"

"These are white collar criminals. Something far more appropriate for our section to be dealing with. Not drugs or the dirty people you seem to prefer." Quaile glowered at Jack and said, "I'm sure you pick on them because of their lower intelligence and it is no doubt easy, but those days are over. If you're not capable of catching the smart crooks then I would suggest that you consider a transfer elsewhere."

"Staff, please. The Russians are big fish. They're planning to go to Costa Rica within the next two weeks. Laura and I should go."

"Absolutely not! As of this moment, you are finished with

them. Pass what you have over to Drug Section."

"We need to do more background work first. Just two more weeks."

"I said no! I'm done for the day. I expect to see you in this office tomorrow morning at o-eight-hundred. Now leave!"

"That son of a bitch!" Laura muttered when they returned to their own office.

Jack glanced at Laura. Swearing for her was most unusual. Her face had gone a blotchy red, which looked all the worse under the red highlights in her chestnut-coloured hair.

"Quaile wants me out of here," said Jack. "I don't know why, but he does. Maybe that's what this is all about."

"Why do you say that?"

"You heard his jab about my abilities and his suggestion I should consider a transfer elsewhere. For some reason, he's got me in his sights."

"Maybe because you'd rather catch bad guys than shine shoes or kiss butt."

"Whatever, but he's the boss. My annual assessment is also overdue. I can just imagine what that will be like."

"What can we do?"

"We need to show him that the Russians are big time. Prove that they're international players. Then maybe he'll see the light of day."

"He said not to work on them anymore."

"I know … and I know it's a lot to ask, but for the next week or two, if we work on them non-stop, we'll prove it. Only come to the office for our morning inspection and then get back out there."

"We can't. He won't let us."

Jack shook his head and said, "There are always guys like

Quaile around. That's usually the biggest challenge in catching bad guys. We just have to get him to give us more time."

"How? He won't listen to us." Laura saw a smile creep across Jack's face. "Don't tell me you have friends in high places, like Ottawa?"

Jack looked at her and shook his head and said, "But I do have friends. I'll see what influence I can dredge up. At this point I have nothing to lose."

"I can't see Quaile ever changing his mind."

"See what happens tomorrow morning," said Jack. "Make sure you're in his office at eight. You won't want to miss it."

chapter nine

Biển's brain didn't want to accept the message that he got from the smuggler in Hanoi. His worst fears were realized. The smuggler's words whirled around in his head like a voice that he couldn't stop.

Hằng died in a car accident when she was crossing the street. Most unfortunate. She is an illegal. They can't get her body. Too many people would be arrested. It would even jeopardize the others when they arrive.

Biển had gasped as he heard the words. The smuggler had continued to speak. *Traffic in America is very fast. You have caused the American family much pain. You should have taught Hằng to be more careful when crossing the street. You are lucky that they are still willing to accept Linh ….*

Now, Biển sat on the floor with his mother. They had plastic chairs inside their room, but Biển's mother always preferred to sit Vietnamese-style on the floor with her legs tucked under.

Biển held the black and white photocopy of Hằng and

Linh standing in front of The One Pillar Pagoda. Minutes later, he put it down on the floor in front of him, afraid that his tears would damage the picture.

Biển knew that his mother had barely survived the war. She had experienced more pain and death in her life than any human should have to endure. He had believed she was incapable of crying anymore, her well of tears run dry. But now, her eyes were wet and she rocked back and forth, her arms folded across her chest and her hands resting on her shoulders.

Biển thought about Linh. He wanted to be the one to tell her, but he knew it wouldn't be possible. She would be devastated. *Mister and Missus Pops … they too must feel the grief … and in three weeks, when Linh arrived, they would have the unpleasant task of telling her that her sister is dead.*

At seven-thirty in the morning Jack and Laura were on their way to work, unaware that at the same moment, Đức was picking up the two Russians in front of their apartment building.

The three men went to a restaurant to discuss business over breakfast.

"We have been checking," said Moustache Pete. "There are many places a ship could come in undetected."

"But it was only a fishing boat going out to sea," said Đức. "My man has his own fishing boat there and his house for the passengers. It is much easier."

"And if the men on the fishing boat that saw the ship unloading have talked, what then? Next time the police could be waiting."

"It is a small town. The fishermen all know each other. My man says he would have heard something if that were true. Next time, if the ship were to come in two hours earlier, there would be nobody around to see."

Moustache Pete and the Fat Man looked at each other and nodded in agreement. "Okay, we do it the same way next time, but if the load is lost, it is you that must pay."

"I understand. It will not be lost."

"The money?" said the Fat Man, gesturing to an attaché case that Đức carried.

Đức nodded and passed it over.

"All there?" asked the Fat Man.

"Yes…. No!" replied Đức.

"What do you mean?" asked Moustache Pete. "Is it, or isn't it?"

"All there except for the young girl. I forgot to pick that up."

"Ah, our insurance policy," said Moustache Pete with a smile as he looked at the Fat Man.

"Insurance policy?" asked Đức.

"Just a joke between the two of us," replied Moustache Pete.

"The money is arranged," said Đức. "He paid all of the deposit the first time, but I gave it back when only one girl came. Please, one moment, I know he works Tuesday to Saturday, but he may not have left for work yet."

Đức used his cellphone and made a quick call. When he hung up he said, "Yes, he is home and will wait, but I must go now."

"That is not a problem," said Moustache Pete. "We will go with you and wait in the car. You can drive us back to our apartment later. Maybe by then the bank will be open and we can stop there first."

Jack stared at Quaile as he made a pretext of looking at them as he sat behind his desk.

"Yes. You look much more appropriate," said Quaile, avoiding Jack's stare. "That is how you should be attired on all occasions. Now, I'm going to call Inspector Penn and tell him that the both of you are now available to …." Quaile paused to answer his telephone.

"May I speak with the NCO in charge, please?" asked a feminine voice.

"You are. This is Staff Sergeant Quaile."

"Stand by, one moment please. I'm going to connect you with Deputy Commissioner Simonson."

"Deputy Commissioner Simonson!" said Quaile aloud.

It was a name Quaile knew well. Deputy Commissioner Simonson worked in Ottawa and was only one rung below the actual Commissioner himself. Someone so far up the chain of command that for him to call someone in Quaile's position was virtually unheard of.

Quaile glanced at the call display and recognized the Ottawa prefix and put his hand over the receiver and looked at Jack and Laura and whispered, "Get out."

"Sorry," said Jack. "I couldn't hear that."

"I have an important call. Get out!"

Jack and Laura obediently returned to their own office.

Back in their own office, Laura looked at Jack and said, "I was afraid to even look at you in there in case I couldn't keep a straight face. Deputy Commissioner Simonson?"

Jack smiled and said, "Quaile would never have the nerve to call him, let alone question what he wants."

"Good one. Who are you using?"

"Remember Bob from Edmonton?"

"Thought he was retired now? Working for the Insurance Corporation of B.C."

"He is, but still has all the contacts. Including someone to provide him with a call forwarding number out of Ottawa."

"If this doesn't work, Quaile will have you transferred."

"I have the feeling that I've nothing to lose."

Quaile drummed his fingers on the desk for thirty seconds, but sat upright when a gruff voice asked, "Staff Sergeant Quaalude?"

"Ah, it's pronounced, Quaile, sir."

"Sorry to keep you waiting. Things are hectic here this morning. What's the weather like out there in Vancouver?"

"Windy and raining right now, sir. Kind of miserable."

"That's good. Listen, I'm calling about the reports you submitted. The Commissioner is personally interested in this."

"The Commissioner! What reports sir?"

"On those two Russians your section is working on. I don't have their names. You must know who I mean?"

"I do sir."

"Their names surfaced in an international investigation we're involved with here. It's a high priority case involving very bad apples. We've discovered that there is corruption at the highest level. Indications are that it is even amongst our own ranks."

"Corruption amongst our own ranks, sir?"

"Yes, Quaalude, I just said that. Now, whatever you get on these guys, I don't want you to dilly-dally with the reports. Send them in pronto! I don't know how you got on to them, but I can tell you, the Commissioner is pleased. There are other countries involved and it's about time we had something to make us look good."

"Yes, sir! My instincts told me these guys were bad from the get-go. Should I have my investigators contact someone?"

"No. Don't talk about this to anyone or have anyone make any calls at this time. Weren't you listening when I said there is a serious indication of corruption?"

"Yes, sir. Of course."

"Simply proceed like normal. We will contact you if the need arises. Just keep those reports coming."

"Would you like me to direct the reports to your personal attention?"

"Jesus … of course not, Quaalude! I have better things to do than distribute reports around the building. My God, what do you think I do here? Send them through ordinary channels as always. You got that?"

"Yes, sir!"

Moments later, Jack and Laura were summoned back to Quaile's office.

"Listen, I've had overnight to rethink what you said yesterday and have reconsidered this whole Russian matter. I'm going to allow you to continue working on them, but I expect results — don't let me down!"

"Staff … are you sure?" asked Jack, ignoring the roll of Laura's eyes. "What about Commercial Crime?"

"That can wait for now. You told me these Russians are worth taking a look at. You better not fail. This is your one and only chance to prove it."

"Will do," said Jack as he and Laura turned to leave.

"Not so fast," said Quaile.

"Staff?" asked Jack.

"I see our overtime budget is healthy at the moment, so don't hesitate to work a few extra hours if necessary."

Upon returning to their office, Laura looked at Jack and said, "Bob was a good operator."

"One of the best. He still is."

Đức parked his car down the street from Pops's house and got out while Moustache Pete and the Fat Man waited. They watched as Đức hustled down the street before disappearing up the inclination of a driveway that led around to the back of the house.

"It is good," said the Fat Man. "This degenerate. He pays us for our insurance."

"Soon the other child will be here," said Moustache Pete. "It will be double indemnity."

Both men chortled.

Jack and Laura were parked near the entrance to the Russians' apartment building and Laura used the steering wheel to steady the binoculars as she looked at a car that just arrived. "Oh, man," she said, passing the binoculars to Jack.

Jack adjusted the binoculars and yelled, "Damn it! That's Đức dropping them off! Damn it, damn it, damn it!"

"Only ten in the morning," commented Laura. "Wonder what they were up to? Maybe just meeting for breakfast."

"Maybe. Would have been nice to know for sure instead of seeing if my tie matched my shirt. Đức isn't usually an early riser. Something was up."

"Stay with the Russians or go with Đức?" asked Laura.

"Let's sit on the Russians. They're our main targets."

It was late in the afternoon when Quaile called Jack and told him to return to the office.

Jack returned and walked into Quaile's office alone.

"Close the door," said Quaile, "and have a seat."

Jack did as instructed.

"What have you learned about the Russians today?"

"This morning they were dropped off at about ten by Đức. Laura and I sat on them all day but they haven't moved."

"You just sat out there wasting an entire shift?"

"These guys haven't been supplying me with their itinerary. They're not a couple of boys who work in offices. It takes time."

"You've had plenty of time. I would have expected a competent investigator to have come up with something more substantial by now."

"Is this what you called us in for? Perhaps if we were still out there, we would have something more substantial," said Jack, crossly.

"Your annual assessment couldn't wait any longer," replied Quaile, "otherwise it would be overdue. I am a firm believer in punctuality." He gestured to the forms in front of him and said, "A few questions. Do you speak French?"

"No," sighed Jack, while checking his watch. "I have passable Spanish and am learning some Russian and Vietnamese, however."

"That's ridiculous!" said Quaile, looking dumbstruck. "Canada is bilingual … French and English. Stop learning those and take French."

"I don't believe the Russians I'm working on know French," replied Jack innocently.

Quaile glared at Jack and said, "How far did you ever expect to get in the RCMP?"

"To the rank of corporal," Jack replied bitterly.

"I didn't ask you what your rank is now! I asked you how far you ever expected to get!"

"I heard you. As I said, to the rank of corporal."

Quaile continued to glare at Jack for several seconds without speaking, before saying, "I don't believe we have anything further to say to each other."

"Neither do I," replied Jack, before returning to his office.

Hằng lay curled on her mattress, her tongue exploring the holes in her gums from her missing front teeth. She knew that soon her father would be expecting her to call. *When I don't, questions will be asked. People will look for me …*

Her thoughts were interrupted by the familiar creak of the passage door. She did not feel the fear she once did. She was still another day away from a red circle on the calendar … and knew Pops would wait until then to do something to her.

Today she expected Pops to smile and mark another X on the calendar, which he did, but he also had a message.

"Your dad thinks you are dead. Killed in a car accident."

Hằng's emotions played havoc with her brain. *Father will be crying because of me!* Then she came to a horrible conclusion — the real reason Pops was smiling. *Nobody will miss me! Nobody will come looking!*

"That's right," said Pops. "Everyone thinks you're dead. Nobody will ever look for you now."

Hằng turned her face into the sponge mattress and wept.

"Do not cry," said Pops. "Soon you will have your sister to love. And I do mean *love!*" Pops snickered as he left.

Eventually Hằng stopped crying and found herself staring at the calendar. She looked past the red circles to something more horrific. *Linh's arrival! It will be soon … and it is up to me to do … whatever … to save her.*

She stared around the room. She knew it well, right down to the number of brass screws in the ceiling. Now, her attention focused on the toilet tank … and a plan began to formulate.

chapter ten

It was eleven o'clock at night when Jack and Laura saw the lights flick off in the penthouse suite. Jack was glad the Russians decided to have an early night. He was tired ... and depressed. He was home an hour later and was glad to see that Natasha was still awake as she lay in bed reading a book. Twenty minutes later, he got in bed beside her as she put the book down.

"You close to catching these Russians?"

"Not that. Quaile did my annual assessment today. It went badly."

Jack sighed and told Natasha about his differences with Quaile.

"In the morning he wants me to bust my ass and find out what the Russians are all about. In the afternoon he does this to me. The guy doesn't have a clue about management."

"You told me before that you didn't think he would last long. You expected him to be transferred soon."

"Now I think I'll be transferred first, if my assessment is any indication."

"To where?"

Jack shrugged and said bitterly, "I suspect I'll be going back to harness, but who knows where. I guess the good news is I'd be working regular shifts. More time to spend with you," he added, forcing a smile.

Natasha gently pulled Jack closer so that their naked bodies could entwine as one, with their heads sharing the same pillow. "As much as I would like to spend more time with you — twenty-four-seven, actually — I know that is not feasible. And going back to uniform? You wouldn't be happy."

"I may not exactly get a choice in this matter," replied Jack.

Natasha lifted the covers and looked at Jack's body.

"What are you doing?" he asked.

"Looking for the man I married," she replied, dropping the sheets. "That guy wouldn't have given up so easily. That guy always found a way to solve a problem."

Jack took a deep breath and slowly exhaled. "Believe me, I've been trying. Laura and I have been putting everything we have into catching these two Russians. I thought that if we did, it might give Quaile reason to reflect. Perhaps adjust his thinking. Now, thinking about how he screwed me on my assessment, I'm not sure that would even work."

"You're tired, stressed, and depressed."

"Tell me about it."

"If you actually took some time off to relax, maybe enjoy life, it would clear your head. Give your brain a chance to re-energize."

"I know," sighed Jack. "What you say is right, but it's a Catch-22. If I take time off, then I might miss something with the Russians … then I'd really be screwed."

"It would still be good to give yourself a small break from it."

"I can't. Maybe in a couple of weeks ..."

"You have to lower your stress level. It's not healthy. Mentally or physically."

"And how the hell do I do that? Quaile's riding my —"

"Shut up about Quaile!" said Natasha angrily. "Complaining about him won't help."

"Then what do you suggest?" snapped Jack in exasperation. "I'm trying damn hard to go by the rules and look what it's gotten me! If I had screwed up or got caught doing something I shouldn't, then fine. I deserve it. But this is bullshit. I know life isn't fair, but it's eating me up inside."

The two of them silently stared up at the ceiling.

Eventually Jack rolled over to face Natasha. "I'm sorry," he said. "That just didn't come out right. I really love you. I think you're an amazing person and sometimes wonder how you put up with me ... and what I do. I just have so many things on my mind. Now is not the time to take a holiday. I wouldn't be able to relax anyway."

Natasha sighed and said, "Yeah, I know. I sometimes wonder myself how I put up with you. Laura once said that I was a brave woman to be married to you."

Jack felt relieved that Natasha wasn't angry. "Laura told you that? That wench! Don't believe anything she says."

Natasha smiled and said, "Of course she was joking, but in a way, it made me think."

"Think of what?"

"Of how much I love you — to put up with all the crap you do put me through."

Jack reflected on his relationship with Natasha since they had met and admitted, "There has been a lot of stress — I'm sorry."

"It's okay," sighed Natasha. "It's not entirely your fault. I brought home my own bag of stress."

"Oh?" said Jack. "Want to talk about it?"

Natasha swallowed and said, "Today I had a patient. A young mom with cancer. She's pregnant with her third and refuses chemo … the only thing that might save her at this point."

"That's awful."

"It makes you think. I can put up with just about anything as long as we're together," she added, bringing her face close to his.

Jack felt her warm mouth linger on his lips. When she pulled away, he said, "I guess we really should remember to put things in perspective. You look around at our apartment, all the things we have … but the really important things in life aren't things."

"Despite what goes on at work," said Natasha, "we have each other. Enjoy life. Every precious minute. Speaking of which, I do have an idea that might help you."

"Right now? You said I needed a break from work."

"Something to make your work more fun."

"I'm listening."

"Would you still like to learn a few more words of Russian? We could start with the parts of the body," said Natasha, with a grin. "Correct pronunciation and memory could be enhanced through a tactile approach."

Jack smiled and said, "Now I know what you mean by making my work fun."

Laura checked her watch. It was 1:45 in the afternoon and for the last five hours she had been sitting in a car with Jack. They were parked where they could observe the front entrance to the Russians' apartment.

She glanced at Jack. Yesterday he had told her about the meeting he'd had with Quaile over his assessment. She had a sleepless night because of it. *I know life isn't fair ... but why do some people go out of their way to make it unfair?*

She cleared her throat and said, "If you end up being transferred because of Quaile, then I'm putting in for a transfer, too."

Jack looked at her and said, "Thanks ... I appreciate what you're saying, but in the long run, that just means the bad guys win. You're a real asset to the section. I'd really hate to see what it would be like if Quaile brought in his own minions."

Laura sighed and said, "Oh, man ... I hadn't thought about that. I know you're right, but I still couldn't work for a man like that. It's barely tolerable with you as a buffer. I'd flip out if I had to deal with him directly."

"I guess you have to do what makes *you* happy ... but don't quit just because of me. Besides, maybe a break for me would be okay."

"Don't try and placate me," replied Laura. "I know you better than that. This is your life."

"Yours, too," replied Jack. "Which is why I don't want you to throw it away on my account."

"I wouldn't be throwing it away. I'd probably be saving myself from being arrested for homicide."

Jack chuckled, turned up the radio and said, "Oh, one of my favourites." He started drumming his fingers on the steering wheel while singing along to Billy Joel's "You May Be Right."

"I thought you liked classical?" asked Laura, more to save her ears than find out the answer.

"All depends on the mood I'm in," replied Jack. "I basically like it all. Classical, country, rock ... anything but heavy metal or opera. One of my favourites is Dr. Hook."

Laura saw him pause to pick up with the words on the radio and quickly said, "You're awfully perky today — considering how you felt yesterday after seeing Quaile."

Jack smiled and leaned back in his seat and said, "I get the point. Sorry. I think one of the most dangerous things I ever did was to try and sing karaoke in a bar one night. You're right, though, nothing like a few hours of sleep to put life back in perspective."

"Somehow I get the feeling that you did more than sleep."

Jack gave Laura a sideways glance and said, "God help Elvis if he ever fooled around on you."

"He'd only do it once."

"Hey, that reminds me. Natasha said you told her she was a brave woman to marry me."

Laura snickered, but didn't reply.

"I told her you were a wench. Not to believe anything you say."

"A wench! Is that what you called me?" said Laura, giving Jack a playful punch on the arm.

"Out of the car," said Jack, seriously.

"I was kidding!"

"No. Our targets. Moustache Pete and the Fat Man.... They're taking a walk."

Laura quickly got out of the car and hustled down the street. She caught up to the Russians and kept pace with them from the opposite side of the street. She used a portable radio to keep in touch with Jack, who would reposition the car as they went.

"They just went inside a business," radioed Laura. "Travel King. Stand by — I'll do a walk past." Moments later, Laura radioed again, "They're just sitting down with a woman. Looks like they're planning on taking a trip."

Laura rejoined Jack in the car and they waited. Twenty

minutes later, the Russians appeared and walked back toward their apartment.

"Do you think they knew the woman?" asked Jack.

"No, I saw them shaking hands, like an introduction."

"Good. Let's chance it and go talk to her."

Jack and Laura introduced themselves to the travel agent and expressed their interest in the two Russians. Elaine introduced herself and said, "I'm not really supposed to do this … but they're flying out of Vancouver a week today. Their destination flight is the city of Liberia located in the northern part of Costa Rica."

Matches the call on the pay phone, thought Jack. He glanced at Laura and saw her nod.

"From there," said Elaine, "they're taking about a forty-five minute taxi ride to the coast. A small town called Playas del Coco — or as us gringos call it, Coco Beach."

"I know that place," said Jack. "I passed through there on my honeymoon."

"You should have booked it through me," said Elaine, with a smile. "Anyway, I offered to get these two guys a rental car but they weren't interested. They did ask that I book them each a room at Hotel Coco Verde, which I did. It's walking distance to the beach and has a pool and a casino."

"They asked for that specific hotel?" asked Jack.

"Yes. Actually I told them that the place has a reputation for a lot of prostitution. Men go there on conferences and sometimes book a prostitute to be with them for the whole time they're there. These two didn't care. They said they were meeting a friend who was going there and had already recommended it."

"No indication of who their friend was?" asked Jack.

"They didn't say, but when I was booking their flight, one of them told me that the date was good because it was two days before the guy arrived that they were supposed to meet. That's all I know. They are there for a week and then are scheduled to return."

Jack gave Elaine his business card and she promised to call him if there were any changes.

On their way back to their office, Laura said, "Our Russians have to be planning on bringing in cocaine. They've been checking the ports, wanting navigational maps — they must have a boat they're using."

"I sort of agree," replied Jack. "Costa Rica is like the skinny end of the funnel for coke coming up from South America. As I recall, someone told me that Coco Beach is the first port of entry for boats coming into the country from the north."

"Did you and Natasha stay at the Hotel Coco Verde?"

Jack laughed and said, "No. A small place called Villa del Sol. Actually it's owned by a couple of French-Canadians. Nice people."

"You said you *sort of* agree. Not completely?"

"If it was cocaine importation, why didn't the bikers cut themselves in on the action … or permanently cut the Russians out? That part still doesn't make sense to me. Maybe it is cocaine importation, but there has to be something else. Something that scared our friend in Satans Wrath — and he doesn't scare easily."

"We've got to go down there," replied Laura. "What chance do you think we'll have with Quaile authorizing that?"

"Last week I would have said none," replied Jack, "but after the number Bob did on him, I bet there won't be a problem," he added with a wink.

Jack's meeting with Quaile was brief.

"I'll okay it for you and Laura to go," said Quaile, "but for the chunk you're taking out of our budget, I can tell you right now … you'd better get results!"

Hằng anxiously waited when Pops carried in a couple of Styrofoam containers of hot Chinese food, along with napkins and plastic utensils.

"Red-circle day," he said, setting the items down out of her reach while he turned on the propane heater. The smell of the food permeated every corner of the room.

Pops used his foot to slide the food over to Hằng.

Hằng ate the food rapidly while Pops sat on the floor, smiling at her. When she was finished, he stood and marked another X on the calendar.

"Two days to your next red circle," he said, before shutting heater off and taking the food containers away as he left.

Hằng stared at the calendar. *This red-circle day was okay. What will I get on the next red-circle day?*

For Hằng, it was better that she did not know.

chapter eleven

"Assistant Commissioner Isaac will see you now, Staff."

Quaile nodded curtly to the secretary and strode into Isaac's office. He saw Isaac gesture to a chair and sat down.

"Good morning," said Isaac. "Update me on this file involving travel to Costa Rica."

"Yes, sir. Corporal Taggart and Constable Secord left yesterday. Liaisons were arranged and the Costa Rican police are accommodating. The two Russians are flying out at five o'clock this afternoon. Corporal Taggart and Constable Secord will assist with coordinating the surveillance with the police down south when the Russians land."

"No indication of who the Russians are meeting?" asked Isaac.

"No, sir. Not at this time."

"What about the Vietnamese? These Trần brothers.... Any indication they are going?"

"No, sir."

"At least on this venture, it does not appear that Corporal Taggart has any personal issues — or potential vendettas," mused Isaac.

"Last week I did his performance evaluation," said Quaile. "I must say, it was the poorest assessment I have ever been forced to give anyone." Quaile saw the raised eyebrow that Isaac cast in his direction. *Was I wrong to ... if he doubts my judgement!*

"I told you to keep an eye on him," said Isaac, "but I expect you to treat him fairly."

"It was fair, sir" said Quaile hurriedly. "The man is a low-life. Shows up to work in the morning with bags under his eyes. Unkempt appearance. Obviously likes to party all night. He lacks initiative to learn new things or apply himself to assignments that I have tried to give him."

Isaac did not reply.

"Are you questioning my judgement?" asked Quaile, nervously.

Isaac stared at him for a moment before answering, "No, I am simply ensuring that he is being treated fairly."

"Well, I certainly stand by my assessment of him. If it wasn't for this investigation on the Russians, I would recommend his immediate transfer but with Deputy Commissioner Simonson calling me and the Commissioner's personal interest, I decided to wait until the investigation is over."

"Paul called you from Ottawa?" asked Isaac in surprise.

"Yes, sir," replied Quaile, feeling somewhat self-important. "It is highly confidential. These two Russians are connected to a major international investigation. Involves corruption. I wasn't supposed to tell anyone. It just sort of slipped — well, besides, I know ... I mean, obviously it is appropriate for you to know ..."

Quaile quit talking when Isaac held up his hand for him

to stop. He waited and listened quietly as Isaac dialled. From snippets of conversation, Quaile realized he had been duped and his ears turned crimson.

When Isaac hung up, he turned to Quaile and said, "Your alleged call from Ottawa was bogus."

"Yes, sir," replied Quaile. "I gathered that from what I heard."

"And you didn't suspect anything?"

"Taggart was in the office when I received the call," stammered Quaile. "How could I? I even remember seeing the area code. It was Ottawa —"

"Likely had a friend do it."

"Sir, this is terribly embarrassing. For a member to pull a stunt like this, well —"

"I warned you to keep an eye on him," said Isaac. "There is something, however, that we need to consider."

"Sir?"

"It would appear that young Jack Taggart is risking his career on the fact that the Russians are worth it. It will be interesting to see the results. Keep quiet about this for now. Give it a week or two and see how all this pans out. We'll deal with the phone call later, although I doubt we could ever prove that he was behind it."

"Yes, sir. Like I said, if you had any doubts about my judgement in regards to his assessment, this incident just goes to highlight the fact that —"

"You can go now, Staff."

Moustache Pete and the Fat Man were both jovial as they checked their baggage at the Delta Airlines counter in the Vancouver International Airport. Their demeanour and self-confidence changed completely just as they were entering the security check-in.

"Hey, comrades!"

Both men turned in surprise and were partially blinded by the flash of a camera. Both were too startled to say anything as the man with the camera turned and hurried away.

The following day, Jack and Laura watched through the tinted windows of a van parked on the main street in Coco Beach. With them was a plainclothes member of the *Fuerza Pública*. This was the name of the Costa Rican police force and the policeman assigned to work with them, Eduardo, spoke English.

"Your two men," said Eduardo, "They are very nervous."

It was a point that Jack and Laura had already observed. The Russians had constantly been looking around them ever since they got off the plane. After checking in to the Hotel Coco Verde, they changed into shorts and singlets went across the street and had lunch at a Cajun-style restaurant, where they sat talking in hushed voices.

The Russians were watched as they finished lunch and took the five-minute stroll down the main street that led directly to the beach. Most tourists stared at the array of gift shops and local crafts, but the Russians seemed more interested in looking at people's faces.

When they arrived at the beach, they turned right and trudged through the cocoa-coloured sand.

Jack and Laura discreetly followed behind, using an abundance of coconut trees farther back from the beach as cover while Eduardo leap-frogged ahead on a road running parallel to the beach that was obscured by buildings and vegetation.

The Russians arrived at the end of the beach and climbed up and stood on some large rock formations jutting out into the ocean. They paused to look back down the beach and Jack was relieved that there was nobody in sight to make them more paranoid.

"These guys are really heated up," said Jack, passing the binoculars to Eduardo, who had now abandoned the van.

"Yes, it is hot," said Eduardo. "Canada. *Mucho frio.*"

"Yes, very cold in Canada," said Jack.

"I think they are fight with each other," said Eduardo, peering through the binoculars.

Jack looked and could see the Fat Man shaking his head and looking at Moustache Pete, who was waving his arms and gesturing in all directions. The Fat Man handed a cellphone to Moustache Pete who took it and flung it far into the ocean.

"Shit! We're burned," said Jack.

"Yes, sun very hot," said Eduardo.

Following their stroll down the beach, the Russians used an Internet facility before returning to their hotel, where they spent the rest of the day drinking and lounging about the hotel pool.

Eduardo attempted to track the Russians' Internet activity on the computer, but told Jack and Laura that it had all been deleted and therefore was unable to retrieve anything.

The next two days passed and, with the exception of another visit to the Internet facility, the Russians did little of interest. They did appear to be more relaxed and now drank copious amounts of Imperial beer while sampling the services of several different prostitutes.

At no time did they appear to meet with anyone of interest — a fact Jack was all too conscious of as he continued to delay calling Quaile to debrief him. Eventually he knew he could delay no longer. He left Laura with Eduardo and went to his room. He found that the phone lines were not working, but after a twenty-minute delay and some apologies from the hotel switchboard, he was able to connect.

"So they're just down there on a holiday!" exclaimed Quaile.

"Something has made them paranoid," said Jack.

"So you're telling me you screwed up the surveillance?"

"The Costa Rican police have been good. Professional enough not to have burned us. Something else must …"

"So you're saying they're just partying and acting like tourists. Obviously then, they weren't up to anything in the first place."

"At the moment they're not, but …." A knock on Jack's door interrupted him and he said, "Hang on, someone's at my door."

Laura was quick with the news. "When you left they went up the street to a place called De La Costa Travel Agency. Eduardo just found out they booked a flight to Cuba. They leave tomorrow and fly to Havana. The agent tried to book them a hotel, but they said they would find one when they arrived. They're booked to come back to Costa Rica, arriving in San Jose five days later and will then head back to Canada."

Jack relayed the news to Quaile as Secord stood next to him, listening.

"Where do you plan on going on holidays next? Spain? Forget it. You and Secord be on the next plane available back to Vancouver. You're finished with this scam!"

Jack didn't reply, his mind racing to find a solution. He knew Quaile wouldn't allow him to pursue the investigation any further. *Phone the Cuban police? They would probably think it was a hoax. Or at the very least, contact Ottawa — and eventually Quaile. Nope, this has to be personal.*

"Did you hear me, Taggart?"

"Staff, I'm feeling really burnt-out. I've got a lot of annual leave to use before year's end. I'd like to take a week off and stay here. I'll pay for it myself. Okay with you?"

A week off, thought Quaile, remembering the short time frame that Isaac mentioned as a deadline to get results. "Go ahead. It's your money. You won't exactly be missed around here."

Laura grabbed the phone from Jack's hand and said, "The same goes for me. I'll be back in the office when Jack is."

"Suit yourself, but realize I'll be checking every penny of your expenses when you get back. As of right now, you're on your own money."

As soon as Laura hung up, Jack said, "Thanks, but no! It's my neck on the chopping block, there's no need to put yours there as well."

"Forget that!" said Laura. "We're partners. It seems to me I've had to remind you that before. Quit trying to cut me out of things. This affects me, too. If we don't get results and go home empty-handed you'll end up being transferred. That will leave me to go begging to Staffing to be transferred as well. Who knows where I'll end up."

"But this could be expensive. I don't …"

"From here, it won't be that expensive."

Jack felt the knot in his stomach. "Thanks, Laura. I really mean that, friends like you are hard to come by, but …"

"*Good* friends are hard to come by. Wouldn't you do the same for me?"

Jack sighed. "You know I would."

"Enough said. I'm going and if you want to join me, you're welcome."

"If I want to join you!"

"Separate rooms, of course."

Jack smiled as he envisioned trying to wrestle Laura off the plane. He looked at her and said, "If we're caught, it could end both our careers."

Laura laughed and said, "Compared to other things we've done? Come on, this sounds like a cakewalk. We're not Americans, so it's not illegal for us to go there. What we do on our time off is our own business."

"We won't be able to do it without help from the Cuban police. We'll need them, otherwise we're liable to lose them as soon as they leave the airport."

"Yeah, so we tell the locals and ask for their help."

Jack put his hand on Laura's shoulder and said, "Think about it. Cuba is a communist country. Going there and contacting them without first getting permission from Ottawa *would* end our careers. If we did that in the States, we might get away with a slap on the wrist, but Cuba is different."

"Guess we'd better not get caught. I've never been to Cuba before. I'd like to see it."

Jack smiled and lowered his hand. "I haven't been there either. I heard the Cubans are really friendly. We'd better hustle. Cash only."

Laura nodded in agreement. "No paper trail."

On the last red-circle day, Hằng had been tortured from items out of the cardboard box. Now, a day later, she held her hand over one eye, hoping to ease the pain as she squinted at the calendar.

Today was marked with another red circle. She had the dates memorized, but kept hoping she had somehow made a mistake. That the circles would magically be gone. They weren't.

Will he hurt me — or bring me a warm meal?

After today, it was five days away until the next date that was circled. *Is he giving my body time to heal?*

Pops had made that circle extra thick as he had gone

round and round with the red felt marker several times on the calendar while grinning at her.

She wondered at the significance of this particular circle — and then she knew.

That is when Linh arrives!

She slowly and painfully eased herself off the foam mattress and took the top off the toilet tank and stared inside for a long time, trying to build her courage. *It is the only possible way to get a message out. I must!*

A creak of the passage door opening told Hằng she would have to wait. She quickly replaced the lid and stood, shaking uncontrollably as she stared at the cardboard box.

chapter twelve

Quaile's briefing with Isaac was short.

"It appears that the Russians aren't up to anything. They're just down there partying and laying around by the pool. I told Taggart to return, but now he's begging for time off. He's stressed and can't handle the pressure."

"Stressed?" asked Isaac, suspiciously. "With the situations he has been in, most members would have flipped out — but he's always remained cool. Are you sure?"

"He told me so. I bet it's over the bogus call he arranged. Probably thought about it later and realized I wasn't the sort to be fooled for long. It confirms my assessment of him."

"Corporal Taggart has always been right in the past. I question how he does things, but it is not like him to go running off on a wild goose chase. Are you sure the Russians aren't up to something?"

"Certainly doesn't appear so. Taggart and Secord both have annual leave coming and asked to take a few extra days off while they're there. Knowing how deceitful he can be … and after he complained of being burnt-out, I decided it was prudent to okay his little holiday. Otherwise I could see him coming back and putting in for six months' stress leave or something."

Isaac sat quietly for a moment, one hand unconsciously rubbing the top of the Bible on his desk while his mind ruminated over what he knew about Jack. *Or what I think I know …*

"Sir?" interjected Quaile. "Perhaps now would be an opportune time to have Staffing find him a uniform position somewhere. If your past suspicions about him are valid and — I mean, I'm sure they are valid, it would place him in a position where he could be more easily monitored."

Isaac nodded, as if in agreement, but said, "Sometimes good investigations still go astray, not that I'm condoning his trip to Costa Rica. Also, we'll never prove he was responsible for your bogus call from Ottawa. Saying he's stressed … time off … what else is he up to?"

"Sir, I don't think he is up to anything other than going down there and wasting tax dollars."

"Give it another couple of weeks to see if anything comes of this investigation. See what happens when the Russians return. We might discover that Corporal Taggart is doing something more serious than making bogus phone calls."

"Such as?" asked Quaile.

"I don't know, but with him, it usually makes headlines. Keep an eye on him."

"And if two weeks pass and the investigation falls flat?" asked Quaile.

"Then he's back in uniform."

Quaile smiled. *Now I know I did the right thing by allowing him to take a week off …*

Jack and Laura waited at the assigned gate in the San Jose
Airport to board their flight to Havana. The area was packed
with passengers, which Jack was glad to see. The only flight
they could get was the same one the Russians were on, and it
was now three hours late.

Eduardo had seen to it that the Russians would be seated
at the back of the plane, where they would board first and get
off last. He also gave Jack a note written in Spanish to pass on
to the captain flying the plane. The note expressed the need
for discretion and also the urgent need for Jack to talk to the
Cuban police about the two Russian passengers who were the
criminals that Jack and Laura were following.

"It will not be a *problema*," Eduardo assured them. "Every
plane from Cuba has its own security officers to make sure
nobody, like members of the crew, escapes from Cuba. They
make sure only the correct passengers get off. You will have
no problems contacting the police."

Jack began to feel uneasy. *Will Laura and I ever leave
Cuba after this?*

"Fat Man is going to the washroom again," whispered
Laura.

Both Jack and Laura held newspapers up to their faces as
Fat Man sauntered past.

"With the amount of rum he had for lunch, I doubt he
can see past his feet," Jack said.

Eventually the boarding call was made and Jack and
Laura found themselves sitting in a crowded and cramped
Russian-built Yak-42 that smelled of aviation fuel.

Jack waited until they were twenty minutes into the
five-hour flight before he handed the note to a stewardess.
She smiled sweetly and said she would give it to the captain.
Moments later, Jack and Laura saw two husky-looking
men dressed in suits come up to them. One bent over and

whispered, "*Policia?* Canada?"

Jack nodded and both he and Laura showed their police identification. The one man handed both pieces of identification to his colleague.

"Passports," the man whispered again.

Jack and Laura handed him their passports. Both men headed for the cockpit with all the documents. Neither were seen again until the plane landed in Havana.

As soon as Jack and Laura stepped from the plane, they were met by eight men, none of whom appeared to speak any English. Jack's limited knowledge of Spanish also seemed to fall on deaf ears.

They were quickly escorted past the crowds and up to the head of one of several long lineups leading to the immigration arrival counters, where they waited momentarily as the customs officer examined the passport of a man in front of them.

Jack saw her examine the passport carefully and, after a couple of routine questions, she stamped a separate piece of paper that was placed inside the passport. This document would be removed from the passport when the person left Cuba. This was standard treatment for any tourist and was meant to protect American visitors from being identified in their own country as having broken the American law by travelling to Cuba.

Jack and Laura stepped forward. Their escorts maintained control of their documents. This time there were no questions and the customs officer quickly completed the documentation process. Jack and Laura were separated and each put into small rooms located behind the immigration counters.

Jack studied the room. *Similar to our own interrogation rooms. Two chairs ... a table against a wall.* The minutes ticked by ... then an hour. *What the hell is happening? The Russians are probably out of here by now — or are they being detained, too?*

Jack opened the door, only to be met by an armed security guard who pointed for him to stay in the room.

"*El banõ,*" pleaded Jack, trying to sound convincing.

"*El banõ?*"

"*Si, por favor. Urgente!*"

Moments later, four men escorted Jack toward a washroom. Three of the guards were the same as the ones earlier, but one was different. Jack could tell by the way the other men acted that he was in command.

On the way, Jack caught a quick glimpse of the Russians. They were standing together, three back in line. Once in the washroom, Jack turned to the new guard and said, "They're about to leave." He gestured toward the bathroom door and said, "*Dos banditos! Vamos! Comprender?*"

The man smiled at him and nodded and pointed to the toilet said, "*Si, el banõ.*"

Minutes later, Jack was walked back toward the interrogation room. He saw the Russians being waved up to the customs counter and stopped and pretended to tie his shoe so that he could observe.

In the few seconds he delayed, the Russians had their papers stamped and disappeared toward where the taxis were parked. *Great. I'm held and they're set free.*

Jack was returned to the interrogation room, but a moment later, the same man he had spoken to in the washroom came in.

"My name is Donato Castillo," he said in perfect English.

"Damn it, you do speak English!"

"I am with the Seguridad de Estado."

"Security of the State. Great. What is …?"

"You speak Spanish?"

"*Poquito* … a little. Your English is much better."

"Then I will tell you in English. You are in a lot of

trouble, Mister Jack Taggart. So is the lady in the other room. Unfortunately for you, someone has talked. We know why you are really here. In a few minutes, you will both be transferred to jail."

Jack remained silent and Donato looked at him with contempt before leaving. Moments later, Laura was brought into the room and they were left alone.

"What's up?" she asked, sitting in a chair to face Jack.

"Did anyone talk to you?" asked Jack.

"Not a word. I'm worried that the Russians might be out of here by now."

"They are. I saw them leave a few minutes ago when I went to the bathroom."

"Then what is going on? Have you been talking with anyone?"

"A man by the name of Donato Castillo just told me that someone had talked and that they knew why we were really here. He said we would be transferred to a jail cell shortly."

"Oh … I see," replied Laura. "They have had plenty of time to go through our luggage and read our files on these guys."

"Exactly."

"So … what now?" asked Laura.

"I guess we could both exclaim that we don't know what Donato is talking about when he said someone talked. We could say that it doesn't make sense because we are being truthful."

"Is that the way you want to play it?" asked Laura.

"Naw. I feel that would be just plain deceitful. If we're going to work together with the Cuban police, we're going to have to learn to *respect* and trust each other."

"Was this Donato taller than the husky types who escorted us off the plane?" asked Laura. "Dark wavy hair, nice teeth?"

"That's him. You said you didn't talk to anyone."

"I didn't. He just stuck his head in the room for a moment

to look at me, then left." Laura winked at Jack and said, "He certainly is a *handsome* man. I bet he catches the eye of a lot of pretty ladies."

"I'm sure. I'd have volunteered to take a polygraph, but he didn't give me the opportunity. Still, I bet he figures out the truth really fast."

"Oh, so you think he's intelligent, too?"

"Guess we'll find out with how long he keeps us waiting. My guess is ..."

"Okay, okay! Enough!" said Donato, as he entered the room. He sat on the edge of the table, looking down at Jack and Laura, and asked, "Was I that obvious?"

Jack shook his head and replied, "No, but both Laura and I work on an Intelligence Unit. We've seen this picture before. As I said, I would be willing to take a polygraph if you wish."

Donato gave a grim smile and said, "Well-trained agents can be taught to deceive the lie detector. The same type of agents who would pretend to need the bathroom and pretend to tie a shoelace so that they could learn what is going on around them."

Jack grimaced and said, "I've heard that such people can be trained in regard to a polygraph, but only to the point of bringing about an inconclusive result. In my case, I am confident there would be no doubt that I was telling the truth. The only thing I would not disclose to you is the name of the informant that started this investigation."

"The note you gave the pilot said you were acting without authority. That your own government was unaware that you were coming to Cuba."

"That is correct," said Jack.

"You are telling me that you are both so rich that you can spend your own money to travel around the world to catch criminals? That is very, very difficult for me to believe."

"Our trip to Costa Rica was paid for by our government," said Jack.

"But not from San Jose to Havana!"

"I'm sorry," said Jack. "I suspect that police officers in Canada are in a far better economic situation than the officers in this country — but you are right. It is extremely unusual. There's more to it than just catching two bad guys. I'm actually hoping to save my career by proving that these Russians are worthy targets."

"Perhaps you should start at the beginning," said Donato.

Jack told Donato everything, starting from a meeting with a high level source who held an executive position with an organized crime family, to the Russians' interest in ports, navigational charts in the U.S. ... and a partially overheard telephone conversation where Moustache Pete said *the shipment will be as white as snow* while arranging a meeting in Costa Rica.

"So your boss does not want you to work on these men and you trick him with a phone call so you can?" asked Donato, somewhat surprised.

"Yes. I must tell you that our source in the organized crime family is a powerful man. He often has people killed. For him to be afraid of these two men ..."

"I understand," said Donato. "Then you lie to your boss and tell him you are on vacation in Costa Rica."

"Yes."

"In my country, to do such a thing, more would happen to you than going back to direct traffic." Donato stared at Jack quietly for a moment before saying, "Your boss, he is what I call ..." he paused and looked at Laura and asked, "*¿Habla usted español?*"

Laura looked at Jack and shrugged her shoulders.

"She doesn't speak Spanish," said Jack. "I think she only

knows the word *cerveza*."

Donato smiled, and continued, "Your boss sounds like a *pendejo*."

Jack laughed and said, "The meaning of that word is used by police forces around the world. For bosses and criminals."

Laura leaned forward in her chair and looked at each man and softly said, "Asshole?" She smiled when both Jack and Donato howled with laughter.

"Okay, my new amigos," said Donato. "We will help you."

"With discretion?" asked Jack. "My bosses will not be informed?"

"I will recommend that it be kept secret. Perhaps you might give me some suggestions on a certain boss of mine," he added, with a smile.

"The Russians … you know where they are?" asked Jack.

"Yes. They are in a taxi on their way to Varadero at this moment."

"Are they booked into a hotel?" asked Jack.

"No. They are being cautious. They told the driver that they would decide on a hotel when they arrived. That is okay. The driver is a member of my staff. Now we must go. We will get you your luggage and then you will ride with me. You will see how the Cuban police catch criminals. If these men, Petya Globenko and Styopa Ghukov, meet anyone, we will know."

Jack glanced at Donato, who gave a slight nod of his head. *I never used the Russians' real names. Just Moustache Pete and Fat Man.* "Did you search the Russians' luggage as well?" he asked.

Donato shook his head. "Not yet. That will be done at their hotel."

"Wouldn't it have been easier here?" asked Laura. "You wouldn't have needed a warrant."

"A warrant?" Donato chuckled. "We have at least one

or two secret officers from the DTI at all major hotels. At customs we did not want the Russians to suspect we had any interest in them."

"The DTI?" asked Jack.

"Sorry, you would refer to them as Intelligence Officers. The other hotel staff does not even know their identity, although, in some cases I think they suspect. It is their job to keep an eye on suspicious people. Very efficient. Do you not do the same thing in Canada?"

"No," replied Jack with a wry smile. "Civil liberties would go berserk."

"Ah, I understand," replied Donato. "Your country has not faced invasions or multiple assassination attempts on your leader. Let alone be faced with an embargo that has alienated you from the world. Such things tend to make leaders more suspicious and defensive. Civil liberties become a luxury we cannot afford."

It took four hours for them to reach the resort area at Varadero and it was eleven o'clock at night when Jack, Laura, and Donato all checked in at the Hotel Acuazul. Moustache Pete and the Fat Man had already checked in at the Hotel Islazul which was part of the same hotel complex, but was a separate building a short walk away.

Jack, Laura, and Donato's rooms were all in a row, with Donato taking the room in the centre. Jack glanced at Donato just as the three of them were about to open their doors. He caught Jack's glance.

"No, you're not," Donato said, reading Jack's mind.

"Of course, not," replied Jack.

"I understand. I would think the same thing," said Donato. "Please ... I insist. You take my room."

"It's okay," said Jack. "I've been bugged before. I have nothing to hide from you."

"I do not want you to think that. Please, use this room and I will sleep in yours."

"What makes you think your own people have not bugged your room as well?" asked Jack. "After all, meeting with two Intelligence Officers from another country … you might be under suspicion yourself."

Donato put his finger to his lips for Jack to be quiet before smiling. He then winked and stepped inside.

Minutes later, the three of them reconvened in Donato's room. "Beer?" asked Donato. Jack and Laura both nodded.

Donato made a phone call and within minutes one of his staff was at the door and handed him a tray with six cold bottles of Bucanero.

Jack didn't know if it was the heat and the high humidity, or perhaps just the stress of a long day, but he decided it was one of the best beers he had ever tasted.

"They have checked in for three days," said Donato. "Now that they are in their room, they seem to be relaxed. I do not think that they suspect any police activity. They converse in Russian, but then, that is their native tongue."

"Do you have someone on your staff who speaks Russian?" asked Laura.

Donato smiled and said, "Cuba has a huge Russian influence. Up until the collapse of the Soviet Union, they provided our country with billions. Now, those days are over. Russia has her own economic problems and has turned away from us. The embargo continues to cause us much suffering. You saw on the way here tonight. Most of our cars are old, running at night without lights. Many people are killed. One of my own children …"

Jack picked up the sudden sorrow in Donato's voice.

Donato realized it himself and looked embarrassed as he quickly changed his tone and said, "I am sorry. I sounded like a beggar. I am not! Enough about that." He turned to Laura and said, "Yes, many members of my staff, including me, speak and write fluently in Russian."

"Russian, Spanish, and English," said Jack. "You're not afraid to learn, are you?"

"You can also add French and German to the list. No, I am not afraid to learn. Perhaps in the next few days we will learn things from each other."

Donato paused to answer another knock at the door. He spoke quickly to one of his men before returning and announcing, "Now, some good news. From what we have heard they have simply come to Varadero to relax and enjoy themselves ... so you two can do likewise."

"That's not good news," said Jack, glumly.

"No, my friend! Let me finish. Then they plan on returning to Havana where they are meeting someone before leaving Cuba."

"Great," replied Jack, returning Laura's thumbs-up sign.

"Do you know if these Russians are dealing with someone who is an Arab?" asked Donato.

"Not that we're specifically aware of. They've made phone calls to several Arab countries. It is possible they could be involved with smuggling heroin or hashish out of Afghanistan. Why?"

"They mentioned a restaurant in Havana that they would be meeting at. Moustache Pete said it would make whoever they are meeting feel at home. The restaurant is called Al Medina. It is the only Arab restaurant in Havana."

"It doesn't really make sense to me," admitted Jack. "If their original meeting was in Costa Rica, it should be with someone from South America arranging to bring a boatload of cocaine to Canada."

"Perhaps Costa Rica was just a place to blend business and pleasure," suggested Donato. "It might be drugs from Afghanistan after all."

"Perhaps," replied Jack. "Seizing a boatload of heroin would be even better."

"We are conducting background checks with Moscow on Moustache Pete and the Fat Man. We will learn more about these Russian schoolteachers."

"Russia?" said Jack, surprised. "If you get anything back at all, I imagine it will be next year sometime."

"We have a much better relationship," replied Donato. "I expect to hear back tonight."

"Tonight!" said Jack in amazement. "Your relationship with Russia is far better."

"I have a question for you," said Donato. "How long does it take you to get information from the United States?"

"Fast … if it is unofficial. Only a matter of minutes," replied Jack.

"For me, it is the same with Russia. Perhaps you and I may help each other in the future," suggested Donato.

Jack nodded and passed Donato a business card.

"Thank you," said Donato, while reciprocating with his own business card. "Now, about these Russians, my staff will handle all the necessary surveillance and investigative duties. They will be monitored every minute they are here, so you can sit back and enjoy yourselves. I will keep you appraised."

"I would like to see whoever they are meeting," said Jack.

"We will have photos — but I understand. I will see what can be arranged. For the next few days, I think you can enjoy the beauty that my country has to offer. For the most part, I will remain by your side. It would not be wise for the Russians to see your faces and I will always be informed of their movements. Another *cerveza*?" he asked, looking at Laura.

Laura shook her head and said, "Thanks, but no. I'm exhausted. I think it's time for me to turn in."

"Likewise," said Jack, getting to his feet.

Donato's phone rang and he answered it, speaking rapidly in Russian, but paused to look at Jack and Laura. "Wait!" he ordered, before returning to speaking Russian.

Jack and Laura each sat back down. Jack saw the surprised look on Donato's face change to that of a frightened man.

Something is terribly wrong …

chapter thirteen

"They're what?" Jack couldn't believe what he was just told. The impact was still sinking in.

"You might call them schoolteachers," continued Donato. "Both of them did teach at various military institutions in Russia. The one you call the Fat Man has his degree in microbiology. Moustache Pete has a degree in history and was a high-ranking officer in the Russian infantry."

The shipment will be as white as snow, thought Jack. *Microbiology … chemical warfare, anthrax?*

"Jack," said Laura. "They were looking at navigational charts around Seattle! Are you thinking what I'm thinking?"

"I think all three of us are," said Jack. *No wonder Damien was scared of these guys! He knew this! Those text books in the apartment he told us about. Sure, maybe they were in Russian, but they were bound to have graphs, maybe a periodic chart of elements or a conceptual flow chart of microbes —*

"Oh, man," said Laura as she started to put everything

together. "This is a plot to smuggle a dirty bomb into the States."

Jack was still thinking of Damien. *If Satans Wrath was linked with terrorists, they'd be slam-dunked by the government of every country they operated in. Half of them would end up in Guantanamo Bay, or secret prisons elsewhere in the world. Maybe never heard from again ...*

"Calls to Iran, Saudi Arabia ..." continued Laura.

"This changes everything," said Donato, quickly getting to his feet. "I must leave for Havana immediately. You will both remain in the hotel until I speak with you. Understood?"

"I understand," said Jack. "We'll be here."

"We're dealing with terrorists," said Laura, as soon as they were alone. "It has to be! It all adds up. "

"Explains why our friend with Satans Wrath was scared and made it clear they were not involved. Tipping us off about them was just his way of covering his ass."

"We're going to have to tell the brass," said Laura. "We can't stay mum about this. We could be talking about thousands of lives here."

"I know, but right now, it's the Cubans who discovered this. It's their ball game. I don't want to do, or say anything ... without their approval."

Laura nodded and said, "Donato is heading back to Havana, I bet we don't see him much before noon tomorrow."

"Yeah," replied Jack, glancing at his watch. "I feel sorry for him tonight."

"How so?"

"How receptive do you think Fidel will be to being woken up at this hour?"

Jack tried to sleep, but found it virtually impossible. By morning, he was just beginning to doze when the hotel came alive. After listening to the movement of hotel guests and the cheery voices of maids going about their business, he finally gave up on the idea. A cool shower helped him wake up before he put on a pair of cargo shorts and stepped out on his balcony. The day was hot, humid, and sunny.

"Can't sleep?" called Laura.

Jack saw Laura on her own balcony and waved her over. Breakfast was included at the hotel, but, not wanting to take a chance of the Russians seeing them, they ordered room service.

Later, from their balconies, they could see the sandy white beaches and azure colour of the sea beyond. Neither one was able to appreciate the magnificent beauty as they paced back and forth in the room, trying to walk off the stress that accumulated with each passing hour.

It was ten-thirty at night when Jack answered the knock on his door and let Donato inside.

"I apologize for keeping you both waiting," said Donato.

Jack noticed that Donato was still wearing the same clothes as yesterday. The dark circles under his bloodshot eyes said that he hadn't been to bed at all.

"That's okay, Donato," said Jack. "Have a seat," he said, gesturing to one of the two chairs in the room while he sat on the bed.

"Anything happen with the Russians today?" asked Laura.

"They drank lots and picked up prostitutes. Nothing of importance. Also nothing of importance found in their rooms."

"Too bad," said Jack.

"Now, on this matter," said Donato, leaning forward in his chair. "We have a crisis that we need to discuss."

"A crisis?" replied Jack. "I think we may have just averted one. I'm sure their meeting in Cuba is just a matter of convenience. If this turns out to be terrorists trying to attack the States, you can just notify them and be done with it. As far as Canada goes, our own Intelligence Service, along with the RCMP, will likely work with them."

Donato shook his head and said, "It is not that easy, my friend. Are either of you familiar with the *Cuban Five*?"

"I never heard of it," said Laura.

"I've heard of them," said Jack. "I once did a Google search of the Cuban Five on the Internet. Lots of info, but it is difficult to understand and know who to believe."

"Then perhaps you will believe *me*," said Donato. "Our country has had many terrorist groups attack it over the years, including threats from expatriates and gangsters who are based out of Miami. In the mid-1990s we managed to get five undercover Intelligence Officers into some of the terrorist groups and uncovered plans to bring a boat full of explosives to Cuba."

"Good going," said Laura.

Donato shook his head to indicate she was wrong, and continued. "Our agents could have simply blown the boat up, but they were concerned that some innocent person could be injured. Perhaps an American citizen. Instead, my government informed the FBI about the boat and gave them documentation telling them who our agents were. The FBI seized the boat of explosives and arrested our five agents. That was in September 1998. They were charged with being spies in the U.S. and are still in prison."

Oh, man, brooded Laura, *sort of like Jack and I coming here …*

"So as you can see, our relationship is not good. We are concerned that the U.S. still considers us a terrorist state.

For someone now to meet on Cuban soil and plan such an attack on the U.S. … it might give them reason to attack us, without having to say they were looking for weapons of mass destruction."

Jack took a deep breath and slowly exhaled.

"Do you understand our dilemma?" asked Donato.

Jack nodded and asked, "So what do you intend to do?"

"We will help, but we would prefer to pass the information through to you. We ask that you not disclose to the Americans where this information came from or that the Russians even came to Cuba."

"You've got our word on that," said Jack.

"After all, it would appear that Cuba was simply picked as an alternative to Costa Rica. Where the meeting takes place should not matter — but we cannot risk that the Americans would feel that way. Our position is that it is *what* is said at the meeting that could be of significance."

"Not *where* it is said," agreed Jack.

Donato nodded.

"So, despite how the States has treated you in the past, you are still willing to help them?" asked Jack.

"Of course. Many innocent people could be hurt if action is not taken. What is your expression? Two wrongs don't make it right? We simply prefer that they never know we helped."

"I won't disclose where the meeting took place," said Jack. "I'll say that to do so would disclose the identity of a confidential source."

Donato gave a wry smile and said, "I presume I am that source."

Jack nodded and said, "I have a reputation for protecting my sources, so that is not unusual. The only problem could be with a Costa Rican policeman by the name of Eduardo. He knows we are here with the Russians, but it is extremely unlikely that he would present a problem."

"I doubt that a Costa Rican policeman would ever connect your investigation, into what you indicated was cocaine importation, with a potential terrorist threat on the Americans."

"Exactly. It is still a loose end, but his interest in the matter was only in relation to what was happening in Costa Rica."

"If he ever did say something, then so be it."

"Eduardo seemed like a good type. He did promise to keep our trip here secret."

"Of course. To protect you from your boss … the asshole," said Donato.

"Yes, the *pendejo*," said Laura.

Donato gave a faint smile and said, "Very good, Laura. Now you know two words of Spanish."

Late the following morning, Jack, Laura, and Donato dressed in beach clothes and walked along a short street leading to the beach. On the way, Jack noticed a chain-link fence and a sign.

"Laura, look," he said.

Behind the chain-link fence was a sign with two small Canadian flags attached. The sign identified the place as the Canadian consulate.

"Open from one-thirty to five-thirty every day except Wednesday and Sunday," commented Laura, reading the sign. "Think we should pop in later and say hello?"

"Hell, no! I don't even want to walk past this place again."

The beach was the nicest of any Jack had ever seen. The sand was white and clean and his bare feet felt like he was walking on warm velvet. Any of the locals he encountered were quick with a smile.

They found a small restaurant facing the beach where

four musicians strummed guitars and beat lively Latin music. They all ordered beer and a quarter roasted chicken that they took down to the beach, where they sat on lounge chairs and dangled their feet in the water. Jack decided that the cold Bucanero tasted just as good as it had the first night he arrived and for a moment, could feel his body start to relax.

Donato received a visit from one of his staff members.

"The Russians are walking this way on the beach," said Donato. "If we go back to the restaurant we should see them pass by."

As they stood under the awning of the restaurant, Laura was the first to comment. "I think that is just about the funniest thing I've ever seen," she said.

Jack saw what Laura was looking at and immediately lost his appetite. "That's not funny," he replied, wondering if the chicken was perhaps a little too greasy.

The Russians strolled past on the beach. They each wore Speedos, along with black socks and sandals.

Later that evening, Jack bought a bottle of rum and the three of them returned to his room.

"Here's to catching bad guys," said Jack, raising his glass of rum and Coke. "No matter what nationality they are — or where they are in the world."

"And to protecting the innocent," added Donato, as the three of them clinked the glasses in unison.

"You have pictures of your family?" asked Jack, a moment later.

Donato nodded, taking out his wallet and showing a picture of his wife, three sons, and two daughters.

"My oldest son died," said Donato softly, pointing at the picture. "It was night. He did not see the car coming. It had no lights. He was nine."

"I am sorry," said Jack.

"It has left a sadness in my wife's eyes for two years now."

Laura swallowed, and said, "Your children look beautiful."

Donato beamed. "They are," he answered, before asking, "You both have children?"

Jack shook his head. "I just got married a year and a half ago."

"That is plenty of time to make a baby," chuckled Donato. "In Cuba, we would have two babies by then. How about you, Laura? Children?"

"My husband and I have been trying for years. I became pregnant, but ..." she stopped and her eyes watered.

"I am sorry, Laura," said Donato. "It was rude of me to ask such a personal question."

"It's okay," she replied. "I really love children. Some day I will have one to call my own."

"Likewise," said Jack. "Likewise."

"Then," said Donato, "When this is over, the both of you must return for a visit. Bring your wife, Jack, and your husband, Laura. You are welcome to share my roof with my family. I would consider it an honour."

"Perhaps the day will come where you are also free to travel," said Jack. "I would also consider it an honour for you to come and stay with me."

Donato nodded, but turned his gaze to the wall, wondering if that day would ever come.

Later that night, Jack went down to the lobby and sent Natasha an e-mail. He told her that he was being well cared for by the Cubans. *They have little, but are willing to share what they do have*, he wrote. *A very proud people. I want to return here some day — with you!*

The following morning, the Russians checked out of their hotel as scheduled. A different member of Donato's staff took on the role of taxi driver and took them to Havana.

Jack and Laura went to pay for their rooms, only to be refused. "It was already looked after," said the desk clerk.

Early that afternoon, Donato told Jack and Laura that the Russians checked into the Hotel Nacional in Havana. A place that Donato informed them was once frequented by Hollywood movie stars and old time gangsters like Al Capone.

Donato had Jack and Laura check in at the Hotel Saint John's. It was a much more modest hotel located about a ten-minute walk away from where the Russians were staying. Jack, Laura and Donato were still in the lobby checking in when Donato received a call.

Donato put his hand over the receiver and whispered to Jack, "It is going as expected. Moustache Pete has already made a reservation tomorrow night at Al Medina. He reserved a table for four people."

"Four?" replied Jack.

"Apparently they are meeting two people," replied Donato. "The Russians are now drinking triple vodkas in the bar at the Hotel Nacional. One moment please," added Donato, as he resumed his phone conversation in Spanish. *"Bueno!"* he said, and hung up.

"Good news?" asked Jack.

Donato smiled and said, "Prostitutes have now been invited to join them. I think tomorrow the Russians will be exhausted and sleep late. Our work will likely not begin until dinner time."

"It will give Laura and me a chance to see Havana," said Jack.

"Tomorrow, perhaps around eleven, I will meet you and

give you both a tour of Havana. Tonight, I ask that you excuse me. I still have work to do and …" Donato paused.

"And you would like to sleep with your wife," added Jack.

Donato smiled and they said goodbye.

After checking into their rooms and cleaning up, Jack and Laura went to a restaurant beside the hotel before returning for a nightcap in the hotel lobby bar.

A vocal trio called the Trio Tesis were singing Latin songs in the lobby. Jack watched as the lead singer poured his heart out in a song entitled "Yolanda." When the trio took a break, Jack discovered that the singer spoke English and purchased a compact disc of their songs.

"You're very good," said Jack. "You show a lot of emotion when you sing 'Yolanda.' Do you know someone by that name?"

"No," he admitted. "But when I sing it, I think of my wife. She is a doctor and has been gone many months. The government sent her to help the people in Belize for six months. Soon she will return."

When he left, Jack turned to Laura and raised his eyebrow.

Laura knew what he was thinking. "It's amazing," she said. "These people are so poor, yet they can still find it in their hearts to help others."

"Not my impression of a terrorist state," replied Jack.

The next morning, Jack and Laura strolled through the streets of Havana. The limestone Spanish architecture of the buildings would have made Havana, at one time, one of the most beautiful cities in the world. Now, most of the buildings were in a severe state of decay and were crumbling down. Inside, whole families lived in darkened vestibules. Mothers swept the limestone dust outside where children used sticks as bats to play ball amongst the rubble.

"Do you see that?" said Laura, gesturing to a young girl holding the hand of a little boy as they came out of a building that apparently was their home. The building was dark inside, with the only visible light coming from a single bulb dangling from a high ceiling on a piece of wire.

"They're spotless," added Laura. "The both of them."

Jack saw the white shirts the children wore. They looked perfect. "I read a newspaper in the lobby this morning," he said. "The paper was called *Granma*."

"*Granma*?" asked Laura. "Sounds like you were in an old folk's home."

"Actually, it is the name of the official newspaper of the Central Committee of the Cuban Communist Party. *Granma* was the name of the yacht that brought Fidel Castro to Cuba in 1956 to start the Cuban Revolution."

"So what's it got to do with these children?"

"The newspaper is not what you would call a free press. But one thing was obvious. They take great pride in looking after and educating their children. There was also an article about them assisting Venezuela with their illiteracy problem."

"Most appear to live in squalor, but …"

"Exactly. They still work hard to improve themselves. You can see it in their faces. I've been through ghettos in Canada where people sat waiting for handouts. Maybe we could learn something from these people."

"I suspect the government of Cuba is too poor to give much in the way of handouts," replied Laura.

Jack and Laura met Donato as scheduled and he took them to a more popular tourist area in Havana. The area was comprised of a few square blocks where many of the buildings had been restored. It was also where the Arab restaurant was located. Another restaurant that was also a microbrewery was just down the street and they went there for lunch.

"You both went for a walk this morning," said Donato. "What do you think of my Havana?"

"Fifty years ago, I believe that this would have been the most beautiful city on the planet," said Jack. "It still is beautiful, but …"

"Yes, I know," said Donato sadly. "The American embargo. It has taken its toll. Medicine, school supplies, parts for automobiles …"

"From what I have seen," said Jack, "the Americans have forced the Cuban people to walk barefoot over the coals … but they have never brought you to your knees."

Donato smiled, and said, "They never will. Still, it is difficult to understand why amends have not been made."

"Allowing Russia to plant missiles here to be used against the Americans — can you really blame them for the retaliation?" asked Jack.

"That was in 1962," said Donato. "I, like most of my countrymen, weren't even born yet. The American mafia was taking over our country. Casinos, gangsters, drugs … was it so wrong to kick them out and invite the Russians?"

"It does seem like a long time to punish someone," said Laura. "Will peace ever be made?"

"I have a theory on that," said Jack, watching Donato's face closely. "I think there is more to it than the missiles. Back in the early 1960s, Fidel was targeted by the Kennedy administration on numerous assassination attempts."

"This is true," said Donato, eyeing Jack curiously.

"JFK was assassinated in 1963," continued Jack. "I think

that Fidel was exasperated and struck back. I also think the CIA is aware of this and will never allow peace between your countries as long as Fidel is in power."

Donato looked around nervously and said, "It is not good to talk of such things. No politics, please."

For Jack, it brought home the realization that he was in a communist country. *Freedom to express or exchange ideas could bring retribution.*

Jack was concerned that he had upset Donato, but within minutes, Donato was smiling and later took them on a drive around the city.

They returned to the Saint John's at four o'clock and the three of them waited in Jack's room. The Russians had slept most of the day, but it was reported that each one was now cleaning up and getting dressed to go out.

Conversation in Jack's room was minimal and stilted, as each wondered what tonight — and the future — would bring.

At five o'clock, Donato drove them back to the vicinity of the Al Medina. He parked the car and took them to a nearby church with a high cathedral entrance.

"You've got an OP in a church?" asked Jack.

"What is an OP?" asked Donato.

"Observation post."

"Yes, I see. It is not a church anymore. The government has turned it into a museum. It is closed to the public at this hour."

Jack was going to ask how the parishioners felt about their church being closed, but decided against it.

Donato led them to a small room in the back and they went inside and closed the door.

"We can't see from here," said Jack.

"It is not to see," said Donato. "It is to listen," he said, gesturing to a mass of electrical cord and recorders on a table. "Others will see for us," he explained. "Don't worry, there will be many pictures. This is for you and Laura to listen. You will hear with your own ears."

"I would have believed you," said Jack, realizing the work Donato went to in setting up this room. He understood why they would not have been allowed entry to the normal facility the Cubans would use for such activity.

Donato smiled and said, "Yes, my friend. I trust you, too. But if it ever happens that someone finds out that this meeting was in Havana, they may not believe what you tell them if you only receive the details from me. It is best to hear for yourselves. You may make notes if you like, but I will also supply you with a tape of what they say. You could record it on your own recorder, if you like."

"Thanks. We'd never be allowed to enter the tapes as evidence in a Canadian courtroom, but it still might be good to have."

Donato received a call on a portable radio and said, "They've just taken a taxi," he said. "They are on their way."

The Russians arrived about ten minutes ahead of their reservation, but their table was ready and they sat down.

Donato turned up the volume on a recorder and Jack and Laura could hear Fat Man and Moustache Pete talking to each other in Russian, over the clink of ice cubes and water being poured.

"I know their voices by now," said Donato. "I will translate for you. Moustache Pete just said something about an incident at the airport. I do not know what airport. He said they still have to be careful."

Jack heard the Fat Man laugh and make a comment.

Donato looked puzzled and translated. "Fat Man said,

that is why they carry insurance. With the police, insurance is always good."

Insurance? Wondered Jack. *Is there a leak? A crooked cop or someone …*

"They've arrived," said Donato. "Two Arab men. Expensive suits, Rolexes …"

Jack heard the conversation switch to English when the two Arabs sat down with the Russians.

After some general polite talk, Jack heard one of the Arabs ask, "So, when can you deliver?"

"Our people in Sweden were successful," said Moustache Pete. "We have two that would be most suitable. Sisters raised by a single mother. They're thirteen and fifteen years old. Both have blonde hair, blue eyes, and, as we promised, their skin is as white as snow."

Jack's mouth gaped open in surprise. "This is white slavery!" he said. "Not drugs or terrorism at all!"

The recorder droned on. "And beautiful?" asked the Arab.

"Of course," laughed the Fat Man. "Their mother thinks they are being accepted as models to do a photo shoot in Morocco. They are both beautiful! As promised, we will make delivery in June. Their mother is adamant about them finishing the school year. "

"And virgins …" the Arab's voice was lost over Jack's outrage.

"These bastards are kidnapping kids to sell to the Arabs to be used as sex slaves!"

Laura saw a sense of relief on Donato's face. A potential crisis with the U.S. had just been averted. She felt relieved herself, until she looked at Jack.

Is he enraged … or in pain? He's been around too long to be shocked by this. Why such anguish?

Back at the hotel in Jack's room, Donato raised a glass of rum and Coke and said, "It went well tonight. I wish you every success in putting these two Russians in jail."

"Hear, hear," said Laura, clinking glasses.

"They will go to jail," said Jack. "If it is the last thing I do on the section, I will see to that."

"Perhaps, now," said Donato, "your boss, Captain *Pendejo*," he added, smiling at Laura, "will realize that they were worthy of your attention."

"Perhaps," said Jack, "except we can't tell him what we learned or that we were even here. He would have us both fired. Regardless, even if I'm not in the section long, I will still get these guys."

"Come on, Jack," said Laura. "Like you said before, Quaile is fast-tracked up the corporate ladder. He won't be around long. We just have to outlast him."

"Moustache Pete and The Fat Man are going down," said Jack adamantly, "one way or the other."

"No problem," said Laura, eyeing Jack curiously. "We just continue to work on them behind Quaile's back. Knowing what we know now, I bet these two are supplying the women for Trần's massage parlours. We could get VPD to help us, or we could help them. Now that we know what they're really doing, it shouldn't take us long to get the evidence we need."

"Jack, Laura," said Donato, "if you will excuse me, I still have work to do tonight. I will be here in the morning to take you to the airport."

Laura waited until they bid good night to Donato, before turning her attention to Jack. "You going to tell me about it?" she asked.

"About what?"

"You're keeping something from me. A secret."

"A *secret*?" Jack spat out the word like it was poison.

"Yes, a secret," repeated Laura.

Jack put his glass down on the table and turned to Laura and said, "It's funny you used that word. Let me tell you about *a secret*."

By the tone of Jack's voice, Laura knew there was nothing funny about what she was about to hear.

"Did you know I used to have three sisters and a brother?" he asked.

Laura shook her head and said, "I just knew you had an older sister, Elizabeth, who lives out near Chilliwack."

"I was raised in a family of *secrets*," said Jack. "My father was a brutal, domineering prick who ruled the house with absolute power. That power included sexually molesting my sisters from the time they were four years old."

Laura briefly closed her eyes and said, "Oh, Jack … I'm sorry. I didn't know that."

Jack sighed and said, "Neither did I, back then. I knew about the physical and psychological abuse … but even as a policeman, I didn't know about the sexual abuse until recently."

"Jack … I'm sorry. Maybe this is something you don't want to talk about?"

Jack shook his head. "That is what the pedophiles like my father want. To keep everything secret. To try and make the children … the victims, somehow think they are responsible. They make the children think that they have to keep the secret to maintain family unity. I'm not embarrassed to talk about it. No victim should be, either."

"How did you find out?" asked Laura.

"My youngest sister, Bonnie, finally found the courage to tell me. Once I knew, then others admitted they had been victims, too. It turns out there were a lot. Neighbourhood children, relatives — even before my father was married, he would visit orphanages and bring candy."

"Classic," said Laura.

"It was classic, all right. My oldest sister left home as soon as she could. Got married, had kids, but died of complications giving birth to her third child. I knew she hated my father and was extremely protective of her children — but I was too blind to put it together."

"Pretty tough to believe that about your own family," said Laura, softly.

"I know. I felt like I was in shock when I found out. Bonnie moved out of the house early as well. I thought it was because of the psychological abuse and the physical beatings. But the signs were there ... and I missed them."

Laura saw the recrimination and guilt on Jack's face as he spoke.

"In any other family," he continued, "I would have suspected it immediately, but with my own, the idea was incomprehensible. Bonnie lived alone in a trailer near Rocky Mountain House and took in all the stray animals that crossed her path. Classic symptoms, yet I missed it."

"Hindsight is twenty-twenty," said Laura. "It is normal not to believe — not to want to believe, something like that even exists. Let alone with your own family."

Jack brushed her comment aside and continued, "Bonnie died of alcoholism a couple of years ago ... another classic symptom. I wanted so much to put him in jail, but none of the victims I found were willing to testify. The real sad thing is, all his victims lived with such a deep shame that they couldn't find the courage to come forward. As a result, dozens upon dozens of other children were molested."

"Where was your mother through all this?" asked Laura.

"That is something else I'm ashamed of. When Bonnie first told me, I naively imagined that my mother didn't know. Of course she knew. All this couldn't take place in a home without her knowing. Later I discovered that when they babysat children, my father would make his selection and my mother would take the other children for a walk so they wouldn't see what was happening."

"What kind of mother could allow that to happen?" said Laura, shaking her head.

"When I first found out and confronted my father, he was afraid he would be arrested. I actually made him write letters of apology. My mother threatened to make life hell on my sisters if I took any action. She reminded me that Bonnie was an emotional wreck and basically implied that if I did anything, her suicide would be on my hands."

"God ... that's awful."

"Tell me about it. Now my father is in really poor health. A good lawyer could delay the proceedings until he dies. Hopefully I can celebrate that day soon. When the bastard first realized I couldn't put him in jail, he would mock me on the phone. He loved to make people angry. I guess it made him feel powerful."

"You said you had a brother?"

"He died several years ago. He left home when he was fourteen. Later, he educated himself, got married, had children and a good life. The odd thing is, despite having received the most severe beatings from my father, my brother still went through life trying to gain his respect and admiration."

"That doesn't make sense."

"I've heard of psychological testing where they would temporarily take away a baby monkey's mother and replace it with a fake one, wrapped in barbed wire. Despite the pain, the baby monkey would still cling to it. My brother was like that. When he turned forty, he died of cardiac arrhythmia. He had continued to befriend and socialize with my father right up to his death, unaware, of course, that my father had an eye on his children as well."

"Where's your father now?" asked Laura.

"Lives in Red Deer. My mother is in a nursing home there. She has Alzheimer's. Maybe nature's way of letting her forget what kind of a mother she was."

"People keeping secrets all those years."

"Yeah. Think how many lives were ruined because nobody had the courage to come forward."

Laura reflected upon what she had just been told and looked at Jack and softly said, "Thank you."

"For what?"

"For trusting me with such a personal thing. For sharing your secret with me."

"These things should not be kept secret. That is exactly what the perverts want. Everyone should know. It's the only way to stop them."

"I agree, but still, thanks for telling me. Helps me understand you better."

"We're operators. We'd better understand each other," said Jack, seriously.

Laura nodded in agreement and said, "I know. Good friends," she said, fighting to keep her emotions in check. "Now stand up."

"What?"

"You heard me."

Jack slowly got to his feet. Laura wrapped her arms around him and hugged him tight.

"Thanks," he said. "Sorry to unload that on you."

"It's like you said. It's not the victims who should be ashamed. Now, two things," said Laura, as she let go.

"What's that?"

"Number one, pour each of us another rum. Number

two, let's figure out how to nail these Russians. I'm with you, whatever it takes."

Jack nodded. "Thanks," he said, his voice sounding hoarse. "As soon as we're back in Canada, I'm going to notify Interpol. We've got a couple of phone tolls from the Russians to Sweden. Shouldn't take them long to put a stop to things on that end."

Laura was silent as Jack poured each of them another drink and said, "What about Quaile? You know he won't let us work on them when we return."

"Maybe he will when we get the proof we need. As Donato said, Cuba is only the meeting spot. Nobody needs to know. We can work with Commercial Crime during the day like Quaile wants, then go after the Russians at night. Like you suggested, we'll work with VPD, too."

"I'm with you," said Laura. "Let's get these guys ... whatever it takes."

"Thanks," said Jack, quietly.

chapter fourteen

It was Tuesday morning at eight o'clock when Jack and Laura presented themselves in Quaile's office.

"You two have a nice vacation?" Quaile asked.

"It was okay," replied Jack.

"So, it is apparent that you wasted your time, along with the office budget, by following the Russians to Costa Rica."

Jack and Laura glanced at each other, and Jack said, "We heard from a reliable source since our return that they're both involved in human smuggling. Abducting young girls or women to be used as prostitutes. I've already notified the authorities in Sweden, where we heard they are obtaining two young girls."

"Really? Prostitution, you say? A week ago you said it was cocaine," replied Quaile.

"I may have been wrong about …"

"Or they might be doing that, too," said Laura.

"Human smuggling, prostitution, whatever; that's for

Drug Section, Immigration, or City Vice. Not our concern. Now that you're back, are you ready to go to work on what you should be working on?"

Laura was about to protest, but caught the slight movement of Jack's head, indicating his disapproval.

"Well?" asked Quaile.

"Ready to go to work," said Laura, sullenly.

Jack noticed that Quaile's eyes remained fixed on him longer than was normal. *He knows something … Cuba?*

"And you, Jack? Ready to apply yourself now?"

"You bet."

"Good. Commercial Crime is having a general debriefing at one o'clock this afternoon. It will be a good time for you to catch up on what is going on."

Later that morning, Jack was at his desk reading when Quaile came in and asked, "What are you doing?"

"Just updating myself on legislation and case law concerning fraudulent transactions relating to contracts and trade."

"Good," said Quaile, before leaning over and whispering, "Perhaps you should also brush up on the Motor Vehicle Act."

"That would make more sense than studying French," replied Jack.

Laura saw the angry look on Quaile's face as he stomped out of their office. "What was that all about?"

Jack sighed and said, "I think he was just telling me that I'm being transferred to Highway Patrol. We may not have much time. We need someone inside one of the massage parlours to help us connect the Russians with the prostitution."

"Sorry, Jack. I don't think my husband would appreciate me working undercover as a prostitute in a massage parlour."

"Couldn't you at least ask him?" He waited until Laura

smiled back at him and said, "Okay, be that way. That leaves us with the option of getting an informant. Guess I'm the one built for that job."

"What? Acting drunk and horny?"

"You got it. I'll start with Đức's place out in Surrey."

"Didn't your friend from VPD Anti-Gang tell you these guys are dangerous? Kids with machetes?"

"What's your point?"

"If things go wrong, it would be nice to have someone there who knows these people and could lend a hand."

Jack nodded in agreement and reached for the telephone.

Detective Rocco Pasquali listened to Jack's request and said, "Hey, I'll be glad to help. I didn't have anything planned tonight. Be good to get out of the city, even if it is just to Surrey."

Hằng knew that it was now or never. She took the lid off the toilet tank and disconnected the chain from the leaver and let it fall to the bottom of the tank. She stared inside for a moment and whispered aloud, "This is the only way, Linh. The American police are smart. They are like scientists. It will work."

It has to … as long as I'm found in time.

chapter fifteen

It was eight o'clock at night when Jack left Laura and Pasquali in the car and walked into the Orient Pleasure.

Better time to make a selection, Jack decided. *Late enough for the after-work crowd to have left and early enough to avoid the arrival of the bar crowd.*

"Have you been here before?" asked a stocky young Vietnamese man behind a counter. His accent was heavy, but his English was passable.

"Not this particular joint ... no," replied Jack.

"One hundred for a room," the young man said. "You pay me now. We rent the room."

"What kind of ... massage does that include?" asked Jack.

"What kind, is up to you and the girl," he winked. "We just rent the room."

"Listen, mate," said Jack. "My needs are sometimes a little different. Last time I was in a place like this, the girl didn't speak a word of English. Hard to tell her what I like.

Your girls speak English?"

He smiled and said, "One girl speak good English. Her name is Jade."

Jack paid the money and a minute later found himself alone in a small room with an attractive Vietnamese woman who was about eighteen years old. She was wearing a red wrap around her waist with a black emblem of a dragon on it. Her top was a short-sleeved white blouse unbuttoned enough to show most of her bare breasts when she bent over. A single-sized bed with white linen sheets and a chair were the only furniture in the room.

"So what you like?" asked Jade.

"Straight sex," said Jack. "I already paid the guy out front. I better not have to pay you, too."

"No, you no suppose to talk about that. What kind of sex you want?"

"Normal. You on the bottom and me on top."

"You don't need English for that," said Jade, unbuttoning the rest of her blouse before releasing the tie on her wrap to reveal that she was naked underneath. "All girls understand that."

"Put your wrap back on," said Jack, "and do up your blouse."

"Oh? You want me to give you hummer first?"

Jack shook his head.

"Blow job," said Jade, while putting her wrap back on.

"I understood you," replied Jack. "No!"

"Why you here, then? You want to fuck me different?"

"Listen to me carefully," said Jack, "and do *not* speak until I'm finished!"

Jade stared back at him, frightened and confused. She was more frightened when he showed her his police identification and said he could arrest her and send her back to Vietnam.

"Please, Mister Police. No. They kill my family you do that!" she said in a hushed voice.

Jack knew the terror in her voice was genuine.

"I owe money for coming to Canada," she continued. "Me no pay and they kill my family in Vietnam. Please ... no take me to jail."

"I will *not* arrest you *if* you help me," said Jack. "You tell me how you came to Canada. Who you work for. Explain everything to me."

"No," said Jade. "I talk to police ... then I die and my family die."

"Nobody will know."

"It is too dangerous."

"If you don't talk to me, then I will arrest you now for prostitution and deport you immediately back to Vietnam. I will also arrest Đức and he will think you did talk. What do you think he will do then?"

Jade gasped and said, "No, please. No do that!"

Jack put his finger to his lips to get Jade to lower her voice again and said, "I keep my promises. You work for me and I will not tell anybody."

Jade sat on the edge of the bed and hunched over to try and stop herself from trembling. Jack sat beside her and whispered, "Start by telling me your real name."

"My name in Vietnamese is Ngọc Bích," she said, while swallowing to hold back the tears. "It means *Jade* in English."

"My name is Jack."

Jade glanced at him and nodded silently.

"So tell me, Jade, how long have you been in Canada?"

Jade held her hands over her face and didn't reply.

"Talk to me, Jade. It is the only way."

Jade put her hands down and stared up at Jack's face. "You can trust me," he said quietly. "Help me and I will help you."

Tears flooded her eyes and she wiped them away with the back of her wrist. "Okay," she said. "I talk." She paused to think, before saying, "I be in Canada three months now. I leave Vietnam four-and-half months ago. Boat take six weeks."

"What boat?"

"I don't know name. It very old. Made to carry big boxes … not people. I come here with many other girls. Maybe forty. We go from boat to fish boat. Then to house. After three day, we put in back of truck. No windows. Then another boat. Short time, maybe two hour. We stay in back of truck. No see. We are told we get job in hotel."

"This isn't a hotel."

"Men lie," she said bitterly. "But no lie about money. I makes much money. I have mother and two brothers and two sisters. They poor. I send money home. Already send six hundred dollar in three months."

"But not from working in a hotel," said Jack.

"Mister Đức will have Giang kill me if I talk," said Jade, changing the subject.

"We won't tell him. Who is Giang?"

"He work for Mister Đức."

"Is that the man at the front who took my money a few minutes ago?"

"No. That Cường."

"What happened when you arrived and found out you would not be working in a hotel?"

"We are brought here. We are told what we must do. What men expect. I say no." She stopped and her body started to shake as she remembered.

"What happened when you said no?" asked Jack quietly.

"Not good to talk to you," said Jade. "Somebody find out and …"

"Jade, we've been over that. Tell me what happened!"

Jade swallowed and replied, "I am beaten by Giang and …" She then stopped and covered her face with her hands again.

Jack gently pulled her wrists down. "Jade, look at me."

She nervously looked up at him.

"Giang raped you, didn't he?"

Her eyes pooled and she nodded. "Not just Giang. By many men and boy who work for Mister Đức," she sobbed. "First night, I count twenty-three times … then I stop counting. If I run away or no work, then men who bring me on boat go to Nha Trang and kill my family. I go to police … same thing."

"Other girls were gang-raped, too?"

"Not so much as me. I say no. Try to fight. They beat me. Giang, he stick gun between my legs," she said, choking out the words. "I say, okay. No fight no more. Other girls smarter than Jade. They say, okay … fast."

Neither spoke for a little while as Jade stared blankly into space as her brain tried to erase what it could not. Eventually she said, "Mister Đức have many bad men and bad boys work for him. One boy, Xuân, very bad. I think he fourteen years old. Xuân much respect Mister Đức. Want to be like him, but now Xuân must do what Giang tell him. Giang in Vietnamese means *river*. With Giang, I tell other girls it mean river of death."

"Why?"

"He sometimes bring drugs for girls. I no take drugs. Other girls say it help you forget. I never forget. I say drugs … it help you die."

"Does Đức sell drugs?"

"No. Giang do that with other men. Mister Đức just sell girls."

"Who is Đức's boss?"

"Mister Đức no have boss. Mister Đức is boss."

Jack brought out a picture from his jacket pocket. It was of Moustache Pete and the Fat Man. "Do you know these guys?"

Jade looked at the picture, and asked, "How you know these two men? They in Hanoi!"

"They're both from Russia, but now they live in Vancouver. How do you know them?"

"They come and look at me and girls before we leave Hanoi on boat. I not know their names. They just look and then we go to boat. I never see them again."

Jack felt a rush of adrenalin. *Solid lead ... but what good is it if Jade can't testify? Even if we protect her, we still can't protect her family ....* "Was Đức in Hanoi, too?" he asked.

"No. Many other men in Vietnam do work there. Mister Đức stay in Canada."

"Đức lets you send money home?"

"Yes. It is good. Maybe good thing I make much money. My family very poor. Soon they buy house because of me."

Jack sighed and looked directly into her eyes. "Does your family really believe you are a maid in a hotel?" he asked, skeptically.

Jade's face darkened. She replied, "Other girls send money home. Some peoples talks. Maybe my family *say* they think I in hotel ..." She stopped talking and burst out crying. Between gasps of air she said, "They no believe that — but they still take money I send."

The sound of her crying brought hurried footsteps down the hall. A fist pounded on the door and a Cường yelled in Vietnamese.

Jack put his hand behind his back and rested it on the 9mm tucked in his belt.

Jade yelled something in Vietnamese and Jack heard Cường laugh and walk away.

"What did you just say?" he asked.

"I tell Cường you want me pretend to cry because you are too big inside me. Okay?"

Jack took a moment to take a deep breath and said, "Okay."

"My family … know," continued Jade. "They know I am whore. They never take me back — but they buy house … so that is good for me to give to brothers and sisters."

"I'll figure out a way to get you out of here," said Jack. "Just give me a little time."

"No. I need send more money home," said Jade.

"Jade, you are smart. Think about it. You need to get out of here."

"No. Too late. I am already a whore. If I go now — I am still a whore. Only a whore with no money and my family die."

"You're not …" Jack paused when he saw that Jade had made up her mind. "Damn it … do you have access to a phone?"

Jade nodded and said, "Sometimes I pick up lunch for people and bring here. Sometimes I go get laundry for beds."

"I'll give you my cellphone and home phone numbers. If you need help, call me. There are other ways to make money."

"Not so much as this," said Jade.

"*This* is costing you too much," said Jack.

"Fruit now rotten," said Jade. "Can never fix now."

"You're wrong. Think about my offer. If you want out, I will do it in such a manner that nobody will know."

"How?"

"Do you want out now?"

Jade paused, and shook her head.

"When you do, I'll figure out a way. You work for me and soon Đức and the two men in the picture will be arrested. Then for sure I will get you out of here safely. Is it a deal?"

Jade sighed and said, "Yes … I deal."

"In the meantime, if something happens, or if the Russians show up, let me know."

"Okay." Jade looked at the clock on the wall and said,

"Only five minute more. You pay for me ... you want?" she asked hesitantly.

"No!" exclaimed Jack in frustration. "I'm here to help you, not to fuck you."

Jade threw her arms around Jack's neck and kissed him on the cheek. He was startled and grabbed her arms to fling her off.

Damn it! Doesn't she understand why I'm here?

He heard her sob and knew that she did. He felt guilty that he had misinterpreted.

It was dark and Linh and her fellow passengers were allowed on deck for a chance to walk and breathe in some fresh air. Linh felt the ship shudder and a sense of dread overtook everyone as the ship's engines slowed. The sound of worried voices arose from different clusters of women around the deck.

Dread was soon replaced by excitement as the message spread like the ripples from a rock being tossed in a pond.

We are slowing down on purpose so that tomorrow night it will be dark when we enter Canadian water!

chapter sixteen

"How did it go?" asked Laura as soon as Jack returned to the car.

"You were gone long enough," said Pasquali. "Hope you didn't get cold feet and stiffen up in there."

Jack ignored the comment and said, "I met one of the working girls. She talked."

Jack relayed everything Jade had told him, including the Russians being in Hanoi.

"Where to from here?" asked Laura, her mind still sickened by what she had just heard.

"I'm going after Giang," said Jack, bitterly.

"How?" asked Pasquali.

"UC. First, I'll gain his trust on a coke deal. Then play it up that Laura and I are opening a massage parlour. Not here, Đức wouldn't want the competition. I'll tell him it's in Edmonton and we're looking for Asian girls because they're popular. I'll ask him if he knows anyone or someone who would want girls to work the circuit for a little variety."

"Hoping he will lead you to Đức," said Pasquali.

"Who might introduce us to the Russians," finished Laura. "It might work."

Jack looked at Pasquali and asked, "You once told me that Giang hangs out at either Lucky Lucy's Bar and Grill, Billiard Bill's, or what was that restaurant?"

"The Mekong Palace," said Pasquali, "But it's closed now. I have to tell you … Giang isn't too susceptible to a UC. We just tried. Giang wouldn't even talk to our operators."

"A couple of weeks ago you told me Giang wasn't all that important," said Jack. "Not worth the price of a bottle of olives for my martinis. What's changed?"

"The assholes, Giang's boys, put the Mekong Palace out of business. The owner was a nice old guy. Worked hard all his life to get his own business, now it's gone."

"What happened?" asked Jack.

"Xuân, being the sweet fourteen-year-old kid that he is, went in there a couple of weeks ago with some of his buddies. He demanded two hundred and fifty dollars of protection money. The owner refused so the gang terrorized the place and threatened to kill everyone inside."

"These are kids?" asked Laura.

Pasquali nodded and said, "Xuân, at fourteen, led the bunch. They held a filleting knife to an employee's throat while they robbed the cash register. Xuân shouted, *you play with God; from now on you have to pay five hundred!* He made a waitress kneel on the floor and fired a round from a semi-auto handgun into the floor beside her. The floor was concrete so the bullet fragmented and went everywhere. When they left, they told the owner that if he called the police they would return and kill everyone."

"What happened?" asked Laura.

"The owner called us. We scooped up Xuân and he's being held. I searched his bedroom myself. The walls were covered with cut-out pictures of guns. Unfortunately for the Mekong Palace, most of the employees quit and customers are now afraid to go there. The owner is trying to sell, but the word is out and nobody is even looking at the place."

"Was Giang involved?" asked Jack.

"The protection money thing would be right up his alley, but nothing we could prove."

"I want Giang," said Jack angrily.

"So do we. As a result of the Mekong Palace we had the narcs do a UC and try to buy coke from him. No luck. Since Xuân got busted Giang is even more paranoid, and if you think Xuân is bad, Giang is even scarier. Wild mood swings. He'll be laughing one second and then go into a rage and slash your throat the next. You know what he did to your CI. He's not the type you can just approach on your own. Our guys had a snitch do an intro and he still wouldn't deal with them."

"Then I'll get him to approach me," said Jack. "Do you know what Giang drives?"

"A new Pontiac GTO sports car. Red. Why?"

"Let's take a drive and see if we can find him," said Jack.

"You got the money on you to buy a kilo of coke?" asked Pasquali. "Giang doesn't deal in the small stuff."

Jack shook his head and said, "Our boss doesn't want us to work on him so we don't have any budget."

"Our department can't afford this. Sorry. How the hell can you even approach him?"

"As I said, I'll get him to approach me," replied Jack. He looked at Laura and asked, "Do you mind giving our narcs a call? See if any operators are working tonight that could spare half an hour to help me?"

"You need an operator?" asked Laura. "What am I?

Chopped liver?"

"Far from it," replied Jack. "If this works, you'll be needed in Act Three."

Jack explained his plan as they drove over to Billiard Bill's. The red GTO was not around so they drove back to Vancouver and headed past The Asian Touch and arrived at Lucky Lucy's Bar and Grill farther down the street. They saw the red GTO parked nearby.

Laura learned that a trained undercover operative from Drug Section by the name of Sammy was available.

"Jack, don't do this," pleaded Pasquali. "They're violent. Knives guaranteed and someone is always packing a piece. They'll slice and dice your ass and feed your body to the rats. I mean that."

"I'll be in and out before you know it," said Jack, while taking off his gun and holster and passing it to Laura. He next gave her his police identification.

"Think about this!" snapped Pasquali. "Nailing a pair of Russians for bringing in hookers isn't worth the risk. We'd be lucky if they each got two years in jail."

"I just met one of the hookers," said Jack. "It's worth it to me."

Jack carried a small backpack in one hand as he shoved the door open into Lucky Lucy's. He dropped the backpack on the floor and stumbled as he picked it up before gawking around as his eyes adjusted to the dimly lit room.

Giang, along with about twenty of his cronies, sat at tables near the only pool table. There were no other customers and everyone except Jack was Asian. The only woman in the place worked behind the bar.

The silence that descended and the glares he received

would normally have caused any sober man to turn around and head back out the door.

"Hooray!" yelled Jack, looking at them. "Men! Not lying, forgetful broads who don't remember to treat a guy like how he should be treated!"

Jack turned to the barmaid and yelled, "It's my birthday today! I'm buying a drink for every *man* in this place! Make mine a gin martini." He paused to regain his balance and said, "Aw, okay sweetie. You're doing the work … you can have a drink, too."

Jack tossed a wad of cash on the bar and said, "If it ain't enough, let me know. If it's too much, keep the change."

He turned to the group of men and shouted, "Sorry guys, I'm not cheap, but I can only stay for one." He paused and said, "What the hell, I bet you guys don't even speak English." He made a motion to drink and said, "Birthday!" and gestured with his thumb at his chest.

By a few of the amused looks and a couple of smiles from the men, Jack knew that he was at least temporarily welcome. He sat in a chair at a table that was one table away from where Giang sat and placed the backpack at his feet.

Act One, successfully completed, mused Jack.

Giang's suspicions were aroused seconds later when he heard Jack use his cellphone.

"Sammy! I'm at a place called Lucky Lucy's. Twelve-hundred block on Kingsway. You have twenty minutes or I'm gone. No more jerking around. Now or never!"

Giang studied Jack carefully. He only appeared to be drunk when he came in. He forgot to sound drunk when he made the call.

Out of the corner of his eye, Jack saw Giang whisper to a couple of the men. Their smiles disappeared and one of them reached inside his jacket, but Giang shook his head and whispered to him again.

Twenty minutes went by and Giang watched as the newcomer slurred his voice and carried on a one-sided friendly banter with those who were enjoying their free drinks. Then the next newcomer strode in.

"Hey, Sammy, over here!" commanded Jack.

To Giang, it was obvious that the man playing the drunken fool was not drunk. *Perhaps a fool, though?*

Sammy approached and stood squinting down at Jack as his eyes focused. "You got it?" he asked.

Jack picked up the backpack from off the floor and it landed with a thud as he dropped it on the table in front of him. "You seen it before. It's all here. Now where's the stuff?"

Sammy gave a pertinent little grin and unzipped his jacket.

"You're looking a little thin these days," said Jack. "I'd say you're down about a kilo from what you should be."

"You got that right," snarled Sammy, pulling his jacket back slightly to expose the handle of a pistol shoved in his belt. "Hand it over and keep your hands where I can see 'em!"

The reaction from the men sitting at the tables was instant. Several reached inside their own jackets and in other men's hands, knife blades appeared and were held ready under the tables.

"Sammy, take a look around," said Jack coolly. "Have you met my friends?"

Sammy glanced at the men sitting around Jack, as if seeing them for the first time.

"Jesus!" Sammy yelled before bolting out the exit.

Jack was already on his cellphone. "Laura! It ain't snowin' tonight. Sammy was gonna rip me. I told you he was no good! See ya back at the apartment."

Jack grabbed his backpack and was two steps away from

the table when Giang shouted a command in Vietnamese.

Several men immediately grabbed Jack by the arms and shoved him back into his chair.

"You're not going anywhere," said Giang.

"Oh shit," said Jack. "You *do* speak English!" He paused as he felt the sharp edge of a knife prodding his Adam's apple toward the back of his throat.

Jack looked up at the circle of men standing around him. "Okay guys, take it easy," he said, realizing that the nervousness in his voice was real. "Stupid thing for me to do. Let me go. I'll just walk out of here and leave the backpack behind."

Giang bent over so his face was close enough for Jack to smell the fish sauce on his breath. Giang sneered and said, "Maybe you will walk out — first, let me see what present you have decided to give me."

Giang picked up the backpack and smiled as he opened the zipper. He looked inside and his smile vaporized. His jaw clenched and the tendons rippled on his neck as he reached inside.

The man holding the knife jerked slightly and Jack felt the abrasion on his throat as Giang slammed the phone book down on the table.

chapter seventeen

"I don't like it," said Pasquali, staring at his watch. "Two minutes and counting."

"Nobody has come flying out through a window," said Laura. "That's a good sign."

"Laura, you copy?" asked Sammy.

Laura thumbed the mike and said, "Go ahead."

"No activity out back. Quiet as a tomb."

Great choice of words, Sammy ... you jerk. "It's quiet out front, too," radioed Laura. "Just keep the alley covered. We'll give him another three minutes. If I haven't heard from him by then, I'll go in for a look."

"Damn it, he could be chop suey by then," muttered Pasquali. "I should have uniform walk through."

Laura shook her head and said, "How often does that happen? If everything *is* okay, that could burn him."

"If everything is okay, why hasn't he called?" responded Pasquali.

Laura didn't reply as she stared at her own watch. *Oh, man … I hate this!*

Jack looked at Giang and pointed to the phone book and said, "Keep it. You never know when you might need to call someone."

Giang stared at Jack incredulously for a moment and started laughing.

Pasquali's words came back to haunt Jack. *He'll be laughing one second and go into a rage and slash your throat the next second.*

"What you just did … that is funny," said Giang. "You are smart, using us like that."

"Glad you have a sense of humour," replied Jack. "I'll buy you all another round on my way out."

"No," replied Giang. "You just used us. I don't like being used."

"My apologies."

"Perhaps you can make that up to me."

"What do you have in mind?"

"I will buy you a drink … for your birthday. And then we will talk." He gave a command in Vietnamese and the man with the knife returned to his own table.

Jack looked nervously at the men around him.

"It is okay," said Giang. "We will talk in private … up near the bar. Don't forget your phone book."

"You can have it," said Jack.

"I don't need it. If I need to reach out and touch someone, I use them," he snickered, gesturing to the men with his thumb.

"Think I could use another martini," replied Jack. "A double, if you don't mind."

"My men scare you?" said Giang. "A double ... yes," he said, giving a shrill laugh.

"Also better phone my girl," said Jack. "Let her know I'll be late. Don't want her to freak out and think Sammy came back."

An hour later, Jack joined Laura and Pasquali back in the car.

"Went well," said Jack. "Giang wants to sell me a key of coke. I told him I was too rattled after what happened tonight to do anything. We agreed to talk in a day or two. I told him I was starting a business in Edmonton. I said that one more dope deal would mean I wouldn't need a mortgage."

"Wasn't he pissed off over the Sammy thing?" asked Pasquali.

"He was irked to start with, but ..."

"Irked?" said Pasquali. He had too much experience investigating gangs to know that *irked* was not a strong enough description for the likes of men like Giang.

"Okay, it was a little tense, like you said it would be," admitted Jack. "But, like I said, he's greedy ... and that won out. Actually, when he calmed down he decided it was funny."

"Nothing about Giang is funny," said Pasquali. He looked at Jack closer and added, "I don't recall seeing that you cut yourself shaving this morning?"

Jack gently rubbed the abrasion on his throat and said, "Okay, he was really pissed off, but he's okay now."

"Damn it, I tried to warn you," said Pasquali.

"You're just upset that you're going to have to fork out some money for a jar of olives," said Jack. "Everything is okay."

Laura eyed Jack's neck and rolled her eyes. "With Act Three," she said, "I *will* be with you."

"You got it. First I'll build up his greed and raise his expectations on the cocaine, then you come in and cancel the dope deal. He'll feel let down and think he's about to lose out."

"I tell you that we can't buy the coke because we need capital to try and entice some girls to start working for us in Edmonton," said Laura.

Jack nodded and said, "Hopefully he'll figure he can still salvage a deal and introduce us to Đức or on up to the Russians."

"You going to meet him tomorrow?" asked Pasquali.

Jack shook his head. "I don't want to appear that eager. I'll have him wait a few days — take away some of his confidence. Give him a bit of a roller-coaster ride on this. One minute he envisions the money in front of him and the next minute he thinks it's gone."

It was midnight when Connie Crane, from the Integrated Homicide Investigation Team, ducked under the yellow crime-scene tape blocking the alley and made her way to the cluster of police officers. They were gathered around behind an apartment building.

Homicide Sections from the B.C. lower mainland, with the exception of Vancouver and Delta, had combined into what was now known as the Integrated Homicide Investigation Team, but was commonly referred to as "I-HIT."

Connie was approaching retirement and had spent much of her career investigating homicides. She was a walking encyclopedia when it came to murder and was considered a valued asset on the I-HIT unit.

When other homicide investigators were initially repelled by some of the more grisly murders they encountered, Connie would just shrug her shoulders and say, "Come on, guys. It's just a body. It won't bite. Let's find out who did it."

Her cool, calculating mind was in high demand and her presence was requested at many scenes. Some cases were easy. Like the time she listened to the sobs of a couple who told another investigator that their baby had rolled off the changing table and died when her head struck the floor.

"Arrest them both," she whispered to the investigator. "Shaken Baby Syndrome. This kid wasn't old enough to roll yet."

Other investigations, like the pig farm, were much more complicated and drawn out, but her energy and determination never waned.

When she got closer, she saw a police officer trying to take a statement from a grubby, bearded man who was sitting on the ground while holding his head and rocking back and forth.

She recognized the chubby profile of a man peering inside the Dumpster with a flashlight as that of her partner. "Hey, Wellsy! What have we got?"

Wells turned around and said, "Hi, CC. You tell me. A lady from the apartment building heard a homeless guy screaming like he was being killed. She called it in. Turns out that Homeless Harry was Dumpster-diving when he found something other than empties."

"Homeless Harry got a record?" asked Connie.

"Nothing serious. Uniform know him. They say poor Harry has a ton of psychiatric problems and is an alcoholic, but is also as gentle as a lamb and generally avoids the human race. Don't think this will help him any."

Connie used her own flashlight to look into the dumpster. A distorted face of a girl stared back at her from a ripped garbage bag. She appeared to be naked and was in a fetal position with her hands up near her mouth.

"Been dead for a while," said Wells. "Most of her skin is abscessed and rotting."

Connie used the end of her flashlight to nudge open the plastic bag a little further. "You're wrong," she said. "Check out the blood. This body is fresh."

Something else about the body did not seem right to Connie — then she saw it.

"Take a look Wellsy," she said, using the beam of light from her flashlight as a wand.

Wells stared for a moment and said, "I see it! What the hell?" he said, stepping back. "What kind of freak — Jesus! What do we have here?"

chapter eighteen

It was three o'clock in the afternoon when Isaac answered his secretary's call.

"Doctor Henckel on the line for you, sir."

"Put her through ... Aggi! How are you doing?"

"Good. One more autopsy and I'm done for the day. What can Leon and I bring for dinner tonight? How about I pick up a cake for dessert?"

"Don't worry about it. Sarah already baked an apple pie."

"Sounds fancy."

"No, not at all. Don't dress up. We're having our first barbecue for the year. Sarah is going to cook a turkey on the rotisserie."

"That's why you invited me! You want me to carve!" laughed Aggi.

Isaac chuckled and replied, "Hey, you've been a pathologist for the last twenty years, I figure you must have learned something!"

"We'll bring some Sauvignon Blanc," said Aggi. "See you at seven."

Aggi returned to the morgue as Connie Crane arrived.

"Good to see you, Connie," said Aggi. "You witnessing this one?" she asked as they walked over to the body just wheeled in from the cold storage locker.

Connie nodded.

"Must be important. Haven't seen you down here in a long time. Better you than those fresh-faced kids you've been sending lately. Half of them can't even keep their lunch down."

Connie didn't reply and for the first time, Aggi took a close look at her. She saw the smeared mascara and the tear-stained cheeks. "My God, Connie ... what is it? You look awful."

"Never made it to bed last night," said Connie lamely, as she pulled the sheet back. "Look ... her thumb ... she has an extra ... thumb ... growing out of the side of it."

Connie's voice was a monotone. It drudged out of her body like she was a robot talking on slow speed. "My partner thought ... she was a freak ... but she's ... just a kid."

Aggi looked down at the body and took one step back in horror.

It was seven-forty when Isaac answered his door and invited Leon and Aggi inside.

"Sorry, we're late," said Leon, looking helplessly at Aggi.

"I forgot the wine," said Aggi. "Came direct from work ... sorry."

The evening slowly progressed from one uncomfortable silence to another. The Isaac's deduced that Aggi and Leon had a fight. Part way through dinner, Aggie dropped her knife and started crying.

"I'm sorry," she said, moving to leave the room.

"Honey," said Leon getting to his feet.

"No," she said, gesturing for him to stay. "I need a minute alone. I'm sorry, everyone. I'm okay. I just need a minute."

Seconds later, Isaac heard the door to his den close.

"Leon?" he asked.

Leon shook his head. "Something happened to her at work today. An autopsy she did on a suicide of a child. She's been doing this for over twenty years. It's been years since I've seen her break down like this."

"I've had a few tough cases in my life," said Isaac. "Suicides of children are never easy. I'll go talk to her."

Isaac sat with Aggi in his den and she temporarily regained her composure enough to talk to him. She rapidly told him the details like anyone in her profession would.

Unidentified Asian female child between the ages of ten and fourteen. Found in a Dumpster in Surrey. Hesitation marks and puncture wounds on her wrists correspond to marks on her hand. Not defensive wounds. She used a thin rod of some sort, likely metal, to puncture and tear open the radial artery in her wrist, causing her to bleed to death. She had been scrubbed ... inside and out with bleach. No DNA. Stomach contents ... nothing ... as was her digestive tract.

After this, Aggi lost her composure. Through intermittent crying spells, Isaac heard about the torture the child had endured. Aggi's words spilled out as a mixture of medical jargon and raw human emotion.

Isaac was stunned as he listened ... and found himself staring at the picture of his own daughter on his desk. *Norah ... killed by a drunk driver ... but this ... Lord, why?*

"Obviously victim to a pedophile who is a sexual sadist," Aggi deduced, while struggling once more to gain control of her emotions. "Marks on her ankle show she was chained. By her condition and the phases of various fractures I would say she's been held somewhere for at least three to four months. Maybe longer."

"Who is the investigator from I-HIT?" Isaac asked.

"Connie Crane attended the autopsy. Incidentally, Connie said that the loss of sight in one of the child's eyes, including how that occurred, will be hold-back information."

Isaac nodded and said, "Corporal Crane's reputation is solid, but I'll still give her boss a call tomorrow. This is not going down as a suicide."

"That's what Connie said, too," acknowledged Aggi. "Nobody — especially a child, could endure such abuse. Obviously, that is the reason she committed suicide."

Isaac agreed.

They were both wrong.

Isaac sat in bed reading as Sarah stood in their ensuite, washing off the last of her makeup. He thumbed through the psychiatric text and scanned the page describing the profile of a sexual sadist:

> *The sadist wants sexual or psychological domination … that may include imprisoning the victim through the use of restraining devices such as chains, handcuffs, plastic ties.… Acts performed on the victim may include whipping, electrical shocks, beating, burning, mutilation, biting, urinating, or defecating on the other person … rape, murder …*

Isaac pondered over Aggi's description of the victim.

Everything that happened to that girl, except the personal touch of murder ... along with the burning, biting, urinating, and defecation. Then again, the child was washed in bleach — perhaps the last two acts had occurred.

"What are you reading, dear?"

Isaac quickly put the book down as Sarah climbed into bed. "Just work," he replied.

Three hours later, Isaac got out of bed and slipped on his housecoat. He found himself sitting in his den, staring at his daughter's picture.

My sweet Norah, you know the pain that Sarah and I have suffered since your accident. Some day we will be together in heaven ...

He turned his gaze to the window and out into the night sky. *The child that Aggi told me about ... does she have parents? When they find out, what will they feel? Unfathomable, even for me to know*

He rubbed his eyes and tried to block the images of what that child had endured. Eventually he resorted to saying the Lord's Prayer.

"You are faster than a monkey with stolen fruit!"

Linh looked up from the deck of the fishing trawler to the rope ladder dangling from the ship above. The young woman who uttered the words waved at her, and started her descent over the side of the ship.

Linh smiled and decided that she had descended faster than even a monkey could.

Very soon I will be together with Hằng — and my new family!

chapter nineteen

It was seven-forty-five in the morning when Staff Sergeant Randy Otto received the call from Isaac.

"Are you still Corporal Crane's supervisor?" asked Isaac.

"Yes, sir," replied Randy.

"Are you up to date on this Asian child found in the Dumpster?"

"Yes, sir," replied Randy. "Found the night before last. Corporal Crane attended the autopsy yesterday afternoon. She said it was a suicide but actually ..."

"This was not a suicide!" said Isaac, harshly. "Try reading section 222 of the Criminal Code! A person commits culpable homicide when he causes the death of a human being through threats or fear of violence to do anything that would cause their death! I don't have the Code in front of me, but that's pretty damn close!"

Randy had never heard Isaac swear before. *What brought this on?*

"Sir," Randy said. "I am familiar with that section of the Code. Your description, as I recall, is accurate. I hadn't meant that we were treating this case as a suicide. I only meant to inform you of that detail before explaining the unbelievable abuse this kid suffered."

"Oh," replied Isaac. He sighed and his voice softened as he said, "The pathologist on this matter is a personal friend of mine who was over for dinner last night. I am only too aware of what this child went through. I am sorry if I snapped at you."

"It's okay, sir," replied Randy. "I have two daughters of my own. This case is particularly upsetting."

Isaac was silent for a moment as he looked at Sarah and Norah's picture on his desk. Now when he spoke, his voice sounded saddened. "I have to admit, I didn't get much sleep last night — and when I did, the whole situation gave me a nightmare."

"I understand, sir."

"I don't want to interfere with your work. It's always top notch. I just want to be kept up to date on the details. Anything you need, you let me know."

"Yes, sir. At the moment it doesn't appear that she was even reported missing. We're checking with schools, hospitals — she has an extra thumb. Somebody must know her."

It was noon and Jack and Laura were sitting at their desks, reading volumes of information from Commercial Crime files in regard to a suspected stock manipulation.

Jack shook his head as he once again glanced at a link-chart where lines and dotted lines told of connections amongst various corporations, companies, and people involved.

"This stuff is unbelievable," he commented. "No wonder

it takes them years to figure out if they can, or even should lay a charge."

"Does give me a new respect for Commercial Crime," said Laura. "I find it boring, but it takes brains to decipher all this."

Jack received a call on his cellphone and quickly jotted down an address. When he hung up, he said, "Come on, time for you to meet someone. It's my new friend from the Orient Pleasure. She wants to talk in person and only has an hour off for lunch. Sounds urgent."

Jack and Laura slowly drove down an alley and Jack stopped the car briefly as Jade quickly climbed into the back seat and lay down out of sight. Jack drove to an underground parking lot where they could talk.

Jade was polite when she met Laura, but focused her attention on Jack. "I have news," she said. "But you arrest Mister Đức, what happen to me?" she asked.

"I told you I could get you out," said Jack. "Safely. Nobody would know."

"I need little more money," said Jade. "To buy house for brothers and sisters. More time."

"If Đức is arrested, it is unlikely he would be in jail more than a day or two to start with. If the Orient Pleasure were to close, he would have someone re-open it someplace else."

"You would allow him?" asked Jade.

"Our judicial system would allow it to happen. We need very strong evidence to arrest people. It takes time and once Đức is arrested, he will simply have someone else take the risk. Even if convicted, he would not be in jail long. This is not your concern. Tell us what is going on."

"You know Cường?"

"That was …"

"He man who take your money when you come to lay with me," interrupted Jade.

"I know him," said Jack, catching a glance from Laura. "The young fellow who works on the front counter."

"Yes, that him."

Jack coughed to clear his throat and said, "Tell my partner that I did not … lay with you."

"Oh!" A look of concern fleeted across Jade's face as she looked at Laura and said, "Jack no fuck me. He nice man."

Laura looked at Jack, opening her eyes just slightly, pretending that she had doubts.

"I hear Mister Đức tell Cường he must rent big truck today after work. Cường take Tommy and go get more girls to come here."

"Who is Tommy?" asked Jack.

"He work at Asian Touch. He Vietnamese, but no speak Vietnamese. Only English."

It was eight-fifteen at night when Jack and Laura drove their car onto the last ferry of the day, leaving from the Tsawwassen terminal. The ferry was bound for Duke Point, near Nanaimo on Vancouver Island. The cube van, being driven by Cường, with Tommy as a passenger, was a few vehicles ahead of them on the ferry.

Two hours later, they disembarked and headed north on Highway 19 from Nanaimo and west on Highway 4.

"Think we're going to Port Alberni?" asked Laura.

"Could be, but my guess is closer to the ocean where a fishing boat could moor."

It was shortly after one o'clock in the morning and they were nearing Tofino before Jack and Laura saw the cube van leave the highway and turn down a gravel driveway leading into the woods.

Jack continued past the driveway and parked on the shoulder of the road. They didn't have to wait long. Less than half an hour passed and the truck reappeared, retracing its path and eventually heading east on Highway 4.

"Back to the ferry," suggested Laura.

"Good thing," replied Jack. "Be hard to explain to Quaile what we're doing on Vancouver Island instead of listening to whose filing cabinets we're going to seize in a couple of years."

"That's right," said Laura. "I forgot. There's a meeting with Commercial Crime at eight tomorrow morning."

"Hopefully, Quaile will think that's where we are," replied Jack. "I'll call Commercial Crime in the morning and say we're tied up and to start without us."

They followed their quarry, catching the first ferry from Duke Point, departing at five-fifteen in the morning. They disembarked two hours later in Tsawwassen and by seven-forty-five they had followed the truck to a residential address in Richmond.

Jack kept his head turned as if he were talking to Laura and drove by just as Cường was backing the truck up a driveway to a home with an attached garage.

"The truck's too big to go inside," said Laura.

"I'll turn around and drive past again."

"Tommy eyed us going by," warned Laura.

"We'll make it look like you dropped me off," replied Jack.

Laura switched places with Jack and slowly drove past the house again. She caught a glimpse of several Asian women being ushered inside the garage.

"You can get your head out of my lap now," she said.

"I don't know," replied Jack. "Feels sort of comfortable. Think I'll take a nap."

A second later, Jack yelped as Laura twisted his ear and sat up.

"Now what?" she asked.

"Find a good spot to watch with the binos and hope that our Russian friends show up. If they do, I think we should call in the troops and make arrests."

"And if they don't?"

"Let's see what happens," replied Jack, tersely. "We need the evidence on them, not these peons."

"You heard what they do to break these women in."

"I know."

"Brutally gang raped by Giang and his bunch."

"Damn it, Laura! Don't you think I've been thinking of that?" said Jack angrily. "Pull over here, it's a good place to watch," he added, as he picked up the binoculars.

"We can't just sit back and let that happen," she said, letting her own anger boil over as she parked the car.

"What are we supposed to do about it? If we arrest these peons and don't connect the Russians, they'll continue to get away with it. They'll pick other people besides the Trầns. There are lots around the globe who are more than willing to deal in human flesh."

"As long as men support it, there will always be women being victimized," said Laura. "Jade can identify the Russians as being in Hanoi. If she testified, that should count ..."

"For nothing," said Jack. "She can't risk testifying now. Even if she could — so what? Two guys looked at a bunch of pretty woman. There's nothing to tie them into the business end of this. We need hard evidence. Boats, documents ... maybe someone with the courage to step forward and do what is right ... instead of keeping secrets!"

Laura knew that the rage Jack felt wasn't directed at her. *He's got the same look on his face as that night in Cuba, when he told me about his family.*

"Believe me," said Jack. "I am not done with Đức and Giang. But it's the Russians who are at the top of my list."

"So you're going to sacrifice these women, if need be, to catch the Russians."

Jack sighed and said, "Yes, because in the end, it will save more women."

"Providing we catch them. Otherwise this sacrifice is for nothing."

"We *will* catch them," said Jack, with determination.

"I don't like it," said Laura. "The whole idea sickens me."

"If it didn't sicken you, I wouldn't want you as a partner," replied Jack. He handed the binoculars to Laura and said, "Cường and Tommy are just leaving, but take a look at who just arrived."

Laura adjusted the binoculars and saw that two mini-vans had arrived. The drivers were walking toward the house.

"We've got two of the Trần brothers," she said. "Thạo and Hữu."

Jack swallowed a surge of bile. *Where are the Russians ... and where is Đức?*

Jack and Laura watched as the two brothers disappeared inside the house. Thạo reappeared by himself and the overhead garage door opened briefly to allow him to back his van inside.

Minutes later, the overhead door opened and he drove away as Hữu repeated the process and also drove away shortly after.

"Dividing up the girls," said Jack. "Maybe Đức is just late. He'll probably show up with a van soon. Maybe the Russians will be with him." *Maybe, but not likely ...*

Đức did arrive soon — alone in his car.

Laura looked at Jack and said, "Guess there are no girls left."

Jack nodded silently, watching as Đức walked up and knocked on the door.

"Figure he's here to pay for their storage?" asked Laura.

"Probably. No Russians," said Jack, feeling depressed. "I bet he already paid them."

"Maybe we can get a warrant for bank records," suggested Laura. "See if we can link them and the Russians. Quaile will think a warrant like that is for Commercial Crime."

"You can try, but I think by the way the Russians throw cash around, you're not going to find much in the way of a paper trail. This isn't a Commercial Crime type file."

"Speaking of that," said Laura, "it's eight-thirty. Maybe we should head over to Commercial Crime."

"Yeah, let's give it a minute. If Đức leaves right away, I'd like to follow and see if he does meet with the Russians."

Đức spoke briefly with someone at the door before returning to his car. Seconds later, he drove it inside the garage.

"What's he doing?" said Jack. "This isn't his house."

"Maybe a mistress," suggested Laura.

Seconds later, the overhead garage door opened again and Đức drove away.

"We're following him," said Jack, as his hopes returned. "Mistress, my ass. There's nobody with him in the car. He drove inside because he didn't want anyone to see what he was picking up."

"Had to be," said Laura. "He wasn't in there long enough to be doing anything else."

Jack smiled and looked at Laura and asked, "What else would a boat bring in from Vietnam?"

"Heroin," she said.

Jack gave her the thumbs up sign and said, "With Giang now being my new buddy, I could push the dope angle and get him to introduce me to Đức for that. He might even get more time than he would for being a pimp."

"I thought Đức didn't deal drugs."

"Everyone says he doesn't deal coke. My money is riding on heroin."

The tires squealed as Laura turned a corner and manoeuvred the car through traffic to catch up. Đức was driving a block ahead of them and was obeying all the traffic regulations.

"He doesn't want to get stopped," commented Laura.

"Corporal Taggart, from Commercial Crime," blared a feminine voice over the police radio.

"Go ahead," answered Laura, while grabbing the microphone that dangled from the steering column. "He's listening."

"Taggart! Where are you!" yelled Quaile into the radio as he nudged the secretary aside.

"Damn it," said Jack, glancing at Laura. "The asshole decided to drop in on Commercial Crime this morning. He knows we're not there. Give me the mike."

"Taggart! Where are you?" asked Quaile, again.

"Sorry, Staff," answered Jack. "I picked up Laura this morning and then we had car troubles. The engine keeps cutting in and out on us."

"Park and tell me where you are exactly. I'll send a tow truck."

"Shit," whispered Jack, before thumbing the transmit button again, "We're just about at the office. It appears to have corrected itself. Probably just condensation in the gas. We'll be there in fifteen."

Jack sighed as he met Laura's gaze. "Yeah, we'll get to the dope through Giang. Go ahead, better step on it."

Laura quickly turned the car around and they sped off in

the opposite direction.

"Up ahead, Linh!" yelled Đức. "Look! See it!"

Linh stuck her head out of the trunk into the back seat compartment and looked up at the sign that Đức pointed at.

Canada–U.S. Border! "I see it! I see it!" she said.

"Pull the seat closed! Quickly!" yelled Đức.

chapter twenty

Quaile did not wait for Jack and Laura at the Commercial Crime office. He requested — and was granted — an immediate meeting with Isaac.

"Sir, it's about Taggart," said Quaile. "He refuses orders and shows a total disregard for others. I just came from a meeting that was to have started an hour ago at Commercial Crime. Taggart was to be there at eight and as far as I know, he still hasn't arrived. It's embarrassing. I radioed him and he said he was having car problems. I'm sure he was lying."

"He's late for a meeting and you feel you need to speak to me about it?" asked Isaac.

"There's more to it than that, sir. I took a call from the Vancouver City Police this morning. They were looking for one of their detectives and believed he might be at our office. It turns out that Taggart has been working on a project that I ordered him to drop weeks ago."

"That investigation where he went to Costa Rica?"

asked Isaac.

"Yes, sir." Quaile leaned back in the chair, shaking his head. "What a fiasco that was. Taggart now says those two Russians may only be smuggling prostitutes into Canada to work in a couple of Vietnamese massage parlours. I told him to either turn it over to Immigration or City Vice. It is certainly not of the quality of file that I expect our office to engage in."

"Maybe Corporal Taggart is burnt-out," said Isaac.

"He seems clueless about what he should be doing. On top of that, he is a bad influence on the people under him. Morale in the office has deteriorated considerably. I respectfully suggest that his time has come."

Isaac nodded thoughtfully and said, "I agree," and reached for the telephone. He paused and said, "It's funny. This isn't how I thought Corporal Taggart would leave the section."

"Sir?"

Isaac shook his head and said, "With his history, I expected he would either end up in jail or dead."

Quaile listened patiently as Isaac talked on the phone. When Isaac hung up he turned to Quaile and said, "It's done. Have Corporal Taggart report to Inspector Schaff in Staffing immediately."

Jack and Laura arrived at Commercial Crime just as the meeting ended, so they returned to their own office.

"Got a call from Elaine at Travel King," said Jack, as he listened to his voice mail. He quickly dialled her number and spoke with her.

"Well?" asked Laura when Jack hung up the phone.

"Moustache Pete and the Fat Man just booked a trip to Vietnam," he said. "They reserved a room at a place called the

Hotel Happy Holiday in Hanoi next Wednesday."

"Only six days from now," said Laura.

"They fly out of Vancouver at noon the day before. Takes over twenty hours to get there."

"They're arranging another boatload," said Laura, excitedly.

"For sure. Maybe we can get the Vietnamese police to nail them. I'd rather serve two years in a jail in Canada than one month in a Vietnamese prison. This could turn out really great. I'll make some calls and see who we can liaise with …"

"Corporal Taggart," said Quaile, announcing his arrival into their office.

"Staff, sorry about missing the meeting this morning. We just came from there. I've got the minutes of the meeting so …"

"So *can* it, Taggart! You're to report to Inspector Schaff in Staffing immediately. After which, you are to return and empty your desk!"

Jack sat in a stunned silence as his brain flashed random thoughts and images like a remote control changing channels at hyperspeed. *The Russians … not too late … Laura can do it … Jade … the others … someone has to get them out … I've been caught at something … what?*

"Cat got your tongue, Taggart?"

Jack stood and walked toward the exit, feeling like he was still in a trance. He looked back at his desk and the rows of filing cabinets that he had invested much of his life into filling. *Laura looks like she is going to cry … hope she doesn't quit. Don't let the bad guys or the assholes win …*

"By the way," said Quaile, "did you really believe that I fell for that fake call from Ottawa? For your information, I just played along to see what you were really involved in." Quaile glanced at his watch and said, "You'd better hurry. I bet the longer you keep Inspector Schaff waiting, the farther north you'll be sent."

Jack heard Quaile's voice behind him as he headed down the corridor. "As for you, Secord, consider yourself on notice! You're only here still because I know Taggart was a bad influence on you, but …"

Linh felt the car come to a stop and she heard the overhead garage door close. She clasped her hands in anticipation, waiting for the lid to open.

Will the first face I see be Hằng? I think so!

The trunk opened and she saw only Mister Đức and a big man standing beside him. She smiled politely and tried to hide her disappointment.

"Hello, Linh. I'm Pops," the big man said, while reaching down to help her out of the trunk.

Linh was too excited to accept help and scrambled out on her own.

"Hello, Mister Pops," she said, extending her hand.

Pops smiled and shook her hand.

"I am happy to meet you," she said, pleased that she had memorized the phrase correctly. "Where is Hằng?" she asked, breathlessly.

"We'll talk about that in a moment," replied Pops. "Come inside."

Linh followed Pops to the door leading into the house, pausing only to smile politely and wave to Mister Đức as he left.

"We'll put your stuff in your bedroom," said Pops. "Then we will sit in the living room and talk."

Linh was awed by the sight of her bedroom. She picked the stuffed bear up off the bed and on impulse, gave it a hug before resting it back down with its head on the pillow.

"Are you hungry?" asked Pops. "It is almost lunchtime."

Linh smiled and said, "Hằng is in school!"

Pops stared at her a moment before taking her by the hand and leading her to the living room where they sat on the sofa. "I have some terrible news," he said.

Linh felt the dread in her heart. "Hằng?" she whispered.

"Yes. It is about Hằng. She died in an accident. She stepped out from behind a truck parked on the street and was hit by a car. I am so very sorry."

Linh burst into tears and felt Pops's arm around her shoulders. She turned and clung to his sweater, burying her face into his chest.

"It happened six weeks ago," said Pops. "We called your dad to tell him, but you had already left to come here. I feel so bad having to tell you the news. My wife wanted to be here when you arrived, but her mother is in hospital and is very sick."

Linh continued to cry softly for an hour, before a combination of stress and fatigue allowed her to doze off as she snuggled close to Pops.

"What happened?" asked Laura, as soon as Jack returned.

Jack tried to smile and said, "It's not all that bad. Lower Mainland Traffic Services in Burnaby. I'm supposed to start Monday."

"Highway Patrol! This is already Thursday — how can Quaile do that?"

"He couldn't, which means the big guy wants me out."

"What are you going to do?"

"I think I'll take a couple of days' leave. I'm lucky. It's not a physical move so it won't interfere with Natasha's work."

"Jack … I'm sorry. Oh, man," she said in frustration. "I

meant what I said before. I'm giving Staffing a call right now. There's no way I can work for someone like this. I'd end up putting on coveralls and calling you in the night to bring a shovel."

"Laura, no," said Jack. "Please don't, at least not yet. We've come too far on this thing with the Russians to let it drop now. We're close."

"You're the one who is already in with Giang. What can I do by myself? I need —"

"I'll still be handy to help out when I'm not writing tickets. I could still do the UC on Giang and introduce you, or maybe someone from VPD. The important thing to me is that we finish what we started. I also plan to get our friend in the massage parlour out of there when things do go down."

"How do you do that without jeopardizing her family? You heard her. If they think she ran away or came to us … people will die."

"I figured out a way, but —"

"Exactly!" said Laura. "You're good at this stuff. I can't do it on my own!"

"You won't be on your own all the time. I told you I'd help. Promise me you'll stay on and fight this battle."

Laura was quiet for a moment, staring down at her desk. When she looked up, she said, "Okay, but then I'm out of here as soon as Moustache Pete and the Fat Man are in jail … or dead."

Jack chuckled in spite of how he felt. "Maybe I have been a bad influence on you. You know, there was a time, before I met Natasha, when I would have gladly arranged for these two guys to die. But now I feel like my own life is worth something. I don't want to lose what I have. I've been doing my best to do the right thing. You should, too. Promise me you won't take any unnecessary risks. Catch these guys by the book. If you were to screw up, I would always blame myself for having started you down that path."

Laura sighed and reached across and put her hand on top of Jack's. "I feel awful about all this, but don't worry about me. I love my husband and I want to be a mom someday. I'll leave the shovel in the trunk."

"Good, it's settled. I'm going to call Natasha," he added, reaching for his telephone.

"Honey, I'm sorry," said Natasha, after Jack relayed the news to her. "You were afraid this was going to happen. I guess you were right."

"It's okay," said Jack. "Really. Sure, I'm not exactly ecstatic about it, but just think … regular shifts. No informants calling in the middle of the night — or when we're … you know. I've been doing this for seven years. The change may do us both good. Also won't have to figure out what to wear each day. Hope you love a guy in uniform."

"I don't care what you wear," said Natasha, "as long as you're the same man underneath."

"Ah … you love me naked. That part won't change."

"I meant you. What's in your heart. Which will change if you're not happy."

"You're in my heart. It's you that makes me happy."

Natasha remained silent.

"We'll talk over dinner," said Jack. "I'll cook something special, maybe chicken cordon bleu. I'll pick up a bottle of wine as well. We'll look at this as a celebration of a more stress-free lifestyle."

"Better make it two bottles," said Natasha. "I'm going to have to be really drunk if you expect me to swallow the bullshit you're feeding me."

It was three o'clock in the afternoon when Pops gently awakened Linh.

"It's a good time for you to call your dad," he said. "He will be worried and will want to know you arrived in the States. You can talk to him for as long as you want. I understand you have a grandmother too?"

Linh nodded.

"Talk to her as well, if you like. With what has happened, I am going to figure out how to bring them both to America. Wouldn't it be nice if you were all together?"

Without Hằng, that is not possible, decided Linh.

Between crying spells, Linh talked for over an hour.

Biển felt that his heart was already broken, but the sound of Linh's tears and being unable to hold her made him realize that his heart still had room for much pain. He asked Linh to be strong and to remember that they only had to look to the sky to know that Hằng would be watching and waiting to see them some day.

When Linh finally ran out of words, she slowly relinquished the phone to Pops, who hung it up.

Pops smiled knowingly and said, "Come, there is a special hiding place I must show you. It is to be used if the police should ever come before the proper papers are in place."

chapter twenty-one

At eight o'clock Friday morning, Laura walked into Quaile's office. She looked at him in disgust and slowly turned around in a complete circle in front of his desk.

"Hi, Laura," said Quaile, sounding friendly. "You look fine. There's no need for you to do this anymore. Your attire is completely appropriate now."

Laura didn't comment and turned to leave.

"Where is Corporal Taggart this morning?" asked Quaile. "He hasn't been excused from this."

"He's taking the day off," replied Laura.

"I haven't signed a leave form for him! Tell him to get in here!"

"I'm sorry, did you think I meant he was on annual leave?" asked Laura innocently. "He called in sick. Would you like him to bring a note from his wife? She's a doctor."

"I want his desk cleaned out before the end of the day," said Quaile. His tone with Laura was no longer friendly.

"Sure, Quaile, I'll do that," replied Laura.

"It's Staff! You will refer to me as *Staff* — and do so in a respectful tone!"

Laura placed the palms of her hands on his desk and leaned over so that her face was close to Quaile's. He instinctively pushed himself back in his chair.

"When it comes to human qualities, you are a very small man," she said. "They should never give power to a small man."

The blood rushed to Quaile's face as he tried to think of an appropriate response.

Laura turned and walked to the door. Just before she left she said, "And another thing, Quaile. I don't respect you enough to call you by anything else … except *asshole!*"

Later that afternoon, Laura sat in a car parked close to the Russians' apartment. She had a shoebox on her lap and carefully looked at the contents. Believing she had control of her emotions, she picked up her cellphone and called Jack.

"I've been sitting on the Russians since nine o'clock this morning," she said. "They haven't left their apartment all day. I saw lights come on earlier, so I know they're home."

"What about Commercial Crime? Quaile will have your ass if he knows you're still working on the Russians."

"Yeah … Quaile. I saw him this morning. I definitely felt vibes that he doesn't like me. I bet I'm next on the chopping block."

"Why? What did he say to you?"

"Nothing, really. It was just the look on his face when I left his office this morning. Call it woman's intuition. I sensed that he doesn't like me."

"Laura, you promised," said Jack.

"I know what I promised," she said evenly. "We're close to nailing these two. Don't worry, we'll get them before he can push me out the door."

"Just don't do anything to jeopardize your career," replied Jack.

"You once told me that you had to be able to look at your own face in the mirror when you shaved. I don't shave, but I do put on makeup. I have to be able to look at myself as well."

"Your record is exemplary. Clean. Don't go and …"

"Which is why it will take time for Staff *Pendejo* to kick me out. Speaking of which, he wasn't going to authorize leave for you this morning, so I told him you had called in sick."

"Thanks. I spoke with my new boss on Traffic Services and asked to take next week off. He said it wasn't a problem and I could back-date the paperwork when I arrived. Sounds like a nice guy. His name is Mike Hewett."

"Anyone would be better than Quaile."

"Now my week is clear to help you. After what has happened, I thought we should take this weekend off to clear our heads. Then meet with Pasquali on Monday and do the UC on Giang."

"Good, that's what I thought, too. Besides, it will be better to let Giang stew about it. We won't look so anxious."

"Set it up with Pasquali for around noon. I'll call you Sunday night."

"Jack … there's another reason I called. I … Oh, man," she said, as her voice wavered.

"What is it? … Laura?"

Jack heard her sigh, and she said, "I cleaned out your desk for you. I've got a shoebox here with your stuff. Coffee mug, pictures of Natasha, your niece and nephew, your little buddy Charlie taking his first step …" She paused as her voice cracked and she swallowed and continued. "You know, stuff like that. I was going to drop it off for you on my way home tonight."

"Oh ..." Jack paused as the feeling struck home. *Seven years of my life bundled into a shoebox.*

"Maybe I shouldn't have done this without asking," said Laura, sensing his pain. "I just didn't want the asshole gloating around watching you do it."

"I was going to come in and do that this weekend. Thanks, though. I really appreciate it. It would have been tough for me."

"I have to go," she replied.

Jack heard her crying before she fumbled to shut her phone off.

It was late Friday afternoon when Isaac waved for Connie Crane to come in and take a seat in front of his desk.

"I hope I'm not interfering with your schedule, Corporal," said Isaac, "but I just called Staff Otto and he said you were in the building and would be the best person to bring me up to date."

"Yes, sir. Randy called and told me. We still have no idea as to the child's identity, but our investigation is progressing. Lab results indicate she had close to two hundred times the normal level of dioxin in her blood. This, combined with a birth defect of an extra thumb and other factors, indicates that, in all likelihood, she is of Vietnamese heritage. Not only that, but it would indicate that she is from an area that has been heavily contaminated with Agent Orange. My guess is she was originally from the central part of Vietnam, in the area the Americans referred to as the DMZ during the American–Vietnamese conflict."

"The demilitarized zone," said Isaac.

"Yes, sir. That's it."

"An extra digit. Surely the Vietnamese must be able to identify her?"

"We've checked. As abnormal as that would be here, it is common over there. Many children are still being born with such defects. Others with no limbs. It's a result of all the defoliant the Americans dropped back in the late 1960s and early '70s."

"So where does that leave us?"

"Locally, we're tracking down sexual sadists: people who have a history of lighting pets on fire and the like. But as I'm sure you know, there are easily over a thousand in our area who are on the National Sex Offender Registry and likely that many more that we are not aware of."

"Learning the identity of this child would be a significant step," said Isaac.

"Sir, we are trying. I've made inquiries with the local Vietnamese community. Some are more than willing to help, but others are either suspicious or afraid of the police."

"Then step up the pressure on the Vietnamese police. An extra thumb, even if it is common over there — a child is missing. They should be able to narrow the list down. There can't be that many children who emigrated here from Vietnam who would match this profile. Check with Immigration. I'll call our embassy in Hanoi if you like, and help get things moving over there."

"Sir, that has already been done. I suspect the real problem is that the child was likely smuggled into Canada."

"Smuggled?" Isaac's mind returned to a conversation he had with Quaile.

"The police over there are being very cooperative," continued Connie. "But the problem they face is that people are not overly willing to come forward. The Vietnamese government is a communist regime and everyone knows they do not take kindly to their citizens being smuggled out."

Connie stared at Isaac but he remained pensive and quiet.

"Sir," she said, "I don't mean to sound pessimistic, but we're trying to identify a kid that nobody has even reported missing. We're looking through stacks of files on perverts that ... well, it's a little like looking for that proverbial needle in a haystack."

Isaac stared intently ahead and Connie had the feeling that he was only half listening.

"Believe me," she continued. "I want to catch this sick ..." Connie paused, glancing at the Bible on Isaac's desk, and continued, "this sick person. Whoever did this ... well, the profile indicates he'll do it again. This case is a priority for our whole office. We won't rest until —"

"Have you checked with Intelligence?" asked Isaac.

Connie sat back in her chair. "Ah ... no, sir. We're not looking at this as organized crime. The profile indicates a person acting alone. Probably single, keeps to ..."

Isaac raised his hand, signalling for Connie to stop and said, "Check with Intelligence. Corporal Taggart was working on a file involving human smuggling. Constable Secord was assisting him. The main culprits are Russian, but I believe it also involved local Vietnamese criminals."

"I wasn't aware of that, sir. I'll go to their office and talk with Jack immediately."

"Um ... I spoke with Staff Quaile this morning," said Isaac. "He indicated that Corporal Taggart was home with the flu."

"I know Jack, sir. He's dedicated. He won't mind if I call him."

Isaac shook his head and said, "No, there's a bit of a ... situation ... with Corporal Taggart at the moment. He's been transferred and is no longer with Intelligence."

"I wasn't aware of that, sir."

"It only happened yesterday."

Isaac was about to suggest that Connie speak with Constable Secord, but he remembered that she was the reason Quaile called him this morning and thought better of it. *At least for now.*

Later that night, Isaac sat alone in his den, holding the picture of his daughter in his hand when Sarah entered the room. He quickly put the picture down.

"Sorry," he said. "I'll be right out. Didn't mean to abandon you for the evening. Just needed a few minutes to think some things out."

"A few minutes?" said Sarah. "Honey, you've been in here for two hours, ever since dinner."

"Has it been that long?" he asked, genuinely surprised.

Sarah walked over and stood behind him and bent over, wrapping her arms around the front of his chest. "She was beautiful, wasn't she?" said Sarah, looking at the picture on the desk. "I miss her, too."

Isaac nodded, but didn't speak.

"Are you going to talk to me about it?" asked Sarah.

"About what?"

"About why you've hardly spoken a word to me ever since Aggi and Leon were here for dinner. Now tonight, it's worse. Something happened today, didn't it?"

Isaac swivelled his chair around, wrapping his arm around Sarah and sitting her on his lap. "You would have made a great detective," he said.

"Doesn't take much detective work to figure you out," she said. "Not after thirty years of marriage. You've only acted this way once before, when ..." she didn't finish, but glanced at the picture and back at her husband's face.

"I'm sorry," he said.

"Can't you talk to me about it?"

Isaac took a deep breath and slowly let the air out before replying, "I'm troubled over a homicide case."

"The one Aggi told you about?"

Isaac nodded.

"You've encountered horrific cases before."

"I know, but now, after losing Norah, it bothers me more."

"Now you know what some other parent feels like after losing a child."

Isaac nodded.

"We've had to learn to accept it. The pain never goes away … but time makes it more bearable."

Isaac looked into his wife's eyes. *No parent could ever accept or understand what this little girl went through.*

"You're worried that you won't be able to solve the case?" asked Sarah.

Isaac nodded, but his mind was elsewhere. *Lord, surely you can show no mercy for whoever did this?*

"Well, as you always said … you just pick the best person for the job and let them do it. What else can you do?"

Her words echoed and replayed themselves in Isaac's head.

If I were a criminal … a child molester … who would be the last person I would ever want on my trail?

"What is it, dear?"

"I think you've given me a message," replied Isaac.

A few minutes later, Isaac kissed his wife goodbye at the door.

"I should come with you," she said.

Isaac shook his head and left by himself. It was the first

time outside of a normal religious event that he had gone to church in the evening.

It was also the first time that he felt justified in asking for forgiveness.

chapter twenty-two

It was seven o'clock Saturday morning and Jack lay in bed, staring up at the ceiling while Natasha slept soundly with her head on his chest. He didn't know if it was the headache that awakened him, or the fact that his tongue felt thick and sticky in his mouth. He also had the urge to drink a litre of water. That would awaken Natasha, so he lay there as his brain regressed on his own life … and what had gone wrong.

A knock on their apartment door startled him.

Natasha's eyes flickered and she said, "Who is that?" She looked at their bedroom clock and added, "At this hour! Damn it, I feel ill. You got me drunk!"

"Coming!" yelled Jack as he put on his bathrobe and dropped his 9mm into the pocket.

He could only find one slipper, so he left it and padded barefoot to the door and stood to one side, gripping the 9mm in his pocket before waving his other hand across the peephole.

No shots … good sign. He squinted into the peephole.

"Jesus!" he said aloud, stepping back while releasing the grip on his gun.

"Who is it, honey?" asked Natasha.

Jack cast a glance at Natasha, who had slipped on her bathrobe and appeared behind him. He didn't reply as he quickly opened the door.

Natasha had never seen the man before.

"Do you mind if I come in?" the man asked.

"Are you executing a warrant?" asked Jack, while looking out in the hall to see who else was there.

Natasha thought her husband was joking. He wasn't.

The man seemed taken back by the comment, but smiled and said, "No. It's not that kind of a visit. I came here to ask for your help."

Jack nodded and motioned for the man to enter before closing the door behind him.

"I'm sorry to awaken you at this time of the morning," the man said, looking at Natasha.

"And you are …?" she asked.

"Excuse me. My name is Jacob Isaac," he said, offering his hand. "I, uh, work with Jack."

Natasha shook his hand and asked, "Are you on Highway Patrol?"

The question caught Isaac off guard, but he grinned and replied, "Not anymore. Years ago, yes. Only for a short time."

"Didn't write enough tickets?" asked Natasha. She turned to Jack and said, "That's the way for you to get out of there. Don't write any tickets and the ol' man, as you call him, will transfer you back."

"Honey," said Jack. "This is the … uh, Assistant Commissioner Isaac. He's the top boss."

"Oh," said Natasha as her cheeks developed a crimson glow. "I'm really sorry. I didn't mean to …"

Isaac chuckled and looked at Natasha and said, "I am an old man ... but I would really prefer it if you called me Jacob."

Natasha looked at Jack and said, "I think I'll take a shower."

Minutes later, Isaac sat at the kitchen table while Jack made coffee. He eyed Isaac curiously. *Must be something pretty damn serious for him to come here — let alone on a Saturday at this time of the morning.*

"It is something serious," said Isaac, reading his thoughts. "I would like to delay your transfer," said Isaac.

"For a few years?" asked Jack, hopefully.

"No. Just temporarily. I would like you to complete your investigation on the Russians. Particularly in regard to their smuggling operation."

"Staff Quaile felt it wasn't worthy of our attention. I don't think he would appreciate me coming back."

"I've already spoken with Staff Quaile this morning," replied Isaac. "He assures me he is in complete agreement with this ... temporary extension."

Yeah, I bet. "I take it something has happened?"

Isaac nodded and the sorrow he felt showed in his eyes. "An unidentified Vietnamese girl between the ages of ten and fourteen was sexually abused and murdered. Corporal Crane is the lead investigator and thinks she may have been smuggled into the country. Would you be willing to help?"

"A young girl sexually molested and killed?" said Jack, vehemently. "You bet I'm willing to help."

If Isaac had any qualms about Jack's initiative at completing this temporary assignment, he didn't now, after hearing the tone of his voice.

"I believe Corporal Crane is currently working on the case at this moment," said Isaac.

"I'll call her and start work immediately," replied Jack.

"Good. Somehow I believed you would," he said, standing up. "Please apologize to your wife for me again. I realize it is early."

Jack was seeing Isaac out the door when Isaac turned and asked, "Do you believe in God?"

Jack was taken back but remembered his exclamation when he first saw Isaac at his door. "I'm sorry about that," he replied.

"About what?"

"That I said *Jesus* when I first saw you this morning. I just wasn't expecting it."

Isaac smiled to himself. *I'm not Jesus … maybe just a servant.* He looked at Jack and said, "I would have buzzed, but someone was just leaving so I entered. That is not why I asked. You don't need to answer if it makes you uncomfortable."

Jack stared at Isaac momentarily and said, "Both Natasha and I are atheists. Why?"

"Because I think He believes in you."

Two hours later, Jack and Laura sat in the I-HIT office and listened to Connie as she updated them on the nature of the file and the steps they had taken to date.

Jack gave Connie a brief account of their investigation into the Russians who were smuggling women to use as prostitutes for the Trâns at the Asian Touch and Orient Pleasure massage parlours.

He outlined the Trân brothers' criminal history and how the one called Đức headed a vicious gang of approximately fifty thugs. He also told Connie about the trip to Costa Rica, but did not tell her about the added excursion to Cuba.

"What do you think?" asked Connie. "Is there a connection?"

"The pathologist thinks the child was being tortured over a period of at least three or four months," noted Jack.

"That's according to the various bone fractures," replied Connie.

Jack looked at Laura, but didn't speak.

"Come on, you guys," said Connie. "Do you know something?"

"I've got a Vietnamese friend," said Jack, "who was smuggled by boat into Canada about four months ago by the Russians."

"That fits!" said Connie. "Who's your friend? I want to talk to her."

"Confidential informant," said Jack. "The same person who confirmed that the Russians were in Hanoi and that they looked at the girls before they boarded the boat."

"Didn't you submit a report on what your CI told you?" asked Connie. "I never read anything of that nature."

"Quaile wouldn't allow us to work on the Russians, let alone the Vietnamese, so I've never put specific reports in on the CI. I just found this out last week. The CI is someone I've been developing on my own. I've also done a bit of UC work on another character by the name of Giang who is a Vietnamese drug dealer and works for Đức."

"UC?" asked Connie. "Are you buying drugs from him?"

"Not yet. I've been doing this out of my own pocket."

"How much you out of pocket?" asked Randy, who had been standing behind Jack and listening.

Jack turned in his seat, unaware that Connie's boss had been listening.

"Well, counting drinks for the drug dealer and his friends, plus a hundred just to talk to my CI, I'm out about two hundred and fifty. It's no big deal."

Randy nodded and said, "Come into my office before

you leave and I'll give you five hundred dollars. Consider it payment to a confidential informant. A receipt from your CI isn't necessary the first time. If you need money, overtime approved, rentals, travel, anything … forget about Quaile. You talk to me. We're running this show. Understood?"

Jack smiled and said, "Understood. Do you think when it's over you could use an extra corporal on your section?"

"And constable," added Laura.

"Have you looked at the photos of the vic'?" asked Randy, curiously.

Jack and Laura shook their heads to indicate they hadn't.

Connie passed a large brown manila envelope over to them and Jack took the photos out. The picture on top was an alley, after which the pictures progressed to the Dumpster and the torn garbage bag with the child's face staring up. More pictures showed the child's body after being removed from the garbage bag.

"Still interested in coming over?" asked Randy.

"I feel nauseated," said Laura, pushing the photos away.

"Likewise," admitted Jack. "Also makes me determined to want to find out who did this to her."

"I'd love to have the both of you in here," said Randy. "We have serious stuff sitting on the back burners that we just can't get to. More stuff is arriving every day. Connie told me about your transfer yesterday afternoon, Jack. I'm sorry. I called Staffing immediately to see if I could get you in here. I was told to forget it. There was no changing it."

Jack picked up a picture of just the victim's face and turned to Connie and asked, "Do you have a smaller version of this one that I can have?"

"To show your CI?"

Jack nodded.

"I can scan it down to wallet size if you like," said Connie.

"That would be even better."

"The Orient Pleasure open on Saturdays?" asked Randy.

Jack nodded. "Seven days a week, three-sixty-five."

"Let me know immediately after you've shown the picture," said Randy, before walking back toward his office.

Jack looked at Connie while gesturing with his thumb toward Randy. "You're lucky, you know."

"You're telling me," said Connie. "He's not afraid to come out and work either. Surveillance, take-downs, you name it. He's the best boss I've ever had — even if he does make me drink Scotch."

It was one o'clock when Jack entered the Orient Pleasure. He had forgotten that Đức spent his lunch hour there and they passed each other in the doorway as Đức was leaving. Đức looked up at him and smirked before continuing on his way.

Jack glanced after him. *I want so bad to choke your skinny little neck and bash your head into the floor until you talk ...*

"Oh, you come back, big guy," said Cường. "You like Jade, yes?"

Jade sat on the edge of the bed with Jack. "I glad you come," she said. "I hear Mister Đức tell Cường that more girls come in six week. I think I go to United States when that boat come."

"Why do you think that?" asked Jack.

"Girls on next boat not so old like me."

"You're what, nineteen?"

"Some men like girls not so old like me," said Jade. "I go to United States and you put Mister Đức in jail and I no be sent back to Vietnam."

"Jade, this life ... I have another way, but first, I need to ask you to look at a picture of a girl's face."

"Okay, Jack. Show me picture."

"It's not easy to look at. It's a young girl. She was tortured … blinded in one eye. I need you to take a good look … she may not be easy to recognize," added Jack, as he handed her the picture.

Jade gasped, dropping the picture on the floor as she put her hands to the sides of her face and commenced rocking back and forth on the bed.

Jack picked up the picture and said, "You know her!"

"No," replied Jade. "Can no be. Maybe make mistake. Picture not Hằng."

"Hằng?" replied Jack. "Who is Hằng?"

"She have two thumb, one hand?" whispered Jade, lowering her hands from her face.

"Yes."

Jade uttered a sound like a wounded kitten and the tears flowed down her face. "Her name Hằng," she said, choking out the words. "Who do that to Hằng?"

Before Jack could answer, Jade started crying and he pulled her close to his chest and held her. He heard a Vietnamese woman holler something from the next room, but Cường hollered back in Vietnamese and the woman giggled and then was quiet.

It took ten minutes before Jade quit crying enough to speak. "Hằng on boat with me, but not same hole on boat. Everybody on boat older than Hằng. Me … Hằng … we good friend. Like sister. She go to United States and live with American family. That all I know."

"That's all you know? What about her last name? Parents?"

"Smuggler tell us no talk about our name or family," cried Jade. "They say if police catched someone … it better not know.

They say they have people with us on boat who tell if someone talk too much. That person have to swim back to Vietnam."

"So there is nothing else you know?"

"Hằng telled me her mother from Dong Ha. Much Agent Orange. That why Hằng have two thumb. But how Hằng talk … I don't know … I think she live in Saigon."

"You mean Ho Chi Minh City."

"Communist from North say that. We still say Saigon. I see Hằng when father bring her to smuggler before we leave Hanoi. He ride bicycle, so maybe Hằng no live in Saigon. Hằng and father meet smuggler in Ba Dinh district of Hanoi."

Jack asked Jade a barrage of questions, but she had little else of value to offer and became more upset with herself for not knowing. Eventually he asked, "Would you like out of this place now?"

Jade trembled at the prospect and said, "My family in Nha Trang. They …"

"They will be okay," said Jack. "I have a plan where you could leave and they would not think you ran away. We will talk about that in a minute."

"Where I go? Where I sleep? Food … money?"

"I have a friend. Her name is Holly and her husband died last year. She has two small children. A five-year-old named Jenny. She has a boy named Charlie, who just turned two this month. Charlie is unable to walk. Holly has … some money. She is looking for a live-in nanny."

"Live-in nanny?"

"A woman to live with her in her house and help her look after her children. I've already talked to her. She will pay you enough that you can still send money home."

"No more men fuck me?"

"No more working in this … this rape factory," said Jack bitterly. "In time, I would be willing to testify at an immigration hearing for you. With how you have helped, along with the danger for you and your family if you were to return, I think we could work something out. Maybe for everybody."

Jade started crying again and buried her face in Jack's chest. "I like to do that, Jack," she sobbed. "I work hard with kids. No more pretend smile and happy so men fuck me."

chapter twenty-three

Jack left the Orient Pleasure and walked a block away before Laura picked him up. He told her what he had learned as they drove back to the I-HIT office.

"So the Russians are directly involved with the victim!" said Laura, making no effort to hide her anger.

"The victim has a name now," said Jack. "It is Hằng."

Laura knew what Jack was getting at. They were no longer dealing with just another unknown or a statistic. Putting a name to the victim made it personal. A lot more personal.

"The Russians brought her here," continued Jack. "But who she was passed on to is anybody's guess."

"Probably Đức or one of his brothers …"

"Possibly. One of them could have sold her to someone else or maybe it's someone else the Russians know."

"She was supposed to go to the States."

"I know."

"So how did she end up in a Dumpster in Surrey?"

"We know she has a father. Maybe living in Hanoi. Speaking of which, the Russians are arriving there next Wednesday."

"We've got to go, too."

"Definitely. With Randy, I bet that won't be a problem."

"So in the meantime, we pass this on to the Vietnamese police. Maybe get Connie to dig up phone tolls from all the businesses and see if she can match them to any perverts."

"I don't even want to think how many that will be … or how long it will take," replied Jack.

"Not much else for us to do until then, other than get permission to go to Hanoi," said Laura.

"There is another thing that needs to be looked after."

Laura waited for a moment before asking, "What?"

"In regard to the young woman I just talked with. I promised her I would get her out by tomorrow."

"Tomorrow!"

"She's really upset. I wish I could do it today."

"How? Without endangering her family … or her? Can't it wait?"

"No. It has to be tomorrow. The Russians arrive in Hanoi on Wednesday. We should be in Hanoi a day ahead to make sure everything is arranged. With the time difference, we have to leave here on Monday."

"What's your plan?"

"It's sort of … a delicate matter. Just between the two of us."

Oh, man …

It was late that same afternoon when Laura and Connie sat together in a car parked near Lucky Lucy's. A team from Drug Section was also on surveillance on nearby streets and confirmed Jack's movements up until he opened the door and stepped inside the bar. After that he was on his own.

"You're lucky you and Jack gaffed a trip to Vietnam," said Connie. "I've always wanted to go there."

"Why doesn't Randy send you, too?" asked Laura.

"It's not him. Court. I'm starting a three-month murder trial on Monday."

"I've done a bit of foreign travel," said Laura. "Not always as glamorous as it seems."

"Yeah, I heard you were in Colombia last year."

Laura smiled and said, "Believe me, that was no picnic, either. Foreign travel isn't as much fun as everyone thinks. Between time zones, work, and jet lag, you don't usually get to see much. The taxpayer's dollar doesn't allow for much sightseeing."

"Speaking of dollars," said Connie. "I'm still a little confused. How does Jack scoring a kilo of cocaine from this Giang character really help our investigation?"

"It might get him an introduction to Đức," replied Laura. "Jack thinks he might be dealing heroin as well as being a pimp."

"Even if he does, that is a far leap to having Đức tell him if he knows anything about Hằng."

Laura eyed Connie casually. *She's right … but how do I get her off this topic and to quit thinking about it? I can't tell her what Jack is really up to with Giang …*

"Jack is pretty persuasive," added Laura. "You'd be surprised how convincing he can be."

"He must be, to convince Randy."

"I suspect Isaac approved it personally," continued Laura. "He must have, I've never seen approval granted this fast before."

"So what are you worrying about? We've got nothing to lose."

"Nothing to lose! How about our budget? We'll be down by thousands of dollars to buy the dope, which in all likelihood, will only end up with a low-life like Giang on the hook. You were on Drugs, you know how it works. Giang will spend so little time in jail that it will be worth it for him, especially if he gets to keep the money."

"It's not your money," said Laura, pretending to sound irritated.

"Comes out of our budget and that affects other investigations."

"Ten to one says you're craving lots of chocolate right now."

"Laura! For your information, I am not having my period."

"Sorry. Actually it's me who wouldn't mind a chocolate bar right now."

"Yeah? Come to think of it, that would be good. I deserve one. I've been working out lately, have I told you that?"

Laura smiled.

Jack sat at a corner table with Giang and negotiated the purchase.

"Tonight," said Giang. "You come back here at nine o'clock."

"Tonight? Here? Not likely!"

"Why? I show you the stuff and you can go get the money."

Jack shook his head and said, "Someone already tried to rip me here. This is your turf and I've never done business with you before."

"How do you want to do it?"

Jack chuckled and said, "Well, I live out in Surrey, but

you probably don't want to go out there either. Maybe some other …"

"No, you want Surrey," said Giang quickly. "That's fine with me."

Jack feigned surprise and said, "Okay, good. Except not tonight. I want it light out, so I can see. I'm willing to meet you in an alley somewhere. You come alone in a car and I'll walk up and meet you. I don't care if you have a piece. You can point it right at me. Once I see the dope, give me a minute to grab the cash from where I'll have stashed it and then we're done."

"That's okay with me," replied Giang. "I was in Surrey a long time ago. Played pool someplace. I think the name of the place was Billiard Bill's."

"I've seen that place," replied Jack. "It's on the second floor of some building."

Giang nodded.

"How about the alley behind it at noon?" suggested Jack.

Giang forced himself not to smile. He nodded and shook hands with Jack.

"One more thing," said Jack. "Because I don't really know you yet, I want it done in two trips."

"Two trips?"

"Yeah, just to be on the safe side. I want to buy half a kilo from you and make sure everything is okay. If it is, in ten minutes or so, I return with the rest of the money for the other half."

Giang smiled and said, "That's okay. It is good to be careful."

"He's out," crackled the radio as Jack left Lucky Lucy's.

Laura grabbed the microphone and replied, "Copy that."

"Just getting in his wheels," the voice continued. "Gave

me the thumbs up."

"Good," replied Laura. "See you back at I-HIT."

An hour later, Jack met with all the investigators and gave a debriefing.

"It went well," he said. "Giang wants to do it at noon tomorrow. He picked a place out in Surrey. It's …"

"The Orient Pleasure?" said Connie.

"Close," replied Jack. "A block away in an alley behind a pool hall. He will come alone in his car and I'll approach on foot. He is willing to let me examine the kilo before seeing the money. I think I'll just take the money with me. He won't be expecting me to have it. We'll do the deal on the spot and it's finished."

"Would be nice to follow him and see what he does with the money," said one of the narcs.

"No," said Jack. "He is really paranoid. This isn't just a dope deal. It's a murder investigation. I don't want to take any chances on blowing this. If Giang gets wise, I'll never meet Đức."

"You're the guy sticking your neck out," said Randy. "It's your call on that."

"If it goes as planned," said Jack, "You'll see me stash the dope in the trunk of my car. Then we all meet back here."

"How long before you make contact again?" asked the narc.

"Give him a week to cool down let him think I'm putting the stuff out. I don't want to do anything that would make him suspicious."

"That will work out," said Connie. "You're taking off to 'Nam on Monday. By the time you come back, it will be just right."

"I want the Russians," said Jack. "They're the ones ultimately behind all this. With any luck, you'll identify the pervert before we even come back. With evidence on the Russians, we'll be able to take down the whole damned lot!"

At twelve-thirty Sunday afternoon, Jack walked toward the red GTO as it pulled up and parked in the alley behind Billiard Bill's. He approached the driver's side and Giang wound down the window.

"Half an hour late," commented Jack.

Giang shrugged, his right hand holding a pistol that rested on his lap. "Accident on the Port Mann Bridge. Down to one lane," he said.

Giang reached under his seat with his other hand and passed Jack a white plastic bag. "Take a look," he said. "Two baggies. Each half a key, just like you wanted."

Jack peered in the plastic bag and saw two clear bags of sparkling white powder. "This better not be baking soda," he said.

Giang grinned and said, "No, go ahead. Test it if you want."

Jack shook his head and said, "It looks good."

"Then go get the bread," said Giang.

Jack smiled and opened his jacket to reveal a paper bag shoved in the inside pocket of his coat. "Got half of it right here," he said, passing the bag to Giang.

Giang smiled as he looked inside at the money. "Thought you were going to stash it until you saw the coke?"

"If you were setting me up for a rip, you would think I didn't have it on me. You'd also bullshit and say you wanted me to go get the money before showing me any coke."

Giang nodded and said, "You know this business."

"I like staying above ground," replied Jack, as he removed one of the clear plastic bags and put it inside his jacket pocket. He gave the rest of the cocaine back to Giang and said, "Now, give me about ten minutes or so, and I'll come back with the rest."

A minute later, Jack put the half kilo of cocaine in the trunk of his car before giving the thumbs-up sign for the surveillance team to meet him back at the I-HIT office.

It was a quarter to one when Jack walked inside the Orient Pleasure and approached Đức, who was behind the counter.

"Hey, you!" said Jack. "Where is Giang?"

"He's not here. Who are you?" asked Đức.

"You obviously work for him," said Jack. "Tell him I've changed my mind. I want to purchase two girls for my parlour in Alberta now. Not just one."

"What are you talking about?" demanded Đức.

"I bought the one from him … what's her name? Jade? Now I want … oh, never mind," he said, glancing at his watch. "He told me to meet him in the alley behind Billiard Bill's. I was just hoping to catch him before he left. I'll tell him myself."

Jack left the premises as Đức hurried to the rooms at the rear.

"Where is Jade?" screamed Đức, at the young woman in the room next to where Jade worked.

"She left an hour ago. She said Giang was going to buy her lunch."

Jack stood in the alley and paid Giang for the second half of the cocaine. He was about to make some idle conversation, but the sound of voices and running feet coming down a stairwell told him it was time to leave.

chapter twenty-four

Jack walked into the I-HIT office and placed the two bags of cocaine on top of a desk.

"Mind if I sit here to write my notes?" he asked Connie.

"No, go ahead," she replied, glancing at her watch. "What took you so long? Stop for gas on the way back? We were getting worried."

"No, sorry," replied Jack. "I just took the long way. Wanted to make sure I wasn't being followed."

"Everything go okay?" asked Laura.

Jack gestured to the kilo on the desk and said, "Smooth as silk. Giang trusts me now. I don't think it will be a problem to get him to introduce me to Đức."

"Yeah," replied Connie. "Then figure out how the hell you bring up the subject of Hằng without making him suspicious."

"I'll think of something," replied Jack. "Now, please give me an hour or two of peace while I make my notes."

An hour later, Jack was still writing when Randy Otto

came out of his office and said he received a message from some uniform members that they wanted Homicide to attend a car fire in an industrial area.

"An off-duty fireman was driving past and saw the smoke," said Randy. "He had an extinguisher in his car and put the flames out before things got too badly burned. Partial crispy critter slumped over in the passenger side. Looks like knife wounds to his throat and face. The fire was started less than fifteen minutes ago, so let's get on it."

Connie started to get up but Randy said, "Connie, you've got too much to do and still have a trial to prepare for. Wells, you take the lead on this."

"What kind of car was it?" asked Jack, glancing up from the notes he was writing.

Randy picked up a portable radio off a desk and said, "I'll find out." He radioed and asked the officers at the scene.

"Red Pontiac GTO," came the reply.

"Giang's car!" said Connie, looking at Jack for a response.

Silence descended over the I-HIT office as everyone turned to look at Jack.

After several long seconds ticked by, Randy said, "How did you piece that together, Jack? What made you ask what type of car it was?"

Jack shrugged and said, "An hour ago I handed Giang more money than most of the punks he hangs out with would see in a lifetime. If Giang is the crispy critter … I'm guessing he doesn't have the money now."

"You know," said Laura, "he did do the deal in the alley behind Billiard Bill's. A lot of the gang who work for Đức hang out there. Wouldn't take much for someone to look out a window from above and see the deal go down."

"Damn it," said Jack, throwing his pen down on the desk. "If it is him in the car, we just blew a lot of money for nothing."

Connie stared at Jack. *I always did think it was for nothing …*

It was four o'clock when Jack saw Natasha and Jade sitting at a table at the Red Robin restaurant in the Metrotown Mall in Burnaby.

Jade was now wearing slacks and a blouse that was buttoned up to her throat. Her long black hair that once hung halfway to her waist had now been cut to just below her ears.

"Hi, honey," said Jack, before kissing Natasha on the cheek and sitting down beside her. He looked across at Jade and said, "Hi. How are you holding up?"

The stress had brought dark circles to Jade's eyes. "Okay," she replied, with little enthusiasm, before asking what was really on her mind. "Mister Đức, he angry?" she blurted.

"No, not with you. Everything went well. Đức has … received a lot of money from Giang for you."

"He angry with Giang?"

"Don't worry about Giang. The important thing is that you're okay. Đức does not think you ran away and he has received a large amount of cash as compensation."

The relief was evident on Jade's face and she gave a genuine smile for the first time in several months.

"You like?" she asked, gesturing to her clothes.

"I like it very much," replied Jack. He looked at Natasha and said, "I see you got her a haircut. Not a bad idea, although where Holly lives, it wasn't …"

"That was Jade's idea," said Natasha.

"It looks nice," said Jack, smiling at Jade.

"I no have to look pretty for men," replied Jade.

Jack gestured to the shopping bags piled next to Jade

and turned to Natasha and said, "Hey, honey, it looks like you girls have been having fun."

"It has been fun," said Natasha.

"I pay you back, Jack," said Jade. "Much money you honey pay for me."

"No, Jade," said Natasha. "I told you, this is our gift to you."

"No," replied Jade. "Too much. I pay back some day quick. You no worry."

"We'll talk about that later," said Jack. "I've called Holly, the woman you'll be working for. We're to meet her at five. We have to get going."

"In North Van'?" questioned Natasha.

Jack nodded and said, "But she wants to meet me at a place in some strip mall near her house. She said she has a surprise to show me."

"What place?"

"She wouldn't say. She said I would know when I got there."

Minutes later, they placed the shopping bags in Jack's car and Jade sat in the passenger seat while Jack said goodbye to Natasha.

"Did you know she didn't even have any underwear on?" whispered Natasha.

"How would I know that?" replied Jack.

Natasha paused, smiled and said, "Correct answer, Officer."

Jack drove slowly through the strip mall, grinned, and parked the car.

"You see Miss Holly?" asked Jade.

Jack shook his head and said, "No … but she'll be in that

coffee shop over there."

As they approached the coffee shop, Jade said, "It closed. Sign say grand open … something."

"Grand opening, tomorrow," said Jack, as he knocked on the door.

Holly was quick to unlock the door and hugged Jack and beckoned them inside. After Jack introduced Jade, Holly said, "So what do you think? My own place now!"

Jack looked around. The room was spotless and red-and-white checkered tablecloths were already in place. "This looks great," he said.

"I'll have flowers on every table tomorrow morning. What do you think of the name?"

"*The Torn Twenty*," said Jack. "I like it."

Holly gestured to an item on the wall behind the cash register. Jack saw that it was a framed twenty-dollar bill that had been torn in half. The glass held it in place and allowed for a small space between the two halves.

"Why you put money in picture?" asked Jade.

Holly smiled and said, "I used to work for someone in a coffee shop. That was the best tip I ever received," she said, glancing at Jack. "It came in two pieces. It brought me luck. Now I have my own place. Speaking of which, we should get going. I've got a girl babysitting from next door. I said I would be back in time for her to be home for dinner."

A short time later, Holly and Jack watched as Jade sat on the living room floor playing with Charlie and Jenny.

Charlie sat on the floor propped up with his back to the sofa while Jade pretended to drive a small plastic car up his arm and onto his tummy where she said, "Oh, car stuck!"

Charlie squealed and giggled as Jade tickled his stomach.

Linh saw that Pops was about to leave the room and she shook as she crawled naked toward the toilet to wash the urine from her head. The chain rattled on the floor and he looked up.

"You worthless little beast," said Pops, "tonight I have a treat for you. It's not a red-circle day, but here," he said, reaching into the box at the far end of the room.

Linh glanced at the calendar on the wall and back at the box. Her clothes were in that box … along with metal objects that Pops would sometimes clang together while he looked at her, telling her she would have to wait until her first red-circle day to find out what surprises awaited her.

He pulled out a jacket and threw it at her.

Linh put it on. It wasn't her jacket, but it looked familiar — a look of horror crossed her face and she looked up at Pops.

It was the response Pops wanted. He laughed, and moments later Linh heard the passageway door creak shut and she was alone.

She slowly put her hand in the pocket and felt the tissue paper containing the pearl necklace from Ha Long Bay.

chapter twenty-five

At nine o'clock Monday morning, Randy drove Jack and Laura to the Vancouver International Airport.

"What do they use for money over there?" asked Randy.

"The Vietnamese dong," said Jack. "A hundred dollars Canadian is worth approximately 1.5 million dong."

"You're kidding, right?"

"No, dead serious. When I checked with the bank I figured I'd need a wheelbarrow to pack it around," he chuckled. "Apparently they have really large denominations. They also don't allow you to take the dong out of Vietnam, so you don't want to get more than you're going to spend. Banks outside of the country don't carry it, but you can get it at ATMs in Vietnam. I'm also told that the American dollar is widely accepted."

"I'd like to go there someday," said Randy. "Hell of a long flight, though."

"Tell us about it," said Jack. "Leaves at noon and we don't

arrive until ten-thirty tomorrow night. Even with the time difference, it's still twenty-and-a-half hours' flight time."

"We're going to be tired puppies," said Laura.

"At least the Russians will be in the same boat when they fly out tomorrow," said Randy.

"I'm impressed you got permission for us to go this fast," said Jack.

Randy grinned and said, "A lot of phone calls to a lot of people who aren't used to working weekends. It was good to let them know how the rest of us work. What was really nice was being able to tell them to call Isaac direct if there were any problems. There weren't. Funny how that works."

"You'll confirm the Russians do board tomorrow?" asked Jack.

"I'll do it personally. Any changes and I'll let you know. Are you being met at the airport in Hanoi?"

"Yes, the Canadian Consulate arranged for a local to pick us up. I think the title was a Doctor Sơn, from the Interpol desk of the General Department of National Police."

"A doctor?"

"Probably in criminal behaviour. He speaks English."

Randy gave Jack a sideways glance and asked, "Has Quaile had anything to say to you about this?"

"Haven't spoken with him, or seen him since last Wednesday when he sent me to Staffing."

"Good. Consider yourself on loan to our office until this is finished."

"With pleasure."

Isaac called Randy Otto later that morning and Randy updated him on the investigation. When Randy told him about Giang being murdered, Isaac shook his head. *So it begins …*

"This is right after he met with Corporal Taggart?" asked Isaac.

"Yes, sir. It had to have been within the hour."

"And where was Corporal Taggart when Giang was actually murdered?"

"In our office making notes. He certainly wasn't responsible."

No, he never is. It's always a coincidence ...

"We're checking the possibility that Giang may have been responsible for Hằng's death."

With Taggart involved, that would explain why he's dead. Of course, it would just be a coincidence ...

"But it doesn't appear likely," continued Randy. "He doesn't have any previous history of deviation that would fit the profile. Long record for violence, drugs, extortion and the like ... but I don't think he's our man."

"What about Đức or the Russians as viable suspects?" asked Isaac.

"Đức doesn't fit the profile, either. We're not sure about the Russians. Still waiting to hear back on their history, but on the surface, I would say not. I think it is someone they know, however."

"Keep me apprised. If anything happens to the Russians when they arrive in Hanoi, I want to be called, day or night."

"If something happens to the Russians, sir?"

"I meant *with* the Russians," replied Isaac, before hanging up.

It was eleven-thirty Tuesday night before Jack and Laura retrieved their luggage and arrived at the Vietnamese customs counter. The customs agent motioned with his arm and a man quickly came forward and introduced himself as Doctor Sơn.

Doctor Sơn was a short, stocky man and Jack estimated that he was in his mid-fifties. He looked friendly and gave a firm handshake. Soon after, Jack realized that Doctor Sơn was of average height in his country.

"Your name is like the star up in the sky?" asked Laura.

He smiled and said, "No. It is *S-O-N*. In Vietnamese it means 'mountain.' I like it if you just call me Sonny."

Minutes later, they stepped outside the airport to face a cool breeze and a light mist.

"My image of Vietnam was jungle, heat, and humidity," said Laura.

"Down south it is," said Sonny. "Hanoi is much like Vancouver in the winter. Cold and wet."

"You have been to Vancouver?" asked Jack.

"Six years ago. I worked there for two weeks with narcotics investigators to learn how the police work in Canada."

"What did you think?"

"You are fortunate. You have lots of money. Most of us have scooters, old cameras, very few radios ... mostly cellphones. Mostly what we have for listening ... bugs, you call them, is old equipment the Russians gave us during the war with the Americans. You are very lucky. Today, I was able to borrow a car because of your status."

"We have status?" murmured Laura.

Sonny whisked them along their way. Once in Hanoi, Jack and Laura saw that many of the women wore conical hats, suited for rain and sun. Many of the men wore green pith helmets, something else that was left over from past conflicts.

The streets were mostly packed with motor scooters and bicycles. Pedestrians appeared to walk blindly in all directions as they crossed the street. The blare of horns was almost non-stop.

"Aren't these people afraid of being run over?" asked Jack.

Sonny smiled and said, "It is different here. We are a poor country and do not have as many streetlights. It is the driver's responsibility not to hit the pedestrians. It is a good idea to walk slowly when you cross the street and maintain the same speed. Drivers will judge as to which side of you they will pass on."

"Do you get a lot of traffic fatalities here?" asked Laura.

"Oh, yes. Very many."

It was midnight when Sonny checked them into the Hotel Happy Holiday. It was located on what was now a fairly deserted street, a couple of blocks out of the mainstream of traffic. The hotel looked quaint and the lobby was open to the second level where the hotel operated a small restaurant.

"We are on the third floor," said Sonny, pushing the button for the lobby elevator.

After waiting several seconds, Sonny said something to the desk clerk who answered back.

"He says sometimes it gets stuck," said Sonny.

Jack couldn't tell if his tone was apologetic or that of exasperation. "That's okay," he said. "After the flight we've been on, I'd rather walk and get the circulation moving."

When they arrived on the third floor, Jack saw that the portion of the hotel which housed the rooms was built with the middle opened up. It made the place noisier, as did the tile floors, but it also looked picturesque. There was one elevator and one set of stairs on opposite sides of each floor, allowing access up and down to the different levels.

"Laura, you will have this room," said Sonny. "Jack, you will have the room next to her."

Laura put her luggage in her room and went to Jack's room.

"I'll lend you this," said Sonny, passing Jack a cellphone

and business card. "If there is a problem with anything while you are here, please call me."

"Thanks. Much appreciated," replied Jack.

"Tomorrow night when the Russians arrive, they will be staying in the room directly above you," said Sonny, looking at Jack. "I will stay in your room with you. I speak Russian."

"Their room will be bugged?" asked Jack.

"If the equipment decides to work," said Sonny. "I will also have men to follow them wherever they go."

"Great," replied Jack. "I think our faces would stand out in this city."

Sonny smiled and said, "They would. You are both tall ...." he paused and looked at Laura and said, "You, of course, would never be good at following people."

"I'm sorry?" replied Laura, not sure that she heard him correctly.

"You must know that you would not be good for such a duty. You are too beautiful. Men would remember seeing you."

Laura waited until Sonny left and turned to Jack and asked, "Did I just receive a compliment or an insult?"

"I don't know. I'm too tired to think. See you in the morning."

Six hours later, Jack awakened to the echo of people chatting and the noise of tiny rollers on suitcases being dragged across the tiled floors to the elevators. Moments later, he heard the sound of a shower in the room next to him and knew that Laura was up. He met her for breakfast and suggested a walk around the area before noon.

"This is nerve-wracking," muttered Laura, as they crossed various streets. "These scooters and cars are zooming past so close I can touch them."

"The trick is to keep walking at a steady pace," said Jack. "Don't make eye contact with the drivers. I just did and ended up doing a jig while we tried to second guess each …"

"Silk!" shouted Laura. "Tailor-made! Success!"

Laura gestured to a mannequin in a store window wearing a woman's traditional-style Vietnamese dress known as an *áo-dài*. The long gown was tailored to snugly fit the body and two long slits along the side allowed the gown to have free-floating panels in the front and the back. Silk slacks were worn underneath.

Laura was pleased to find that the clerk spoke broken English.

Laura turned to Jack and said, "Can you believe the price? Twenty-two bucks American. This would cost a fortune at home. I like the emerald green dress with white slacks. Do you think Elvis would like it?"

"It'll look great," said Jack.

"Two for twenty dollar each," the clerk told them.

After some discussion with the clerk, Jack ordered a similar outfit for Natasha. "Same figure, only shorter," he said.

Laura whispered in his ear and said, "Tell her to make yours a bit larger through the chest," while indicating her breasts.

"You can explain that to her."

Laura laughed and said, "Tell you what, buy me a conical hat and I will."

Just before noon, they returned to their hotel. As promised, Jack bought Laura a conical hat, along with an extra one for Natasha. The total price for the hats came to two American dollars. As a souvenir for himself, he bought a green pith helmet with a small badge on the front. The badge had a single gold star on a red background to closely match the Vietnamese flag. "How do you like it?" he asked Laura as he modelled the helmet. "Could I pass as a local?"

"Too tall, round eyes, too tall," she retorted.

Sonny arrived at Jack's room on schedule and Laura mentioned that they had been out shopping.

"What do you think?" asked Jack, indicating the green helmet he still wore.

Sonny grinned and said, "Many people use them as rice buckets here, but they are not that good."

"They cook rice in these?" asked Jack.

Sonny chuckled and said, "No, that is what I call motorcycle helmets."

"I've noticed that some helmets have a similar badge on the front with the gold star over an upper background in red and the lower half in blue."

"That badge was special made for when the Communists won the war with the Americans. It was worn by the Northern soldiers when the last push was made to get the Americans out. It is a symbol of reunification between north and south Vietnam."

"Were you in the war?" asked Jack.

Sonny nodded. "I was a teenager and fought for the North, but I also have family in the South. I had an uncle who fought for the South during the war. When the Americans pulled out, he was isolated deep in the Mekong Delta. Later he escaped to Cambodia and four years later made it to America."

"An American citizen now?" asked Jack.

Sonny shook his head, replying, "The Americans told him he was too late. They would not accept him. My uncle went to Canada and became a Canadian citizen. He lives in Vancouver."

"That's good," said Jack.

"The Americans treat you like a lemon," said Sonny.

"How is that?" asked Laura.

"They squeeze you until there is no juice left and then

throw you out," he said, bitterly.

"Tough times back then," said Jack. "Tough decisions being made by bureaucrats who never saw either end of a rifle."

Sonny smiled. "You are right. Now I do not like to talk politics. It is best forgotten. Many American tourists come here now. They are most welcome." He paused and added, "I have found them much friendlier now that I am not shooting at them."

All three laughed and left the hotel to go for lunch to a place that Sonny recommended. They walked through crowded streets and eventually came to a small restaurant where they seated themselves.

Jack pointed to a line on the menu. *Bún bì, thịt nướng, chả giò.* "Strips of grilled pork with noodles?" he asked.

"Yes," replied Sonny. "Your Vietnamese is very good. So is that selection."

"You understand that?" asked Laura in surprise.

"I have a favourite restaurant I go to whenever I'm in Victoria," said Jack. "It's called the Saigon Night. That's number eighteen on their menu. It is what almost everyone orders."

Laura ordered the same selection on Jack's advice and discovered that the meal consisted of a combination of rice vermicelli with shredded strips of grilled pork topped with peanuts and spring rolls filled with shrimp and crab. She also asked for a knife and fork.

"You don't use chopsticks?" asked Jack.

Laura shook her head and said, "I can never seem to master them. I'm afraid I'll end up sticking one up my nose."

"I thought you worked a UC op' in Bangkok?"

"Actually, the Thai are one of the few Asian cultures that don't use chopsticks. They use a fork and a tablespoon. They push the food onto the spoon with the fork and eat it that way. They also tend to order the food on platters for the centre of the table and everyone helps themselves. Very social. Kind of nice, really."

Jack also added several clumps of hot chili paste from a small dish he found amongst the condiments.

"Watch it, Jack," Sonny warned. "Very hot."

Jack nodded and said, "I know. I love this stuff."

Laura found the food to be delicious without the chili paste.

"You both like beer?" asked Sonny. He waited until he received affirmative nods and ordered three bottles of Huda.

Jack picked up the bill when it arrived and discovered that the total was less than twelve American dollars.

They spent the rest of the day sightseeing. Sonny took them to Uncle Ho's Mausoleum and pointed out the Canadian embassy across the street as they approached the mausoleum.

Jack and Laura were warned to look sombre at all times and lower their head to show respect as they entered the mausoleum. Guards with harsh, angry faces ensured that cameras were not taken inside and that people walked single file.

The experience was a reminder to Jack that he was now in a communist country and understood the fear that people developed toward authority.

Beside the mausoleum was a large park with many trees and ponds. Sonny led them down a path to show them where Uncle Ho lived during the war with the Americans.

"I never see any birds," noted Jack.

"People eat them," said Sonny.

"Even the little ones?"

"Yes."

They viewed the small bamboo structure and tiny room with a single bed that had been used by Uncle Ho.

"Did Hô Chi Minh ever marry?"

Sonny quickly glanced around to see who might have

heard the question and said, "Keep your head down. That is not talked about." He saw the bemused look on Jack's face and added, "The official version is no, he never married."

"I guess he was gay," Jack whispered to Laura.

Later that day, Sonny also took them to what was formerly the Hoa Lo Prison. It had been built by the French in 1896 and was home to thousands of Vietnamese who were imprisoned, tortured, and lost their lives.

In 1954 the communist party took over North Vietnam and the building became a state prison. From 1964 to 1973 it also became a prison for captured American pilots who nicknamed it the *Hanoi Hilton*.

In 1993 most of the prison was demolished to make room for commercial property but a small portion of it was preserved for historic value, complete with dungeon-type cells with rows of shackles.

It was depressing, but for Jack and Laura, it was even more so. The shackles were a graphic reminder of a more recent victim who had been chained ... and a reminder of the real reason they had come to Vietnam.

On their way back to the Hotel Happy Holiday, Sonny pointed at a passing motor scooter being ridden by two men. On the back of the scooter was a small cage containing three dogs.

"Look," he said. "Those are dognappers."

"Dognappers?" asked Laura, watching the scooter quickly disappear amongst the traffic.

"Dog meat is considered a delicacy to Koreans. Sometimes to tribes in northern Vietnam also. Men on scooters will drive by and steal dogs."

"In Canada, people on scooters steal women's purses," said Jack.

"Was that really pork we had for lunch?" asked Laura.

Sonny smiled and said, "Yes, you don't have to worry. Dog meat is very expensive. Pork is much cheaper."

Back in Vancouver, Randy passed the taxi containing the two Russians as it entered the perimeter leading to the Vancouver International Airport. He parked his car at the International Departures level and was met inside the doors by Aaron, who was an RCMP officer attached to a special unit at the airport.

At the airport Aaron routinely did surveillance on people as requested by various departments, such as Drug Section. On slower days, he would pick his own targets who looked suspicious, sometimes discovering drug mules or money launderers passing through from city to city or country to country.

Aaron also had the right connections with airline services to obtain information to meet various investigative needs. Aaron didn't look like a policeman and blended into the crowd like any other passenger … except the attaché case he carried also took pictures.

"Not busy today?" asked Randy. "I didn't know whether to call you or not."

"Not a problem," replied Aaron. "You want photos of these guys?"

"May as well."

Moments later Randy saw the taxi arrive and Moustache Pete and Fat Man stepped out.

"These your boys?" asked Aaron.

"That's them."

"You should check with Intelligence. They took close-up pictures of these two just a couple of weeks ago. Man, it really shook them."

"What are you talking about?"

"It's kind of funny, really. I was tailing this guy and didn't know who he was. I didn't find out until later when I scooped his licence plate and showed his picture around the office that he was one of our guys. Staff Sergeant Quaile from Intelligence. He was following these same two guys. Walked right up to them and said, *Hello, comrades,* or something to that effect and took their picture."

"Quaile did that?" said Randy, in disbelief.

"Yeah. These two guys looked so rattled I thought they were going to run out of the airport. I didn't know what the hell was going on, but figure Quaile must have been trying to scare them from taking their flight or something."

"Did you talk to him about it?"

"No, he was gone long before I found out who he was. It was none of my business." Aaron gave a nod toward the two Russians and said, "Here they come. I take it you want to be discreet this time?"

"Definitely," said Randy, through clenched teeth. "And after, I want copies of every picture you took last time they were here."

chapter twenty-six

"It was simply a momentary lack of judgement," said Quaile.

Isaac glowered back at him, pointed to the photos on his desk and yelled, "A momentary lack of judgement! Look at their faces! The only person more shocked is me!"

"Sir, I was following them and was about to take a picture when they turned suddenly and saw me. I considered it a good response. They'd never suspect the police of doing something like that."

"Only if they presumed the police were competent," said Isaac. "This is why the investigation fell flat in Costa Rica! A child was brutally tortured and murdered because of these two men. The same two men you had the gall to tell me weren't worth working on!"

"We didn't know that, then, sir. How was I to know? I believe I made the right decision with the information I had available."

Isaac rested his elbows on his table, clasping his hands together near his chin as he weighed over the scenario that Quaile had just told him. "I'm going to give this some serious thought," he said. "You're dismissed ... for now."

Moustache Pete and Fat Man arrived in their room at the Hotel Happy Holiday as scheduled. Fifteen minutes after their arrival, Sonny took off a set of headphones and turned a dial on a receiver. Both Jack and Laura heard the sound of two men snoring.

"Looks like we weren't the only tired ones," said Laura.

A light knock on Jack's door was answered by Sonny, who spoke quietly to one of his men. He closed the door and turned to Jack and Laura and said, "When they checked in, they asked to be awakened at nine o'clock tomorrow morning."

"It sounds like we can all get some sleep," said Jack.

Sonny dismissed his team after telling them to be back at the hotel by seven in the morning. Laura returned to her own room and Jack and Sonny went to bed while listening to the static noise over the monitor of two men snoring in the room above.

The next day the Russians were awakened on schedule. They took a leisurely breakfast in the hotel while a surveillance team relayed their activities to Sonny, who stayed in the room with Jack and Laura. After eating, Sonny was informed that the Russians had decided to take a dip in the hotel pool.

Jack saw Sonny's face as he wrinkled his nose while talking in Vietnamese over the phone. When he hung up, Jack said, "Let me guess, they both walked to the pool wearing Speedos, black socks, and sandals."

"You speak Vietnamese?" asked Sonny.

Jack and Laura both laughed and Jack said, "No, only a few words ... but we have seen this unfortunate sight before." It was not until mid-afternoon and after the Russians had downed several vodkas on ice while sitting in the hotel restaurant before Jack and Laura received some news of interest.

"They've just met a Vietnamese man," said Sonny. "He arrived in a taxi. They are ordering more drinks."

Minutes later, Sonny found out that the Vietnamese man had flagged the taxi down off the street. "Don't worry," said Sonny. We will find out who he is."

It was early evening when the Russians and their Vietnamese escort left the hotel and crossed a nearby plaza to a restaurant for dinner. After dinner, Sonny reported that the three men had gone to the Thang Long Water Puppet Theatre.

Sonny explained that this theatre was world renowned. He said the puppeteers stood behind bamboo screens in a large pool of water and used bamboo poles to raise puppets out of the water to complete a performance.

Interesting, thought Jack, *but nothing to do with our investigation!*

Following the theatre, the two Russians caught a taxi back to the hotel while the Vietnamese man took a taxi elsewhere.

It was ten o'clock at night when the two Russians arrived in the lobby and checked at the desk for messages. There weren't any.

Sonny put on the headphones as the Russians entered their room. "They are angry," he said. "They expected to receive a message and didn't. Now they are tired and are going to bed — wait they are phoning ... no, they have just asked to be awakened at nine o'clock again."

An hour later, Sonny took off the headphones and turned up the volume to the familiar sound of snoring.

Sonny received a call on his own phone. When he hung up, he said, "Good news for you. The Vietnamese man went to an apartment. We think it is his place because he had a key to the door. His name is known to us. He is the captain of a boat and has been suspected of smuggling drugs in the past."

Jack breathed a sigh of relief. *Much better news than hearing they came for a puppet show.*

Sonny broke off his surveillance team with the order that they be back at the hotel by seven in the morning as usual.

It was after midnight when Jack was awakened from his sleep by the sound of a telephone ringing. It took him a second to realize that the sound was coming over the monitor and not from his own room. Sonny quickly got up and put on the headphones.

Jack quickly put on his pants and ran next door to summon Laura.

The minutes ticked by as Jack and Laura watched Sonny, who was scribbling notes as he listened. "They are arguing," he said. "Both Russians have been talking on the phone. They are angry. They are saying to wait until tomorrow. The man they are talking with ... he is speaking English, but his accent is Vietnamese."

"Maybe the boat captain?" offered Jack.

"No," said Sonny. "The Russians mentioned having met the boat captain on time tonight. He is asking why this person did not meet them earlier." Sonny pressed the earphones closer to his head and said, "The caller said it is the same place as last time and that he would meet them out front."

"Out front of where? Here or the place?" asked Jack.

"I don't know." Sonny muttered something in Vietnamese and ripped off the headphones. Jack didn't need it translated to know that he swore.

"They're on the move?" he asked.

"Yes … and I have no team to follow!"

"You have us," said Jack, grabbing his new helmet. "I'll stoop. Laura —"

"I'll get it," she said.

"Wait," ordered Jack. Above them they could hear the sounds of the Russians' voices. "They're already outside their room," whispered Jack. "Give them a few seconds' head start. If they see us coming out of here at this time of night at the same time as them, the jig will be up."

When the sound of the Russians' voices disappeared from above, Laura grabbed her conical hat and joined Jack and Sonny as they ran down the stairs. The lobby was empty and they hurried out the front doors of the hotel.

A thick mat of black clouds covered the night sky and pieces of garbage were gusting down the street, still wet from an earlier rain. The hotel was well lit, but, within a few metres, the street disappeared into clusters of dark shadows amongst merging streets and alleys.

Sonny ran toward his car, which was parked nearby. "I'll circle the block," he said. "You walk, if you see them, call me on my cell or wave me down."

Seconds later, Jack and Laura saw a taxi nose out of an alley in front of them and they stepped back into the shadows.

"See anything?" asked Jack.

"Not sure."

The taxi sped off down the street and Jack and Laura saw two figures sitting in the back seat.

"Damn it!" said Jack, watching as the taxi put on its turn signal.

Headlights from another car appeared in the alley and Jack and Laura watched.

"Sonny's got 'em," said Laura.

Jack saw Sonny zoom out of the alley without stopping

and speed down the street, turning where the taxi did.

The street was now quiet, void of any human activity except for Jack and Laura.

"That had to be them," said Jack.

"Now what do we do?" asked Laura.

"Back to my room and wait."

They were just about to enter the hotel when Jack shoved Laura up against the wall and pulled her conical hat to one side as he nestled his face into her neck.

"What the …?"

"Shut up. It's them," whispered Jack.

Laura heard the hotel door open and the sound of Fat Man's voice beside her as he spoke angrily in Russian to Moustache Pete.

Laura remained where she was, peeking past the side of Jack's face as the Russians walked past them and stood nearby on the sidewalk. "They're just standing there," she whispered. "Glancing back at us … or maybe the lobby. Looks like they're waiting for someone. What should we do?"

"What kind of perfume are you wearing?" whispered Jack.

"You ass!" whispered Laura. "How could …"

Jack covered his mouth as he sneezed before whispering, "I have allergies to certain cosmetics. Sorry."

"Oh."

"Why do you think I asked?"

"Because you're a man — you know why!"

Jack snickered and said, "You're right … and if I keep standing like this, I'll forget why we're here. Come on, straighten your hat and make a break for the lobby. Just don't look back before we reach the desk."

Jack and Laura hurried inside the lobby and the desk clerk said, "Please don't use the elevator. It's sticking between floors."

Jack had no intention of using the elevator and he took out the cellphone that Sonny had provided him and quickly punched in the numbers. "Busy," he told Laura.

Outside, the Russians were looking down the street and stepped forward as a set of headlights appeared.

Jack hit the redial button again. "Still busy," he sighed. "Sonny's probably trying to get help. Doesn't know he's on the wrong guys."

Jack and Laura watched as a taxi drove up, but the Russians waved for it to continue and stepped back.

"They're waiting for someone to pick them up in a car," observed Jack, heading over to talk with the desk clerk.

"Do you drive a car?" asked Jack.

"No. Motor scooter," he replied.

"Is it at the hotel?"

"The red Honda Helix parked out front," he replied, suspiciously.

"I want to rent it from you."

"No, sorry, I cannot do that."

"I will pay you fifty American dollars."

"Fifty! I don't know … I —"

"That's fifty an hour, I mean."

The clerk smiled. "Here are the keys. Take your time. There is much to see in Hanoi. May I recommend the lounge at the top of the Sheraton? It has a beautiful view of the city at night."

Laura tapped Jack on the shoulder and said, "Their ride just arrived."

As Jack and Laura scrambled onto the scooter, Jack pushed the redial button again and heard the busy tone.

"We're on our own," he shouted to Laura.

Oh, man … Laura wrapped one arm around Jack's waist and, with the other, hung on to her conical hat as Jack gunned the gas and the engine roared to life.

chapter twenty-seven

Jack used all his concentration to dart amongst the tangle of pedestrians and traffic as he followed the car onto a busy thoroughfare through the heart of Hanoi and an area that did not sleep at night.

He skidded to a sideways stop to avoid hitting a woman who was carrying two large baskets balanced on each end of a pole as she crossed the street. The woman uttered harsh words at them in Vietnamese. Seconds later, he was once more weaving, twisting, and turning until he was in a position to keep only a couple of vehicles between him and the car they were following.

Eventually the car left the crowded streets and entered an area where homes, apartments, and businesses were in darkness. Jack slowed, dropping farther behind ... and the farther behind he was the more tense he felt. It was a delicate balancing act. Too close and you are spotted. Too far and you lose them.

The car's brake lights came on and it slowed to a crawl. Jack looked for a place to turn off, but there was none and he knew he would have to drive past. Just as he neared the car it turned into a narrow lane.

Jack continued past the lane and was about to make a turn to come back when Laura said, "I saw the flash of the brake lights in the lane. They may be stopping."

Jack parked the scooter and both he and Laura hurried to the entrance to the lane and peeked around the corner. The street was in complete darkness but they could see the silhouette of a car parked halfway down the lane.

"You going to try Sonny again?" whispered Laura.

Jack looked around and did not see any street signs. "Do you know where we are?" he asked.

"Not a clue."

"Likewise. Come on," said Jack, shutting off the phone. They entered the lane, slinking close to the buildings as they moved toward the car. When they got close, Jack whispered, "That's the car, but nobody is inside."

Laura scribbled the car's licence plate on the inside of her forearm. That way, the information was out of sight and perspiration would not make it illegible later.

Jack glanced around and saw several apartment buildings were crammed into the area where the car was parked.

"Not after all this," lamented Laura. "You don't happen to have a spare street light in your pocket, do you?"

Jack held his breath and listened. *Let me hear a voice … footsteps … the sound of a lock … anything!* His eyes searched the darkness to no avail.

"Let's try the closest apartment building," whispered Laura. "If we hurry, it might not be too late to hear a door or something."

They started toward the apartment as the moon appeared

for the first time that night. Jack felt his pulse quicken and he grabbed Laura by the shoulder. "Over there," he whispered. "Two — no, three people walking."

Laura looked where Jack pointed. She saw the targets briefly outlined in the moonlight just before they disappeared inside another apartment building.

Jack and Laura followed and entered the dilapidated building. It was five stories high and built of cement blocks that had never been painted, inside or out. They heard the sound of the Fat Man's voice muttering in Russian from the stairwell leading up.

They crept up the stairwell after them. The scrape of the men's shoes echoed on the steps from above. Jack saw that the stairwell was open to the corridors, with only a single overhead light giving a dim glow from the middle of each corridor.

Jack motioned for Laura to pause and they heard the sound of the Fat Man panting as he slowly climbed upwards. They allowed a little more space between them before continuing. On the fourth level, they heard the men leave the stairwell and walk down the open corridor.

Seconds later, Jack heard the sound of a knock on a door. He peered around the corner and saw the men being let into an apartment part way down the hall.

"I'm going to give you the cell," he whispered to Laura. "Go back out and try to figure out where we are and call Sonny. Make sure you're far enough away when you do. I don't want anyone hearing an English voice."

Laura nodded and took the phone and started to descend the stairs. Seconds later, she returned and grabbed Jack's sleeve. "Come on, hurry," she said. "Someone is coming up the steps behind us."

Jack and Laura went up another level and listened to the sound of two people approaching from below. Their footsteps indicated that they also headed down the same corridor as the Russians.

Jack and Laura went back down to watch and saw the figures of a woman and a child venturing down the hall. The child pointed to the apartment door that the Russians had entered. The woman bent over and whispered to the child who then scurried back toward the stairwell.

Jack and Laura quickly retreated once more and heard the child running down the stairwell toward the exit before returning to their position to watch.

The woman knocked on the apartment door. It opened a crack and a short conversation in Vietnamese took place. The door closed with the woman remaining in the hall.

Seconds later, the solitude of the apartment building came to an abrupt end. The woman screamed in Vietnamese and the door rattled with the pounding of her fists. Voices shouted out from nearby apartments.

Another explosion of voices came from inside that apartment, with a man yelling in Vietnamese while the Fat Man yelled in Russian. Jack heard Moustache Pete say, "Make that bitch shut up!"

"Fuck you!" yelled the woman in the hall. "Give me Chi … or I'll stand here and yell all night!"

"She sounds like an American!" whispered Laura.

The woman turned and Jack saw her face and said, "She's Caucasian all right. Looks like she's only in her early twenties. Whoever she is, she's liable to get herself killed if she keeps this up."

"Just love foreign travel, don't you?" said Laura.

Jack caught her meaning and replied, "Yeah, especially the part where we're not allowed to carry guns."

The apartment door opened again and another heated exchange took place in Vietnamese between the woman and a man in the apartment. A neighbouring apartment door opened and another man stuck his head out to see the commotion.

Seconds later, Moustache Pete appeared holding a girl by the wrist. He flung her into the hall and stepped back inside, slamming the door shut behind him.

The girl started yelling and Jack guessed she was about eleven or twelve years old. The young woman grabbed her by the wrist and started for the stairwell, but the girl was crying and dragging her feet as she tried to return to the apartment.

The woman ignored her demands and spoke harshly in Vietnamese as she dragged the girl down the hall.

Jack and Laura stepped back before following the woman and girl down the stairwell. They stopped at the exit and watched as the woman argued with her just outside the door. The woman cursed in English, but continued to speak Vietnamese.

"What do you want to do?" asked Laura.

Jack shook his head in wonderment and said, "I don't know who this young lady is, but I think we should talk to her and explain who we are."

"Could blow our whole case if this gets back to the guys upstairs."

"She has guts trying to save this kid. I think we can trust her — let's hope we can do it quietly."

Jack and Laura stepped out onto the sidewalk and Jack took off the green helmet he had been wearing.

The woman and girl quit talking and stared at the new arrivals.

"Excuse me," said Jack quietly. "Does this girl speak any English?"

"Not really," the woman replied," looking at them suspiciously. "Her name is Chi. She only knows the basic manners and to say hello. Who are you?"

"We are both police officers from Canada."

"From Canada!" the woman said in amazement.

"Yes. We are what are sometimes referred to as Mounties. My name is Jack Taggart and this is my partner, Laura Secord."

"I know what the RCMP is," she replied. "I was born in Calgary. My name is Tarah Mulligan."

"You're Canadian!" It was Jack's turn to be amazed. "What the hell are you doing in Hanoi?"

"I was going to ask you the same thing, but first, do you have any identification?" she asked.

Jack stepped closer to discreetly show his badge. Chi knocked Tarah's arm out of the way and saw the badge.

"Công an!" the child gasped.

Jack knew it was Vietnamese for police and put his finger to his lips, but Chi immediately started yelling and broke free and ran back toward the apartment.

"Laura," said Jack. "Grab her and shut her up!"

Laura grabbed her around the waist with one hand and put her other hand over her mouth.

Chi kicked and flailed her arms and started yelling again.

"She bit me!" said Laura.

"Slap a sleeper on her!" ordered Jack.

"We're not allowed to use — Oh, man …"

Laura wrapped an arm around Chi's neck, while using her other arm in a pincer-like move to restrict the flow of blood to the carotid arteries in her neck.

"You sons of bitches!" yelled Tarah. "You're killing her!" she said, making a grab for Laura as the child went limp.

"Jesus, not you too," muttered Jack, moving toward Tarah.

chapter twenty-eight

"What the hell! Put me down!" demanded Tarah.

Jack set Tarah on her feet and she angrily looked around. She was now half a block away from the apartment and on the street around the corner from the lane.

Chi was standing looking at Laura, who was holding her by the hand and saying, "See? Tarah is okay now. She was just taking a nap."

Jack looked at Tarah and said, "I'm sorry. But there are two men in that apartment that we have spent a lot of time trying to catch. They traffic in human flesh ... children," said Jack, pointing to Chi for emphasis. "We've come a long way and can't afford to jeopardize our investigation at this point."

"How long was I out?" asked Tarah, blinking her eyes.

"About ten or fifteen seconds. Are you okay?"

Tarah glared at Jack and asked Chi a question in Vietnamese.

Chi nodded that she was okay.

"Did you have to do that to us?" asked Tarah.

"I'm sorry, but I didn't see any other option. I want to catch these guys. Right now, we still don't have enough evidence to convict them. If they know we're on to them, we lose everything. I really want them to go to jail."

"They should be in jail," said Tarah.

"Does your neck hurt?"

"I'm fine," admitted Tarah, while massaging her neck with her hand. "I wouldn't have known I was out, except suddenly you were carrying me and I'm here instead of down there," she said, using her thumb to point toward the lane. "You freaked me out."

"What are you doing here?" asked Jack.

"I used to teach in Calgary, but got tired of all the spoiled, snotty little rich kids who think the world owes them a favour. I came here and found kids who really need help. I'm a volunteer with The Blue Dragon Children's Foundation."

"I never heard of the Blue Dragon," said Jack.

"It was started by a man out of Australia," said Tarah. "In Vietnam, it is the only social work program for street kids. I operate a soup kitchen just a couple of blocks from here. Some kids don't have any parents or others are from poor families. I entice the children with food, soccer games, music, arts — anything that works. The idea is to try to educate them so they'll have a better option than ending up in prostitution. At the soup kitchen, we teach them to cook and how to be waiters and waitresses."

"Sounds impressive," said Jack.

"If you have time, we have a restaurant called Koto that is run almost entirely by our kids who are older and have been through our program. Many will be able to get jobs in some of the best hotels and restaurants around. We also teach them English, so they'll have an advantage over the others."

"I admire you for having the courage to step forward and do what is right. You've got a lot of guts."

Tarah shrugged and said, "If anyone saw these children … how much they need help … the look on their faces when you do get through to them. Believe me, it is worth it."

"What do you know about the men in the apartment you just went to?" asked Jack.

"One of the street kids told me that Chi was being taken and sent to live with some family in America. She's an orphan here, so I guess it sounded pretty good. When I heard the name of the Vietnamese man who took her, I knew it was probably a lie. He has a reputation for being involved in drugs and prostitution. I found out where Chi was and got her back. No big deal."

"What you did was a hell of a big deal," said Jack. "Think maybe we can walk to your soup kitchen and talk?"

"Sure. For a donation, I'll also make you breakfast."

When they reached the soup kitchen, Tarah brought them inside a long narrow room with a wooden table lined with chairs. They sat down, but it was apparent that Chi was going to try to escape as soon as she could. Tarah argued with her in Vietnamese and Jack asked her what she said.

"I told her she was too young to end up in some brothel in America. She doesn't believe me and says she is being adopted by a rich family and will later work in a nice hotel. Yeah, right! Like I haven't heard that story before! She's only twelve years old, so …"

Chi made a dash toward the door, but Tarah grabbed her by the arm and made her sit down.

Jack told Tarah about another child, by the name of Hằng, who also headed to America last January on a boat and ended up murdered in Surrey.

"Hằng?" questioned Tarah. "It is not that unusual a name

here. What did she look like?"

"She had an extra thumb," said Jack.

Tarah was visibly shaken. "I knew a kid like that. Used to come here once in awhile with her younger sister. She quit coming around Christmas. I asked the younger sister where she was and she told me Hằng had been sent to live with relatives in Saigon. Maybe it is just a coincidence. Agent Orange had caused a lot of birth defects. There are many —"

"I have a picture of her," said Jack, pulling out his wallet. I must warn you, it was taken after she was murdered. It is awful to look at."

Tarah took a deep breath and slowly exhaled before nodding and reaching for the photo. She looked at the picture and immediately started to sob. Chi also looked, but was too frightened to cry and hugged Tarah and asked her a question in Vietnamese.

"Why is she like this?" asked Tarah, ignoring Chi and pointing to the picture. "Her face …?"

"She was held captive for months by a sadist and tortured," said Jack quietly. "Maybe you should explain that to Chi."

Tarah explained the situation to Chi, who immediately started crying. Tarah hugged her and gently whispered to her. Eventually Chi quit crying but she kept her arms around Tarah. There was no longer any fear of her returning to the apartment.

"Would you ask Chi, please, how many others were in the apartment we were just at?" asked Jack.

Tarah spoke with Chi briefly and Jack saw the surprise register on Tarah's face.

"She says there were about forty young women," said Tarah. "Chi guesses that most of the others are between the ages of sixteen to twenty-two. There were also two foreign men and three Vietnamese men in the apartment."

"The two foreign men are the ringleaders," said Jack. "They're both Russian."

"I had no idea there were that many people in there," said Tarah. "I thought it was just a couple of women and Chi who were going."

"Maybe just as well for you that you didn't know," said Jack. "Do you know where Hằng's father is now?"

Tarah nodded and said, "His name is Biển. He lives with his mother in a room off an alley in the next block. He works as a tour guide now. He speaks good English. Are you going to tell him?"

Before Jack could reply, Tarah said, "Or maybe I should."

"We both should," said Jack. He glanced at Laura and said, "Hand me the cell back, I'm going to call Sonny."

"Who is Sonny?" asked Tarah.

"A Vietnamese policeman who has been working with us," said Jack.

"Just a minute," said Tarah. She spoke with Chi, who nodded and left the room.

"I sent her to get Biển," continued Tarah. "I told her just to say that I had some urgent news. You might want to speak with him before he talks with the Vietnamese police. The relationship between the police and the people here is very different from Canada. He might be more forthcoming talking to us alone at first."

"I understand," said Jack.

"Oh," said Tarah, "but I guess you need the police to get the people in the apartment before they …"

"They can wait," said Jack. "I'll talk to Biển first. From what we know, the Russians will have probably have left the apartment by now. All they do is take a quick look to confirm the … quality of the merchandise … and leave. We need to let things proceed like normal for the bad guys and hope we can get more evidence. Perhaps with the Russians talking to the boat captain or paying him. Something to prove their involvement. Their being in the apartment is not enough."

"It might be enough here in Vietnam," suggested Tarah.

Jack nodded and said, "I believe that. But we are trying to solve Hằng's murder. I think the murderer is in Canada. Those are the rules I have to play by."

Tarah nodded and said, "Whoever did that to Hằng ... at the very least, I'd like to see that guy sent here to a Vietnamese jail. It is tough enough over here for ordinary people. Try to imagine what the jails are like."

"No colour TV or private rooms, I suspect," said Laura, facetiously.

"Sorry," said Jack. "If the murder happened in Canada, that's where he'll do his time. You said Hằng had a sister?" he asked, changing the subject.

"Her name is Linh. She is younger than Hằng is ... or was. I think she is about nine or ten."

"Is she still around?"

"Actually, I haven't seen her either for ... my God!"

Pops marked another X on the calendar and looked at Linh, who was curled up in a ball on the mattress, facing away from him.

"Only two days left until your first red-circle day," said Pops. "What special thing do you think the box will hold for you?"

Linh did not move.

"Look at me when I talk to you!" yelled Pops.

Linh remained still so Pops walked over and kicked her lightly on the back of her leg.

Linh yelled in rage and spun quickly, kicking up with her

feet and striking Pops on the shin, before leaping to her feet and crouching on the mattress in anticipation of his next move.

Pops stepped back and smiled with amusement. "That is great," he said. "You are strong … a fighter. You are the type who will endure much. Not wimp out and kill yourself like your stupid, stupid sister! Guess she didn't think you were worth trying to protect!"

chapter twenty-nine

Jack saw Chi enter the room with Biển a few steps behind her. He had a round face that seemed out of place on his thin body. He walked with his shoulders stooped, giving the illusion that his face was even bigger and rounder than it really was. His black eyes looked sadly out over puffy mounds of darkened skin. Jack saw a flicker of optimism when Biển glanced his way.

"Are you an American policeman?" asked Biển. "FBI?" he said, as he shuffled toward him.

"No," said Jack. "We are both Canadian police officers."

"Canadian?" Biển frowned, but said, "I know why you are here." He looked at Tarah and continued, "I am sorry, I told Linh to lie to you before. The news you want to tell me, I already know."

"Tell us what that news is," said Jack.

"That my daughter ... Hằng, was killed in a car accident. Have you brought me her body or her ashes?"

Jack shook his head and said, "Please sit down. First I must ask you to look at a photograph. I have been told that it is a picture of your daughter. It was taken after she died. There are lots of injuries to her face."

Biển sat and his hands shook as he took the photo in both hands. He looked at it for a moment before pressing it to his chest while squeezing his eyes shut, but not tight enough to stop the silent flow of tears.

Several minutes passed in silence before Biển opened his eyes and looked at the picture again. He choked out the words and said, "Hằng ... her face ... did she die quickly? Did she suffer?"

"I will tell you about how she died in a moment," said Jack. "First I would like you to tell me who told you she died in a car accident."

Jack saw Biển's eyes dart around the room before pausing and saying, "I do not know. It was a man I met at the market. He has relatives in America who told him the news."

Jack watched Biển as he spoke. He grimaced at Biển's pathetic attempt to lie. *In Canada, many of the people who lie say they met someone they don't know in a bar. Here it is a market. What is he hiding? Why would he lie about the death of his own daughter ... unless ... damn it!*

Jack cleared his throat and said, "Biển, if you do not wish to tell me who told you of her death, please tell me this. Where is ..."

"I told you, I do not know the person!"

Time to use another approach. "You must be able to tell me how Hằng came to be in Canada and why you believed she was in the United States?"

Biển shook his head and said, "It is late. I need to go. I have to be at work soon," he added, getting to his feet.

"Biển, please sit down," said Jack. "Hằng did not die in a

car accident. She was murdered and her body was found in a Dumpster."

Jack saw the shock on Biển's face as he gasped, grabbing the table for support as he fell back into his seat.

"That is not possible," he said, as his brain grasped for other possibilities. "Perhaps after she was hit by a car she was put ..."

"She was chained and tortured for at least three or four months. Then she committed suicide, but because of what happened to her, it is still murder."

"Chained and tortured! No! You are lying!" Biển's face went red with rage. "You hope to catch the men who are smugglers by using such trickery!"

Tarah burst into tears, startling Jack and Biển, who ceased arguing and stared at her in silence.

Several seconds later, Tarah regained her composure enough to speak in halting sentences to Biển in Vietnamese. After a short exchange of conversation, Biển sat back in his chair and wept openly.

"I told him you were not lying," said Tarah, while fighting to regain her composure. "That the police in Canada would never say such a terrible thing to a parent."

"Biển," asked Jack gently, "where is your other daughter? Where is Linh now?"

Biển's face contorted in anguish and he emitted a moan that filled the room. Tarah moved to sit beside him and put her arm around his shoulders.

Biển looked at Jack and slowly shook his head. "She is in America, too," he finally said, telling everyone what they already knew.

"Perhaps you'd better start at the beginning," said Jack.

Biển told him how he was approached by local smugglers who arrived on his doorstep one morning. He described the events that followed, including a painful six weeks of worry when Hằng made the trip to America.

"She called me from America," said Biển. "I did not send Linh until I knew that everything was as it should be. Then I put Linh on the boat. She too, called me from America."

"When?" asked Jack.

"One week ago," replied Biển.

Jack and Laura exchanged a glance. That was around the time they had followed the cube van to Vancouver Island and back to Richmond.

"Did Linh sound okay?" asked Jack.

"She was crying because she was just told by Mister Pops that Hằng was killed by a car. She said Mister Pops was very nice … but she was sad."

"Did she say how she was smuggled into the United States?"

"A man drove her across the border in a car. She saw the signs saying it was the United States border. She was excited to see the signs."

"She just went through the border as a passenger in a car?" asked Jack. "Didn't they ask for proof of …?"

"No, no," said Biển. "I asked her the same thing. She said she looked up and saw the signs but then pulled a handle to hide and the police at the border did not see her. I do not think that she was supposed to tell me that on the phone, but she was crying and not thinking very clearly. I think it was the same for Hằng. She also told me about seeing the sign."

"Jack," said Laura. "She was in the trunk!"

"Folding rear seat," said Jack, feeling nauseous.

"It was her that day who Đức …" Laura couldn't bring herself to finish as the realization sank in as to how close they had been to Linh.

Jack briefly clenched his jaw to quell his tears.

"You know where she is?" asked Biển excitedly.

Jack shook his head and said, "No … but we do know who one of the smugglers is in Canada. The one, perhaps, who drove her in the trunk of the car."

"You must find her," said Biển. "She is not as strong as Hằng. She is like her name."

Tarah saw the puzzled look that Jack and Laura gave each other and said, "The translation of Linh means *Gentle Spirit*."

"Hằng's spirit is strong," said Biển. "She would not commit suicide, knowing that Linh would be coming to such a place."

Hằng's spirit is strong — don't you mean, was strong? thought Jack. He looked at Biển and said, "I'm sorry. Our medical examination was very thorough."

"How did she die?"

"She used some type of metal rod to … to make herself bleed. By the marks … and marks on her hand … we know that it was self inflicted."

Biển looked at Jack and said, "If that is true, she did not do it for herself. It would be for Linh. She loved her very much. She promised me that she would do whatever was necessary for her sister. If she died, it was to save Linh."

Silence descended on the room for a minute as everyone became lost in their own thoughts. Eventually, Jack placed his hand on Biển's shoulder. "We will find her," he said, forcefully. "We will also find out who did this to Hằng."

Biển nodded silently.

"I must call the Vietnamese police now," said Jack. "There is a man I have been working with. He will want to speak to you."

"Yes," said Biển. "I will wait."

Jack called Sonny and explained the situation. He handed the phone to Tarah to give directions, while watching as Biển walked over and opened the door and stepped outside.

Is he going to take off? Jack glanced at Laura who had also noticed and they quickly followed.

Biển stood on the doorstep. For the second time that night the clouds parted, giving his face an eerie complexion as he looked up at the moon. He dropped to his knees and started crying, while speaking Vietnamese and looking up to the sky.

Jack felt Tarah's hand touch his arm and he turned and whispered, "We didn't say anything to him. He just came out here. Maybe he needs time to be alone."

Tarah shook her head and said, "The translation for Hằng is *Angel in the Full Moon*. Look up. He's not alone."

chapter thirty

It was six o'clock in the morning when Sonny dropped Jack and Laura off at their hotel with a promise to call them in a couple of hours after he spoke with his superiors.

As soon as they were alone, Laura said, "Jack ... we had her. She was in the trunk ... we just let her go."

"I know."

"I feel like crying. I'm so angry and frustrated," said Laura, her eyes brimming with tears.

"It was me who let her go. It was my call."

"I'd like to chain Đức to a wall. He'd talk."

"As nice as it is to fantasize, we don't have the time. We've got to do something, fast. "

"What do you think of this Mister Pops? Likely not his real name."

"My guess is it falls in the realm of the nickname for Dad. I'm going to call CC."

Jack called Connie Crane to tell her what they had learned.

"How the hell did she end up back in a Dumpster in Canada?" asked Connie. "And now her sister is with the guy, too? Jesus fucking Christ!"

"Đức is the key," said Jack.

"Yeah, like he's going to talk," said Connie sarcastically. "I'm not even sure if we have grounds for a warrant. Even if we did, if we search and don't find her, she'll be killed once they realize we're on to them."

"Check the border crossings," said Jack. "See if Đức has been across. If Hằng did die across the line, why bring her back? I think this happened on our turf. Probably in the Surrey area. That's where she was found."

"Đức is running hookers — maybe he's got a special place built just for the perverts."

"A possibility. Actually, it's a sickening possibility — the Orient Pleasure is in Surrey. Get on it. You've got to get into his places for a look."

"What about your informant? Don't you have someone connected to that place?"

Jack sighed. "Not anymore. Besides, if that friend had known about it, I would have been told. You've got to get a warrant and search everywhere."

"How, without tipping our hand?"

"Call Rocco Pasquali with the City Anti-Gang Unit. Get him to help. If VPD takes out the warrants under a prostitution investigation, the bad guys may not clue in as to what we are really after. Make it look like the RCMP is just assisting them with the places outside of Vancouver."

"That might work."

"You've got to do this without mentioning my informant in the warrants, or anything to do with Hằng and Linh. Also, don't mention anything about how the girls arrive at the parlours. Keep the warrants as simple as you can. Do both massage parlours as well as their homes and any other building they own. Search everywhere. Attics, basements, out-buildings, hidden dungeons under garage floors … look at everything."

"Dungeons under garage floors?"

"I've seen it done for grow-ops. Hidden trap doors under workbenches. Search everywhere. Look for hollow panels. Use the narcs to help. They're good at it."

"What if we don't find her? We could still be signing her death warrant if they get scared."

"And if you don't search and she is there, she may die anyway. It's a chance I think we have to take."

"Damn risky chance for Linh."

"Do you have a better idea?"

Connie was silent for a moment and replied, "No."

"They take credit cards at the massage parlours. Maybe you can match some names to your pervert list."

"I'll do that. Especially perverts who live in nice homes."

"Both Hằng and Linh told Biển they were in a very wealthy home, but the standards here are different. Any home with more than a couple of rooms or two toilets is considered wealthy by Vietnamese standards."

"I'll keep that in mind."

"If you identify any perverts, take a look and see if they used the credit cards to purchase construction materials leading up to last January."

"Will do."

"Laura and I will catch the next flight back. We're bringing Biển back with us."

"Why?"

"Because he couldn't afford the ticket himself. I've already spoken to our Vietnamese contact. He says it won't be a problem, if we pay for it."

"No, I mean why …"

"Damn it, Connie, think about it! If your kid was over here, would you be sitting on your fat ass over there! We owe it to him! One of his kids is murdered and the other one missing!"

The silence that followed reminded Jack how tired and exasperated he was … *Now I can add rude and thoughtless to the list.*

Jack sighed and said, "I'm sorry, CC. I haven't slept all night. You haven't met the father. I just did. I feel for the guy. He fits the grandfather image more than a dad. Don't take it literally about the fat ass comment. It's just an expression."

Jack paused, but Connie didn't reply.

"I mean, you're in good shape. Buns of steel …"

Connie laughed out loud and said, "I was just yanking your chain. I know what my ass looks like. I was just wondering if you had ever noticed. I'll talk to Randy. We'll think of a suitable reason for you to bring Biến."

"Appreciate that. Maybe say you want to drive him up and down the kiddie stroll in Vancouver and see if Linh is one of the kids turning tricks for the perverts there."

"That'll work. What about the Russians? What are the Vietnamese police going to do?"

"They're being really cooperative. They appreciate our concern with Linh. They'll keep gathering evidence, but won't touch them until we ask. If you get the warrants and find Linh, they'll grab the Russians over here. Neither of them would ever see the light of day."

"Better than the twelve or eighteen months they might get here."

"Right now, I don't care. Just find Linh."

"To get the warrants under the guise of prostitution and coordinate with City, it will probably take a day."

"If you get them signed before Laura and I get back,

don't wait for us."

"Believe me, we won't. Talk to ya later."

When Jack hung up the phone Laura looked at him and said, "That was a good idea you had about matching perverts to construction materials."

Jack shrugged and said, "Except the list of known pedophiles on the lower mainland, not to mention licence plate data included from those who pick up children on the kiddie stroll, is what, over a thousand? Linh doesn't have that much time."

"It's still a good idea. You really would be good on Homicide."

"I'm not suited for it. I hate pedophiles and bullies who abuse children. Makes me think of my own father too much. Put me in that section and the murder rate would go up, not down."

Jack, Laura, and Biển boarded a flight leaving Hanoi at 11:05 that same morning. With the time difference, they were scheduled to arrive in Vancouver forty-five minutes later on the same date. In fact, it was almost twenty-five hours later.

It did not help Jack's peace of mind when he discovered that Moustache Pete and the Fat Man were on the same flight and flying first class.

So much for Sonny gathering more evidence on them …

Jack and Laura were still three hours out of Vancouver over the Pacific Ocean when Connie received confirmation that the Vancouver City Police had obtained the search warrants.

She met with teams of police officers who were a combination of both Vancouver City Police and RCMP. The briefing was thorough and everyone assigned knew their duties.

Two VPD plainclothes officers, posing as customers, would be sent inside The Asian Touch massage parlour in Vancouver. Two RCMP officers, also posing as customers, would enter the Orient Pleasure massage parlour in Surrey at the same time.

The job of the *insiders* was to stop anyone who tried to burn or flush evidence when the raid commenced. They would be given exactly two minutes. Hopefully long enough to gather evidence of prostitution, but a short enough time to hide the fact that they were not going to be customers and that they were carrying weapons and wearing Kevlar vests under their shirts.

Three hours after the search warrants were signed, multiple teams of officers in Vancouver and Surrey waited at their assigned locations at the ready.

Connie gripped the police radio in one hand and watched the seconds tick by on her watch as she sat parked with her partner near Đức's house. Eight other officers assigned to her team were parked close by.

"Now! Now!" echoed across police radios and Connie leapt from the car and ran to the front door of Đức's house. The sound of splintering wood from the rear told her that other officers had just gained entry ahead of her.

Elsewhere, squads of officers were entering the massage parlours and smashing their way into the homes of the other Trần brothers, as well as two apartments belonging to employees who worked at the parlours.

Hopefully the sounds of splintering wood, breaking glass, and yelling would momentarily shock and paralyze anyone to delay them from grabbing a weapon.

Hopefully, Connie realized. *But not always …*

Within a few seconds, all the places being searched were secured and all those found inside had been handcuffed. Connie breathed a sigh of relief. *Nobody hurt ...*

The initial search being conducted by Connie's team yielded nothing. Now a more careful search was being conducted. Every room, ceiling panel ... anything new that had been built ... rugs to be looked under for trap doors.

Connie answered her cellphone and discovered it was Jack.

"Just landed and cleared Customs," he said. "Anything?"

"We're doing the searches now. Started about fifteen minutes ago. Doesn't look good. I'm at Đức's house. He's got an attached garage. I'm going to look at it again."

"Could you use a hand?"

"Got lots of help. No use burdening you."

"What about the other places?"

"So far they've got a bunch of credit card receipts. Also a lot of red-faced guys lying around handcuffed wishing they were wearing pants ... but nothing of real interest."

Jack sighed and said, "Call me if ... you know. I'm going to the office and then will find a hotel room for Biển."

"Talk to ya later."

"There's one other thing."

"What's that?"

"The Russians came back on the plane with us."

"Shit!"

Connie entered Đức's garage. It had a cement floor but she noticed some partial sheets of plywood lying on the floor under a work bench. She got down on her hands and knees to take a closer look. The sound of running footsteps approached her from behind.

"Connie!" came the excited voice of a young officer from her team. "Something you should see in the basement!"

"What?" she replied, trying to maintain a professional calm while her pulse quickened.

"A wall with wooden panelling. I knocked on it. Sounds hollow in one place!"

chapter thirty-one

Jack arrived at his office and plunked himself down behind his desk as Laura went to find an extra chair for Biển.

Jack called Natasha at work to let her know he was back. Not home. Just back. He then listened to the messages left on his office phone.

He hung up just as Laura wheeled a chair across the office floor for Biển to sit on. "I took this from Staff *Pendejo*'s office," she said. "He's not around. Probably not back from lunch." Laura glanced at Jack and raised an eyebrow and asked, "What's with you?"

"Isaac wants to see me immediately upon our return," replied Jack.

"What about?"

"I don't know. Maybe I should have Natasha call and ask. She's on a first-name basis with him."

Jack met with Isaac and was asked to give a quick debriefing on what had transpired in Vietnam.

After Jack told him, Isaac nodded and said, "Staff Otto had basically filled me in on the details. How is the father holding up? Does he speak English?"

"Yes, sir. His English is excellent. As far as holding up goes ... he is doing as well as could be expected under the circumstances."

"I would like to meet with him shortly and assure him personally that we will do everything possible to find Linh and apprehend whoever is responsible," said Isaac. "Now, however, there is another matter I wish to speak to you about."

Jack listened as Isaac told him about Quaile's *lack of good judgement* in regard to taking a picture of the Russians as they boarded the flight to Costa Rica.

"Lack of good judgement, sir?" seethed Jack. "I would call it obstruction of justice."

"I can see on the surface how you might feel that way. However, I spoke with him and he explained that they caught him off guard and he reacted in a manner that he hoped they would think a policeman would not do. He was so upset by being seen by them that he was too embarrassed to come forward and admit it earlier. I'm sure he would never make the same mistake again. However, it is also obvious that his judgement in his assessment of you may have been flawed."

"*Flawed*, sir?" said Jack sarcastically.

"We all make mistakes, Corporal," said Isaac flatly. "Perhaps I am making one now, by cancelling your transfer to Traffic Services."

"You are letting me remain here on Intelligence, sir?"

Isaac nodded and said, "You were correct in your judgement to work on the Russians."

"I believe that Staff Quaile disagreed strongly with that

point of view on my last assessment," said Jack.

"I appreciate that your last performance rating was less than satisfactory. Far below what you have normally achieved. Staff Quaile and you obviously had a personality conflict. With that in mind ... and considering all the circumstances, I will see to it that a new performance rating is completed by whoever is selected to replace Staff Quaile."

"To replace Staff Quaile? I appreciate that, sir!"

Isaac frowned and said, "We all have different abilities in different areas. I can see that, perhaps because of your background and experience, you have a more analytical mind when it comes to how organized crime functions. I'm sure that Staff Sergeant Quaile will be well-suited for the administrative position that he is now being transferred to."

"When is that effective, sir?"

"At the end of the month."

Jack tried hard to look solemn.

"In the meantime, I would strongly advise you to put your differences behind you. We all have our strengths and weaknesses. The administrative position that he will soon be responsible for is an important one ... that I suspect you would not perform well in."

"Yes, sir. I'll keep my interaction with him professional at all times. In fact, to show there are no hard feelings, I have a box I can lend him to pack up his personal belongings."

Isaac locked eyes with Jack for several seconds before adding, "I will be watching you closely. You step out of line and I will come down on you hard. Understood?"

"I would expect nothing less."

Jack arrived back at his desk and Laura looked at him and said, "So?"

"In a nutshell, my transfer to Highway Patrol is cancelled. I'm staying on Intelligence. Quaile is being transferred at the end of the month."

"Are you serious?

"Very."

"That's unbelievable," said Laura, getting to her feet and gripping each of Jack's hands. "I feel like we've just won the lottery. What happened?"

Jack glanced at Biến and replied, "Quaile burned the Russians at the airport before they flew out to Costa Rica. That's why they were so jumpy."

"Intentionally?"

"No doubt in my mind."

"That jerk!" Laura glanced at Biến and said, "I'm sorry."

Biến didn't respond and it was obvious that his mind was elsewhere.

"Anything more from CC?" asked Jack.

Laura shook her head.

"I'm going to call her. Isaac wants to meet Biến right away. "Why don't you take him in and introduce him?"

Connie used her flashlight to knock on the wood panelling. There was no doubt that approximately one metre of the wall sounded hollow along a portion of the wall that one would have expected to be up against the cement walls of the basement.

"Shall I kick it in?" asked the young officer. "There doesn't appear to be any handle or anything to pull it open."

"Did you try pushing on it?" asked Connie.

"Pushing? We want to open it, not close it."

Connie used her hand to push on various locations. She was rewarded by the sound of a metallic click and a portion of the wall opened outwards a crack.

"Magnetic push latch," said Connie excitedly. "Got the same thing at home on a cabinet," she added, putting her fingers in the crack and pulling outwards.

The section of the wall opened and Connie unconsciously held her breath.

The area she looked into was a large notch in the cement foundation that was meant to be a roughed-in fireplace. All it contained was a dresser and she swallowed as she tried to hide her disappointment.

The young officer pulled a drawer open. It was packed with money.

Two hours later, Jack, Laura, and Biển met Connie at the I-HIT office. After introductions were made, Randy took Biển into his office to explain some of the steps that had been taken in the investigation. He also had Biển look at mug shots of members of various Asian gangs on the lower mainland.

Randy didn't expect it would yield anything, but he knew it made Biển feel better to think he was helping.

"Everyone demanded lawyers immediately," said Connie. "Đức and Cường are in Surrey cells right now. They're going to be transferred to City lockup within the hour to face a joint indictment of keeping a common bawdy-house. Maximum sentence is two years. I expect everyone will be charged and released tomorrow morning on a promise to appear. Most of the women will be held for now and likely deported."

"If we can't keep these guys in jail, at least we can piss them off," said Jack.

"That's not all," said Connie. "Đức will really be pissed. We found where he keeps his money. It was hidden in his basement. Over a half-million in cash ... and get this. It also included the money you used to buy that kilo off of Giang.

Might help if we could ever pin Giang's murder on him."

"I'm sure members of his gang were responsible for the actual dirty work," said Jack. "Still, that's good. He was trying to hide the paper trail. Proceeds of Crime should be happy."

"Yeah, them and the taxman both."

"What about credit receipts?" asked Laura.

"Got boxes of them. Lots with criminal history. Also dumped the phone records. Besides massage parlours, they just started operating as an escort service, too. We've got a ton of numbers, most of which are hotels. It's going to take time."

"Linh doesn't have time," said Jack, quietly. "Do you think anyone twigged as to what we were really after?"

"I don't know," said Connie. "I don't think so. It went out over the media as a low-interest prostitution bust. All the media wanted to know is if there were any judges or politicians caught. They were told not this time. Some may not even bother to run it."

"So now what do you intend to do?" asked Jack.

Connie shrugged and said, "We can try for a wire, but my guess is we're better off looking for leads amongst the credit slips and phone numbers. We've got a criminal profile. A male, under the age of fifty. May fantasize by looking at pornography or lingerie catalogues and drawing pictures of chains and ropes on the female models. Likely suffering from other mental disorders as well."

"Not suffering like his victims," said Jack. "I agree with you about the wiretap. Unlikely anyone would ever open their mouth about it over the phone. But working through mounds of paper in the hope you'll find the guy? We don't have time for that bullshit!"

"I know what you're thinking ... but you so much as glare at a prisoner these days and a judge will rule the statement inadmissible."

"Why does everyone think I'd torture the guy?" said Jack.

"Wouldn't you?" asked Connie.

"I actually do have a better idea. It's even legal. Hard as it is for you to believe that," he added, looking at Connie.

"I'm all ears ... except for my buns of steel," replied Connie.

Jack ignored the comment and said, "It would be nice to hear what the Trần brothers have to say when they're all put together today."

"These guys have been around. Even if we did have a wire, once we put them in a nice quiet cell to listen, they'd clue in."

"Not what I had in mind. How about putting someone in the general holding cell at City with them? Do it before Đức and Cường even arrive. Someone who speaks Vietnamese."

Connie shook her head and said, "Try and find an operator who speaks Vietnamese ... good luck. I know the City has someone who does, but he works the street and is well known."

"We've got someone," said Jack.

"Yeah? Who?"

Jack pointed at Biển.

"You nuts? He's the father! We can't do that! They're liable to kill him, especially if they find a wire."

"So we'll stick some other operator in there for protection. Someone to stay in the background. Biển could gesture when he wants out. I'd do it, but Đức and Cường have both seen me."

"Christ, we can't ask him to do that. Besides, the brass would ..."

"Biển will want to help. He speaks their language and definitely doesn't look like a cop. Put him in for a couple of hours and take him out."

"The brass would never allow ..."

"The brass have nothing to lose. Linh does, if we don't find her."

Connie took a deep breath and slowly exhaled before saying, "They won't trust him. He's a stranger."

"I'll give him a quick course on UC. I've got a story he can give that will make them want to be his friend."

"That would have to be some story. These guys will be pissed off. We took their money and their girls. They won't be in the mood for making new friends."

Jack smiled. The steam had gone out of Connie's protest. It was no longer about not doing it. It was about how to do it.

"We use that to our advantage," said Jack. "Biển can say he got off the plane from Hanoi today and was arrested when the hotel taxi-van delivered him from the airport to the hotel lobby. He can say a nice young Vietnamese woman was also on the plane … and just happened to be going to the same hotel where she got busted for bringing in heroin. All he has to do is wink and say, of course I never met the lady … and she really doesn't know me. Đức will think Biển is a watcher."

"A watcher?" asked Connie.

"That happens regularly," explained Laura. "Someone who is on the plane with the mule to make sure they're not arrested and turned into informants before completing the delivery. The mules often don't know who is watching them, although the list of possibilities narrows once they leave the airport. Same goes for the police, if they are watching."

"With Đức's background, he'll know all this," said Jack. "It will make sense to him. Usually there isn't enough evidence to charge the watcher … but making them sit in cells to sweat for a while wouldn't be unusual. With Đức having his girls taken away, it will really help."

"Help? How? He'll be pissed off!"

"That's just half the story I'll get Biển to say," said Jack.

"Then he will say that a lot of nice young women smuggle drugs into Vancouver. That will really bait the hook. Especially when he implies that the same girl never gets used twice."

"Perfect!" said Laura.

"It'll work," added Jack. "Trust me."

"Bait the hook?" asked Connie. "Explain this, will ya? I work homicide cases, not dope."

Laura smiled and said, "Đức is bound to ask what happens to the women after they make the delivery. When Biển shrugs and says, who cares? Đức will jump on the opportunity to try and get them for the parlours!"

"Exactly," said Jack. "They'll treat Biển like gold — at least they won't hurt him."

Connie didn't reply as she silently ran the scenario through her brain.

"It might be a new angle to try and get to Đức if everything else fails," said Laura. "We could later get Biển to introduce a real UC operator to Đức at a later date."

"We all know what happened to Hằng," said Jack. "Let's hope that it is not a later date."

"Think Biển could keep his cool if they talk about Hằng or Linh?" asked Connie.

Jack stared at Connie and said, "If he ever wants to see Linh alive, he'll have to keep his cool."

"Hell of a thing to ask a father to do."

"I know … but it's him or nobody."

Pops's mouth flopped open and he quickly turned up the dial on his car radio as he drove home from work. The news about the police raids on the massage parlours was brief, but it was enough to tell him that the Trâns had been arrested.

He gripped the steering wheel with both hands and looked

in the rearview mirror. He found he was holding his breath and exhaled, before subconsciously taking short, shallow breaths.

He took an extra few minutes to drive around his neighbourhood, looking for any sign of the police before slowly heading up his driveway. He watched his rearview mirror closely as he followed the driveway past the side of his house and to the garage attached to the rear. He pushed the automatic garage door release on his sun visor and pulled inside.

He sat in his car for a moment, conscious of his hands still grasping the slippery steering wheel. His armpits felt sticky and damp. He hated being afraid.

The idea that anyone could arrest me for doing what I do in my own house is unbelievable! This is my house! I have the right to do what I want!

Linh heard the passage door open and the sound of Pops grunting with something. His head came into view and he stood up. She saw that he had reeled in a garden hose. He looked at her without speaking and departed, only to reappear a moment later.

This time he had something different in his hand.

Linh shrunk back on her mattress as Pops slowly walked toward her, slapping a baseball bat in his hand with each step.

chapter thirty-two

$\mathbf{B}$iển followed Jack's instructions carefully. Once he was placed in the holding cell, he went and stood by himself. It didn't take long for Thạo and Hửu to approach him and ask what he was in jail for.

Biển carefully gave the story that Jack told him to give. Stopping, as Jack suggested, at the point where he was arrested when he arrived at the hotel. The rest of the story was to be saved for when Đức arrived.

Thạo and Hửu were amiable, but eventually started talking about their own problems and explained to Biển that they were businessmen who owned massage parlours. They said they were somehow swept up in a police raid. Evidently, it would appear that some of the girls who worked for them may have been doing something illegal behind their backs.

The sound of the cell door opening caught everyone's attention.

"Our brother!" exclaimed Thạo. "And Cường!"

Thạo and Hữu rushed to meet Đức and Cường as they were placed in the holding cell. Biển quietly walked up behind them.

"They found my money," said Đức, angrily in Vietnamese. "Years of work. Now half of it gone!"

Half of it? thought Biển. *Important to tell Jack. Important to remember exactly who said what …*

"And the girls … gone!" yelled Đức, flicking his fingers for emphasis. He saw Biển and lowered his voice and said, "Who is this?"

Thạo took him aside and whispered in his ear while Biển watched nervously. Đức nodded before approaching Biển and introducing himself.

In the next few minutes, Biển found himself answering a barrage of questions from Đức about his flight over. Hanoi … the old quarter. Shops and stores.

Đức was polite and explained that his curiosity was because he was originally from Hanoi. It would be natural that they would know many of the same places. His memory was also bad, and Biển had to remind him of the names of several streets.

Biển was not fooled. Jack had warned him to expect questions. For Biển, it was easier than he imagined. All he had to do was tell the truth about the city he lived in.

"About your problems now?" asked Đức. "Do you have a lawyer?"

Biển shook his head. *Time now for the second part of Jack's story.* "I don't need one. I will not be here long. The young woman who was arrested … she does not know me. I know many young women," he smiled, "but they do not know me."

Đức nodded, but his brain was active. "On a plane … if you travel often … perhaps in time they might think they know you?"

Biển forced another smile and said, "It is my understanding that such women are only used once. The police might become suspicious if they fly too often."

"What do you think would happen to such women after they arrive in Canada?" asked Đức.

Biển shrugged his shoulders and said, "It is my understanding that they are paid to come here. Once that is finished, who cares?"

Biển saw the gleam come to Đức's eyes. "My fellow countryman, we should get to know each other better. My lawyer has told me that my brothers and I will no doubt be released on these nuisance charges tomorrow morning. If you do not have any plans, we could all meet for lunch and celebrate with a more appeasing type of food than is served in here."

"Perhaps," said Biển, not knowing if Jack would allow this.

"May I suggest a restaurant called the Sacred Phoenix? It has both Asian and Western food. Say, around one o'clock?"

"I will try to make it. I have many important calls to make, but I will try."

Thạo, Hữu, and Cường listened patiently to Đức and Biển as they spoke, but finally Thạo could wait no longer. He grabbed Đức by the arm.

"This situation that we are in ... could it be because of Petya and Styp'?" Thạo asked.

"Why would you think that?" asked Đức.

"Because of the two girls," replied Thạo.

Biển stared intently with his mouth hanging open, afraid his heartbeat would drown out the words he was hearing. *Petya ... Styp' ... it is the names we seek!*

"It has nothing to do with them," said Đức. "This is just a matter of prostitution. It is the Vancouver police who are behind this. Surrey is only a coincidence. The RCMP is only helping the Vancouver police."

Surrey? wondered Biển. *A third man who was also arrested? Petya, Styp', and Surrey … all important names to remember for Jack.*

"It was stupid of them," said Thạo. "I still do not understand why they did that. We would have paid them more money if they had let us keep them."

"Thạo is right," said Hửu. "Why did you drive the girls to that place for Peter and Styp'? There is much demand for them in our business. Men pay much money."

"That is what they wanted," shrugged Đức.

Biển looked at the big man watching him from the back of the cell. *Peter … Styp' … they have Linh!*

Biển scratched his throat and the big man started yelling for the guard, saying he wanted to speak to his lawyer.

The guard arrived and told the big man he would have to wait. Biển was being released first.

Biển was led into an office where Jack, Laura, and Connie waited.

"I have the names," said Biển excitedly. "Write them down! Quick! The two men who have taken my daughters."

Connie grabbed her pen and notebook.

"Their names are Petya and Styp'!"

"Shit," said Connie, putting her pen away.

"There is maybe a third man," said Biển. "His name is Surrey!" Biển looked at the three forlorn faces looking back at him. "What is wrong? Do you not know these men?"

Jack cleared his throat and said, "Petya, or Peter as it is called in English, is a Russian we have been referring to as Moustache Pete. His partner is Styopa. They are the two men Laura and I followed to Hanoi."

"They have Linh! Arrest them now! Search their houses!"

"They share an apartment together. It is not a house. They do not have Linh."

"Then it is the man called Surrey! Do you know him?"

"Surrey is a *city* near Vancouver. It is where Hằng was found. It is not a person." Jack saw the tears fill Biển's eyes. "Tell us what you heard," he asked softly.

"Thạo spoke with Đức when he arrived. He asked him if they might be in jail because of Peter and Styp' over the two girls. I am sure it is Hằng and Linh they talk about!"

"Please ... tell us the rest," said Jack.

"Đức said it had nothing to do with them. He said it is only because of prostitution. He said the Vancouver police are behind it. He said Surrey is only a coincidence."

"Did he say what kind of coincidence?" asked Connie.

"No. Thạo said it was stupid of Peter and Styp'. He said he did not understand why they did that. He said they would have paid them more money for my daughters."

"He said they were sisters?" asked Jack.

"No ... he said girls ... but I know he is talking about my daughters. Then Hữu asked Đức why he drove the girls to that place for Peter and Styp'. Đức said it was because that is what they wanted."

"What place?" asked Connie.

"Now I do not know," cried Biển. "I believed he meant to one of the homes of the three names I told you."

"Take it easy," said Jack. "What you have done has helped us."

"I did not do this right!" shouted Biển. "I should have asked questions!"

"No," replied Jack. "I told you not to ask any questions. That would be very, very dangerous for Linh."

Biển grabbed Jack's sleeve and said, "But now we know that Đức and those two Russians know where they are. You can find them easy now." His eyes flashed and he added, "I would like to be there when they talk!"

Jack closed his eyes while briefly massaging his temple with one hand.

"What is it, Jack?" asked Biển. "Why are you still sitting here? Linh is in great danger!"

"It is not that easy," explained Connie. "We know that they do not have Linh. If we question them about it, then they will tell whoever has her to kill her and hide her body."

"You do not ask them politely!" yelled Biển. "You are the police! You make them talk! Do not let them talk to anyone until Linh is safe. You must act now!"

"I'm sorry, Biển," said Connie. "It does not work that way in Canada."

Jack looked at Biển and thought, *I'm sorry, buddy, there was a day I would have glady beaten the information out of them. I just can't. Please understand, I have someone I love in my life now. I have to do the right thing.*

"It has to work that way!" said Biển. "It is my daughter's life! She is a child!"

Jack looked at Biển and sighed. *Why do I feel so much shame and hate myself if what I am doing is the right thing?* "Biển … no," said Jack. "You said that Hữu told Đức that he should not have driven the girls to that place."

"Yes, that is right."

"'That place' … does not mean that Linh is still there. It could have been a temporary drop-off place. Neither Đức nor the Russians may know exactly where she is. Even if they were made to confess … they may not know where Linh is now. Whoever has Linh might hear about it and kill her."

"Then what will you do?" asked Biển.

"You have given us a good lead," said Jack. "We can now focus our attention on Đức and the two Russians."

"It sounds like whoever has her is known to both Đức and the Russians," said Connie. "We have phone records. I will work on it tonight with many investigators. If there is a common denominator, we will find out."

"Is there anything else they said?" asked Laura.

"There is only one more thing," said Biển, bitterly. "Đức mentioned that you only found half his money."

Connie glanced at Jack and Laura and said, "I've already got Proceeds of Crime looking at his financial transactions."

Jack nodded and looked at Biển and asked, "Did you tell Đức about using lots of different girls to smuggle heroin?"

"Yes, I told him," replied Biển. "He did not ... what do you call it? Steal the bait."

"Biển, believe me," said Jack. "We will find her. You've got my word on that."

Biển nodded as he silently committed one other piece of information to memory.

The Sacred Phoenix at one o'clock.

chapter thirty-three

Linh tried to ignore the sound of the bat slapping against Pops's hand as she got to her feet. Until now, she had remained defiant ... angry at the man she knew had killed her sister.

Pops had been wickedly controlling. A slice of bread ... perhaps allowing her to temporarily have an article of clothing to lord his power over her. But he had not caused any physically lasting pain. With the exception of her fighting with him and being slapped and punched when he first chained her up and tore off her clothes, she had not yet suffered much physical torture.

There were times when he would urinate on her, but he seemed to take more joy with marking an X on the calendar each day, while verbally tormenting her about the box that was out of her reach and what she might expect on the red-circle day.

Linh had refused to show any interest in the calendar or the box ... at least when Pops was in the room.

Tonight, something is different about his face. He does not look as evil — he looks … afraid! The bat … the hose … because I do not play his game, he is going to kill me!

"Please, Mister Pops," said Linh, pointing at the calendar. "I must know. Tomorrow is the first red-circle day. Please tell me! What is in that box?"

Pops stopped and stood staring at her. He was panting, as if he had just been using the exercise equipment that Linh had seen in the basement when she first arrived.

"Mister Pops! I must know. Don't make me wait. Please … tell me now."

Pops turned to look at the calendar and looked at Linh and smiled. "It *is* your first red-circle day tomorrow," he said.

Abruptly he stepped forward again, raising the bat menacingly over her head and she stepped back.

"No!" Pops shouted. "I will not tell you now! You will wait until tomorrow." He lowered the bat and, almost as an afterthought, he said, "It is Saturday tomorrow. When I come home from work I will be off for the next two days. I think it will be best if I give you all the surprises during that time."

Linh watched as Pops leaned the bat up against the box and placed another X on the calendar. He stared at her intently before gathering up the hose and disappearing back out the passageway.

It was eleven o'clock at night when Natasha heard Jack arrive and the noise of his suitcase landing on the tiled floor at the front door. She was ready for bed, but he had called so she waited, watching the *The National* on CBC.

"Let me guess, don't tell me your name," said Natasha teasingly, before kissing him warmly on his lips. She stepped back and looked at him again. "I'm not sure … maybe if

I use a little more passion." She kissed him again, taking her time and running the end of her tongue around his lips before stepping back.

"Now do you remember who I am?" asked Jack.

"I've certainly narrowed it down to a short list."

"Really? How many names are on that short list?"

"Unfortunately, quite a few. Do you have any distinguishing marks or scars to jog my memory?"

"I can't remember. Maybe if you allowed me a moment to take my coat off and undress we could find out."

Natasha smiled and hugged him again. "I missed you. I'm so glad you're back. Travelling to all these exotic places … with another woman, I might add."

"Speaking of Laura, you didn't happen to buy her a certain bottle of perfume, did you? As a bon voyage present?"

Natasha furrowed her eyebrows and said, "No, I never … ah, ha! Your allergies."

"I did get you a little something," said Jack, handing her a large plastic bag.

Natasha peered inside the bag. "A conical hat!" she laughed, quickly trying it on. "What do you think? Perfect for the rain we're getting this time of year."

"Looks adorable, but the outfit isn't complete. There's more. I just have to unpack it."

Natasha followed Jack into the bedroom and watched him unpack.

"You must be exhausted," she said.

"Managed to catch a couple of winks on the plane, but not much."

"How did everything go? Earlier, when we talked, you said you were putting the father into jail with them."

"Partly successful," said Jack. "He learned that the two Russians and one of the Trần brothers likely know where Linh is, but that is all. Homicide will work through the night on it. Laura and I are meeting with them in the morning."

"These guys are monsters," said Natasha. "They should be ..."

"I know," said Jack. "Let's not talk about that now."

"Sorry." Natasha changed the subject and said, "I bet you're glad that Jacob recanted your transfer."

Jack paused and grinned. "Yeah, Jacob to you. God to me."

Jack found the package wrapped in soft tissue paper and handed it to Natasha. She tore it open and saw the silk gown.

"Traditional Vietnamese gown," said Jack. "I hope it fits."

"It's beautiful!" said Natasha. "Thank you," she added, kissing him on the cheek. "Give me a minute in the bathroom to try it on. You finish unpacking."

Minutes later, Natasha decided that the outfit looked really good on her. It was tailored to fit the curves of her body perfectly. She leaned into the mirror and re-did her makeup, before lightly tossing her hair with her hands.

"What do you think?" she asked, walking into the bedroom and giving a wave of her arms to show off her new outfit.

Jack didn't respond. He was sprawled across the bed, sound asleep.

Connie glanced at her watch when she saw Jack and Laura walk up to her desk. It was eight o'clock in the morning. She stifled a yawn before asking, "What did you do with Biển?"

"We told him we'd meet him today for lunch. How did you make out?"

"Nada. Nothing. Most everyone in our office has been up all night and we don't have a thing to show for it."

"No third party connection?" asked Laura.

"Not a fucking one," said Connie, angrily. She looked at Jack and said, "So now what the hell do we do? They'll all be released in a couple of hours and we still don't have a clue as to where she is."

"At least now we know that Đức and the Russians probably have a good idea as to who has her," said Jack.

"So what?" said Connie. "After yesterday, they'll all be too paranoid to go anywhere near where Linh is. Besides, they have no reason to. It's not like we have a clue. If we do risk putting surveillance on them and they spot it — you both know what will happen."

"You're tired," said Jack. "You've been up all day and all night."

"Christ," said Connie, dismissing Jack's comment with a wave of her hand. "I even considered telling Đức that the charges might go away and his money might reappear if he had something of value to give us."

"They would figure that out pretty quick," said Jack. "You'd be signing Linh's death warrant. Not to mention that Đức is involved with this. He has his own ass to protect."

"Yeah, I know."

"Go home, get some sleep," said Jack. "It's easier to think of a game plan when you've had a little shut-eye."

"Yeah? Well you just had some. Do you have a game plan?"

"So you don't have any surveillance planned on Đức or the Russians?" asked Jack.

Oh, man … I don't like the sounds of this, decided Laura.

"No," said Connie. "Like I said, we don't dare chance it."

"I agree completely. Just wanted to make sure."

Connie glanced at her watch and said, "Damn it, I'm already late to talk to Isaac. He wants to be debriefed personally on this twice a day. So what are you two going to do?"

"Look for a new informant," said Jack. "Maybe some way to get in through the back door."

"Yeah, well … good luck."

Laura waited until they were in the car and looked at Jack and said, "I heard you in there."

"Heard me what?"

"You're pleased that they're not being followed. I know you, it's more than just not tipping them off. What's up? What's this about getting a new informant?"

"Two of them," said Jack. "Moustache Pete and the Fat Man."

"You can't be serious. They'll never turn! You ask them anything and Linh will end up in another Dumpster."

"We won't ask them anything. All we have to do is get them to tell us."

"What, some kind of UC? The Trâns didn't take the bait with Biển."

"A UC, but we keep Biển out of this."

"How? You got an angle to get in with the Russians?"

"Yes."

"Even if we do gain their trust … I doubt that they would ever talk about it. Or if they do, they're smart enough not to give away any details that would let us locate her."

"That depends upon our approach," replied Jack, giving a grim smile. "I think I figured out something from what Biển told us last night. The part about the Trâns wondering why the Russians didn't sell them the girls for more money."

"I remember."

"So why didn't they?"

Laura paused and watched as a group of school children walked across the road in front of them. She glanced at Jack and said, "I don't know. Maybe doing someone a favour."

"These guys deal in human flesh ... children," said Jack, gesturing to the group crossing the road. "They don't do any favours unless there is something in it for them."

"Such as?"

"Remember what we heard in Cuba when they were waiting to meet with the Arabs at that restaurant? The comment about an insurance policy?"

"Vaguely."

"They talked about the incident at the airport and how they had to be careful."

"Quaile."

"No doubt. Then Fat Man made a comment saying that is why they carry insurance. He said that with the police, insurance is always good."

"I don't get it."

"I think that is the reason they sold off the girls for less money. They want a pervert to have them. I think they know where Linh is, or at least know how to find out."

"The girls are their insurance policy!"

Jack nodded. "If either of them gets taken down with anything serious, they're going to use the girls as their insurance policy to walk away."

"That ... that is so sick."

"I know."

"We don't have enough evidence to nail them for smuggling. As far as the courts would allow, all we have is mere association with the people we do have evidence on."

"I know, but ..."

"A UC will take time to gain their trust."

"Who said anything about gaining their trust? That is definitely not part of the UC I have in mind."

"So I take it there was a reason why you didn't mention

this plan to Connie?"

"I wouldn't recommend you tell anyone about it."

Laura sighed. "Okay ... how, where and when?"

"*How* ... is we kidnap them. *Where* ... is outside their apartment building. *When* ... is right now."

Oh, man ...

chapter thirty-four

Jack and Laura drove over to the Russians' apartment building and parked where they could watch the front entrance.

"Curtains are still pulled," said Laura, as she scanned the penthouse suite with binoculars. "Still sleeping."

"We'll wait. I'd better call Biển and tell him we can't make lunch."

Or dinner either, if we end up in jail, thought Laura.

Jack used his cellphone and called Biển's hotel. The switchboard put the call through and Biển answered the call on the first ring.

"Biển, it's Jack, I take it I didn't wake —"

"Any news?" asked Biển. "Connie … did she find something?"

Jack grimaced and said, "I'm sorry, she didn't find anything concrete yet." He heard Biển's forlorn sigh and continued, "But there are plenty of leads to follow. Laura and I are working on something now. That is why I'm calling. We won't have time to meet you today for lunch … I don't know about supper."

"That is okay," replied Biển sadly. "I wasn't able to sleep last night. All I can do is think about …." Biển stopped and said, "I have a bad headache. I will try to sleep or maybe go for a walk. If you have news, please call me. Otherwise I will call you when I have rested."

"Biển … hang in there. Laura and I are working on this. We are doing everything possible."

Not everything, Biển thought, as he hung up the phone.

The hours ticked by slowly for Jack and Laura as they waited in anticipation of what they were about to do.

At one o'clock, Laura sighed and said, "The blinds are still closed."

Jack glanced upwards and nodded to indicate he heard, but his mind was brooding elsewhere. *Today, two more men may go free for allowing children to be sexually exploited, abused … and in this case, murdered. Free … just like you, Douglas Henry.*

Jack tried to wipe the image of his father from his mind, but it seemed the harder he tried, the more the image persisted. *Funny, I don't even want to say he's my father … even in my thoughts I prefer to use his first and middle name … but he is my father. Even worse, I'm a policeman and still can't arrest him without someone willing to come forward. Victims … remaining silent … allowing the continued exploitation of other children. How many would have been saved if only one had the courage to come forward earlier and put a stop to it?*

"What about going up there and just hauling them out?" suggested Laura, interrupting his anguished thoughts.

Jack shook his head and said, "They've got video in the lobby. If this goes sideways …." Jack decided not to end that sentence. It wasn't necessary to dwell on that possibility. The image of his father returned. *How many died like my sister Bonnie? Or did some prefer the needle over the bottle?*

Douglas Henry ... you are able to spend your final days in perverted pleasure, knowing you are still able to inflict pain and anger on your own son — I wish there was life after death and a hell waiting for you ...

Jack felt relieved when Laura once again interrupted his thoughts. "What if it does go as planned," she asked. "Then what happens to us?"

"Saving Linh is more important."

"I wasn't meaning that we shouldn't. It's just that with you ...." she glared at Jack and added, "never mind."

"With me what?" asked Jack, as he took his turn with the binoculars.

"The ideas you come up with."

"You don't like this idea?" he asked, while refocusing the binoculars. "You'd rather yank out their fingernails?" *Even for you, Douglas Henry, I would not do that. You are like a rabid dog. You should be destroyed — without feeling. Feeling anger would only make you happy.*

"No, torture is not an option I would use," said Laura. "Although I have to admit, the idea has occurred to me, only I'd remove another part of their bodies."

"Sometimes I fantasize, too ... about a lot of people."

"You're a man, I bet you do. Telling Connie she has buns of steel. Do you undress all women with your eyes?"

Jack smiled, despite how he felt. "I prefer to use my fingers —"

"Jerk."

"And there is just one woman I save that for."

"Oh."

"Trust me, Connie has never entered my fantasies. Besides, that is not what I meant when I asked you what you meant about my idea."

"It's good. That's why I asked. What if this *does* work? Do you have a story to explain it all to everyone else? One that would keep us employed? Not that it matters, if we find Linh alive, it will be worth it."

"Hadn't really thought that far ahead yet. But — the blinds have just opened!" said Jack, passing the binoculars back to Laura.

Biển stepped through the doorway into the Sacred Phoenix and looked around the restaurant. He was immediately hailed by Đức.

"I'm glad you made it," said Đức, while gesturing for his two brothers to make room while Cường hurried to obtain another chair.

Biển nodded and said, "So is it true? Is the food better here than … our last hotel?"

Đức laughed and said, "That hotel was truly a nuisance. The room service was totally inadequate. As you can see, we were all released — I should say, vacated, from that hotel this morning. I have been told by my lawyer that it is unlikely that I will ever have to return to that hotel, although the bill for it will be expensive. And you, my friend? How does it go? You still look upset. Will you have to return to that hotel?"

"I was not charged with any crime — but I am very tired," said Biển truthfully. "I did not sleep last night."

"Perhaps with a better meal in your stomach and some wine, it will help you to relax. Today, it will be my treat."

It was three o'clock before Moustache Pete and the Fat Man walked out the front entrance of their apartment building and sauntered down the sidewalk. They each carried telescopic umbrellas, but kept them closed. The darkening clouds were only threatening at the moment and the Fat Man held his umbrella by the cord on the handle and swirled it in an arc as he walked.

Moustache Pete was the first to notice the dark car pull up to the curb a short distance ahead of them — and the attractive woman who stepped out from the passenger seat as they approached.

The man driving the car also got out and walked toward the rear of the car just as Moustache Pete and the Fat Man were about to walk past.

"Police!" the woman yelled, while pointing a pistol at Moustache Pete's face. "Don't move!"

Moustache Pete and the Fat Man's mouths gaped open and they saw the flash of a badge in her other hand.

"Both of you, put your hands up!" yelled the man behind them.

Moustache Pete and the Fat Man both turned to see a second gun being pointed at them. They put their hands up and Moustache Pete asked, "What is this about? What have we done?"

"You fit the description perfectly," said the woman, "of two men who clubbed and robbed a man in an alley just two blocks from here."

"It wasn't us," said Moustache Pete, glancing at the Fat Man, who let out a big sigh and began to smile.

"Gee, I've never heard that before," replied the woman, sarcastically. "Put your hands on the roof of the car and back your feet away. You're going in for a lineup."

Within seconds, Moustache Pete and the Fat Man found themselves handcuffed with their hands behind their back and placed in the back seat.

"You will see that it is not us," said Moustache Pete as the man buckled their seat belts across their laps. "How long will this lineup take?"

"Shut the fuck up, Petya Globenko," the man hissed. "I don't want to hear a word from you ... ever."

Moustache Pete's eyes opened wide and his mouth hung open.

"You know who we are?" asked the Fat Man in astonishment.

"Same goes for you, Styopa Ghukov," the man snarled. "You're finished. We know all about you." He handed the woman the keys and said, "You drive. I'll watch these bastards."

Moustache Pete and the Fat Man exchanged nervous glances. There was no denying the rage in the man's eyes.

This is somehow personal to him, Moustache Pete realized. *I am sure we have never met ...* He looked at the woman's face in the rearview mirror and fell back in his seat as she peeled away from the curb. He glanced back at the man beside her. The man sat sideways in the seat watching them.

When they stopped at the next set of traffic lights, the woman leaned across and kissed the man on the cheek and the nape of his neck. "You did it," she said softly. "I love you."

"Told you I would, babe," he replied. "A little pre-wedding gift for you," he added with a grim smile. "What did you think when I said, *put your hands up!* Did I sound like a real cop? I always wanted to say that."

The woman chortled and said, "You did sound like one. Doesn't CSIS teach you how to arrest people?"

Moustache Pete and the Fat Man quickly exchanged a few words in Russian and Moustache Pete looked at the man and said, "You are with the Canadian Security Intelligence Service!"

"Ah," the man said, looking at the woman and adding, "Our

two Ivans in the back seat are cluing in." He glanced at them and said, "Just for your info, my fiancée *is* a police officer."

"But you are not," said Moustache Pete. "What is this about? Where are you taking us?" he demanded.

"Relax, Ivan. You would have been arrested by my office tomorrow morning anyway. I'm just doing it a day early."

"Arrested for what? We have done nothing wrong."

"No, not yet. But we know that you were about to."

"My brother!" yelled the woman, her eyes burning with anger as she looked in the rearview mirror. "You sons of bitches! He was in the World Trade Center when it collapsed. He was the only family member I had left!"

"I don't understand!" yelped The Fat Man.

"The Trade Center?" asked Moustache Pete. "We had nothing to do with that. You have made a mistake. We are retired schoolteachers. You have arrested the wrong men."

"Maybe you had nothing to do with the Trade Center," she said, "but your friends did."

"Our friends?" asked Moustache Pete.

"Only this time you've got something far more murderous up your sleeves," said the woman.

"If I were you," said the man, raising his hand and wagging his index finger to emphasis the point, "I would just sit quietly. If you want to talk, I suggest you do it later tonight when you arrive in Guantanamo Bay."

"Guantanamo!" exclaimed both men from the back seat.

"Yeah, I don't really believe in the extradition process. My buddies in the CIA feel the same way."

"You cannot do this!" said Moustache Pete. "I wish to call the Russian embassy. It is my right."

The man shook his head and said, "My friends down south have assured me that you will speak to nobody again … not even each other, for as long as you live." He gave a sinister grin and added, "Except for their interrogators, of course. I think they will make you say plenty."

"You will stop the car immediately," said the Fat Man. "We have the right to call the Russian embassy," he demanded.

"You ignorant, dumb bastards," said the man. "Who do you think it was, Styopa, who told us about your degree in microbiology? Or your degree in history, Petya? How you did not teach at all — except at military institutions."

Moustache Pete and the Fat Man glanced at each other in surprise.

"Believe me," the man continued. "Russia's only interest in you now is to ensure that you do end up in the hands of the Americans. The war on terrorism has united many countries. Russia, Cuba — countries who used to be enemies … have now united."

The man glanced at the woman and added, "Except for fucking Vietnam. They're still too hung up on past conflicts to cooperate on anything. I can just imagine how many more terrorists we would have discovered if they had cooperated." He turned to the men in the back and said, "We do know you went there as well."

"Your own people at CSIS, they will find out if you carry out this … this plan," said Moustache Pete.

The man sneered and said, "My people will be told that you became paranoid over that incident at the Vancouver airport. Remember? Where you had your picture taken just before you went to Costa Rica. You have talked of it. The CIA will say that you spotted CSIS agents following you in Canada and decided to flee to the U.S. where you were arrested."

"That was you?" asked the Fat Man. "You took our photograph at the Vancouver airport?"

"No, that was a Russian attaché. They said it was an accidental blunder, but we know better. You were an embarrassment to them. They hoped to prevent you from meeting with the al-Qaeda operative that you later met in Cuba."

"Al-Qaeda?" said both captives in unison.

"Mother Russia believed they could scare you into returning to Russia so that they could arrest you. Now that we know you met with al-Qaeda in Cuba and plan to attack the States, Russia is more than happy to let the Americans have you." The man looked at the woman and said, "I wonder which would be worse? Russian or American interrogation? Probably the same."

"You're still lucky," said the woman harshly, while glancing in the rearview mirror. "You'll both get to spend the rest of your lives in Cuba — which is a hell of a lot more than I can say for my brother. Personally I hope you die of the heat ... while the rats nibble at your toes."

Biển finished his steak sandwich and took another sip from the glass of red wine. Đức raised a bottle to refill his glass, but Biển put his hand over the top and shook his head.

"What is wrong, my friend?" asked Đức. "You do not like wine? In over two hours you have only had two glasses! Perhaps I should have ordered you a Huda?"

"No, the wine is good," said Biển, but I am tired and should return to my hotel."

Đức nodded and said, "First, there is something I would like to speak to you about. A business proposition. One that could be lucrative for the both of us."

Biển raised his eyebrows in response.

"About the women you ... see ... who fly to Vancouver with packages," added Đức. "I have an idea."

Biển looked looked sharply at Đức and said, "I think that

such a discussion should only take place between you and I. Are you able to give me a ride back to my hotel room?"

Đức smiled and said, "You are absolutely correct, this is no place to discuss issues of a sensitive nature. Let me finish my wine and then I will drive you to your hotel."

Later, Biển slipped a steak knife into his jacket pocket.

chapter thirty-five

Laura glanced at the highway sign indicating the way to the U.S. border and caught Jack's eye. He turned in the seat and said, "Hey, you Russkies! See that," he said, pointing to the sign. "One hour and you will be the most welcome guest of the US government."

"This is a terrible, terrible mistake," Moustache Pete said. "I do not understand why you would think that we are —"

"Shut up!" yelled Laura. "One more peep out of either of you and I'll pull off in some farmer's field and shoot the both of you!"

Jack glanced back at the Russians before looking at Laura. "Honey, I love you, but please settle down," he said, affectionately squeezing her shoulder as she drove. "For my purposes, it would not hurt if these men decided to cooperate now and give us the names of other al-Qaeda agents that they are involved with."

"Let the Americans talk to them," she said. "I don't need

to hear them yap."

"They could have information valuable to Canada," Jack replied. "Other lives could be at stake here." He looked at the Russians and said, "I know you will tell everything eventually. It is inevitable," he shrugged.

Laura shook her head silently and stared ahead in anger.

Jack eyeballed Moustache Pete and said, "How about it? With your military background, surely you know that, in time, you will be broken. The longer it takes, the more painful it will be. Why not make it easier on yourselves? You have no people to ever rescue you … or even a country to go to."

"You are wrong," said Moustache Pete. "We are not terrorists. I swear on my mother's grave."

"You are foolish not to cooperate," said Jack, "unless of course, you are a masochist and enjoy pain. The two Arabs you met at the Al Medina restaurant in Havana? Well, one of them has been under watch for years. He is very high up in al-Qaeda. A financer, I am told. As you have now probably figured out, he is only allowed to operate so that we can identify people such as yourselves. Do you deny meeting him there?"

"No, I do not deny that, but —"

"Your interest in navigational charts …." Jack said, letting out a laugh before continuing, "You really are poorly trained. I was even in the West Marine store with you a little while ago when you were asking about Seattle and inquiring about navigational charts for Puget Sound. You should remember my face. Believe me, the Americans were not amused by that."

Moustache Pete tipped his head back, briefly closing his eyes while shaking his head.

"Vietnam is the only country that refuses to cooperate. Tell us who you met there, it might go well for you. You were in the military. You know what is in store for you if you do not cooperate."

The tears rolled down Fat Man's chubby cheeks as he pleaded, "We are not terrorists … please." He looked at his friend and spoke rapidly in Russian, but stopped when Jack leaned over and backhanded him across the face.

"Either speak English or shut the fuck up!" Jack yelled.

"Sir," said Moustache Pete. "Believe me when I tell you that I did not know that the gentlemen we met in Havana were —"

"Gentlemen!" yelled Laura. "You call cowardly killers gentlemen!" She glanced at Jack and said, "That's it, I'm looking for a place to pull over. The other side of the tunnel … past Deas Island … there's some bush along River Road."

"It was simply a figure of speech," said Moustache Pete quickly. "Personally, I did not care for either one of them."

"Yeah, right," Laura replied.

"You are a police officer," pleaded Moustache Pete, before taking a sideways glance at the Fat Man. "We have some information that is very valuable to the police. You can check it out. We are smugglers … not terrorists. If you let us explain — just stop and talk to us for fifteen minutes … we can prove it."

"They're looking for a chance to escape," said Laura, speeding up. "Watch 'em."

"We are handcuffed!" cried Moustache Pete. "We can't escape. You are a police officer … you may even know of the crime that we wish to tell you about."

"What? Somebody importing vodka illegally?" said Jack, contemptuously.

"No! Someone … a little girl … she is in great danger," said Moustache Pete. "Promise to let us go and we will tell you how to find her. It will save her life."

Laura lowered her head so that her eyes could not be seen in the rearview mirror and stared ahead without speaking.

Moustache Pete turned to Jack, but he had turned his back to him and also sat quietly staring out over the hood of the car.

"Please," said Moustache Pete. "Do not treat what I say with indifference. I am not lying. This little girl … we have heard that she had a sister who was murdered by the same man. If it is not true, then you can give us to the Americans. But you will see that it is true. Please …"

Jack and Laura discovered that they were now at the most difficult part of their charade. Something they hadn't expected just happened.

They knew that if seen, the tears in their eyes might give everything away.

"I hate this time of year," said Đức, starting the engine as Biển got in the car beside him. "It is barely four o'clock and it is getting dark already," he said, while turning on the windshield wipers.

"I have something I want you to look at," said Biển, handing Đức a folded piece of paper.

"What is it?" asked Đức.

"Look … and you will understand."

Đức unfolded the paper and looked. He gasped when he looked at the black and white photograph of Hằng holding Linh's hand. His hands shook as he turned to look at Biển, but froze when he felt the serrated blade of the knife slice a jagged line under his chin, before stopping with the point pressing into this throat.

"These are my daughters!" yelled Biển. "Look at them! Look closely at their beautiful faces! Look at how old they are! Look at their eyes — so full of life!"

Đức looked down at the photograph as droplets of blood from his chin dripped onto the picture. He was still in shock when Biển repositioned the knife so that the tip was directed upwards under the bottom side of his rib cage.

Pops had just arrived home from work and was hanging his jacket in the closet when he heard the knock at his back door. He hesitated, but heard Đức's voice and opened the door.

Đức's wide eyes and pasty-white face stared up at him. Another Vietnamese man stood behind him. *Why is Đức clutching his throat? Blood is seeping through his fingers!*

Pops moved to close the door but he was too late. Biển propelled Đức forward, smashing him against the door and stepping inside the foyer behind him.

"My daughter!" yelled Biển. "Take me to her now or I will slash his throat and yours right after!"

"Your daughter?" Pops replied.

"Linh!" yelled Biển. "Linh!" he yelled again.

"She cannot hear you," said Đức, nervously. "I told you, he has a room in the basement. I am sure she is okay," he added, looking nervously at Pops for confirmation.

"Take me to her, or I will kill you now and find her myself!" said Biển.

Pops stepped back and said, "Okay, okay." He pointed to the stairs leading to the basement and said, "She's down there."

"No," said Biển. "First ... Đức, you hold the back of his shirt as he walks. I will hold you. If you let go of him, you will die first!"

Pops slowly led the way into the basement and opened the hidden door.

"Linh!" yelled Biển. Her screams and the sound of her sobs answered in a hysterical response.

"See? She's in there, waiting for you," said Pops. "Go and see her," he said, gesturing to the passageway entrance.

Biển started crying, but shook his head. "You go first," he said.

The sound of Linh crying and screaming now howled out of the passageway like a megaphone.

"I didn't hear you," said Pops. "Go to her. She needs you!"

"No!" screamed Biến. "You go first!" he yelled so there could be no doubt that Pops heard him.

Pops nodded and Biến watched as he struggled through the opening.

Biến clung on to Đức and shoved him through the passageway ahead of him.

Seconds later, Biến's mouth dropped open in shock at the sight of his naked daughter standing in chains.

He was more horrified to see a pistol in Pops's hand with the end of the barrel stuck in Linh's ear.

"You have a choice now," said Pops, calmly. "You can put the knife down or hold it and watch me shoot your daughter … and then you. Although I must admit, I may do it in the reverse order."

"No! You put the gun down or I will kill Đức," replied Biến, quickly putting the knife back to Đức's throat.

Pops started laughing and said, "I was going to kill him anyway for bringing you here. Please … go ahead. You can kill him now and I will not even try and stop you. I would consider it a favour."

Biến jerked his arm, as if he were going to cut Đức's throat. Đức cried out in fear and Biến saw the disappointment flash across Pops's face at the ruse.

"Okay," sighed Pops. "I'll tell you what I am going to do. I am sure that someone probably knows that you came here with Ducky Boy. If I stay, I know that it is just a matter of time before I am found. Put the knife down and let Đức chain you up at the other end of the room. Do that and I will not hurt you or your daughter. Đức and I will leave and when we are safe, we will call someone so that you are found — if you have not been found already."

Biến looked at Linh, who shook her head before yelling at

him in Vietnamese, telling him to escape fast.

Biển knew that he could not do that — no more than he could get to Pops before his daughter was killed.

Pops smiled when Biển threw his knife down on the floor.

"Chain him up," ordered Pops, "then bring me the key."

Đức led Biển over to the far side of the room and picked up the length of chain. A padlock with a key in it hung from one of the links in the chain. He fastened the chain tightly around Biển's ankle, nervously approached Pops, and handed him the key.

"What's wrong?" asked Pops. He chuckled and added, "You didn't really believe that I meant to harm you, did you?"

Đức didn't reply.

"I meant to fool him," said Pops, gesturing toward Biển with the barrel of his pistol. "It worked. I didn't think you would believe it!" he chortled, patting Đức on the back.

Đức smiled nervously.

"Do you think anyone knows he is here?" asked Pops.

Đức shook his head.

"I didn't think so," replied Pops. "How is your neck? Do you need stitches?" he asked, sounding concerned.

"It is not deep," said Đức. "I think it has stopped bleeding, but it is painful."

Pops nodded and said, "I think we should extract a certain amount of revenge on this man for what he has done to you. Don't you agree?"

Đức was no longer afraid and his face showed his anger as he turned and looked at Biển. "Yes. Very much so."

Pops smiled and said, "Good. I think you will find this amusing." He walked over and ordered Biển to lie on his back on the floor in front of him. Biển hesitated and Pops said, "If you do not want your daughter hurt, you will obey me completely!"

Biển did as ordered. He closed his eyes but his mind could not block out his daughter's crying as Pops urinated on his face.

"Okay, you pathetic excuse for a father — a father who would allow his own daughters to be sold and raped! Get on your knees and look at me!"

Biển did as instructed.

"Take one last look at your daughter. I wonder what will happen to her?"

"Please, Mister Pops," begged Biển. "You must be a man of your word. You promised not to hurt us. Please! I will not tell anyone. All I want is to go back to my own country."

Pops said, "Really? Oh, okay," he said, turning away, but laughed and spun around and said, "It is time for you to say goodbye to your daughter. Is there anything you wish to say to her?"

Biển looked up as Pops stepped back a short distance before aiming the pistol at his face. His mouth opened to yell to Linh that he loved her as his mind reeled with what he could possibly say to make Pops change his mind.

"Too late," said Pops. He smiled and said, "Pop," and squeezed the trigger.

A bright red dot instantly appeared on Biển's forehead and the blood ran down the side of his nose as he slumped sideways onto the floor.

chapter thirty-six

Laura found a bush-filled entrance to a farmer's field, pulled in, and parked the car. The fear on the Russians' faces showed that they were now acutely aware of their new surroundings.

Fat Man was sweating profusely and his lips had taken on a bluish hue. He looked at Jack and gasped, "Please … my chest … the pain, it has gone to my neck, shoulder … arm. I think I am having …" He stopped talking and started panting heavily.

Don't die on me now, you fat bastard!

Jack saw the concern flicker across Laura's face. *Not now, Laura! You're supposed to act like you want them dead!*

Laura looked at Jack and said, "I think he's —"

"Yeah!" said Jack loudly, interrupting her. "Fat Man looks like he is about to have a heart attack. Good! One less cell needed at Guantanamo." Jack's voice returned to a normal level and he added, "He probably wouldn't survive the interrogations anyway. As long as Petya here is healthy, who cares?"

Laura momentarily turned away from the Russians. *Oh, man —*

"Cut to the chase," said Jack. "What is this nonsense about two girls?"

Moustache Pete's eyes betrayed his fear as they flickered between the Fat Man and Jack. "The business we are in," said Moustache Pete quickly, "it is only importing women to work in hotels. Illegal as far as immigration goes, but nothing to do with terrorism."

"Yeah, sure," said Jack. "What does the hotel business have to do with Puget Sound and meeting with al-Qaeda?"

"I did not know the Arab was connected to al-Qaeda. He told us he wanted some young women to work in a hotel. Our interest in navigational charts was purely a matter of interest as to where we could bring people in."

"So this Arab killed some girl?"

"No! Not him. Someone who lives here, in Vancouver. We heard, through a business associate here, that he sold two young girls to a monster of a man who killed one of the girls and is holding the other girl in chains. They are sisters. One of them, her body has recently been found by the police."

"I would have heard of it," said Laura.

"No, my mistake," muttered Moustache Pete. "It is not Vancouver police. It is the RCMP in Surrey. Please check, you will see that I am telling the truth."

"This story," said Jack, "it will not take us long to find out the truth. If you are lying, it will go *very* hard on you."

"We are not lying. If we prove this, will you let us go?"

"Of course I would, if it was true. It would still take time to sort things out. I won't be able to stop my office from arresting you, but you'll have about a fourteen-hour head start."

"We would still be arrested?"

"I can't guarantee anything that the Americans would ... or

would not do. You know how they operate. The secret prisons they have all over the world. Still, if you are telling the truth, you would not be detained forever." He pointed his finger at the Fat Man and added, "So you, fat boy, if you are lying to us, you may as well continue with your heart attack. If you're not lying … then relax, because I will let you go."

"We are not lying," panted the Fat Man.

"Then you have nothing to fear from the two of us," said Jack. "I can assure you that I will let you go tonight. You might want to take the opportunity to try and find a place to hide until your story is checked out by my friends down south. Although hiding may prove difficult. The Americans have most of the holiday spots on the globe well covered."

"We are telling you the truth," said Moustache Pete.

Jack glanced at his watch and looked at Laura and said, "I never did confirm with my friends waiting at the border that we picked them up. We can delay for a little while. I can't see why these two would make up such an absurd story. They're cuffed and can't escape. If they're lying, I'll definitely make sure that their interrogators are told about it. It would cost them dearly, they must know that."

"Yes, we would not lie about such a thing," said Moustache Pete. "It will be easy for you to discover we are telling the truth. This place, where the monster lives, it is even close to the border."

"We don't have anything to lose," said Jack, looking at Laura. "Let's just sit quietly for a moment and let me figure out all the angles. If they are being truthful, I will let them go."

A few minutes passed and the natural colour returned to Fat Man's face and his breathing became normal. Laura caught the slight nod of Jack's head and she resumed her role. "Come on," she said, looking at Jack. "Let's drive them to the border. This is bull."

The Fat Man gasped.

Jack held up his hand as if to stop Laura from talking and looked at Moustache Pete and asked, "What is the name of your alleged business associate?"

"Đức," he replied immediately. "He owns a massage parlour in Surrey called the Orient Pleasure. He has two brothers. They own another massage parlour in Vancouver called The Asian Touch."

"I have heard of that place," said Laura. "We busted it yesterday."

"See!" said Moustache Pete, giving a worried look at the Fat Man who was beginning to take shallow breaths again. "We are telling the truth."

"Yeah, right," said Laura. "It was in the news. You probably read about it."

"No! I did not — well, I did, but that has nothing to do with the two young sisters. Call the police in Surrey. You will see."

"Why don't you do it, sweetie?" said Jack. "What if he is telling the truth?"

"Yeah, I guess that won't hurt," she grumbled, getting out of the car.

The men watched intently as Laura got out and walked around the car with her cellphone at her ear. She got back inside and said, "A girl's body was found. Unidentified. There is nothing about any sister."

"That is her," said Moustache Pete. "She is Vietnamese, right?"

"I was told Asian," said Laura.

"See? I am right. The police do not know about the sister, but I do."

Laura glanced at Jack and said, "Maybe they are telling the truth. Could your office be wrong about these guys?"

"CSIS … make a mistake? I can't see that happening. If we did, it was because of something the Americans told us." Jack saw the glare that Laura gave him. *Sorry … getting into my role too much …*

Jack pretended to cough and said, "There is no doubt about the Arab they met. He was confirmed by multiple independent sources —"

"Not about the Arabs, about these two? You told me you had two bona fide terrorists here!"

"Well," Jack paused, "the investigation is still continuing, but their contacts and affiliation with the Arab was confirmed. This could still be a delay tactic," he said, glancing suspiciously at the men in the back seat. "Perhaps trying to put us off while the police run around playing footsy with this Đức character. Maybe trying to find some house with a kidnapped girl that may not even exist."

"No, it does exist!" said Moustache Pete.

Laura glared at him. "I suppose you are going to tell us that we just have to go ask Đức and he'll tell us where she is," said Laura.

"I know the house," said Moustache Pete. "We were there once and waited in the car while Đức went inside."

"What's the address," Jack snapped at him. "Quick!"

"I … I do not know."

"It's all bull," said Laura.

"No. It is no bull," replied Moustache Pete. "I know it to see it, but I just don't know the address."

"How do we get to it?" asked Jack.

"You keep driving toward the border on Highway 99, but you take the last exit. It is 8th Avenue. You turn right. From there, I can take you to the house."

"What street is it on?" asked Jack.

"I don't know. If you drive, I will recognize it."

Twenty minutes later, Laura turned on 8th Avenue as directed.

"Go straight," said Moustache Pete, "but slow down — I need to look."

Moments later he argued briefly with Fat Man before speaking English and saying, "Yes, turn right here."

"It's on this street?" asked Laura.

"No, farther yet. Keep driving. I remember it is on the side of a hill."

"We're in White Rock," commented Laura.

"Please … keep driving. I think you turn here."

Jack felt the tension in his body increase with every turn the car made. He realized he was holding his breath and wiped the sweat off the palms of his hands on his pants.

"No, this is wrong," said Moustache Pete. "Go back. Maybe it was the next street …."

Jack glanced at Laura and saw that her body was rigid and the frustration was evident in her face as she slammed on the brakes to turn around.

Biển felt stunned as he blinked his eyes. He felt the painful mark on his forehead as Pops and Đức roared with laughter.

He looked up at Pops who pointed the CO_2 pistol at him again and said, "Pop," before firing another pellet. Biển cringed and felt the pellet ricochet off the side of his head.

"You shouldn't flinch," yelled Pops. "That is how Hằng lost her eye!"

Biển screamed out in rage and leapt forward, clawing at the air like a madman as Pops stepped back out of reach.

"How ferocious," said Pops, "I should take you to a taxidermist after and have you stuffed. You would look good standing near my fireplace." He smiled and said, "Maybe now you know why I am called Pops!" Again he said, "Pop," and fired another pellet, striking Biển on the back of his hand as he covered his face.

Biển cringed but he lowered his hands as he heard Pops moving away.

Pops tossed the pistol into a box and looked at Bien and said, "You are fortunate that you arrived today." He pointed at a calendar and said, "It is a red-circle day. A day of surprises for Linh. Actually," he said, glancing at Đức, "a day of surprises for all of us."

"Please," begged Biển.

Pops waved his hand, gesturing for Biển to be silent.

"Unfortunately," continued Pops, "because of your arrival, all her surprises will be today. You will watch. If you do not watch ...," Pops gestured to the steak knife on the floor, "I will start by cutting off your daughter's ears ... then other parts of her body."

Biển watched in horror and revulsion as Pops slowly took off his clothes, flexing his muscles as he did so.

Đức stood with his back to the wall, watching intently.

"Please, sir, please don't," begged Biển.

"Keep asking politely," said Pops. "If you ask enough, maybe you will convince me to stop. But if I see you looking away — if you even blink, I will toss you one piece of your daughter each time."

Linh screamed as Pops grabbed her. He shook her by the arm and said, "And you, my little fighter. You will do everything I say or I will cut your father to pieces before your eyes!"

chapter thirty-seven

"That's it!" said Moustache Pete, gesturing with his head toward a house that Laura was driving past. "The place with the hedge and the driveway that goes to the rear."

"You are certain?" asked Jack. "The place we are driving past now — the house in darkness?"

"Yes," both men said from the back seat.

"Maybe he's not home from work yet," suggested Laura.

"Maybe," replied Jack. "Turn around and park a few houses down on the opposite side. Time for you and me to have a private talk."

Moments later, Jack and Laura stood outside the car. "Now what?" she asked.

"I'd like to scoop a licence plate or something. Figure out who really lives here. With what this guy has done, if it's him, he'll definitely have a history."

"Like setting pets on fire when he was a kid," said Laura with disgust.

"If that is the case," continued Jack, "I'll call Connie and she can send in the troops and we'll sit back with these two. If it's confirmed, we'll let them go as promised."

"How do you explain that we found this place?" asked Laura, gesturing with her thumb at the two Russians. "If anyone finds out what we did with these two, we're finished. Not to mention that a judge will probably rule that we put the administration of justice into disrepute and toss the evidence."

"As far as I'm concerned, these two fine gentlemen in the back of the car are our informants. There is no need to get into how they were ... cultivated."

Laura nodded. "And as informants, we keep their identity secret."

"It's not like I expect them to stay once we release them anyway. They'll be running for the airport."

Laura looked toward the house and said, "Do you think they're telling the truth?"

Jack looked up at the night sky as the full moon momentarily shone through a break in the clouds. *That's eerie ...*

He glanced at Laura and said, "Yeah, I think they're telling the truth. Looks like the driveway might lead to a garage out back. I'm going to grab my flashlight and picks out of the trunk."

"You're not going inside the —"

"No. I'll check the mailbox, if there is one, and then the garage for a plate. If I'm lucky, the garage will have a window. If it doesn't, or I can't see in, I'll pick the lock if there's no alarm system."

Laura opened the trunk and Jack reached for his briefcase, removing a penlight flashlight and a small leather case from it and put them in his pocket. He looked at her and said, "If there aren't any cars, I'll come back and we'll wait here. Tap the horn twice if a car arrives and I'll take off through the back. I'll have my phone, but I'm shutting it off."

"Good luck."

Jack casually sauntered down the sidewalk while glancing at neighbouring houses. The ones with lights on made it easy to see that nobody was looking out. He turned into the driveway and walked toward the house. He could see a slot in the front door for mail. *So much for that idea …*

He followed the driveway to the rear and peeked around the corner at the back of the house. The back porch light was on, as well as a light from inside the kitchen. Another light shone out from the ground behind some bushes close to his feet. It came from a sunken window well and he tried to peer inside, but blinds blocked his view.

The garage extended out on the far side of the back door. The overhead garage door faced him, but he could not see the far side of the garage or the rear, where he hoped to find a window to look in — or a door where he could pick the lock unobserved.

He quickly surveyed the situation. The light from the porch did not extend to the back fence, where an ample supply of bushes would provide cover.

He crept back from the house and slowly made his way across the backyard, crouching to keep his silhouette even with the bushes around him. He was at the midpoint in the yard when he realized that the back door to the house was wide open. His pulse quickened as he quickly knelt beside a shrub.

Bushes rustled close to him and his body tensed before realizing that it was just the wind. Slowly, he turned his head and scanned the backyard again. The house backed onto a lane, but the only access was a small gate beside a wooden structure that held garbage cans. He did not see anyone and waited. With the wind picking up, and the hint of more rain to come, it did not make sense that someone would leave the back door of a house open for long.

Moments later, a car drove slowly down the lane behind him. He held his breath as the headlights flickered past the cracks between the board fence behind him, hoping that the headlights would not reveal his silhouette to anyone who might look out from the house.

Without warning, the small gate to the lane smashed back against the fence.

Jack instinctively reached for the butt of his 9 mm that stuck from the holster on the back of his hip. He waited, unaware that his mouth was open as his body went into survival mode … acutely listening for any sound of danger.

The gate smashed a second time and Jack realized it too, had been left open and was simply at the mercy of the wind.

He took out his phone and used his jacket to shield the light as he jabbed the numbers. The sound of the wind covered the tone that each number emitted as he dialled.

Laura took the call on her cell.

"It's me," whispered Jack. "I'm hiding in the backyard behind some bushes — the back door to the house is open … but I don't see anyone around. Lights on in the kitchen and basement. I'm going to wait a few minutes. A gate to the lane was also left open. Maybe the owner popped over to the neighbour's place or something. Would be just my luck to have him come back as I'm leaving."

"Anything I can do?"

"Just hang tough where you are, this might take awhile. If a car comes, lay on the horn a couple of times and I'll leave through the back gate."

"Got it."

"I'm shutting my phone off. See ya later."

The longer Jack waited, the more his curiosity got to him. *What the hell, I'm not a cat …*

He got to his feet and crept toward the gate in the lane and quietly slid the bolt to latch it shut. A hole cut into the wood would still allow a hand to reach through and open it, but he hoped the noise would alert him first.

He stood erect and walked straight toward the back door. *If someone comes out I'll say I was walking past in the lane — noticed the door was left open and was coming to close it like a good Samaritan.*

As he neared, he saw a smear on the door. *Muddy hand print …* He stepped closer, his eyes looking past the door and into the foyer behind. *A couple steps up to the kitchen — more steps leading down to the basement.*

He took another look at the door. *That's not mud!* He looked at the bloody handprint and glanced down at the linoleum floor. *Bright red drops of blood leading to the basement stairs — not even congealed yet!*

The muffled sound of a girl's scream came up the basement staircase.

Jack jerked his pistol from the holster and raced inside.

chapter thirty-eight

Laura accepted the next call on her cellphone and recognized her husband's voice.

"What are you up to?" Elvis asked. "Want me to put dinner on the stove?"

"Oh, hello," said Laura, as she sat sideways in the seat, watching the two Russians, who were listening closely to her conversation. "Yes, I'm just out with that good-lookin' fiancé of mine. We're shopping."

"I see," replied Elvis, who was not unaccustomed to the coded phone conversations he had with his wife when she was working undercover. "Bad time to chat?"

"That sounds nice," replied Laura. "*Tomorrow* night would be fine for dinner."

"Maybe I'll call Natasha and see if she wants to join me for dinner tonight," Elvis chuckled. "I bet she's available."

Laura smiled and hung up.

Jack ran down the basement stairs while fumbling to turn on his phone. The first room he entered contained weight-lifting equipment and he followed the sound of a man's laughter and a girl crying to the next room.

He saw a small panelled door that was partially open in the wall and quickly pushed the redial button on his phone.

Busy signal! Not now, Laura!

Another scream caused him to yank open the passage door and crouch down to enter. The sound of the man's laughter abruptly stopped and Jack knew he had been heard. His finger tightened on the trigger and he pointed his gun in front of him as he scrambled through.

The first thing Jack saw was a naked man staring at him. The man's arm muscles bulged as he gripped a naked young girl by her hair. The girl had a length of chain wrapped around her ankle.

Jack started to rise out of the passageway and screamed, "Police! Don't —"

A flicker of movement out of the corner of Jack's eye caused him to lurch to one side, but he wasn't fast enough. His wrist went numb instantly and his gun clamoured to the floor.

Đức!

Jack ducked as a second swing of the bat breezed through the hair on the top of his head.

Jack stared at Đức's face and saw Biển chained to the floor in the background.

"You!" shouted Đức. "I know you!" he snarled. His eyebrows furled over his eyes in a look of hate and he stepped forward, swinging the bat with both hands as Jack leaped farther back.

"Behind you!" shouted Biển. "Pops!"

Jack turned and placed a side kick at Pops's naked midriff, causing him to let out a loud grunt and stumble back. Đức reached for the gun on the floor, but Jack stepped forward to kick him in the face. Đức saw it coming and stepped back, putting both hands back on the bat and raising it over his head.

Jack raised his left arm to try to block Đức's forearms, while pulling his right fist back to deliver a blow.

Biển's second cry of warning coincided with a vicelike grip as Pops wrapped his arms around Jack's waist, lifting him off the floor.

Jack gasped for air as he felt the muscular arms tighten under his rib cage. He instinctively used the heel of his shoe to kick back and scraped down the front of Pops's shin.

"Get his gun!" yelled Pops.

Đức stepped forward to pick it up but Jack gave a well-aimed kick and sent the gun flying through the passageway. Jack writhed and twisted his body. He knew that he could not free himself before Đức reached the gun.

By the smile that appeared on Đức's face, he knew it, too.

"Okay, you got me," said Jack, letting his body go limp. Pops lowered Jack's feet to the floor but did not relent on the pressure around his waist.

"Hurry up," said Pops. "Get his gun."

Đức bent to go out the door and Jack yelled, "Hey, duck face!"

Đức looked up just as Jack spit on his face.

An unintelligible sound emitted from Đức's throat and he immediately stepped forward and cocked his arm to punch Jack in the face.

"No! Get his —"

Pops's words were drowned out by Đức's vomit-sounding wretch as Jack kicked him in the groin, partially lifting him off the floor.

A gurgling rumble continued to emit from Đức's throat

and he doubled over in pain. Jack grabbed Đức by his hair, jerking his head upright, while simultaneously landing a karate chop to the back of his neck with his other hand.

Đức's neck broke the first time, but Jack still managed to whip his victim's head back and deliver a second blow before Pops managed to twist him away.

"Get up!" screamed Pops. "Get up!" he yelled, before realizing that Đức would never move again.

Jack reached behind his head with both hands in an attempt to grip Pops's head and gouge out his eyes with his thumbs, but discovered that the numbness had gone from his wrist and the sharp pain that replaced it told him that Đức's swing with the bat had broken a bone.

Pops spun around fast, bashing the side of Jack's head against the wall, before crashing to the floor on top of him and delivering a violent punch to Jack's midriff.

The air exploded out of Jack's mouth like a burst balloon. For a few seconds he was helpless as he lay sprawled on his back, trying to gulp in air as Pops sat on top of him.

Jack was only partially aware of Linh's scream as she crashed to the floor when Pops yanked on the chain. Seconds later he felt a loop of chain around his neck.

Jack tried to claw at Pops's face with his good hand, but Pops leaned back and positioned his knee, pressing Jack's arm to the floor before putting a hand on Jack's forehead, pushing his head to the floor while sitting upright and yanking on the chain around Jack's neck with his other hand.

Linh screamed and came flailing at Pops with both hands. He dropped the chain and punched her in the temple. She fell in a dazed clump to the floor.

Pops picked up the chain again, yanking it tighter around Jack's throat.

Jack felt the darkness swooning in on him. His struggle

was becoming weaker.

Their eyes met and Pops smiled down at him, before leaning back and reefing harder on the chain while Jack's legs kicked involuntarily as his body craved for air.

Pops position now gave Jack a little more movement with his good hand.

Got ya!

Laura answered her cellphone again.

"I could use some help," yelled Jack. "I found Linh."

"You what? Where? Is she okay?"

"Yeah, but I'm not. Get in here! Leave the guys in the car and go around back of the house. The door's open. Just follow the noise!"

"What noise?" asked Laura, while stepping out of the car onto the quiet street.

"It sounds like this," said Jack.

Laura heard a long, high-pitched scream over her phone and Jack said, "It's the sound of a guy getting his nuts crushed. Want to hear it again? Listen …"

Moments later, Laura saw Jack's gun and picked it up as she scrambled through the passageway door with a gun in each hand.

"Who are you? Two-gun gringo?" asked Jack, as she entered the room.

Laura saw a naked man on his hands and knees as Jack knelt beside him with one hand clenching the man's scrotum. In front of her, Đức lay motionless on the floor while Biển and Linh, both with chains on their ankles, clung to each other in the middle of the room.

"Biển? What … Jack? What is going on?" asked Laura.

Jack wrenched his hand tightly, leaving Pops screaming

and writhing on the floor behind him, before walking over to retrieve his gun from Laura.

Jack pointed his gun at Pops, as Laura bent over to look at Đức.

"I broke his neck," said Jack, with a nod of his head toward Đức. "He's either dead or paralyzed. He's not talking so …"

Laura put her fingers on Đức's neck. After a couple of seconds she shook her head and said, "He won't be talking again. Mind telling me what the heck just happened?"

Jack quickly told Laura what had happened.

Laura pointed at Đức and said, "They didn't teach that at the Academy."

"No," said Jack. "That was extracurricular. Bush Survival 101."

"Bush Survival?"

"Learned how to wring a duck's neck," said Jack, before turning to Biển, who was holding Linh. She was sobbing in his arms. "How is she doing? That was quite a punch."

"She says she is okay," sobbed Biển.

"Mind telling us how you got to be here?" Jack asked.

Biển used his hand to wipe the tears from his face. In short, halting sentences, he told them of the invitation he had received to the restaurant and what led up to him finding Linh.

Biển pointed at Pops's clothes piled on the floor and said, "The key to the padlock on my ankle is in his pants.

Jack glanced at Laura and said, "Do you mind? My wrist hurts … and maybe Pops will think I can't shoot with my other hand and try to escape."

Pops glared up at Jack from where he lay on the floor.

Laura holstered her gun and quickly freed Biển. She tried to open Linh's padlock but the key did not fit.

"Where is it?" demanded Laura, pointing an angry finger

at Pops. "The key! Where is it?"

"Fuck you," replied Pops.

"I'll cover him," Jack whispered to Laura. "Go back to the car and take the cuffs off the Russians. Kick them out and tell them they've got twenty minutes to get out of the area. That should give them enough time to find a payphone and call a cab." He gave a nod of his head toward Pops and said, "Once he's cuffed, I'll pick the lock on Linh's ankle."

"That sounds good except for one thing," said Laura, "and I'll take care of that right now!" She looked at Biển and said, "Take Linh and move to the far side of the room."

As Biển and Linh complied, Laura walked over to Pops and said, "Get up on your hands and knees! Now!"

Pops slowly obeyed.

"Crawl," ordered Laura. "Hands and knees only. Go over to the other side of the room."

"Fuck you."

Jack hid a smile when Laura placed the barrel of her gun between his buttocks and cocked the hammer back.

"You see him, eh, Jack?" she said. "He tried to grab my gun and escape."

Pops quickly crawled across the floor to the chain that had held Biển moments before.

"Now," Laura demanded. "Put that chain on your own ankle. Tight! Then padlock it!"

Pops did as ordered before glaring up at her.

"So how does it feel?" asked Laura. "You better get used to it. You'll be spending the rest of your life in a cell."

"Fuck you."

"You pathetic piece of drivel," said Laura. "You don't even have the brains to form a proper sentence."

"Fuck you!" yelled Pops again in rage.

Laura looked at Jack and said, "I'll go get the cuffs out of the car. If you're up to it, I think you are probably safe to take a crack at the padlock while I'm gone."

"I'm up to it. It's my wrist that's broken, not my fingers. Hang on a second," said Jack, as he walked over to a large box in the corner. He looked in the box and saw some box cutters, pliers, a CO_2 pistol, candles, matches, an electric cattle prod, and an assortment of girls' clothing. *That son of a bitch! I want to kill him so bad …*

Laura also looked inside. "Oh, man," she muttered. "I better get the cuffs. If I stay here, I will shoot him."

Jack reached in and pulled out a jacket to give to Linh. "Hurry back, we've got some things to discuss."

Biển weakly pointed at the jacket and started to cry while Linh buried her face in his neck. Laura paused and glanced at Pops, who was now smiling. She hurried to the car.

Moments later, Laura returned, dangling a set of handcuffs in front of her. "It's done," she said. "I left yours in the glove box."

"Our terrorists?" whispered Jack.

"Took off on the run. How you making out?"

"Doing okay," said Jack, as the lock sprung open and he helped Linh to remove the chain from her ankle. When she was free, she immediately turned to wrap her arms around Biển's neck once more as he kneeled beside her.

"Cuff him," said Jack. "I'll cover."

Laura ordered Pops to lay face down on the floor while she cuffed him with his hands behind his back. She was about to use the key to release the padlock and take the chain off his ankle when Jack said, "That can wait a minute. Come here, we should talk about some things first."

Jack and Laura stood by the passage door and turned their backs so they could talk in private.

"We've got to get Linh to a hospital," whispered Jack.

"While you were getting the cuffs, Biển spoke with her. She says she wasn't sexually abused, but even if she wasn't, she's still traumatized."

"So let's call an ambulance and bring in the troops."

"For sure, but now there is no need to make up our informant story. Let's just say that we did follow Đức and he led us here. We'll say we didn't realize Biển was with him until —"

"No!" screamed Pops in a high-pitched voice.

Jack spun around and saw Biển running toward Pops with a knife in his hand.

"Biển, no!" yelled Jack, as he leaped, tackling Biển around the legs and sending him crashing to the floor.

By the sound of Pops's anguished squeal, Jack knew that he was too late as he grabbed Biển by the back of his shirt and flung him off.

Pops looked up from the floor, his eyes wide with fright as he lay on his side.

"He stabbed me!" Pops said, as his eyes became fixated on the knife handle protruding from the side of his chest — and the deep, dark-coloured pool of blood spilling out onto the floor.

Jack saw that Laura had grabbed Biển, dragging him backwards as she restrained him from behind, wrapping one of her arms around his throat, while using her other hand to bend his wrist up high behind his back.

Linh cried loudly, ran up and tried to pull Laura off.

"Pull it out," pleaded Pops.

"Not a good idea," said Jack. "Lie still."

Jack spun around, grabbing Biển by the front of his shirt.

"Why?" Jack demanded.

"If you were a father, you would know why," retorted Biển.

"You are *still* a father!" sputtered Jack. "You've got Linh to take care of! Who will look after her now?"

Biển stared dumbfounded down at his daughter. His knees buckled and he sank to the floor sobbing as Linh hugged him.

Laura let him go and reached for her cellphone, but Jack put his hand on her arm and said, "What are you doing?"

"Calling an ambulance."

"They'll never make it in time," whispered Jack. "Look at the colour of that blood," he said, pointing to Pops. "It's in his liver. He'll be dead before he ever makes it to the hospital."

Laura stared at Pops before looking back at Jack and whispering, "So what are you saying?"

"I'm saying if you do that, Biển will be arrested for murder and Linh will end up in an orphanage in Vietnam. Is that what you want?"

"You know I don't."

"Call the ambulance, you fuckers!" gasped Pops. "What are you waiting for?" he asked, before clenching his teeth in pain.

"We don't really have a choice," whispered Laura.

"Yeah … we do. I'm sick of going by the book. Sick of hating myself."

Oh, man. The old Jack is back …

chapter thirty-nine

Laura quickly helped Linh find all her clothes in the box while Jack spoke quietly with Biển. She didn't need to ask if Biển was willing to go along with Jack's plan. Biển's nodding of his head and the warm embrace he gave Jack was answer enough.

Jack approached Laura and said, "He says he is certain that Linh can do it. She's a little girl who is very traumatized. Nobody would dare push her too much at this point."

"Hope you're right," said Laura, before telling Biển to take Linh out to the adjoining room to get dressed. She watched them leave before checking the chain on Pops's ankle and taking his handcuffs off.

"Thank you," said Pops. "The chain?"

"That stays on," said Jack.

Laura walked to the passageway and turned to take one last look around the room.

It was a memory that would haunt her forever. A place

where the walls and floor had been covered in red enamel paint. A colour she knew, that was picked for a reason. The drain on the floor completed the look.

She gazed at the dirty and blood-stained foam mattress beside a toilet that had the lid held on by two steel bands. Briefly, Laura wondered if Pops was afraid his captives might use the toilet tank lid as a weapon.

A large calendar on the wall with splashes of red circles caught her eye. Beneath it, a box of horror. It wasn't a prison cell, she decided. It was an abattoir.

She looked at Jack and gave a silent nod, before wiping off the key to the padlock and dropping it in the box.

Jack followed Laura out through the passageway.

"Where are you going?" cried Pops. "You can't leave me in here!"

"I'll be right back," said Jack.

At the back entrance, Jack went up into the kitchen while Laura took Biến and Linh to the car. She placed them in the back seat and got in the front and waited.

Jack found a tea towel, left the house, and went out into the lane. A minute later, he returned to the basement and scrambled back through the passageway.

"You called an ambulance … right?" asked Pops.

"No," replied Jack, carefully picking candles up out of the box by their wicks.

"You have to hurry! I might die!"

"I'm surprised you haven't died already," said Jack calmly, as he walked around the room and set the candles down in various locations.

"You can't do this! You will call an ambulance right now!" Pops demanded harshly.

Jack looked at him blandly and said, "The illusion of power and control … right to the end. I know about that. I was born into that element. I figured that by now you —"

"No," cried Pops. "Please … don't torment me like this."

"Ah … now it comes. That's more the tone I expected. The bully reveals the insecure coward that he really is."

"Don't," Pops said weakly.

"Don't what?"

"Don't torture me like this. I'm scared — look … I've wet myself."

"So you have," observed Jack.

"You see? You've won! Please … call the ambulance now."

"Won? I haven't won anything! This isn't a game. It isn't my intention to torture you."

"Good," gasped Pops. "You'll call now, right?"

"Wrong. You are like a rabid dog. I take no delight in destroying a rabid dog any more than I would wish a dog to be rabid. I am simply doing it because it is the right thing to do."

"You can't! You'll go to jail for this. For the rest of your life!"

"A chance I'm willing to take."

Jack dropped the last candle on the floor close to Pops. They both watched as it rolled to a stop.

Pops looked up. He had a look of bewilderment in his eyes, which increased more so when Jack picked Đức up off the floor and dropped his body on top of the candle near Pops.

"What are you doing?" asked Pops.

"You can hold his hand and take him with you when you die," replied Jack.

Pops went to speak, but winced, grabbing his side while watching Jack light the four other candles he had placed. Their meaning became clear when Jack disconnected the propane heater and turned the propane tank on.

"Turn it off!" sputtered Pops.

Jack turned off the lights and briefly watched the flicker of the candles before ducking down to leave.

The sound of the hiss from the escaping gas permeated the entire room.

"Take me to the hospital," pleaded Pops.

"I'm sending you someplace else," replied Jack. "Say hello to my father for me, when he joins you."

Jack got in the car and Laura started it up, drove to the end of the block, and parked. Everyone sat in silence and a minute slowly ticked by.

The sound of a muffled explosion and the shattering of basement windows caused Laura to glance in the rearview mirror.

She looked at Jack, who remained staring straight ahead. "Jack?"

"Take Linh to a suitable payphone," he said, without turning his head.

chapter forty

Connie was back at her office working when she answered the telephone from Jack.

"What are you doing?" he asked, cheerily.

"We're going to pull another all-nighter," replied Connie. "Going to keep working until we find this bastard. You sound happy?"

"Got some fantastic news. Linh is okay!"

"What? What are you talking about?"

"She escaped. Laura and I are with her and Biển at Surrey Memorial right now. She's traumatized, but is going to be okay."

"Jesus Christ! Jack! How —" Connie started crying and couldn't finish her sentence.

"She was locked in some dungeon in a basement someplace by a man she only knew as Pops. Tonight some other man came in with Pops and they started fighting. She used the opportunity to escape. I guess the poor kid ran for blocks before she calmed down enough. Later she got some money off a guy and used it to call home in Hanoi."

"Who gave her money?"

"Some good Samaritan. She was crying and said she was lost and wanted to call her father. The guy probably didn't realize where her father lived. He gave her some money and walked away. Linh called and her grandmother answered and gave her the number to Biển's hotel. He called me and Laura and I grabbed Biển on the way and we picked her up."

"Jesus! You should have called me as soon as Biển told you."

"I would have, except Biển said she was really freaked out. He was afraid she would take off if anyone else showed up. He told her to hide in some bushes and not move until he got there personally."

"I'm on my way over," said Connie. "We have to get to this phone booth. I'll call the Dog Master."

"Laura will meet you at the main entrance. I've got something to do."

"What? Where are you going?"

"I'll be here, but I'm a little banged up. I broke my wrist."

Warning bells sounded in Connie's head. "Jack?"

"It's embarrassing. I was standing on a chair on my balcony cleaning the leaves out of my rain gutter when I took the call from Biển. I was so bloody excited I took a tumble. I'm going in now to get a cast put on. They said I'll need to wear it for six weeks."

An hour passed before medical staff was able to find the time to put a cast on Jack. It covered most of his forearm and the lower half of his hand. He immediately went to the nursing station and found out that Linh had been examined.

He was told that there was no indication of any sexual abuse or serious physical injuries, apart from some bruising around her ankle. She was being given a sedative and was going to be held overnight for observation.

Jack was about to head to her room when he heard Laura talking to Connie as they approached the nursing station. He discreetly zipped up his jacket and flipped his collar up to cover the scrapes on his neck.

"Oh … did you just get here?" he asked as he turned around and feigned surprise.

"Been here and back," said Connie. "Laura took me to the phone booth. The dog lost the scent. How's she doing? I need to talk to her."

"No sexual penetration and no serious physical injuries, but she's severely traumatized. I don't think you should talk to her yet. I was just about to head out of here. Maybe you should talk to her in the morning."

Connie frowned at Jack. "This can't wait. Any clue she could give would help. The bastard who did this knows she escaped. He's liable to do the same."

Connie followed Jack and Laura down the hall and entered a room that Linh shared with three other patients.

Connie saw Biển sitting on the edge of the bed. He was smiling and talking in Vietnamese to Linh as he stroked her hair. Connie did not know any words of Vietnamese, but by the tone, Linh did not sound severely traumatized.

Her suspicions were confirmed when Linh looked up and said, "Hi, Jack! Hi, Laura!"

Biển looked at Connie and she saw the mark on the centre of his forehead.

"How is she?" asked Connie.

Biển's face immediately became sombre and his command of the English language seemed to dissipate.

"Very scared. No talk to police now."

"That's too bad," replied Connie, softly. She gave a fake smile, before her face abruptly turned to business. "What happened to your forehead?" she demanded.

"I fall on bushes."

"There seems to be a lot of clumsiness going on around here tonight," she said, glancing at Jack.

"Pretty wet and slippery out," Jack offered.

Connie smiled at Linh and moved closer and held her hand. "Hi," she said. "My name is Connie."

Linh glanced at Jack and looked at Connie and wrinkled her face, before turning her head away and starting to cry.

"She feels more comfortable with us," said Jack. "Why don't you leave and Laura and I will talk to her."

"That isn't going to happen," said Connie. "I want to talk to her alone … now!"

"Why? She's a child. Someone has to —"

"I'll allow her father to stay," said Connie. "You and Laura … out!"

Connie waited until Jack and Laura left the room before using her cellphone to call her partner.

"Get back to that pay phone. I want it dusted and get the coins done as well. Also get the tolls and times for any calls made from it tonight."

"What's up?" her partner asked.

"I'll explain later. There's a gas station across the street. See if they have any security cameras!"

Over the next half hour, Linh slowly divulged bits and pieces of what she knew from the time she left Vietnam. At times, she trembled as she recalled certain details of her captivity and her fear of the unknown, the impending red-circle day that Pops taunted her with. She cried when she pointed to a jacket on a nearby chair and explained that it had belonged to Hằng.

Connie was gentle and slowly pulled the information from her. Linh's eyes still held a look of innocence and it took all of Connie's professionalism to keep from breaking down and hugging her.

"Now tell me about tonight," said Connie. "I understand that there were two men?"

Linh's eyes immediately darted toward Biển and she said, "Yes, the man who drove me to Pops's house came in with Pops. He is Vietnamese, but I do not know his name. He had a knife, but was bleeding, here," she said, touching her chin."

"Who had a knife? Pops or —"

"No, Vietnamese man had the knife. He was very hate, hate at Mister Pops."

"Angry," said Biển.

Connie looked at Biển and said, "Let her speak please. If I don't understand, then I'll ask you. Okay, sweetie, what happened then?"

"My name is Linh," she said.

Biển quickly spoke in Vietnamese and Connie heard the word *sweetie*.

"Okay," said Linh. She flashed a quick smile at Connie and said, "I am Sweetie." Her face became sombre as she recited how the Vietnamese man made Pops release her. She said the man made Pops take off all his clothes."

"Why?" asked Connie.

"I do not know. I think he very hate at Mister Pops and want to ..." she paused and asked Biển a question in Vietnamese.

"Punish," said Biển.

"Yes, that word," said Linh. "For what he do to me. Mister Pops take off his clothes but try to grab knife. They fight and I run away."

"Can you tell me what the house looked like? Were there

any numbers on the house or did you see any signs?"

"Very dark. I run long time. I don't remember."

Connie continued the questioning. With everything up until tonight, Linh had answered her questions without hesitation. Every question after that caused Linh to glance at her father before and after each answer.

Connie stopped to take an incoming call on her cellphone.

"Have you heard?" her partner asked.

"Heard what? I'm still at the hospital talking to Linh."

"An explosion went off in the basement of some house tonight. Neighbours called it in and the fire crews are at the scene."

"I'm busy, get someone else to —"

"Uniform just called in the plate of a car parked in an alley behind the place. It's registered to Đức at the Orient Pleasure!"

Connie arrived at the scene and let Biển and Linh out of the back seat of her car as Jack and Laura arrived in their own car behind her.

Most of the fire trucks were leaving and those that remained were wrapping up their hoses. The lower half of the outside of the house was scorched above the basement windows, but the rest of the house appeared to be okay.

"Linh?" asked Connie, "Can you remember if this is the house that —"

Linh started crying and buried her face in Biển's chest. Her body shook uncontrollably and Biển hugged her. Connie had no doubt that her trauma was genuine.

Connie's partner ran up and said, "Two bodies were found in a hidden room off the basement. That's where the explosion and fire originated from. A half-sized door leading to the room was blown off by the explosion."

"What caused it?" asked Connie, while staring at Jack.

"Someone disconnected a propane tank that was hooked to a heater in the room. Gas must have run a long time to cause this big of a mess."

"Is one of the victims Đức?" asked Connie, conscious that Jack now matched her stare.

"Don't know yet. One guy is small and fits the description, but they're badly burned. The other guy is a big fellow. He was naked and is shackled by a chain around his ankle. Also has a knife sticking out of his ribs."

Connie's thoughts were interrupted when Biển said something excitedly in Vietnamese. She saw him point up in the sky. The moon had just appeared and shone through a break in the clouds.

Linh turned around and looked up. She quit trembling as she held her father's hand.

Connie saw Jack staring stone-faced up at the moon.

Laura was also looking up … and trembling.

chapter forty-one

Two days after the explosion, Randy and Connie were summoned into Isaac's office.

"Staff Otto ... Corporal Crane, have a seat," said Isaac, gesturing to the two overstuffed leather chairs in front of his desk.

Isaac waited until they were both seated and said, "So ... Staff? What can you tell me about this ... dead pervert in a secret room out in Surrey?"

"Connie is the lead officer," replied Randy. "She is the best one to fill you in on the details."

"Go ahead," said Isaac, while glancing down at the picture on his desk.

"The pervert went by the name of Pops," said Connie. "His real name is Henry Grossman-Warrick."

"I've read the initial report," said Isaac. "Pops will suffice."

"Thank you, sir." said Connie. "As you know, Pops did not have a criminal record but he fit the profile we were looking for in other ways, including a history of cruelty to animals. He was never charged because he was under twelve years old. Later in life, he married and had two daughters, but his wife left him about ten years ago and took the daughters when they reached puberty. She admitted to us now that she left because he was sexually abusing his daughters. Unfortunately, she never reported it. The daughters, either. It gave him free rein to continue."

"Pops decided to get his own girls and step up the abuse," said Randy.

"As far as Hằng's murder goes," continued Connie, "we know that she died using an implement from that room. There was a toilet in the room with the tank lid strapped down by metal straps. We found a broken metal rod in the bottom of the tank, along with an old toilet handle. The rod was part of the lever apparatus used to lift the plunger in the tank. Hằng broke it off and used it to gouge open her wrists."

"For what she was going through, I'm sure suicide seemed like the only option."

"We think she may have done it to save her sister," said Randy.

"To *save* her sister?" asked Isaac.

"Yes, sir," said Connie. "We interviewed a person by the name of Tommy, who worked for Đức. Tommy picked up Hằng and the others when they first arrived off the boat. He said Hằng was obsessed with watching *CSI* on television."

"I'm familiar with the show," said Isaac.

"Because of the show, she was really impressed with how smart the American police were. She said they were like scientists and was afraid they would catch her and send her back to Vietnam. Tommy said he laughed and told her that not all the police were like that. He told her the scientists only worked on dead people."

Isaac briefly tilted his head back and closed his eyes as the true reason for Hằng's action was realized. He sighed, before leaning forward and asking, "So what do you surmise happened the night Linh escaped?"

"From what Linh told us, it would appear that Đức parked in the alley behind Pops's house. An altercation took place because we found traces of Đức's blood in his car, as well as his bloody handprint on the rear door to the house. He died of a broken neck, but had received a superficial wound under his chin first."

"Did you find the pervert's fingerprints in the car as well?"

"No," Connie replied. She glanced at Randy and added, "The passenger side of the car was clean. No prints at all."

"None?" asked Isaac.

"Almost as if it had been wiped down," replied Connie.

"Was it?" asked Isaac.

"I don't know, sir. That was just an observation. Maybe he hadn't had a passenger since he last cleaned his car."

Or was Taggart his passenger? wondered Isaac.

"A theory is, if we go by what Linh told us," said Connie, "Đức chained Pops to the floor and then disconnected the propane tank and went around the room lighting candles. The propane would sink to the floor so he would have had plenty of time to leave before the gas reached the height of the candles. His body was next to Pops and we found a complete candle under his body. He may have gotten too close to Pops, who grabbed him. Đức may have stabbed him, but Pops was a big man and a body builder. He could still have snapped Đức's neck before he died."

"Did he die from the knife wound or the fire and the explosion?"

"That is inconclusive. The autopsy indicates only minute

quantities of soot in his lungs. He may have been on his last breath."

"Hell of a way to die," said Randy. "Being chained there with a knife stuck in your liver and watching the candles flicker while the gas fills the room."

"You seem to have some reservation about what the child told you?" noted Isaac.

"She just didn't strike me as being totally honest," said Connie, "but it was pretty traumatic. Her father wants to take her back to Vietnam, but I'm holding his documentation. There are still a couple of loose ends I would like to clear up. I'd like to interview Linh again in a couple of days. The psychologist feels she is doing well, all things considered."

"You think she is hiding something?" asked Isaac.

"She seemed really straightforward about everything leading up to her escape. After that I felt everything she said had been coached and rehearsed."

"Can't you verify her story?"

"We checked the pay phone she used. A call was placed to her grandmother in Hanoi. Also found the coins with her prints — but only her prints. We know she made the call."

Randy cleared his throat and said, "Tell him what else you found, Connie."

"There is a gas station across the street from the payphone. We managed to review some film footage and it showed Linh making the call in the background."

"Good work. So you have confirmed she was telling the truth."

"About that. Yes, sir. She told us that she borrowed some money from a man. That is on film, too. Unfortunately, the guy never looked toward the camera and he can't be identified."

"Do we need to identify the man?" asked Isaac.

Connie and Randy looked at each other and Randy turned

to Isaac and said, "He appeared to favour his right arm … or wrist, sir."

Isaac looked sharply at Connie and said, "Corporal Taggart has a cast on his right arm. Just out of curiosity, do you happen to know how long he's had it?"

Connie glanced at Randy and said, "Yes, sir. He was getting the cast put on right after he and Constable Secord dropped Linh and her father off at the hospital. He said he broke his wrist when he fell off a chair cleaning the leaves out of his gutter."

"You said there were no other prints on the coins that Linh used?"

"In the gas station film, you can see where the man retrieved a small pouch from his pocket, like someone would keep parking change in. He handed it to Linh, who placed the call before giving it back."

Isaac nodded knowingly. *I bet there were no prints on any of the coins in that pouch.* He looked at Connie and said, "You mentioned a couple of loose ends. What else is there?"

"Just speculation, sir. Trying to prove, or disprove, any other possible theories. If, for whatever reason, Linh did not escape on her own that night, then the question remains as to who helped her and how did that person — or persons — find out where she was?"

"Don't beat around the bush, Corporal. Do you suspect Corporal Taggart or Constable Secord of somehow being involved?"

Connie's face blushed and she looked at Randy for support.

"Sir," Randy said, "when it comes to murder cases, I have to admit that anything that arises as happening by coincidence is automatically suspect. The man on the film favoured his wrist … Corporal Taggart gets a cast on his wrist right after. It would be negligent of us if we didn't investigate that matter a little further."

Investigate a little further, mused Isaac. *Good luck. Many before you have tried.*

"If that theory was actually true," said Isaac, "is it also your theory that Corporal Coincidence set the explosion to — sorry, did I say coincidence? I meant Taggart."

"It certainly destroyed most evidence of fingerprints or DNA in the room," said Connie, "but there's more."

"More?"

"Yes, sir. The father, Biền, had a mark on his forehead. It looked exactly like some of the marks we found on Hằng's body. They were made by the pervert shooting at her with a CO_2 pistol. We found the pistol in the room after the fire. That was how Hằng was blinded in one eye. The pathologist found a pellet — it was hold-back information."

"Did you ask the father about the mark on his head?"

"Yes, sir. He said he fell on some bushes."

"Well, well, well," said Isaac. "Corporal Taggart and the father both happen to fall and hurt themselves on the same night."

"Another coincidence, sir?" said Randy, glancing at Connie as she grabbed her ringing cellphone.

"Sorry, sir," she said. "This could be relevant, I better take it."

"Go ahead," said Isaac. "Use the outer office."

After Connie left, Isaac clasped his hands under his chin while resting his elbows on the table. "Tell me," he said.

"Sir?" replied Randy.

"How did Corporal Taggart find her? Compared to him — even if you include Constable Secord — your office has abundantly more investigators and resources."

"Sir, all this is just a theory that we are trying to prove or disprove."

"I know. Just to tie up loose ends. But as you are well aware, this isn't exactly the first time that some criminals, albeit very evil criminals, connected to Corporal Taggart ended up dead while he is still walking around above ground with the word *coincidence* stamped all over him."

"Sir … everyone in my office is extremely dedicated. I would personally vouch for every one of them. Everyone follows procedure and everyone works very, very hard to bring every case to a successful conclusion."

"I'm not implying that you or anyone in your office is negligent or lazy," said Isaac. "In fact, it is the complete opposite. It is my respect for you personally, that allows me to ask you the question. This discussion is just between the two of us."

"I see," replied Randy.

"I'm not blaming you. If anyone is to blame, it was me who cancelled his transfer out of the section and brought him back into the case."

"Understood," replied Randy.

"So how did he do it?"

Randy took a deep breath and slowly exhaled. "Well, the truth is, sir, we are half expecting to find two more bodies. If we do, I suspect that they may show signs of having been tortured."

"Who?" asked Isaac coldly.

"This morning I learned that the two Russians have both been missing ever since this happened," replied Randy. "We think they knew who Pops was and where he lived. Most of their belongings are still at their apartment."

Isaac slammed his fist on the desk and said, "I want everyone involved in this put on the polygraph! Taggart, Secord — the father, too! Take his daughter and put her with Social Services. I'm not accepting a *theory* that Taggart may have tortured and killed two people! I want the truth!"

"Yes, sir," replied Randy. "I know that Constable Secord had to fly to Toronto today for a court case, but is due back the day after tomorrow. Corporal Taggart is around and both Biên and his daughter are ..." Randy paused as Connie returned and bent over beside him.

"I just found the two Russians," she whispered in his ear, before taking her seat again.

"What was that?" asked Isaac. "What did you just say?"

"I just explained that they were missing," said Randy, looking at Connie.

"Not anymore," said Connie. "I just took a call from a Doctor Son, who works with Interpol in Vietnam. He said both Russians flew back to Hanoi."

"They just came back from there three days ago," said Randy. "This means they would have had to have turned around and gone back almost immediately. It doesn't make sense."

"There's no doubt it's them," said Connie. "Whatever the reason, Doctor Son said the timing was perfect. The Vietnamese police had just raided and detained the ship in port that the Russians were using to smuggle people. The captain rolled and gave up the Russians. They've both been arrested. Doctor Son thinks with the sentences they will get, they'll spend the rest of their lives in prison over there."

"How did Doctor Son get your number?" asked Randy curiously.

"Uh ... apparently Jack gave it to him." Connie looked at both Isaac and Randy and added, "The call was legit."

"How do you know?" asked Isaac.

"I already called the airport and verified the Russians' flight itinerary," admitted Connie.

For a moment, silence descended upon the room. Eventually Randy said, "I guess that one theory I had has proven to be wrong."

Isaac didn't answer and leaned back in his chair as his eyes drifted toward the ceiling. His lips moved slightly before he leaned forward and absentmindedly straightened a picture and a Bible on his desk.

"Sir?" asked Randy, after what seemed an awkward silence.

Isaac looked up and said, "Corporal Crane, see to it that Biển and his daughter receive the necessary documentation to travel forthwith. Should you deem it *absolutely* necessary, you can request that Doctor Sơn follow up on any other questions you might have."

"Yes, sir," replied Connie.

"Good. Now, Corporal Crane, would you please leave. I have another matter to discuss with Staff Otto."

Isaac waited until Connie left the room before saying, "It would appear that we both may have been jumping to conclusions. A real shame if we had levelled false and serious allegations over what turned out to be a simple coincidence. Don't you agree?"

"Yes, sir."

"False conclusions about the torture, that is."

"Yes, sir. That would have been awful."

Isaac nodded thoughtfully, stared at Randy and said, "Regarding the death of Pops and Đức — and the girl's escape. With the Russians being arrested, do you now believe it happened as we were told?"

"No, sir. I don't," replied Randy nervously, looking at Isaac for a response.

"Me, neither," said Isaac. He gave a wry smile and added, "I just wonder how the son of a bitch pulled it off."

Jack walked into The Torn Twenty coffee shop with Biển and Linh. The tears flooded Jade's eyes when Jack introduced her to them and she immediately gave them both a hug. Jack left the three of them at a table to talk in their native tongue while he went to the counter and talked with Holly.

"How is she making out?" he asked.

"Right after you called and told her what had happened, she started crying. She was really fond of that girl, Hằng, who came with her on the ship."

"I know. It took tremendous courage for her to agree to testify."

"Will she have to go back to Vietnam as well?"

"No, I think they have a mountain of evidence against the people on that end. But with Jade's help, we should be able to convict the remaining Trần brothers, along with other people in the gang ... including many of the men who raped her."

"Any risk to her family?"

"The Vietnamese police say not. Their system is different than ours. The bad guys over there won't be getting a slap on the wrist. Any retribution toward Jade's family now would bring them even more severe repercussions. The bad guys know that."

Jack watched Jade unconsciously massage Linh's arm while talking to her. It was a common sign of affection amongst Asian people. "How is she doing as a nanny?" he asked.

Holly smiled. "Fantastic. She wanted to bring Jenny and Charlie to the restaurant, but I got a sitter. I thought this should be a private moment for the three of them."

"So she's working out okay?"

"The only complaint I could have is that she is too hard of a worker. It's difficult trying to get her to take two days off and relax. She would rather play with Jenny and Charlie, or clean house. She's really good with them. Acts like she's their big sister."

"I think she could use a family."

"I like her. It's also nice having another adult in the house. It makes me feel safer. She wrote a long letter to her mother telling her what happened and where she is working now. She hasn't mailed it yet."

"Why not?"

"She wants to ask your permission."

"It's a good idea. I think we should take some pictures of her with you and your family. It would be nice to include. People over there are too poor to have cameras. It would mean a lot."

"She doesn't know how her mother will respond when she finds out what happened."

Jack reflected back on his own mother's bitter response when she knew that Jack had discovered the "secret." He sighed and said, "Jade has had a tough life, but if her mother is worthy of being a mother, she'll respond the right way and not blame Jade. If she's not worthy, she's not worth worrying about."

"I guess so," replied Holly. "But my heart goes out to Jade. I hope it works out. She's told me some things. I know life for her has been hell."

"She's still a good kid. It was her idea to meet Biển and Linh. They wanted to meet her, too. To thank her for having the courage to come forward and testify."

Jack paused, wondering how many countless others would be saved by Jade having the courage to come forward.

"What will happen to Biển and Linh?" asked Holly, nodding her head toward their table.

"They're heading back to Vietnam. Their flight leaves at around eleven tomorrow morning. I invited them to come over and meet Natasha and have dinner with us tonight.

They declined and said they wanted to just be alone. They're anxious to leave tomorrow."

"Can't say as I blame them."

It was eight o'clock at night when Natasha heard Jack arrive home. She lit the candle on the dining room table just as he entered the room.

"What do you think?" she asked, doing a pirouette that allowed the silk fabric of her Vietnamese gown to flare out. "Last time I wore this, you went to sleep before seeing it," she added.

Jack stared at her for a moment. Her hair flowed down to her shoulders and the snug-fitting gown revealed a figure that was absolutely stunning. Light from the candle flickered in her eyes.

"Believe me," he said, "I won't fall asleep tonight. You look incredible."

"You like it?" she asked.

"It's stunning. You're beautiful … and I really love you."

"I love you, too. I feel like you're back to your old self again. The guy I really love."

"I'm not sure what you mean?"

"Yes, you do. It's okay. Just make sure you always come home to me. Promise you won't get yourself killed, or end up on the wrong side of the bars."

Jack felt his eyes water. "I promise. There is one more thing. A very nice man gave me a gift for you today," he said, handing her a silver chain with a large pearl dangling from the centre.

"Jack! It's lovely! Huge!"

"I'm told that if you look at it, you can imagine the moon. He said if you're lucky, and you look at it closely, you might even see an angel looking back at you."

epilogue

1. Petya Globenko and Styopa Ghukov were each sentenced to eighteen years in jail for smuggling and are currently serving their time at Thanh Hoa prison in Vietnam.

2. The owner of the Mekong Palace restaurant went out of business. He feared for his life but did have the courage to attend the trial for Xuân. Although he was the only witness to do so, of the many who had been summoned, Xuân changed his plea to guilty when the owner appeared and was subsequently sentenced to eighteen months of secure custody to be followed by nine months of probation.

   After his release from jail, Xuân was the prime suspect in the stabbing death of three people in a Vancouver nightclub. The three victims had no known gang association and were simply believed to have been in the wrong place at the wrong time. Police had just obtained enough evidence and were on the verge of *charging him for the murders when Xuân wounded and attempted to murder the leader of a rival gang with an automatic handgun. In an exchange of gunfire, Xuân was wounded and died a short time later.*

3. The "Cuban Five" comprised of Gerardo Hernández, Ramón Labañino, Antonio Guerrero, Fernando González, and René González successfully gathered information on a terrorist attack involving a boatload of explosives bound for Cuba. The Cuban authorities notified the FBI, who seized the explosives, but arrested the five undercover Cuban Intelligence officers.

   Despite the U.S. demands for the world to unite in the face of terrorism, the "Cuban Five" have remained in prison in the U.S. since their arrests in 1998.

4. "Tarah," the Canadian volunteer at Blue Dragon Children's Foundation in Vietnam, was instrumental in setting up a network to provide homes for over fifty children and feed dozens every day. Many more children are in need of help. Anyone wanting to learn more about this organization, or wishing to make a contribution to the Blue Dragon, may do so by going online at www.streetkidsinvietnam.com.

5. Justice was denied when Douglas Henry Easton died alone in a hospital in Red Deer, Alberta, without ever facing prosecution for his crimes.

Author's note:
For those who are the victims of sexual abuse — know you are not alone. There are no geographical, social, or economic

boundaries when it comes to the perpetrators and the children they prey upon. If you are a victim, please find the courage to come forward. As part of the healing process, change your perception of yourself from "victim" to that of "advocate" and "survivor." You have the strength within to do it. It is time to identify the monsters and put them away. Our children need protection. Please find the courage to do what is right.